KLAUDEN'S
RING

KLAUDEN'S RING SAGA

KLAUDEN'S RING

AWARD-WINNING AUTHOR
JM PAQUETTE

DEDICATION

To Phil Chamberlin, for the Elevator Game*

*The Elevator Game states that if I do not write during the day, I cannot take the elevator the next day. My office is on the third floor, and I am very lazy. Writing beats the stairs any day!

TRIGGER WARNING

This book contains violence, gore, and a lot of blood spatter.

TABLE OF CONTENTS

ACKNOWLEDGMENTS

Writing a book seems like such an isolated undertaking, but so many others hover along the sidelines; this page is for them. I raise my metaphorical pen in salute to the greats who have come before, in whose words and worlds I have wandered through many a long night: J.R.R. Tolkien for the mythology, Stephen King for the audacity, Diana Gabaldon for the wittiness, Margaret Weiss and Tracy Hickman for the fantasy world, and all the others who have made me laugh and weep with their tales. I roll my d20 in honor of the roleplaying games that allowed me to create so very many characters (and to the DM who loved pool effects and gave my mage "Vampirism"). I raise my mug of tea (Thanks, Lisa!) to my fellow Ink Slingers, without whose steady encouragement I might never have actually finished Hannah's story. I take my hat off to Nicole Dragonbeck, who not only creates amazing fantasy worlds, but translated my crazy crosshatches and chickenscratch marks into a delightful map. Thanking my family goes without saying—much appreciation to Remi (who gave Ev a bath while I was busy writing at night), to Ev (for making me put the laptop down and come play), to Freyja and Nebi (for making me get up and stretch while taking them outside), and to Greyhame (who always keeps my feet warm when he isn't yowling). And of course, I have to thank Erika Lance for being the superhero to my Nobbits, but I wanted to make her wait until the very last line. She knows why.

I

Well, this isn't the worst thing that could happen, Hannah thought when the first goblin smashed through the front door of her little smithy.

Aside from losing her head or getting speared through the heart, Hannah had little to fear from the invader. It wasn't like it could kill her. There were few who could.

Then again, she decided, seeing four more goblins piling through the splintered door with weapons raised, *perhaps today isn't the best day to test those odds.* It had been a late night, after all, and she hadn't memorized more than the basic spells that morning.

She reacted to the intrusion almost instinctively, her right hand throwing the hammer she held to smash the first creature in the face. The impact earned her a squeal of outraged pain, and the goblin fell to the side. Her left hand dropped the tongs, took a second to get a firm grip on the half-molded pot resting on the anvil, and gritting her teeth as the hot metal seared her skin, she flung the item at the next goblin as it entered, catching it center mass. The hot metal smoked as it connected with the leather chest plate the creature wore. This goblin shrieked too, but more in surprise than real pain, and it swiped the pot aside, pig-like eyes narrowing as it charged forward. Hannah saw that the one behind it had a bow nocked and decided it was time to reconsider the situation from safer ground. Ducking behind the anvil, she heard the slap of several arrows as they snapped against the hardened iron side. Not one to linger when the enemy knew where she was, Hannah rolled away, squeezing her small frame into the little space between the water tub and the belly of the forge, the heat baking through the metal and warming her face. She couldn't stay there very long before things got way too hot, even for her.

She knew she would survive. She always did. Her vampiric body could recover from almost anything so long as she had fresh blood. Still, knowing she would survive and finding a way out of this place before her skin began to blister were two very different things.

Escape. Run. Survive.

That seemed simple enough.

The goblins lingered in the customer area of the shop, on the other side of the wooden beam that served as a counter, but moving carefully around the small shelf that held the pots and pans that kept her in business, hovering beneath the walls that held the few weapons which drew in the travelers. She could hear the creatures breathing out there, their hearts beating with the excitement of the hunt, and if she took a moment to concentrate, she knew she could get a rough sense of their thoughts.

Why bother? They were goblins. Their desires weren't a mystery. Every goblin Hannah had ever met had only been interested in slaughter.

Of course, she admitted ruefully, the ones she had seen were fighting for their lives in her father's arena or fighting her for their life when she got desperate for blood. *There is a chance that my exposure is somewhat limited. Maybe there are some peace-loving goblins far away from here,* she considered, *only interested in family and good meals and whatever else mortals cherish.* Even so, those kind souls didn't matter now, as their relations were certainly entertaining entirely violent intentions toward the small blacksmith of Talperin.

What are they even doing here?

Hannah forced herself to focus. She could worry about the goblins' intentions after she was safely away from them.

Or standing over their corpses. Either way.

Hannah was fairly sure these goblins didn't realize that the red-haired girl cowering near her forge was a magic user, and not just any magic user, but one trained by Kelvin Malbrek, one of the greatest wizards her people had seen in centuries. Then again, Hannah's magical aptitude had nothing to do with Malbrek. She had been a terrible student, lacking focus and, more importantly according to her father's magician, respect, but power she had. Klauden van Sherinak, to whom she had been promised since before she was born, had taken her aside to teach her the words to unlock the power within. She could see his face now, a hand running through his blonde hair, ink-stained fingers settling against his chin, could hear the heavy sigh of her exasperated friend: "Just two spells, chaivin! Surely your brain can memorize these few lines."

Hannah smiled as she recalled Klauden's name for her. *Chaivin*, a word in the old tongue meaning fiery, though whether he meant the endearment as a reference to her hair or her temperament, Hannah was never certain. She wondered what he would make of her now, trapped in her own shop with barely enough magic ready to protect herself from mere goblins.

Hannah racked her brain for the simple spells she had memorized that morning. They weren't battle spells. *Why would I need anything offensive for a day at the forge?* The closest thing to a battle she'd had since her arrival in this village several months before was the occasional struggle with her meals, and even that wasn't really a fight. Men were always willing to spend a few quiet moments with her, eager to nuzzle in closer to her heart-shaped face, her bright eyes, her pale skin. Sometimes, she didn't even need a spell to daze them at all. Some just let her feed on them, staring at her with hungry eyes as she cut them, and she knew what they imagined was happening, saw it as she drank their blood and gained their memories. Sometimes she wanted to bite them instead, to make them pay for such thoughts, but she never did. Hannah did not leave fledglings in her wake. She was too careful for that.

All her care seemed a waste now. If she had to face these goblins as the vampire she was, revealing her true self to the villagers, her position as simple blacksmith in this place would be gone. She would have to start all over again somewhere else. Finding this smithy had been a stroke of great luck. The wounded blacksmith had been wandering in the woods when she found him. The smell of his blood was too much, and after days spent wandering in the wilds, she had been desperate. She had bled him dry, absorbing his knowledge of fire and steel as she drank his life, and when she arrived in Talperin the next day, it was too easy to talk her way into using his smithy.

Apparently, the villagers never really liked the last blacksmith. Hannah was charming, if a bit strange, and she charged less for her work.

They accepted her without much trouble. Hannah glanced around at the small work area she had inherited.

Maybe I can still keep this quiet. I have the hypnosis spell ready to go.

Hannah shook her head. Hypnotizing one goblin would leave four more ready to kill her. It wasn't enough.

What else? Fire to kindle the forge. Light to allow me to work late if I wanted. Ice to cool my water if I wanted a drink... She paused, head snapping up to stare at the forge next to her.

Deciding it was worth a try, she brought the words in her mind, then recited them in a slow methodical whisper, feeling the cold sear down her arm and through her hand. She waited until the last second to press her hand flat against the hot belly of the forge, raising more blisters on her palm as she released the spell into the metal. Then she threw herself as hard as she could out of the little hidey hole and across the building, her small body rolling over the sandbags she used to keep her personal living space somewhat separate from the work area, just as the forge exploded, the combination of intense heat and cold too much for the aged metal to withstand.

Hannah ducked into a ball, shuffling her shoulders as something hot hit her back and slid to the ground with a sizzle. With her ears still ringing from the sound, Hannah sat back to consider the scene. The forge had broken apart, shards of metal impaling two of the goblins who lay motionless nearby, their hands still clutching rusty short swords. The flames had gotten two more, the singed corpses still twitching a little as Hannah stared at them. The final goblin was nowhere to be seen, then Hannah noted a wet pile of sludge next to where the water barrel had been.

Vaporized.

She sat for a moment to collect herself, running her unburned hand over her face and grimacing a little as a hunk of hair came free from her forehead with a wet splat. Apparently, she had not escaped the explosion either. She looked down at her clothes, the worn leather apron scorched through in places, her brown skirt and shirt ragged around holes that revealed bright pink skin. Burned, but not badly. She could still pass for mortal. She rubbed her forehead again, smearing the blood on her apron and feeling the length of the cut on her scalp. Not bad at all. She would heal. With blood, she would heal even faster.

The straw of her bedding was smoldering in the flames, and Hannah knew she had to leave before the rest of the building went up in smoke. She grabbed her bag, tossed a few belongings inside, her traveling cloak over her shoulder, then crawled back to the front counter area to shove her few best knives into her belt. She left the pots and pans, cursing to leave the swords, but was enough of a realist to know that she would never use the weapons. Hannah had always been a knife and dagger girl.

She surveyed the remains of her shop one last time, trying to decide if she cared that the place where she had spent so many monotonous hours over the last five months was burning down, but then her eye caught the hammer still lying on the floor by the front door. She bent to pick it up, settled her bag and her cloak into place on her shoulders, the small hammer's familiar weight swinging in her hand.

This might even be fun.

II

Hannah slipped sideways out of the remains of her front door, pressing her body against the wall as she considered the situation. The smithy sat near the edge of the village, so she should be able to flee into the surrounding woods if things were as bad as they seemed.

There were three other shops at this end of the street, then the wide-open field where Margo Dancy grew her berries and a few hundred wheels of dirt path leading into the woods. The village wasn't very big, claiming only a few hundred residents at capacity, and it had no walls or defenses to speak of. The mayor and his personal guard could use their swords in extremity, but things had been peaceful for years. The people had grown to expect that the most trouble they might encounter would be a drunken traveler who could sleep it off in the back room of the general store. The idea that the entire village would be attacked by goblins was unthinkable.

Hannah knew goblins didn't attack like this, and yet as she stood motionless, her brown clothes blending in with the wooden building behind her, she watched as an entire score of goblins chased defenseless villagers down the street. There should be screams, she noticed, seeing the wide-open mouths of the people running past her, then realized that the explosion must have temporarily deafened her. She sank down on her haunches for another moment, the heat of the fire inside her shop making the wall warm behind her back.

A lot of villagers had the same idea that she had entertained: run for the woods and the distraction of trees. Judging by the number of goblins pursuing them as they ran, falling under an onslaught of arrows or caught from behind by metal weapons, Hannah realized that Talperin wouldn't survive this attack. There were just too many of the invaders.

Not one to wait around to see if her predictions were accurate, Hannah changed her mind, picked up her skirts, and fled down the small alley that ran beside the smithy to the back of her shop, dodging the growing flames and closing her eyes as she made her way through the worst of the smoke. She wasn't worried about being able to breathe. Her kind could breathe, and did, but they didn't need to, and holding her breath was easy enough as she considered her options. She could try to run into the woods from here. She might run into some goblins there. *One or two I can handle, but if I run into a group of them, who knows how things will work out?*

It's probably too risky to flee on foot anyway. I need a horse.

Hannah looked to her right, down the street that began behind her smithy, contemplating. There would be horses in the stables. Talperin was always filled with convenient travelers as a well-known rest spot off the Tel Road, and she could definitely find something useful, but getting to the other side of town where the inn and stables were might be a challenge. Hannah hunched down again, blending in with her surroundings.

She began to twist the silver ring on the middle finger of her left hand as she debated. She always did that now, a nervous habit she had picked up south of the mountains. It started the night she rented a room in the first town she encountered after fleeing her father's castle. The men who burst into her room that night had thought to find a helpless victim. Instead, Hannah learned her lesson as she feasted. She would not be so foolish again. In the lands south of the Vanya Mountains, she was no longer Lady van Kreeosk, First Daughter to Magnus van Kreeosk, lord of the oldest and most powerful stronghold among her people. Now she was just Hannah Blacksmith, daughter of no one and beholden to none.

There was a freedom in Talperin, a life without the many restrictions of her father's castle, but there was danger as well, even more than she had ever imagined. In any of her considerations of what may go wrong living among the mortals, something she seldom did, a veritable army of goblins had never occurred to her. There had to be someone powerful behind this attack. Hannah did not want to wait around to find out who it was.

Alright then, she decided. *A horse first*. That meant she had to get across town to the inn and stables. She could do it. Her wounds weren't that bad, and she knew how to avoid being seen. Her hearing had returned. She took several purposeful steps to the right, looking from side to side and reaching out with her senses. There were more goblins coming down this street as well, and Hannah slipped to the nearest hiding spot: an overturned wagon in the street. She hunkered down behind it, hearing the goblins storm past on the far side, and she was about to move again when something touched her knee.

She looked down to see one of the villagers, an older man that she knew by face but not name. He was nice enough, she recalled, always offering her a polite "Morning, lass" as they passed in the street. Now that pleasant face was pale, a small trickle of blood running from one corner of his mouth, and Hannah saw he was lying mostly underneath the wagon, his chest crushed by what had been the bench seat. She knew immediately that he would not live long. His heart was already straining, and now that she had noticed him, the scent of prey nearly overwhelmed her restraint. Hannah had been consciously ignoring the scent of blood in the air, the sound of panicked heartbeats all around her. It would be too easy to lose herself in the haze, the frenzy of bloodlust, and she took a slow, calming breath before preparing to move on.

The carter reached out, his fingertips brushing against her knee, and Hannah looked down at him again. She shook her head, willing him to be silent, to leave her alone. His eyes were pleading as he gasped.

"Please..." he whispered, blood shining on his lips. Hannah rocked back on her heels, ignoring the bloodlust that rose in her, the sudden need to have him. She closed her eyes and shook her head at him again.

There is nothing I can do for you, she mouthed to him, readying herself to flee. She didn't notice just how close her hand was to him, and he suddenly gripped her fingers with surprising strength for one so far gone. His eyes blazed at her, and she had several flashes of pleasant exchanges over the last few months. "I'm sorry." She stumbled over the words, a sudden surge of guilt obscuring the bloodlust.

You know what to do, he mouthed to her, no longer able to speak the words, but still Hannah could sense his pain, his struggle to draw each breath. His heartbeat, slow and labored, echoed in her skin, thrummed along her senses. "Please!" he cried, the sound a wheezing gasp. She sighed, giving in to the inevitable. She couldn't just walk away now. She saw her father's sneer in her memory, knew how disappointed he would be in her, how disappointed he always was in her. Fighting the urge to obey that expression, to turn away and save herself, she looked at the man again, lower body smashed and broken, his heart slowing, his pain intensifying as he struggled to breathe.

You cannot save him, she heard Klauden's voice in her head.

I know, she told the memory of her old companion, feeling the truth in his words. *But still, I can do something.*

She nodded at the old man with what she knew was a reassuring look on her face. "Look at me," she said quietly, mind focusing on the words that would bring forth the spell. It was easy—she had been hypnotizing victims since childhood—and she felt the spell run out of her as her lips moved along the sounds, the power sinking into him.

<*Calm,*> she thought at him. <*Easy. Just be.*> She felt the man relax, saw the tension leave his eyes as he no longer noticed the pain. When he was still, his eyes eased shut and his grip on her hand slackening, Hannah took her other hand and gently touched his cheek.

"<*Go,*>" she said softly in the language of her people. He wouldn't understand the word, but he would know the meaning. "<*Let go.*>" She felt him take another shaking breath, still pained but not focusing on the feeling as her spell held his emotions in check. She waited until he let the breath out, and in the space before his struggling body tried to take another one, she snapped her hand sharply to the side, abruptly ending his life. She released his hand, resting it in the dirt of the road.

Such a waste.

She looked again at the blood trickling from his mouth but felt no bloodlust now. The dead held no appeal for her. It wasn't that she couldn't drink the blood of the dead—she'd never heard anyone say that it would harm her—but she had never wanted to try. The blood she needed was always fresh and vibrant, easing her hunger and her bodily pains at once. She imagined that cold blood would probably help at least a little bit if it wasn't too old, but she had never been desperate enough to find out. More shrieks and the sound of many footfalls coming down the road toward her roused her from her thoughts.

I stayed here too long.

She glanced around the barricade that the wagon made, dismayed to see a trio of goblins coming at her from both sides. Two would pass on her side of the wagon. There was no way they wouldn't see her crouched there.

Hannah hitched up her skirts and ran for the nearest building. Shouts followed her, and she heard the *twang* of several bowstrings. Hannah was fast when she wanted to be, but it was a close thing. The arrows *thunked* into the wooden doorway around her as she rolled through, skirts flying in a rather unladylike fashion as she regained her feet.

She recognized the smell of the tanner's shop. Without pausing, she continued her flight straight through the store, bashing into shelves and knocking things to the floor as she barreled through a back door into the main leather-drying area. Hannah's nose screamed in outrage as the fumes hit her, and she tried not to inhale as she fled through the racks into the next street. She immediately cut to the right again, this time risking a direct path to shelter as she tried to get closer to the stable.

The street she was on now was still full of people, screaming as they ran in all directions. The goblins after Hannah took off after easier prey. She also ran but knew enough not to run from bowmen in a straight line. Others on this street were not so lucky. Men and women cried out in pain and terror as she passed them, goblin arrows drawing blood and knocking people on their faces. Hannah hadn't known goblins were such good marksmen. She added the observation to the growing list of things she hadn't known about the creatures. As the crowd around her began to thin, Hannah knew her time was limited. She had not avoided all of the arrows pelting down the street, and though her body could survive the wounds, she was still slowing, her heart beginning to pound as she lost more blood. Before she was the last figure standing on the street, Hannah ducked down an alley to the right and flattened herself against the wall.

This was a bad idea.

The arrows in her back and shoulders jammed home, and she groaned in annoyance, sinking down on her haunches to make a smaller target as she began wiggling the arrows out of her body. There were five of them all together, and two of the arrowheads left gaping wounds that had her worried. One was on the back of her thigh, just above the knee. It was still sluggishly bleeding, something that rarely happened. Hannah usually healed faster. Her body had already started to run down. The other arrow had gone through her side, a clean hit that she was able to pull through, but she could feel blood running down her back and across her hip. For the first time, Hannah considered whether she might not escape the destruction of Talperin.

She gritted her teeth as she stood, ignoring the pain as habit instructed, and wobbled a bit as the world shifted dangerously beneath her feet. Things were worse than she thought. Taking a deep breath to steady herself, she allowed the bloodlust to come forward—just a little. Any more and she might lose herself in the feeding. That was too dangerous. It was one thing to hide among the mortals, to pretend to be one of them; it was quite another to let herself loose among the goblins, earning much more attention than her reputation as "Simple Human Girl" could handle. She needed what her father would call delicacy. She sent her senses out in a searching arc, seeking that slow rhythm of blood that would give her strength.

She didn't have to wait long. A goblin passed her alley, and she launched herself at its back, arms wrapping like iron bands around its chest as she latched on to its neck. It tried to squeal, but her weight and surprise attack bore it to the ground, and despite its struggles, Hannah had a solid hold on it. Wrinkling her nose a little at the stench, she struck hard and fast, the blood flowing into her, soothing her aches and erasing her pain. She waited until the creature stopped struggling, her hand pressed hard against its face, and lingered even though the idea of feeding on a goblin repulsed her.

The things a girl has to do, she thought distractedly, then pain flared in her wrist. She looked up at the arrow lodged there. Following the direction of the shot, she spied the goblin running across the street at her, and she launched herself at it. Flying high on the singing blood in her veins, she leapt right at the goblin's chest, arms wrapping around its neck and legs hooking around its middle. It was too surprised to fight as she latched on to its neck, and they fell to the ground, dirt and blood spattering them both. When this goblin stopped moving, Hannah tried to remind herself why it was so important to be running. The grunting of nearby creatures brought her back to the moment and she cursed. Her little antics had drawn unwanted attention.

The blood was helping; of course, it was helping. Her body surged with strength and energy, but she also had the other effect of the bloodlust: a sense of distant euphoria, a mad desire to stand and absorb the feeling. Blood stupid, she had called it in her youth, her reaction to feeding that made her refuse to take blood in the midst of battle. The others hadn't reacted that way; only Hannah lost the benefits from the renewing blood—increased strength and speed as well as memories—because she simply stood there to absorb the power, perfectly defenseless.

Hannah shook her head, determined to stay focused. Her vision blurred into a wall of goblins, then crystallized into the perfectly absurd image of fourteen goblins running right at her. She could maybe handle five at her most desperate and prepared. She scuttled back, slipping onto her butt, then managed to gain her feet and run full tilt away from them. She didn't care where she went, plans to reach the stable and horse lost in the sudden panicked need to flee. She ran as fast as she could, ducking and weaving as the arrow strings snapped behind her.

She reached another doorway and smashed through it, her brain dully informing her that she had just broken the front door of the inn, and she ducked to the side. The dull tromping of many feet followed a few steps behind.

This is bad.

Hannah rolled into the room, small form sliding underneath the big table near the door, and she had a moment of inspiration. She grabbed the table leg as she went beneath it and tugged, flipping the table onto its side. She nearly decapitated herself in the process, but when she did manage to stop sliding and hunker down, she now had a rather effective oak shield between herself and the goblins.

At least I can make a stand here.

Hannah took a moment to take stock. She was bleeding badly, trapped by over a dozen goblins piling inside. Her head was swimming with bloodlust, and the only magic at her disposal was a light spell and a small fire spell. She briefly considered lighting the place on fire. It would distract the goblins, certainly, but a quick look behind her at the bar was enough to confirm that this place would explode from all of the liquor inside. Hannah could recover from a great deal, but fire was one of those things that had always been on her "death first" list. She couldn't even imagine the pain as she recovered, skin knitting itself back together. She shuddered. Fire was not an option.

Well then, she thought, *what to do? Curl up and die. No. Hide here until something else came up. No. Run like hell and get pelted. No. Find some weapons and fight back. Ah, that one has promise.*

She glanced around, eyes lighting on the table leg lying broken on the floor. She snapped it in half, then risked a quick look above the table's defense. Her hand let the stake fly, then she ducked back behind the shield, but she heard the surprised gasp as her weapon found its mark in a goblin neck. Counting on her attack to distract them, she used the next moment to throw not only the other half of the table leg, which impaled another goblin with a meaty *thunk*, but also two of her daggers, her training paying off as both blades landed in eyes. *Four down*, she thought as she ducked again. *Only ten to go.*

This is hopeless. I have to get out of here.

She scanned the rest of the room behind her. The bar wasn't too far away. She could probably get behind it and only take some small hits. *What then?* She tried to remember the layout of the inn. She had been here often enough, but then, she'd always been preoccupied with her next victim. Hannah shook her head.

Always be prepared, her teacher had told her. Imagining his reaction to this scene, she could hear Kelvin Malbrek's voice dripping with disdain. *How disappointing, Lady van Kreeosk, but,* and here there would be a deep sigh of long frustration, *not surprising.*

Fine, she decided. *I'm a bad student. But you know what I am good at? Improvising.*

Hannah crouched on her toes, hands already finding four more blades, then stood up and let loose with another volley. Three of the daggers hit their marks, but the remaining goblins were not going to let her get another round off. They charged at the table, weapons raised. Hannah risked an insane backflip that would have made Klauden roll his eyes, bumped up against the bar, then reversed direction, lifting her legs up and rolling backward again over the bar. She landed in an awkward heap on the far side, but she had gained time. The bar stretched almost the length of the room. She grabbed two bottles of liquor from the shelf under the bar and got her feet beneath her, ready to smash the next goblin that came into view.

Unfortunately, that was when the table came crashing over the bar, smashing to pieces as it landed on her. When she finally regained her senses and crawled free of the mess, the goblins were everywhere. A pair of strong arms grabbed her from behind, another latched on to her hair, and two more yanked her feet out from under her. Hannah went down with a snarl. She was fighting, yes, flailing and clawing and snapping with teeth that were suddenly useless under the pile of heaving goblin flesh.

Hannah mustered her final dregs of strength for one moment and managed to lift the entire pile off the floor, but then something hit her very hard on the head, and the world wobbled dangerously.

Hannah's strength ran out of her, and she collapsed, boneless, her last sight a puddle of alcohol next to her head, the wine running from the remains of a smashed bottle. She had a moment to contemplate what her father would think of such a pitiful demise before the world turned red, then gray, and then everything was darkness.

III

Hannah was only aware that she was awake because she heard something that she couldn't identify. *Is that shuffling feet?* There was thumping, and some kind of squealing sound, but she couldn't make any sense of it. She forced an eye open, confused at first as she tried to focus on the sight before her. She blinked hard and opened both eyes, watching as the blur sharpened into a broken bottle sitting in a puddle of wine. The wine was thick with something else, and Hannah's vampiric senses suddenly screamed with her need. One of the goblins must have been cut by the glass. She rolled over and had her face in the puddle before she could stop herself, sucking the spilled blood and wine from the floor. She licked the puddle clean before she regained control, some strength coming back into her body. A body, she realized, that was screaming with wounds.

The goblins.

She sat up slowly, brushing aside chunks of broken table, focusing again on the sounds coming from the far side of the bar. She got carefully to her knees, dangerously off balance, before crawling to the end of the bar to glance around it into the room. The sounds were more distinct now, a squeal that definitely marked the death of a goblin, and some grunting sounds of exertion that must be whoever had distracted it.

Hannah got her feet underneath her and risked a slow look around the side of the bar. Her hand automatically latched on to the nearest weapon, a bottle sitting on the bottom shelf, and she held it tightly as she took in the scene.

There was a man in the bar. Not just any man, but a fighter, a tall figure in black leather who was cutting down the remaining goblins with ruthless efficiency. As she watched, the newcomer dispatched two goblins with a double thrust to each side, then twirled neatly aside from another beast's stabbing short sword and kicked the creature in the chest, sending it crashing into the bar in a splintering of wood. The fighter then turned to the remaining three and, after leaping up on the counter and easily beheading one, engaged in a deft match of baiting and ducking with the remaining duo. The two goblins seemed to get a feel for his rhythm, both moving in to strike at the same time, and Hannah felt a sharp pang of fear for the warrior.

Her worries were quickly quelled, however, when he stepped easily out of the way of both blows and turned, not even waiting to watch the creatures stab each other, instead focusing on the goblin who had regained its feet after the encounter with the bar. The man strode confidently forward, stepping easily over the fallen bodies of the other goblins, spinning his two blades casually.

He is amazing, Hannah thought stupidly. *Just look at the way he moves!* The goblin's pitiful defense was almost hard to watch as the man easily knocked the beast's blade aside and ran it through. He paused for a moment then, eyes scanning the room for other attackers, and that was when Hannah realized that she wasn't looking at a man.

His eyes were too slanted, his cheekbones too high, and she noted, as he tucked away a stray bit of shaggy black hair, his ears were long and pointed at the top. She took a moment to steady herself.

An elf, her mind hammered. *An elf! An elf standing right in front of me!* She had heard so many stories of the mysterious race that lived to the east of her people's land in the mountains, tales of the elves with their strength and stamina and power. Elves were the only race that matched hers in longevity, living hundreds of years in their fine city by the sea. She had known she would eventually run into an elf in her travels south of the Vanya Mountains, but this was just too lucky to ignore. She should take him now when he was unaware. His blood would heal her entirely, and then she could get out of this town and away from the goblins.

Yes, the rational part of her responded, *you could run right out of here and smack into another reinforcement of goblins. Even with his blood, could you make it by them?*

Hannah considered. Even with the boon of Elven blood, she was tired, her spells almost tapped out. She looked back at the figure as he sheathed his blade, carefully wiping the weapon free of goblin blood before replacing it with a movement so practiced that she almost missed it. He considered the other blade he held for a moment, hand considering weight and balance as he moved the short sword in a few quick thrusts, then shook his head and dropped the weapon to the floor. Hannah realized he must have picked it up from one of the goblins while he was fighting.

He really was amazing to watch, she thought again, suddenly reminded of her father's deadly tournaments, games where newly turned fledglings had their chance to prove themselves worthy, where fighters blessed with the blood gift fought with sharpened instincts and heightened awareness. None of them could compare to the display she had just witnessed, and Hannah was curious if all elves were as skilled as this one.

What would the blood gift even do to one already so skilled? Hannah tried to stop her thoughts, tried to formulate a plan, but all she could think about was how fast he had moved. Even Vailen van Joosen of the Third family had not been so fast, and he had been the best in their House with a long blade. Of course, Hannah could destroy him with her daggers, or her magic, but for an elf to have such raw skill was mind-boggling. Hannah wondered what else the elf was capable of doing.

She would have to do this very carefully, she decided, straightening her legs a little as she got ready to stand up. The wound on the back of her thigh had stopped bleeding, but it ached as she straightened the muscle. Her knees creaked loudly in the sudden silence, stiff joints popping as she moved, and the elf snapped his head in her direction, hand going to the hilt at his belt. He hesitated when he saw her, and the intense look on his face vanished, replaced with a rakish grin.

"Ah," he said, head cocking to one side, "are you the one they were after?" He seemed to regain his composure then, as if realizing he had somehow said the wrong thing, and the grin disappeared, replaced by a polite concern.

Hannah was uncertain how to respond. She reminded herself that he couldn't know that anyone was after her, that she had fled her father's castle, that the goblins were a coincidence, that none of this had anything to do with her, and then tried to cover her awkward silence by getting to her feet. She quirked an eyebrow at him, trying to decide how to play this.

"I wouldn't say that," she replied evenly, eyes scanning the carnage of the room to find her blades. She spotted some of them near the remains of the front door, and her hand tightened on the bottle she still held near her hip. Just because he had killed the goblins didn't mean he was on her side. Not all smiles meant friendship. Hannah had learned that early, having given many supposedly friendly smiles in her life.

The elf took a slow step toward the bar, hands reaching the scarred slab and splaying out as he leaned over to glance at the destruction on her side. "Well then, what would you say?" His eyes caught on the wreckage behind the bar, and he glanced at her, a laugh catching in his throat. "Is that a table?"

Hannah shrugged, aware of the way the movement made her arms ache, and she realized that she was still quite wounded. She wasn't bleeding anymore, but a quick glance down showed that she was covered in blood. "It was."

The elf dipped his head in approval. "Well done," he told her, approaching her with a casual confidence that made Hannah like him. He was just so ... open. His eyes widened a little as he took in more of her appearance. "Are you hurt?" he asked suddenly, concern evident in his voice. He stepped closer to her with bit more urgency.

"I'm fine," Hannah started to say, but then he was right in front of her, and the smell of him, the rush of his strong heartbeat, echoed in her skin, and she had to look away, suddenly unsteady on her feet as the bloodlust washed over her. She closed her eyes, allowing her hair to cover her face, concentrating on not losing her focus, then the feeling passed. He was just another person again, not something she needed to devour in order to survive.

Hannah allowed herself a moment of outrage. She was a born vampire, not subject to these powerful spells of bloodlust like a mere fledgling, and the fact that she was so close to losing herself was a sign of just how badly she was hurt.

Hannah ignored the other possible reason; now wasn't the time to think about that. She returned to the problem of the moment. Her body would need a few days to recover, a few days while she would be vulnerable.

A few days with an elf for protection wouldn't be such a bad thing.

"Fine?" the elf echoed. "You're covered in blood!" His hands reached out to her, a finger brushing the line on her forehead from the forge explosion, and he pushed a red curl out of her face. His touch made her skin tingle, and she stood there for a second, staring up at him. He was tall, but not huge, long limbs thickened with muscle and hair tousled from fighting. She saw that one of his front teeth was chipped, and his cheek had a thin line of blood from a sword nick. "Child," he said, concern growing as she stared at him, "are you alright?"

"It's mostly their blood," she replied, hands brushing absently at her clothes, which were stiffening as they dried. "And I am no child."

He sniffed, looking her up and down, no doubt taking in the simple brown skirt, the plain brown shirt, the worn apron, her tousled hair, her blood-smeared face. There was nothing untoward in his manner, simply a reassessment of his first impression. His eyes stopped briefly on his way back down to stare at her shoes. Her boots were the only thing she had kept from home. They were well-made, comfortable, and obviously not something a blacksmith would own. Fortunately, the people of Talperin never noticed her shoes. Hannah noted the look, making a point to remember just how observant the elf was. She idly lifted a foot, placing one boot on top of the other, and realized that she had something wedged in the bottom of her foot. She would have to pry it out when she got a chance. The elf looked back up at her face without mentioning her boots. "You can't be out of your teens," he declared.

"I'm twenty-two," she lied, back on more familiar territory. The mortals always thought she was younger. She might still be considered young by her people's standards, but if she told him she was actually eighty-two, he might think she was crazy. "My people have always been small," she added, watching his face calculate. She remembered the bottle in her hand and set it on the bar with a sheepish grin. "I guess I don't need this."

The elf grinned at her again, his manner subtly shifting as she grew in his estimation. "Are you sure? I know I could use a drink right about now."

"Maybe later," she told him. "After we get away from here." She took a tentative step away from the bar, gentle on her foot, head swimming only a little as she tried to walk toward the door and reclaim her daggers.

"Maybe you should sit down." The elf's voice echoed oddly, and Hannah realized that she was now leaning back into something solid, something that smelled like the elf's chest. "Here." And then strong arms were lowering her to the floor.

"I'm alright," she said, but her voice seemed thick and syrupy to her ears. Maybe she would have to kill him now anyway.

Have I ever been hurt so badly?

Something pressed against her lips, and she opened them, relieved when cool liquid filled her mouth. It wasn't the warm heat of blood, but anything would help at this point. That was when the fire caught up to her, and she swallowed hard, coughing a bit as the liquor seared her throat. She was suddenly very awake and aware, consciousness that had started to fade at the edges snapping back into focus.

"Another," he said and raised the bottle to her lips again. She swallowed this one more carefully, only coughing a little, but her eyes teared as the burn slid down her chest. He waited, hunkered on one knee in front of her, a steady arm holding her shoulder. "Better?"

Uncertain of her voice, she took a deep breath. She actually did feel better. The elf gave her a searching look. "Can you stand?"

"I think so," she said, then tried it. She was slow and a little shaky, but the world was solid and steady, and she thought she would be fine.

For now.

The elf stared into her eyes for a long moment, then he traced his finger in front of her eyes, a quick gesture back and forth that blurred a little in her struggling vision. Hannah was about to ask him what he was doing when he spoke again. "Did something hit you on the head?"

"A lot of things hit me on the head. And everywhere else."

The elf reached out and held both of her arms steady. "Head injuries can be funny things," he told her. "You might get dizzy at odd moments. Hold on to me. We don't want you falling down as we try to get away."

"Where are we going?" she asked as he led her to the door, pausing as she collected her blades and slid them back into place.

Whatever the elf was going to say, it was lost in a loud explosion from the street. When Hannah could hear again, it was a shout from an unfamiliar voice, "Rory!"

Hannah looked at the elf who had hunched down in front of her, his body blocking the open doorway. He gestured her away as he peered cautiously out of the door, body hugging the side of the doorway to make a smaller target if any enemies should linger outside. He turned his head, mouth forming words, but before he could say anything, Hannah's mind flashed red, and without thinking, she tackled him, knocking them both to the floor beside the doorway just as a blast of flames exploded where he had been standing.

Hannah felt the magic tingle in her fingers, knew that a powerful user had sent the fireball, and again her body reacted without consulting her mind. She stood up, an arm suddenly infused with something close to her normal strength shoving the elf back down as he tried to rise with her, and she leaned out of the smoldering doorway. The street was hard to see, blurred by the fire and haze of the heat, but the words were already coming out of her, a chant that she eventually recognized as the dismissal spell, and that spell didn't need her to see the spellcaster, just the spell itself.

As the magical fire faded away, Hannah was amazed that she had even known the spell. She didn't remember memorizing it. As she stood there, the street appeared, and Hannah saw several figures engaged in close combat with goblins. She heard a sharp curse that must be the wizard, then the clash of steel drowned out everything. A hand grabbed her shin, and she was yanked back into the relative safety of the inn where the elf pulled her down hard to the floor. "—crazy?" She heard the tail end of the question as he pushed her behind him again, then he knelt in the doorway, body protectively blocking the danger. He glanced out quickly and gave her a severe look that clearly meant "stay here." Hannah sat where she was and watched him duck out of the door into the fray.

She waited a moment, listening to the sounds of his entry into battle. There were some more surprised shrieks from goblins, but Hannah tried to hear the others out there. *How many companions does the elf have?*

She had narrowed it down to three: a female, a low gruff grunter, and another male. She took a moment to take stock of herself, looking down her body with a critical eye. Her shirt was ruined, smeared with blood and torn in several places. Her skirt was in slightly better shape, but the hem was torn, and a rip ran halfway to her knee on one side. Her father would not approve. Such obvious displays of skin disgusted him. Her people enjoyed their share of bare skin, but only in carefully designed dresses cut to accentuate curves that Hannah never had.

She sat down hard on the floor, pulling her foot close, determined to deal with it while the elf wasn't looking. Her boot was mangled, the leather sole pierced with a chunk of glass that began life as an ale bottle. She wiggled the piece, pulling it out of her flesh and away from her boot, dismayed to see the rest of the boot collapse in her hand once she pulled it off her foot. Tossing the glass aside, she pressed her foot hard against the floor to stop the sluggish bleeding. She frowned as she replaced the boot, wrapping her laces tightly around her foot to keep the leather in place. *I definitely need new boots.* It was a shame; they were nice boots.

With her feet sorted out, she looked down at her body. Her apron was still almost in one piece, but Hannah decided it was time to take it off. The newcomers outside were taking care of the remaining goblins, so she shouldn't need the extra layer. She folded up the leather, then scanned the room for her bag. She found it casually tossed to one side and still virtually unharmed. She said a brief thanks to the gods for that as she got carefully to her feet. There was blood left on her clothing, but nothing she couldn't realistically blame on the goblins. She knew her face was a mess, but that too was explainable. She ran cautious hands over her limbs, making sure she didn't have any other arrows that she had missed. It was one thing to be a hurt human girl. It was quite another to be a miracle survivor. Hannah had learned to be careful south of the Vanya.

Another loud explosion echoed outside, and Hannah decided to risk a glance at the street. She shuffled forward, peeking out near the bottom of the doorway, but there was too much smoke, and her ears were still ringing. She decided to see what she could find with her senses instead and fell gracefully to one knee, eyes closed, focusing with that small, secret part of her being. She sent a slow wave out into the street, trying to identify who was still out there, glad that this kind of magic never required words. It was just part of her, this ability, something she could do easily. Of course, Klauden and Vailen could sense so much more when they tried, but for life south of the Vanya, Hannah's limited ability was sufficient.

Hannah found the elf at once. His presence was loud and vital, and though she wanted to linger there, to see if she could read more into him, she moved on, knowing that she needed more information. She found one of the elf's companions next, someone small and dense—Hannah thought it might be a dwarf. She ranged over two goblins, but they were struggling feebly, near death now, and found another human, probably a man. He wasn't nearly as vibrant as the elf, but he was definitely present, though no one she recognized. She stumbled on to the remains of what had probably been the goblin wizard, though his essence was fading fast, the magic around him disappearing into the air. Hannah was about to stop, to return to herself, when she felt something that made her blood run cold.

Holy magic, she thought as the searing cold seeped into her—the only power that could completely incapacitate her kind. When faced with divine powers, Hannah had been taught that any child of the mountains should flee. She had only felt it once before, but the incident had stuck with her. The priest had been a captive in the castle, and certainly not a danger to them, but Hannah had listened to Malbrek's lesson that day and really heard him when he explained what the man was and what he could do to them. Divine magic was more effective on fledglings, those changed by the blood gift, but even born vampires were subject to its whims.

"Mark this," Malbrek had told her when he saw the fear on her face, "as you rarely mark anything I say, lady, and I tell you, if you ever come across it again, you should flee." He moved closer to her then, eyes burning into hers as he spoke. "Especially a young whelp like you. A girl-child who cannot call her magic is no match for such power." He had looked behind her then, to where Klauden was no doubt standing. Hannah knew that her friend had probably approached slowly and quietly, as he sometimes did, but that he had her back and was looking at Malbrek with that cool indiscernible expression that always made Hannah wish she could read his mind. Hannah knew Klauden would always protect her. That was what betrothed mates did for each other. Malbrek had laughed then, low in his throat. "Though if you have this one with you, well, then you might survive. Perhaps."

Hannah pulled back into herself immediately, goosebumps rising on her skin as she wrapped her arms around her chest. She took a deep breath and tried to calm her racing thoughts. *Divine magic*, her mind hammered at her. *Run away. You must get away.*

As she got to her feet, Hannah decided that she didn't have much choice in the matter. She was too wounded to go anywhere on her own. Wiping a hand across her face, she made sure no blood lingered around her mouth. She thought of her teeth at the last minute, hurrying back to the bar to find an unbroken bottle. She swished the liquor in her mouth, then spat, happy to see the pink. She swished again, mouth burning at the sharp reek of the alcohol—she must have bitten her cheek in the confusion—and at the last moment, decided to swallow. She might need something to help her through the next few minutes.

IV

Hannah waited until the fighting had ceased before poking her head out of the doorway. She took a long look at the street, which until this afternoon had been a familiar place with recognizable buildings and mostly friendly people. Now it was a jumbled mess of smoldering wood and unidentifiable mounds of wreckage. Hannah took a slow, halting step through the door, careful now that her boot wasn't trustworthy. It wouldn't do to fall flat on her face just as she was making introductions. Her father had taught her better than that. Granted, the boots weren't nearly as challenging as the four-inch block heels she had sometimes worn back in the castle, but that was a lifetime ago. Hannah doubted she would ever wear such shoes again.

The victors of the goblin rout stood in the middle of the street, heads close together in discussion, but the elf looked up when she appeared. He gestured to her, directing everyone's attention, and Hannah limped toward the group, moving much more slowly than she needed to, feigning more weakness than she felt, but she was up on the balls of her feet, ready to bolt if the moment went badly. Not that she could get very far in her condition, but she could try.

There were three others standing near the elf—a tall man dressed in black, a short dwarf bristling with red hair and axes, and a female elf. Hannah couldn't stop herself from staring at the sheer beauty of the female's face. She was elegant, her face exquisitely formed, her hair long and blonde and flowing back from her face into a perfectly bound braid, her seemingly simple clothes made of fine material and well-cut to accentuate her figure. Hannah felt a sharp undeniable jolt of pure jealousy. She had been like that, once upon a time. Perfectly coiffed, always expertly groomed, her appearance everything in her father's castle. Living south of the Vanya had changed her priorities somewhat, but she was still Lady van Kreeosk enough to wince at the quality of the elf's clothing. Even her boots were fabulous.

Hannah glanced down at her own substandard clothing, shirt and skirt scorched and getting crispy as the blood dried. Her hair was probably a disaster, curls tangled every which way, and even her hands were filthy with dirty nails like a child. She restrained the urge to hide them behind her back as she had when a little girl. The memory of those times spent hiding from her father, hoping he wouldn't notice just how dirty she was from exploring the caves, gave her strength. This elf, however immaculate, wasn't her father. Hannah didn't need to impress her. Standing up straighter to emphasize every inch of her five-foot frame, Hannah raised her chin as they approached.

"Who is this?" It was the man who spoke, and his voice was not friendly.

"This is a survivor," the elf replied sharply, and Hannah knew that he didn't like the other man's tone either. At least she had an ally there, for now. "This is..." He looked at her. "I never did catch your name."

"Hannah," she said and bent her head a little in greeting as was customary among the people of Talperin. It wasn't quite the curtsy the elves should expect—if what she and Klauden had read in their history books was true—and certainly more than the dwarf would require, but Hannah knew that the mortals here varied a great deal in their introductory customs. She thought it best to stick with the local guidelines—a small incline of the head as a gesture of respect, nothing like status or subjugation suggested. It was a far cry from the rules of greeting at Hannah's father's castle. Something inside Hannah thrilled a little at the very idea of getting away with greeting someone new with so little a gesture.

The female elf curtsied gracefully, a move that spoke of long years of practice. "I am Lira Dinuviel Galadron." Hannah made a note, smugly satisfied that at least those books had been right about Elven names. *That is a mouthful!* But in Lira's melodic voice, it sounded musical and just right. Her own name was gruff with hard edges, as were most of her people's, an echo of the language they spoke, a tongue not known south of the Vanya. If Hannah had been glad for anything when she fled her home, it was that she had a gift for languages, and the common tongue of the

Southerners had been something she actually learned under Malbrek's (and Klauden's) tutelage.

"My pleasure," Hannah replied in the Southern custom. She waited for the others to go on.

The dwarf acknowledged her with a brusque "Gorn Haversont" and went back to scanning the street. He was clearly not interested in further conversation. Hannah noted the easy grip he had on the axe at his belt, the rugged hands of a long-time fighter. His clothes were travel-stained but of fine quality, as she judged such things. He had been on the road for a while, but he was well-equipped. His hair was long and red, twisted into two braids that lay across his shoulders and blended into the long beard that covered his chest. The bottom of the beard was tucked into his shirt, a consideration for battle. Loose hair could be a detriment.

"Nice to meet you," Hannah said, and though the dwarf didn't reply, she didn't think it was an insult. He just didn't seem like much of a talker. She turned her attention to the man, and he scowled at her, obviously not impressed by the scorched and battered blacksmith of Talperin, but a dark look from the male elf made him straighten his shoulders and address her. "Jamison Hunter," he said brusquely.

"My—" Hannah began, but Jamison cut her off, stained travel cloak snapping as he turned to speak to Lira. He did not look at Hannah again.

"Are we going to stand around all day? There may be more goblins around. We should be moving."

Lira glared at him as if judging his poor manners, but she did seem to consider his words. "We should go, Rory," she said, looking at the male elf.

"Rory?" Hannah asked. "Isn't that a little short for an elf?"

"Oh gods, my apologies." Rory's face reddened for an instant as he realized that he had never properly introduced himself. He stood up straight, then gave a bow from the waist, one arm gracefully extended to the side as he spoke. "Rorinvalranus Tallerin at your service." Hannah tried to remember the foreign syllables, but she caught the suddenly curious look on Lira's face, a surprise quickly there and then gone. *What did Rory say to shock her?*

"And you?" Rory prompted. "Are you just Hannah?"

Hannah fought a sudden urge to tell him her name, to introduce herself as she once was, as Hannah van Kreeosk, First Daughter to Magnus van Kreeosk. Though the names would mean nothing to these people, the titles might raise suspicion, and Hannah wanted no reason for that. She went with her introduction of the past few months. "Hannah Smith," she said, holding out her hand in greeting. The elf shook it politely, noted the wound on her wrist, and pulled her hand close, using the bottom of his shirt to wipe the skin clean. Hannah tried not to stare at the small band of skin the motion revealed as his armored chest plate lifted with his shirt. The elf's stomach was smooth and tanned, and she caught the edge of what was probably a sword scar across one hip. *A real fighter then*, Hannah mused. She tried to guess how many other scars he had.

Since living among the Southerners, Hannah had come to realize that she was fascinated by the marks that wounds left on mortals. Her kind rarely scarred, no matter what type of wound they sustained. The idea of smooth lines marking old wounds was somehow intoxicating, a map of one's history. A fighter like this may have a dozen scars.

Hannah bit her lip, consciously calming her growing excitement. This was not the time for such feelings.

"Smith? As in blacksmith?" Rory was asking, holding her arm out in the light. Hannah's fingers were very aware of the warm skin of his palm as he released her hand. "You should keep that clean," he told her. "It's not bad, but you never know with goblin weapons. Lira can probably help you with it if you like. Her god likes to bless people on occasion."

Hannah shook her head at once, looking up at the elf's cool expression. So, Lira was the one with the divine magic. Hannah would have to be careful here. "Thank you, but I'm fine." When Lira nodded, Hannah said, "My forge is just over there." She gestured, then turned back, face sheepish. "I mean, it *was* just over there. There may be some water left in the barrels in the back. I'd like to rinse off if I can."

"Sure. We have a little time." Rory ignored the incredulous look on Jamison's face. "So, what happened?" he asked. "What I mean is, how did you survive?" The others leaned in to hear her story, and Hannah decided to play up her part as a wounded mortal.

"I was in my smithy when they attacked. I managed to escape, but not before my forge caught fire."

"*Your* smithy?" Jamison asked, disbelief in his voice. Hannah didn't miss a beat. She had grown accustomed to men's surprise at her occupation.

"*My* smithy," she replied, "as in belonging solely to me." She looked at the others to see if they would raise any objection. When they said nothing, she continued, "The goblins came in fast, but I got away." She considered whether she should tell them about her magic outright. Rory already knew—he had seen her spell against the shaman—and he didn't seem to mind, but Hannah had learned that the mortals only mastered magic after long years of training in special schools. Hannah appeared too young to have mastered any semblance of magic yet, although in truth, she could have done the mortal training twice over by now. She decided not to say anything specific yet. "I was able to get away," she repeated, "and I thought I could get a horse from the stables if I was quick and quiet enough, but they caught me outside the inn. I barely managed to get inside, but they had me cornered." She looked at Rory with honest gratefulness. "I wouldn't have made it out alive if you hadn't found me."

"So, all those goblins were after you?" Jamison's voice was sharp, dripping with fresh disbelief. "A paltry blacksmith?"

Rory rolled his eyes, but his gaze didn't stray from Hannah's face. She found his complete attention enticing. Of course, men always listened when she spoke, but that was when they were cozy and alone, after she had plied them with soft words and hints of desire. Rory had none of that. He was just honestly interested in what she had to say. It was somewhat unnerving—yet completely satisfying. Hannah bit her lip a little, only forcing herself to stop when she realized that she was rubbing her front teeth with her tongue, a move that always led to poor choices. Her hunger rose in a low rumble. She stopped herself and turned to address Jamison instead. "This paltry blacksmith bested three goblins all by herself," she told him boldly, though in truth, she knew she had killed many more than that.

"Three, huh?" Jamison gave her a once over, a cruel smirk on his thin lips. "Did you smile at them, pretty wench?"

"Only before I hit them with these," she said, pulling a dagger from her belt and tossing it lightly in his direction. He was too stunned to move, and her blade sank into the soft dirt between his feet. He looked at it, then up at her, and Hannah watched the hatred move across his face. The dwarf let out a guffaw, and Rory grinned at her. That hadn't been a good idea, but she had to show this group that she was worthy. Otherwise, they might leave her behind. She needed them.

For now.

Lira leaned down gracefully and plucked the dagger from the ground, then handed it handle first to Hannah. Her fingers brushed Hannah's as she reached for the blade, and a jolt went through Hannah. She stood frozen for a second, trying to register what had happened. Her hand was numb, her arm ice cold, and the hair on the back of her neck stood up.

Divine magic, she thought, then the moment was over. The elf stepped back, a concerned look on her face as Hannah wobbled a little. "Are you alright?" she asked, and there was a genuine note to her question. Hannah stared hard at the elf. *Does she not know? Did her magic not tell her what just happened?* Deciding to take her luck where she found it, Hannah put a hand to her forehead, feigning weakness.

"Fine," she told them. "My head—"

"Sit," Rory told her, and he took her arm, letting her lean heavily on him.

"It's nothing," she said, pushing weakly against him.

"It's always nothing right before you find yourself on your back," he commented. "You hit your head. You need to rest."

Hannah shook her head hard, ending the moment. "I'm fine, really," she said and delicately removed herself from his arm. He let her move away, but she thought there was a moment of hesitation, as if he hadn't wanted her to stop touching him. That thought allowed Hannah to recall the feel of his hand on her arm, but she stopped the bloodlust even as it stirred. *Not now,* she told herself. *Not yet.* "Thank you," she said.

Rory glanced at the rest of his companions, the calculating look of a leader, and said, "We should leave soon."

"I said that before," Jamison grumbled. Rory ignored him.

The elf turned back to Hannah. "You can come with us if you want."

"Where are you going?" she asked.

Rory shrugged, looking at his friends again. It was Lira who spoke. "We are heading south."

"Upsen," the dwarf muttered. "We'd a' been halfway there already if we didn't keep running into the damn mudcrawlers." He kicked at a goblin corpse angrily.

"More goblins?" Hannah asked. "Beyond Talperin?"

"Many more. Your village isn't the only one to be destroyed. We were following a group of goblins that joined up with this raiding party."

"Raiding party?" Hannah echoed, wishing she could think of something better to say instead of simply repeating his words. From what she knew, a raiding party was maybe a dozen warriors, but then she realized that she was thinking of a dozen of her people—a group perfectly capable of slaughtering a hundred people without trouble. *How do the mortals calculate such things?* Numbers had always boggled her mind. The castle she was raised in had maybe a hundred people in all—a third of whom were of the blood and the rest servants and slaves. She had learned the counting words from Malbrek, but she had never really seen such numbers in reality until she came south. And even then, she knew that for mortals, Talperin was a small village—nothing like the great eastern cities of Firene and Warin.

The elves shared a look. "We can tell you the rest as we move," Lira said. "It isn't safe to stay. There are always more of them, somehow."

"Can I just collect some belongings? I grabbed my bag, but I'd like to see if I can salvage anything else," Hannah asked.

Rory nodded agreeably, turning to Lira. "I'll meet you by the stables, then. There aren't any horses, but we can head toward the Tel Road." He turned to Hannah then. "Lady?" Hannah felt a thrill as the word left his lips, an echo of years in her memory.

"Not lady," she told him as she led them away. "Just Hannah."

"I meant no offense." He shrugged then, a disarming grin forming. "Old habits are hard to break sometimes."

Hannah laughed a little. *Where did he learn that habit, and what lady was he addressing?* He was handsome after all. Hannah knew some women who would have swooned over him even without that Elven blood. She thought of her own struggles to resist following old patterns. "I know what you mean."

"Do you?" The question was direct, an honest inquiry that reminded Hannah of the way Klauden sometimes looked at her, when he truly wanted to understand something that she had said or done that he found incomprehensible. Hannah mimicked his shrug, suddenly shy in the face of that look and the memory it conjured.

"Sometimes, things get ingrained in a person," she found herself saying, a sudden urge to tell him something true overwhelming her common sense. "One has to remind herself that such customs are not necessary."

"What customs could be so ingrained in so few years?" he asked, holding her arm as they crossed some wreckage that had once been the wall of a house.

Hannah gave him a sharp look, pulling away from him in sudden irritation. "You think that because I am young that I am not subject to the same thing? That your, no doubt, hundreds of years make more of a habit than the entirety of my existence?" At his suddenly apologetic face, she smiled, her ire vanishing as fast as it had come. "It's alright. I wouldn't expect an elf to understand."

Rory gave her a long appraising look and told her, "You may be young in years Hannah, but you have more wisdom than many of my kind gain over their long centuries. I beg your pardon for my insensitivity." He stood at attention, then bowed from the waist, a gesture so precise and formal that Hannah had to repress a giggle. *What good are such manners in the middle of nowhere?*

Hannah marveled at the odd blend of courtesy and spontaneity in him, that such formal manners could exist within someone who so clearly enjoyed a good laugh. Then again, she realized, thinking of her own behavior in her father's castle, maybe such balancing acts were not as uncommon as she thought. "You don't need to be so formal," she told him. "I'm no lady, and you haven't offended me."

A grin replaced his serious look. "No lady, perhaps," he observed, "not anymore, but as you said, some habits are hard to forget."

Does he know who I am? Who I was? Looking at his open face, she didn't think so. Instead, she thought that maybe he just saw her a little bit more clearly than anyone else did. She saw him give her boots another glance as they walked through the devastated village. "You're going to need some new shoes," he said casually. "Those will not do."

Hannah chose not to answer the unspoken question. "I'll have to find some on the way to..."

"Upsen," he supplied helpfully.

"Upsen," she repeated, leading him down the street where her forge had been. "Have you been there?"

Rory stepped easily around the sprawled form of a goblin. "A few times. It's a bustling place, and the people are interesting, but I'll always take the woods or a small place like this over a big city."

"You're not a city person?"

He shook his head. "Not Upsen," he told her. "Why? Do you prefer the big city?"

It was Hannah's turn to shake her head. "I don't think so."

"You don't know?"

"Let's just say I haven't made up my mind yet." Hannah knew she should stop talking, that being so easy with this elf was dangerous, but she couldn't help herself. She liked him. And he had saved her life.

"Well then, I hope to be there when you do decide," he commented, a slow smile crossing his face. Hannah was suddenly aware of him again, his pulse pounding against her senses, the temptation growing as his heart sped up a little. She bit her lip, viciously turning her attention to other matters. They stood before the forge now, the smoking remains still standing, but barely.

"Come on," she said to relieve her awkwardness. "I'll show you what's left of my smithy."

THE ELF

Lira Dinuviel watched the weather with growing unease. They were in the middle of the Wilds now, having traveled two days down the Tel Road before abandoning that well-traveled path and heading south, skirting the mountains to the west as they headed to Chrypsen Forest.

She had tried to persuade the few people they passed to get off the main road as well, but to no avail. The small herds of survivors were frightened, desperate for answers they were sure lay just down the road at the next village. Rory tried to explain that the next village might not be there, that goblin bands were destroying villages and small towns all over the area, and the people nodded at him, knowing that he spoke the truth, responding to his charisma the way people normally did to the Tallerin, but they stayed on the road anyway, unwilling to risk traveling so near the Venris Gaps.

Lira understood their fear of the Gaps, a land dotted with caves and prone to sudden cave-ins, a place that few travelers returned from. Some said the holes in the ground were actually portals to other realms. Lira didn't believe any of that, but she had never been there herself, and now wasn't the time to go exploring. They weren't going through the Gaps anyway, she tried to tell them, but it didn't matter.

She shook her head, letting them pass. Some people would never listen to reason, even when they knew better in their hearts.

Looking at the small rise of the Chrypsen Forest in the distance, the few trees currently around her dwarfed by the solid cover of greenery ahead, the mountain foothills to her back, she reminded herself that they were commoners; they didn't know what else to do. Most had never been more than a few miles from the places they had been born, and they were all just struggling to survive. She tried not to judge them harshly.

Not everyone felt her place in the world so clearly; Lira was lucky to know she belonged beside her Tallerin—as his friend if never more than that. She had known it since childhood, though she and the Tallerin were not particularly close growing up. Lira had always known him, always known he would make a fine leader for her people. When that whole mess with Galina happened and the Tallerin fled the city, Lira went with him. A second pair of eyes was always useful on the road, she had told him, and she still believed it was true. Besides, she had lied, she wanted to see more of the world than inside Valerius's Temple, beyond the great city of Firene and into the Wilds.

She was so young then.

Even with her prayers and her faith that she was in the right place, Lira sometimes doubted the path she found herself on. A hundred years ago, she would never have imagined that she would leave the safety of the Temple, that she would travel as her sister Maya had done, that she would find herself in the company of the Tallerin, that they would have picked up bedraggled companions in the midst of what appeared to be a goblin uprising or that she would find herself standing in the middle of nowhere with rain in her immediate future. Even Valerius could not have prepared her for this life.

Pausing to glance at the Tallerin, though, Lira was glad she had come with him that day. "For luck," he had said, "for laughs"; "For the unknown," she had replied, and they smiled at each other. For a brief time, Lira thought that smile meant something, but now she knew better. The Tallerin was not for her—and after traveling with him for so many decades now, Lira was glad of it. Rory was a great companion, but not at all what she wanted in a mate. She thought about it more often in the recent years, and staring at the gray, cloud-filled sky gathering above her head, Lira decided that perhaps a life that involved warm beds and a roof at night wouldn't be such a bad thing after all.

As she slowed, eyes watching the sky, Rory followed her gaze. He sent her a silent message with his expression, asking if she thought they might need to stop soon. She pursed her lips, considering. Lira noticed that when Rory slowed, Hannah did as well. The girl rarely took her eyes off the elf. Part of it might be hero worship for the one who had saved her, but Lira knew better than that. The little creature was hunting, but there was something else there, something Lira had sensed from their first meeting back in Talperin, something more than mere hunger. Hannah was a vampire, a cursed creature to be sure, but she didn't seem like anything Lira had read about in her days at the Temple, and her years on the road had taught her to be cautious—and that meant patience. If the girl tried anything, Lira could stop her with her divine power. Until then, she would wait.

Besides, she had always been ... curious. It wasn't that she deliberately left dangerous things running around—she just liked to see how dangerous things would play out. *Call it experimentation,* Lira justified, *call it foolishness, call it what you like, but it's the way I am.*

Though things would certainly be easier if she could watch these things from inside a warm inn. She knew that she would be soaked through within the hour.

Rory caught her eye, read her longing for shelter, and shrugged, smiling a little. Lira shook her head, glaring at him. Nothing ever seemed to bother the elf. It made him an excellent traveling companion, but sometimes, she found his equanimity annoying.

"Looks like a little rain," he commented with a grin. He almost looked excited about the prospect.

Lira looked behind her as the dwarf hurried and fell into step between them. "What is it?" Rory asked. "Something wrong?"

Gorn gestured to the sky. "The weather."

Rory looked up. "It just looks like rain."

"A storm," Gorn told them. "A bad one, and soon. We need shelter." The dwarf took in a long breath, sniffing deep in his wide nose.

Rory cocked his head. "You read the weather?"

Gorn grunted. "I do."

"I never knew a dwarf that could do that," Rory commented, then looked at Lira. She raised her eyebrows, not sure what to make of the dwarf. She had heard of those who could read the weather, could smell storms on the wind, but she had never met anyone with the ability.

She asked, curiosity winning, "But how do you know it will be anything but a normal shower?"

"I know weather, and I know my nose," Gorn replied, one hand absently stroking his beard while the other rested casually on his axe handle, "and my nose says get inside."

Rory nodded, seeming satisfied. "How bad will it be? Will trees do, or do we need a cave?"

"Trees will fall," Gorn predicted. "A cave if we can find one." They all glanced around them, and their gazes slid west to the mountains in the distance. It wouldn't be too hard to find a small cave nearby. The foothills were filled with small hollows and pockets, echoes of the Gaps to the north. If they couldn't find an actual cave, they were sure to find an overhanging rock that should serve.

"A lot of wind, then?" Rory confirmed, lips pursed as he considered. Lira knew he was calculating the distance to Upsen, but they were still a few weeks' travel from the port city, and that's only if they kept a steady pace and eventually rejoined the road south of Chrypsen Forest. If they stayed on their current path and cut through the forest to avoid the goblins, it could take well over that.

Gorn glanced over at the humans, noting the girl's slight frame. "Wee Hannah could be blown away." After a beat, Rory looked at Gorn, decision made.

"I'll go east," he said, taking off into the few trees. Gorn disappeared into the foothills in the opposite direction.

Lira watched them go, then turned back to the rest of her traveling companions. Hannah stood awkwardly where she was, staring after the spot where Rory had disappeared. Jamison stood a few feet away, his face a mask of irritation as always. When he saw her looking at him, the look shifted to something more friendly. Lira suppressed a shudder. Human men were so ridiculous sometimes.

"We're going to get a little rain then?" Jamison asked. When she nodded, he said, "I have a spare cloak with me. You can use it to stay dry if you like."

Lira tried to appreciate the gesture but was unable to while he kept looking at her like that. She had joined the Temple of Valerius in order to get away from looks like that. Apparently, they followed her even into the Wilds.

"What does he mean?" the girl asked, and Lira turned to her, surprised that she would speak. Hannah hadn't said a whole lot since joining the group, spending her days watching the woods around them and her nights in deep sleep. Lira assumed it was because the vampire was healing. The old books had said vampires could go days between feedings, but the time was coming when the girl would need more blood. Lira was curious what she would do. *Will she go for Rory as she clearly wants? Or will she surprise me?*

Lira wasn't a fool. She could see how Rory looked at the girl, and it was those looks that had finally convinced her to keep waiting. Her prayers had helped as well, and though she knew that it was her duty to destroy demons like Hannah, she also knew that it was her duty to see her Tallerin happy again, and it had been years since Rory had looked at anyone with anything more than polite interest. Not that the elf had lived like a monk, but he hadn't been the same since the business with Galina. Even now, Lira couldn't think of that woman without sneering a little. She remembered her coming to the Temple, bragging about how she was going to marry the Tallerin, how someday she was going to be the queen of Firene, even though everyone knew Rory's cousin Marten was king. As Warmaster, Rory was next in line, but Marten was healthy and young, sure to rule for centuries yet.

Lira hadn't liked Galina, hadn't thought her good enough for Rory.

And then they met Hannah. The little vampire was a match for Rory, a woman who could hold her own in a fight, whose lifespan as a vampire matched the long lives of the elves—a woman who made Rory grin as he hadn't in years. She stared at Hannah now, wondering how she had made it south of the mountains. The old stories mentioned the vampires but never one so far from home. Hannah probably had a fantastic story.

"The dwarf?" Lira asked. "He means he can smell storms."

Hannah cocked her head. "Is that something you learn to do, or is it something he can just do, like magic?"

Lira shrugged. "I'm not sure. You should ask him. I think it's something a magic user could learn in time, but maybe his is natural. What about your magic?"

"Mine?" Hannah asked, looking uncomfortable.

"Yes. Were you born with it, or did you learn it?"

"Both." After a pause, the girl said, "I can do some things just because I can, but others I had to learn. I memorize spells."

"I have heard of the school of wizardry in Upsen."

When Hannah bent her head as if she knew the name, Lira decided to push the girl a little bit. "Is that where you studied?"

"No," Hannah said quickly. "I didn't learn in a school. I had a tutor."

"You must have come from a wealthy family, then," Jamison put in, and Lira remembered the man was still there. "Where are you from?"

Hannah was about to answer when Rory returned. The elf was slightly out of breath as he gestured back toward the trees.

"A cave this way," he explained, pointing with his free arm, "not huge, but enough for all of us to fit inside."

They waited for Gorn to return—he hadn't found another cave, but he had found a decent overhang, and he seemed pleased to hear Rory's description of their night's shelter. They set off into the trees, pushing through low-lying brush and scuttling over twisting tree roots. Hannah tripped once and nearly fell, her foot catching on a root, and Lira saw that one of her boots was split in half, held together with laces. Rory caught her with a quick hand on her upper arm. Lira watched as the elf tried to pretend his help was a routine affair, and the girl tried to hide her embarrassment at having tripped at all. Lira grinned, asking herself if someday she would play coy with someone. It didn't seem very likely.

They reached the cave just as the first heavy drops fell from the sky, the rain swiftly picking up into a drenching layer that flattened the tree leaves and caused the dirt to morph into splashing mud. They trudged the last few feet inside, pushing wet hair behind ears as they mopped their dripping faces. Hannah lingered outside for a few more seconds, allowing the rain to wash her face and soak her hair. Lira thought she might stand there long enough to drench her clothes, which, even though not covered in blood anymore, were a bit travel-stained. A flash of lightning and a crack of thunder overhead changed the girl's mind.

Rory had spoken the truth when he said the cave wasn't huge, but it was large enough for all of them to stretch out on their bedrolls, and they even had enough room to stay back from the opening and the lashing rain that slanted inside. Rory piled some dirt against a side wall and built a pyramid from the wood he had gathered. Lira sat by as the elf tried to light the fire, the sparks from his flint jumping into the brush he had stuffed under the branches, but the wind was toying with him. As Lira watched, a promising swell of smoke blew first back into the cave with a whoosh, then forcefully into Rory's face with a sizzle of sparks.

Without a word, Hannah was beside the elf as he cursed and wiped at his eyes, ash smearing across his forehead. She spoke a low word as she held her hand over the wood, and Lira watched the magic swell below her hand, a blue light bursting into flame. She had always been intrigued by magic; her powers were different, a gift from Valerius, and though she could feel Hannah's spell echo in the air, it was alien to her magic. Rory said something to the girl in a low voice, and she smiled shyly. Lira didn't think anyone had complimented her before. She seemed awkward in her reply. Lira considered getting closer so she could hear their conversation over the rush of the wind but decided against it. She was close enough to act if the girl tried to hurt the Tallerin. Rory deserved some privacy.

The rain was coming down in sheets now, the hazy afternoon light all but gone, but the area in front of the cave mouth was illuminated every few seconds by bursts of lightning, the flash followed by thunder that echoed in Lira's chest.

Lira leaned against the cave wall near the opening, settling in as her companions prepared for a night's rest. Their patterns were familiar to her now. The dwarf would lean against the wall, axe laid across his lap, and begin snoring almost immediately. He had done so from the first night they had found him on the road, the lone survivor of a goblin attack on the caravan he had been guarding. They found Jamison the same way—huddled in the remains of a burned-out barn as the goblins ravaged the small village. Lira, Rory, and the dwarf had made short work of the remaining goblins, and Jamison had decided to come with them to Upsen. Lira sometimes regretted their offer of safety in numbers, especially when Jamison would stare at her as she unbraided her hair for her nightly prayers. Rory would lay out his bedroll with the precision of a soldier—some habits would never fade. He would also cook if anything was available—tonight's fare was a thin soup made from a small score of rabbits they had caught earlier in the day. Hannah was still figuring out how to live on the road. The girl laid out her blanket awkwardly, then she sat and fought with the contents of her bag for a bit, surreptitiously watching Rory as he cooked.

The girl had a rather fancy bowl for her dinner, an ebony piece with carvings around the edge, and she was careful to wash it each night after they finished eating. Lira marveled that the vampire would eat, and after close observation, she saw that Hannah rarely ate the food Rory cooked but just moved it around her bowl. She did drink the liquid though.

It is just a matter of time now, Lira thought.

Lira was considering sleep when a bright flash followed by a thunderous boom that she felt in her teeth jerked Hannah out of a restless sleep across the cave. The girl had been lying near the fire, her eyes long since drifted closed, but now she sat upright, and Lira saw the demon reflected in her eyes, a red flash in the night. She watched as Rory sat up from his own bedroll, leaning over to place a hand on Hannah's arm. The girl started, obviously not entirely awake, but then she settled, eyes on the elf's face. Rory leaned down to say something to Hannah, and the girl let out a low chuckle, face brightening in the dark. Lira wondered if the red eyes had been a trick of the firelight. Hannah's eyes were a bright green, a shade that reminded her of deep forests and wide leaves. Rory settled himself back on his bedroll then, body turned to face Hannah, and she lay down on her side facing him. There was a low conversation, the words inaudible above the rain splashing down outside.

Lira watched them until they both fell asleep again, ready to act but relieved that she didn't have to.

V

They came across the cabin a week later. Hannah's boots were in serious protest, the leather rubbing her foot raw as they trudged through the storm debris. She cursed again, wishing that the remains of the general store in Talperin had held a pair of shoes that fit her. The skirt and shirt had been easy enough to find, though they smelled like smoke and were not quite her size, but the only boots had been made for a much bigger man, and the cobbler had not survived the attack to make her a new pair.

Still, even with her aching foot, Hannah was relieved to get out from the shadow of so many trees. She didn't like the deep forest. Mountains she could mark and identify easily, but trees all looked the same to her. She knew that if her new traveling companions were to leave her alone in those woods, she would not find her way back to the road easily.

Hannah wrapped her arms around herself at the thought, glad that her sweater at least had survived the attack. She could do without the clothes she had left home in, but Klauden had acquired the sweater from one of the slaves, and though she didn't really need the warmth, it was a comforting reminder of home. It was a simple weave, a dark brown jacket that came down to her mid-thighs with big wooden buttons down the front that kept it closed over her new shirt and skirt, and she was glad for it now as she stood thinking about the forest behind them.

She had only left the group once so far, in the middle of night when everyone was asleep, including Jamison who was supposed to have been on watch. He only needed a slight nudge from Hannah's spell to nod his head forward, and by the time she tracked the lone goblin, cornered him, drank her fill, and found her way back to the low embers of the campfire, he was still out. Hannah knew she was gambling with the others' safety by leaving him spelled, but if she didn't feed regularly, there would be a bloodthirsty monster in their midst soon enough.

As she stared at the little house, so quaint amid the small open green field, the sunlight was warm on Hannah's face, and she took a slow breath, relishing the feel of the air even though she technically didn't need to breathe, more relieved than she wanted to admit for the small break in the damn forest.

They would pass through more trees on their way, but they were nearly halfway through now, according to the elves, so there was no real danger of getting lost. The Tel Road was due south, parallel to the forest's southern edge, and they could have gone that way, but the elves preferred trekking through the endless woods. Rory said they would eventually reach the Marin River and follow it south to the port city.

Though Hannah wasn't a huge fan of water—she couldn't swim—it was certainly better than the idea of getting lost amid those trees and going mad from bloodthirst. One could probably wander for days without finding another person, and Hannah would never be so desperate as to drink from animals. In fact, she didn't think animals could sate her anyway, and the idea was so repulsive that she thought she would probably choose death. Then again, she knew it was easy to think such things while standing in the sunlight on the open ground; it would be quite another if she ever found herself in such a bind.

She opened her eyes to glance at her companions. She didn't want to feed on any of them except, well, maybe Jamison, and definitely Rory if she let herself think about it, but if things went poorly, she knew she was Magnus van Kreeosk's daughter, and would do what she had to do.

Betrayal was one thing; debasement was something else entirely.

Hannah was deep in these musings when she saw the front door of the house bang open to reveal a tall woman in a faded red dress rushing out to them. The woman ran right for Rory, her skirts flying out behind her, and her sizable bosom bouncing in her bodice. The woman's hair was a mass of black curls that trailed down her back and covered part of her face. Rory caught her lunge with a gentleman's calm, arms cradling the woman to his chest, and Hannah realized that what she had mistaken for anger was actually sobbing. The woman was babbling so fast that Hannah couldn't understand her over the panicked beat of the mortal's heart. When she pulled back, Hannah saw that her face was red with strain and streaked with tears.

Hannah didn't like the way she clutched at Rory's chest. The elf wasn't holding her close, but he was holding her upright, hands on her arms as he tried to soothe her with calm words.

Hannah looked away, trying to hide her disgust. She'd met mortals like this, humans who lost their minds under some minor stress and fell into madness. This woman was clearly on the brink of a breakdown. Hannah didn't want to stand around and watch it happen. She looked around to see how the rest of her companions were reacting. Gorn was scowling, his feelings clear. Lira had leaned in, trying to decipher the woman's babbling, and Jamison was at the elf's elbow, feigning interest in the woman to gain Lira's approval.

The tall human always seemed to have his head tilted toward the elf. Hannah knew desperation when she saw it. Lira didn't seem remotely interested in Jamison's suit, but she was too politely aristocratic to make him stop. Hannah found herself enjoying the man's awkward advances and chuckled every time Lira sent him away with an elegant shake of her golden hair.

She hadn't been so polite to her own suitors in her father's castle, but that was because everyone knew she was betrothed to Klauden. When Vailen van Joosen, of the Third family in the castle, made his advances, Hannah laughed in his face, mocking his aspirations, claiming he would never be First family. Watching Jamison's seemingly fruitless pursuit of Lira, Hannah wondered what Vailen was doing now, how he was pursuing his path into aristocracy without her in his sights. A brief flash of Livenna, her father's other daughter, crossed Hannah's mind, but she shook her head. Livenna was Kargin, not first born, and even lower class than Vailen himself. Then again, she realized, mind returning to the scene before her, none of that mattered. She would probably never find out what happened in her father's House now that she had left. The world south of the Vanya was all she had.

The woman seemed to have calmed down and was speaking more clearly, but as Hannah turned back to look at her, she saw that the stranger had not released her grip on Rory, and she fought to hold back a scowl.

"What is it?" she asked, heart suddenly light when Rory gave her a smile. She shook off the feeling, focusing on the situation. *What the hell is wrong with me lately?* He was food, nothing more. She cut off the thought as she stared at the crazed woman huddled against Hannah's future prey. She was nearly as tall as Rory, her black hair in long ringlets that framed her red face, and Hannah tried to make out what she was telling them.

"It's my Jason!" the woman wailed, and Hannah restrained an urge to strike her. Hysterical women had always grated on her nerves. That was part of the reason she hypnotized her meals. She couldn't stand histrionics. "He's gone," the woman cried, "and demons have taken his soul!"

Hannah halted. That was something different. Her annoyance faded, and she listened more closely, piecing together the story as the woman calmed down. After more soothing words from Rory, she seemed to regain control of herself and invited them inside. Hannah marveled at a woman who could be tearing her hair one moment and serving tea and biscuits the next. They learned that her name was Molly, and her beloved husband Jason had been attacked in the woods while hunting a few days before.

"Attacked by what?" Lira asked, sipping at her teacup as if this was the most normal thing in the world. Hannah could see from her expression that the tea was quite good. She sniffed her own teacup, debating whether the tea would leave her in cramping agony for the night. Hannah could eat some normal human food, and she did, but sometimes it left her writhing through nights when the only relief lay in fresh blood. They were near the road now, but Hannah hadn't seen other travelers. Blood might be scarce. She wasn't willing to risk it, not until they had reached some more people. She pretended to take a small sip, letting the tea brush against her lips, then set the delicate cup down on the table.

"I don't rightly know," Molly said, her normal voice lilting in an odd accent. Hannah didn't want to admit it, but she had always been fascinated by the way others spoke, and she had to force herself to listen to what Molly was saying rather than how she said it. "It was a bite mark for sure, and on his neck. Clean punctures for a wild animal though."

"What kind of wild animal? Did Jason say?" Rory asked, and Molly shook her head, black curls dancing around her face.

"Not a wild animal at all! Jason said he didn't know what had happened, figured he must have bumped his head in the fall, and it seemed fine that first night, but then..." Molly's voice trailed off as she stared across the kitchen table, apparently seeing the man who wasn't there.

"What then?" Lira prompted in a gentle tone.

Molly turned red-rimmed eyes in the elf's direction, and big slow tears spilled down her suddenly flushed cheeks. Hannah felt the sudden tug of her rushing pulse as it sped up, the pull of her blood almost magnetic in the small room, and she looked quickly away, focusing instead on the small details of the teacup on the table, trying to hear the woman's words and ignore her blood. "Then he started raving," Molly said sadly. "He was burning up with fever and rambling about a man in the woods and red eyes in the dark, and then he just up and ran out of the house into the night. I haven't seen him since!" Her lip began to quiver, and Hannah looked away again, disturbed by the woman's sudden shift in mood and the jerk of her heartbeat but terrified by the implications of what she had just said.

A man in the night with red eyes who left clean punctures on his neck.

Jason had been bitten by one of her people: a vampire. The only question left was who had bitten him. Had it been a pureblood, Jason's odds of survival were fairly good. Many humans could survive the transition to become fledglings. The first few years were a little rough until they got the bloodlust under control, and people could always mark them by their blood tears or the way they stopped aging, but they gained most of the abilities that Hannah's people had: strength, speed, longevity, and the thirst—always the thirst. A few people even survived the bite unscathed, remaining completely mortal.

But if he had been bitten by a fledgling, that was a different story. Some victims survived to transform, especially if the fledging's maker was old and strong, but there were some who went mad with the change, transforming into the fehalon, deranged feeders whose only purpose in Hannah's life had been to serve as challenges in her father's tournaments.

It has only been a few days, Hannah thought. If the vampire was still nearby, she could sense him. She could find out who it was and determine Jason's fate. Hannah didn't want to think about the implications of a vampiric presence in these woods. She didn't want to think that someone may be hunting for *her*.

"Red eyes?" Rory was asking. At Molly's nod, he shared a long look with Lira. Hannah observed the silent conversation that caused both of the elves' heartbeats to speed up a few beats.

"And he said he was attacked by a man?" Lira prompted. Molly nodded again, this time noting the meaningful look on the elves' faces.

"Why?" she asked, voice breaking. "What does it mean? Do you know what it means? What happened to my Jason?"

Again, there was one of those looks, and Hannah knew that kind of communication wasn't forged in a few weeks on the road. Rory and Lira had known one another a very long time indeed. In fact, the only other time she had seen such a connection, she had been on one end of it, and Klauden had been sharing volumes with the subtle lift of an eyebrow, the minor motion of a finger. Hannah had a long moment to ponder just what the elves were to one another, and she wondered why the thought bothered her so much.

Apparently, Hannah thought, *today is a great day for dodging the obvious.*

Rory placed a reassuring hand on Molly's, and his voice was soft with sorrow. "I am sorry, Mistress, but your husband is lost."

"What do you mean 'lost'?" Molly's eyes were wide, her lip trembling again.

"It's likely that Jason was attacked by a vampire," Lira told her, and Molly's eyes closed as she absorbed the news. "Victims of such attacks do not survive."

"But he came back!" Molly said, eyes opening in one last desperate attempt.

Rory shook his head. "It wasn't him, or rather, it *isn't* him, not anymore. It's the nature of a vampire attack," he explained. "The victim may remain himself for a short time, but after a few days, the demon takes over, and the good man you once knew is gone. Your husband is dead, Mistress Saffron," he said, not unkindly. "What lives in his body is a demon from the depths of hell. It has to be destroyed or it will use your husband's body to cause even more trouble."

"He is right," Lira said in a solemn voice. "There is no cure for such an attack." She shook her head sadly. "The only solution is to destroy the beast. It is the only way to save his soul from the underworld."

Hannah held her breath. This was what they would say about her if they knew. Such rumors were created by her people, true, but that didn't make them any less ridiculous when she heard people credit them as truth. *They honestly believe that vampires are demons?* She wanted to scoff. There were far greater evils in the world than people who needed blood to survive. Hannah imagined that real demons, if there were such things, would be offended by the comparison.

"But a vampire?" Molly asked. She began to shake her head vigorously. "No," she stated. "My Jason wasn't out at night." She looked desperately from Rory to Lira and seeing no sympathy there, turned to Hannah. "Vampires only come out at night," she told the vampire. Hannah cleared her throat as if in preparation to say something, but Rory saved her the trouble of dispelling that particular rumor.

"No, Mistress Saffron," he told her gently. "Vampires may prefer to hunt at night, but they have been seen during the day as well." He looked uncomfortable for a moment, as if discussing such matters before Hannah was inappropriate, then shrugged, speaking to Hannah. "Vampires are very real and very dangerous, day or night."

Hannah solemnly guarded her face.

"What—" The widow choked, then regained some of her composure and asked quietly, "What will happen to my Jason?"

Rory's face grew serious as he turned back to her. "He isn't your Jason anymore," he repeated. "He may look the same, but the good man that was your husband is gone."

"Gone?" The woman was on the verge of more hysterical crying. She looked at the three of them again, the force of her desire for a different truth making Hannah almost pity her.

Lira spoke gently, a hand reaching out to comfort the woman. "His spirit will find peace," she told her. "I promise. We will see to it."

"How?" Molly sniffed, coughed, and made a visible effort to pull herself together. "What can you do?"

"If he returns," Rory explained, "which is doubtful, we can see to it that his soul is redeemed." He gave the woman a serious look. "Only his soul," he said forcefully. "We cannot save his body."

Hannah heard the coldness in Rory's voice and tried to repress the shiver that wanted to shake her. He would say such things about her if he knew. *What else do these elves think they know about my people? Do they know about purebloods?*

Hannah ignored the suddenly loud voice of her father and her teacher echoing in her head: *Kill them all! Kill anyone who knows too much about us! We survive this way only because no one knows exactly what we are. Once the mortals figure out our existence, they will find ways to destroy us.*

"Yes, I know," Molly said sadly, voice heavy with acceptance, eyes closed as she dropped her head. "I knew it wasn't him, not at the end. I think maybe he left so he wouldn't hurt me. Near the end there, he looked like he was struggling with something inside."

Hannah knew it was probably the bloodthirst. Not every new fledgling became one of the fehalon, and if he was struggling, that was a good sign. There was hope for Jason Saffron, even if these mortals couldn't see it.

"That's often how it happens. The victim may retain some memory of himself for a little while, but it fades, and then all that remains is the monster." Rory lowered his head as if debating whether or not to say something. Hannah thought he decided against it, choosing to say only, "I am sorry, Mistress."

Hannah considered the elves. They spoke as if they had actually faced a fehalon before. The people of her father's castle did not bite victims at random. Magnus was very clear about the punishment for that. But there were other Houses in the mountains, and perhaps Gerter van Lartner and Pietor van Kistling weren't so particular about what their people did. Or it could be a stray, a random attack—such things happened even with the harshest penalties—but Hannah didn't think so. It was too convenient and too close.

"So, there's no hope then?" Molly asked, and Hannah felt the tension in her words, the hope she wanted them to validate, the smallest chance that her man would return and recover. Hannah thought they should probably tell her that, in a few days, goblins were likely to overrun this small homestead and her demonic husband would be the least of her worries.

But then she felt a sudden inexplicable urge to reassure the woman, to tell her that Jason Saffron was fine, or would be fine, likely, and they could still live together—that is, if she didn't mind letting him feed from her. There were ways to keep her from being turned. It was the bite that did it, something in the saliva, Hannah remembered Malbrek lecturing about it, but people could be bled easily enough. Hannah had always fed from the human servants in that way. There had been whispers that some Kargin did more than just feed on their servants, but Hannah had never really paid attention to that.

The idea was so ... repugnant. To feed was one thing; to force the slaves into anything more was monstrous.

Most of the slaves were willing enough to serve anyway, at least the ones Hannah had met. There had been a few who resisted, but Hannah's magic had always been enough to calm them. She had never bitten anyone she intended to let live, and Hannah had access to plenty of food as First Daughter. Most of the time, she let them go after bleeding them into a cup, but she couldn't deny the part of her that thrilled at their deaths. *They are mortal,* she told herself. *They die anyway.* Not that her people were immortal, of course—they were just long lived, like the elves and dwarves. It was only the humans who died so quickly. Jason Saffron would now be spared that fate if he hadn't turned fehalon.

She looked around the small kitchen. The simple table and chairs, the delicate tea set, the worn wooden cupboard were so ordinary, so commonplace. *What made this farmer deserve the blood gift?* If it was a random attack, fate was playing with her.

I have to know, she decided. She had to find this Jason and deal with him.

Of course, she could find him. She only had to reach out with her senses. She could find another of the blood. It wasn't even the kind of magic that required words. It was harder to sense the fehalon since they were usually a little crazed but not nearly as hard as sensing a fledgling who had learned to hide himself or as easy as sensing another pureblood—born vampires of her father's House were easy to sense. Even now, she was vaguely aware of Klauden at the edge of her senses. She knew he was hundreds of wheels away in her father's castle, likely with his head buried in some ancient book from the library.

She had sensed the others when she had left, but they had faded as time passed and the distance between them grew. Only Klauden remained now, and Hannah was glad to know that even though she couldn't see him or talk to him, she could at least feel that he was alive. He could probably sense her too, but no one else could. Not anymore.

She had another moment of gratefulness for the spell Klauden had used to hide her from Malbrek, knowing that she would have been found long ago without Klauden's help. *If they are even looking for me,* she reminded herself. Her father was probably glad to be rid of her.

She dragged her thoughts away from her old friend to focus on the present. The elves were still leaning forward, talking to Molly in low voices. She knew that Jamison and Gorn were minding the exits, Gorn standing idly by the kitchen door, out of place with his axes amid the simple furnishings, and Jamison back in the big room near the front door. Hannah needed to be alone if she wanted to find Jason Saffron. When she opened her vampiric senses, her eyes would glow red. Her companions couldn't see her like that.

She looked at Rory, deciding.

"We can try to find him," Rory was saying, "but it won't be about saving him."

"He's lost," Lira said, "but we can try to redeem him, at least."

"How?" Molly asked.

"The demon has possessed his body," Rory explained. "We can release him from that."

"If you kill his body," Molly finished, and Hannah was surprised at the sudden steel in the woman's voice. Her surprise must have showed on her face because Lira gave her an odd look.

"Are you alright, Hannah? You look ill."

She willed her face to calm itself. "I just need some air," she said. "I'll be outside for a bit."

Hannah was almost to the door when Rory spoke. "Be careful out there." Hannah turned back to look at him, pausing for a second too long to stare at those brown eyes. Gorn opened the door and gave her a look as she passed through it.

Once outside, she walked away from the house, heading toward the outlying buildings. The house was surrounded by a barn connected to a stable, and there were several smaller sheds farther away from the forest. Hannah guessed they held farming implements since they were nearer the small field. She waited until the barn was between her and the house, then reached out with her senses. The magic was comforting, familiar as it crawled up her arms and through her legs, and suddenly, she could see everything with a clarity that defied the late afternoon light.

Where would Jason Saffron go? He couldn't know how to hide himself, not as new as he was. As she sent out the power in a questing wave, the answer came almost immediately. *Where else could he go?*

Jason Saffron was still at home.

VI

Jason Saffron was hiding in his barn. Hannah moved quickly, slipping inside without opening the back door all the way and shutting it quietly behind her. She advanced into the dim interior a few steps and stopped. She didn't need to allow her eyes to adjust. When she invoked her innate ability to see in darkness, the barn was awash with contrasting lights and darks. Hannah marveled at how long it had been since she had used her magic like this. She really needn't have worried so much when they were in the forest. With such clear vision, she would have been just fine. It was so easy to forget herself among so many mortals.

Hannah mulled over whether the time had come to leave them, but then shelved the thought for future debate. They were still in the middle of nowhere, and goblins were about, and apparently, a rogue vampire was biting victims and abandoning them to seek shelter in barns. Now was definitely not the right moment.

A rogue vampire? Seriously? That's what you're going with, huh? Hannah willed the voice in her head to silence, unwilling to admit anything else. *It couldn't be Malbrek,* she assured herself. There was no reason for her father's magician to be hunting her. Magnus van Kreeosk was probably glad that his troublesome daughter was gone. And Malbrek certainly wouldn't leave a fledgling alone in the middle of nowhere like this. Unless...

Hannah's mind finished the thought for her. *Unless he wants to send you a message,* she knew. *Unless he wants to taunt you.*

No.

It doesn't mean anything, she insisted. It was a coincidence, nothing more, and finding Jason Saffron would only confirm her suspicions.

She stood in the middle of the barn, a huge open space with the smell of hay and horses. She could sense Jason off to her right, his presence a low thrum against her skin. He didn't feel like the other mortals, but he wasn't entirely a fledgling yet. She could tell right away that he wasn't a born vampire like her, but she knew his body was still making the shift from human to fledgling. He smelled good, as all mortals did, but he wasn't as appealing. Jason's blood was losing whatever she needed. Hannah knew that Klauden would have understood this, would have known why the human wasn't making her teeth tingle and her jaw ache with need. Hannah knew she should have paid more attention in Essentials.

Hannah could see Jason clearly against the wall, his form distinct against a background of wooden slats in grays and blacks, red eyes glowing in the dim light, and she knew the use of her nightvision was glazing her eyes the same shade of red. She had to make this quick.

"I know what you are," Hannah said bluntly, focusing on the figure before her, knowing this would only enhance his fear, the terror she could feel rising from him in waves, "and so do those inside." She decided this was enough and pulled back her magic, focusing solely on her remaining nightvision. She didn't want to know any more about Jason Saffron than she already did. As she spoke, Jason ducked, his figure disappearing behind a pile of crates stacked between two posts.

"What am I?" the voice was slurred, no doubt by teeth he was not used to yet. It must be disturbing to have teeth that lengthened inside the mouth after a lifetime of them not moving. Hannah couldn't imagine her own mouth without her teeth's ability to grow. *How bored a mortal tongue must be.*

"You are fledgling now, forced to survive on the blood of other living creatures," Hannah explained in a way that would make sense to him, knowing that whatever state he was in, he already felt the truth.

He was obviously not one of those who would fully recover from the bite. Hannah had seen such victims grow and mature into full-fledged kindred, but she had also seen others debased into mindless feeders. Looking at him, she felt some of her tension release. If he had been one of the fehalon already, she would have had to kill him herself—she wrinkled her nose in disgust at the thought. Those unfortunates were not tolerated for long among her kind, usually finding a messy end in the endless tournaments. Hannah didn't want to think about how difficult that would make her current situation. The fehalon were loud and dangerous, and she couldn't have contained him without the aid of her new companions— and that would raise more questions. No, Jason wasn't fehalon. At least, not yet. Sometimes a perfect fledgling would go bad, though. Some said it depended on the individual.

Which way would Jason Saffron fall? Hannah didn't know, but she also knew it wouldn't matter. Rory would kill this man on sight, for no greater crime than being victimized. It made Hannah angry, not for poor Master Saffron's fate, but because she knew the elf would do the same to her if he ever found out her true nature. The thought hurt her for some reason, and she was suddenly determined anew to have him before she ran out of chances.

"How do you know?" the fledgling whispered, voice carrying from his hiding place. "Who are you?"

"I am one who might help you if you listen to me." *What am I talking about?* the rational voice in her head demanded. *This is an unauthorized fledgling, a bottom feeder. I should kill him and get it over with.*

There was a silence, then, "I am listening." The slur was gone. It seemed that he had gotten control of his new teeth. "What can I do?"

"You can run, flee now, and never return. If you do come back to this place, you will destroy your wife. Save yourself the pain. Leave, and fast, before they find you." Hannah didn't know why she was saying this. It wasn't as if she cared about the man; she had taken her own share of humans just like him, though Hannah had made it a matter of principle to finish off her victims so they never had to endure this crisis. In her long life, Hannah had never made a fledgling.

Gods. Two weeks with the damn do-gooders and here I am trying to save a damned farmer from the inevitable.

"But why?" Jason was asking, his voice bubbling. Was the man weeping? "Why do I have to leave? Where should I go?" Hannah wanted to look away—it was always humiliating to see a man cry. Her father had taught her that only weaklings cried, and there were weaklings among the fledglings. They were easily marked by the blood tears they could not hide. A wise fledgling, like Kelvin Malbrek, her father's second and Hannah's teacher, had learned to hide his emotions immediately when he was transformed. Even pain couldn't conjure tears from the man. This mortal could barely contain himself, and all that she had done was warn him from danger. She sighed. Sometimes these mortals were so pathetic.

Hannah walked deeper into the barn. Jason did not try to evade her approach. In fact, he was simply sitting, his hands in his lap, looking utterly dejected when Hannah stopped before him. He looked up at her, his eyes wet and puffy, his mouth swollen, his teeth protruding awkwardly from sensitive gums. She knelt before him.

"Your eyes—" he began, but she cut him off.

"Look the same way yours do right now," she explained. She grabbed his hands and started to pull him to his feet. "Listen, there are people here to kill you. If you want to survive, you've got to get out of here."

"What will become of me?" the man wailed, and Hannah suddenly understood the attraction between husband and wife. She shook him.

"You will live," she stated, willing him to accept her advice.

"But like this? How can I?"

"You must," Hannah said, letting him go. He slumped back to the floor. "If you would live, go now. I will not give you another chance." She stepped away from him, uncertain why his eyes should grab her own the way they had. She didn't care about him, not really. *Honestly though,* she thought, *what chance does he have on his own?*

"Help me," he whined, his pleading eyes boring into hers. She steeled herself, jerking the man to his feet.

Hannah shook her head in frustration. "I *am* helping you. Go."

"Save me!" he yelped, throwing himself at her. He was in her arms before Hannah realized what was happening, his hot blood tears soaking the front of her sweater. "Please!"

She stood there, her arms held at a distance, aware of how close his neck was to her own eager mouth. *He is already doomed,* she thought. *Why not finish him off?*

"I cannot save you," she said softly. "There is no salvation for you." Her voice grew stronger. "But you can *live* if you are strong enough, and such a life isn't always a bad thing."

"But to live with such thoughts, such desires..." His voice trailed off. "How can I live like this? I am not myself!"

As much as she might want to continue the conversation, Hannah knew that the others would come for her soon. Time was running out. *How can I help him in one moment and abandon him the next? Is he my responsibility if I do send him away?* Hannah shook these thoughts away. It wasn't like her to think of such things. It wasn't in her nature to think so far ahead, and it certainly wasn't in her to care about random fledglings.

What is happening to me?

"What is it that you wish?" she whispered, leaning closer to him. He smelled good, fresh and masculine, so different from the goblins she had been reduced to lately.

Jason raised his head, winced as his sensitive teeth surged to full length again, then seemed to decide something. "I wish for peace," he said clearly, then bent his head back down to her shoulder, exposing his neck. "I will not become a beast. Finish it."

Hannah didn't realize she had decided to oblige him until her mouth began moving toward his neck, closing the gap between them in seconds. She didn't speak again, cutting off the internal protests before they could begin. A man was standing before her, asking her to kill him. He may not completely have the blood that her body craved, but he still had some mortality left in him, and that small part called out to her, the very slow thump of his heart suddenly pulsing in her fingertips. It wouldn't be enough, never enough, but she had had nothing but goblin for days and days. The echo of human blood, however weak, was enough to make her abandon all thought and act. She didn't even have to worry about biting him.

She enclosed him carefully, one arm going behind his neck to hold him steady when he began to sag against her, the other wrapping around his waist. Jason Saffron was sturdily built, his muscles hard against her hands. Hannah let herself savor the moment, then bit him, her teeth sliding home with a jolt like ecstasy.

There was no need for restraint with this mortal—he wanted to die. Some of those brought to her back home had been like this, had sought death in her arms, and she had always loved the freedom in biting them. Even blood in a glass was preferable to the goblins she had been reduced to, but this moment was all pleasure. She drew him into herself, feeling his body relax against hers as his memories ran across her mind.

Hannah watched the haphazard impressions of the attack in his mind. The images were hazy, twisted and distorted as he recalled them. One moment he was walking back home on a route so well known that he didn't have to keep his eyes open to know where to place his feet, and the next, he was on the ground with something large retreating into the distance, head aching and skin tingling with the change. Hannah knew what Jason did not understand. He had been spelled, hypnotized as she sometimes did to her victims to make them pliable, and his only real impression of the attack was the large shape speeding away.

She wondered why the vampire had stopped short of killing him. It didn't seem to make any sense. She certainly wouldn't have left him alive. The bonds between master and the changed vampire were strong, and she had read enough stories of vampires who had died when their fledglings did, a connection that seemed a foolish risk to Hannah. True, it could gain the master a devoted follower who was unable to disobey, but such a great cost didn't seem worthwhile to Hannah. Sure, fledglings could grow quite strong in their own right—wasn't Kelvin Malbrek, her teacher, a turned vampire? Not that anyone would say so to his face any longer.

She mused briefly in the haze that the blood always called down across her thoughts, wondering what had befallen Malbrek's maker. It wasn't her own father, she knew that, but she didn't know if she should be surprised at the question or more surprised that it had never occurred to her to ask it before. Since leaving home, Hannah had moments like this with increasing frequency, sometimes astounded at how very little she had thought to question in her father's castle. Back home, it just hadn't seemed to matter. *Not that it does now*, she thought distractedly. *What is it to me anyway?*

She let herself sink back into the moment, relishing the feel of the blood in her mouth, the magic of his life echoing in her skin, the soft weight of his body starting to lean into her a distant burden.

She had a brief moment as Jason started to sag against her when she thought she felt someone else, a presence distantly connected to the man sensing his impending doom. It must be the one who had bitten him. Her mind tried to remind her that maybe the vampire was Malbrek, and this was a trap. She didn't think so though. The bond between master and fledgling held over great distances and even unto death, with some hinting that master shared his fledgling's pain, and vice versa, but if Malbrek was the maker, he should have been closer, sharing the death with his creation. Hannah reached out with her senses again, trying to find that presence, but she and Jason were alone. If the maker shared any bond with his fledgling, Hannah couldn't sense it. She didn't think the maker had severed the connection—she didn't even think that was possible—but maybe the person could hide his presence. Deciding she could think about it later, she surrendered to the moment.

She was still caught up in the blood-stupid daze when the shouting started.

VII

Hannah wasn't sure at first what was happening, her mind lost in the euphoric haze of Jason's blood, and she struggled to regain her senses. Jason Saffron had no hesitation. He was weak, his body nearly drained, and Hannah marveled at his ability to move in such a state, but move he did. The fledgling shoved her to the floor, hunching down and taking two stumbling steps to the right, clearly meaning to flee to the back of the barn where she had first found him. Hannah went down in a heap, willing her limbs to obey and cursing as she tried to order her mind. Her eyes were closed, and she had a brief moment of clarity when she started to open them. *Your nightvision!* She shouted at herself. *Don't let them see your eyes!* Deciding that she was probably better off playing the victim in this scene, she lay unmoving on the dirt floor with her eyes closed, trying to piece things together by the sounds around her.

There was a lot of motion and confused words. She heard mumbling and an echo of magic swept across her skin—mortal magic, though. She hadn't realized that one of her traveling companions could call the power. *Could that be Molly?*

She heard the telltale ring of a blade being drawn from a scabbard. That would be Rory. There was some scuffling that might have been Jason trying to get deeper into the barn, but before Hannah could wrap her head around the action, Lira began to chant. The divine magic caused Hannah's skin to tingle painfully, obliterating the small hint of magic she had felt just seconds before, the power building fast and streaking across the room, not aimed at Hannah but so close that the echoes made her head ache. She opened her eyes, needing to see what was happening, and she saw the white-hot light engulf Jason Saffron as he crouched against the far wall. He tried to scream, his face stretched into agony, and then he was melting, his form disintegrating as Hannah watched, disappearing into that light until there was nothing but a shadow, a vague shape where he had been, then there was nothing at all—emptiness. The light faded with a hollow bang that resounded in Hannah's own bones, the force of the magic sizzling in her own blood. Jason Saffron had been obliterated.

There was a distant echo in Hannah's head, a scream of surprise and frustration that seemed terribly familiar, then the sound was gone. It took her a moment to place the voice, but finally her memory clicked, and Hanna's skin ran cold. It had been Kelvin Malbrek's cry that she had just heard, his frustration when the link between he and his new fledgling had been severed by Lira's power. *He was using Jason Saffron to get to me*, Hannah thought with chilling clarity. *He is coming for me.*

Lira took a shuddering breath in the sudden silence. Hannah kept staring at the spot where Jason had been. Her body ached with the echoes of the divine magic, the pain of such a fate. After what seemed like a long moment, she turned to see Lira, the elf standing, still haloed by the after-effects of her power, her long blonde hair settling in loose strands around a face flushed with exertion and excitement. The elf saw Hannah looking at her, and Hannah shivered.

Such power, she thought. She had known that divine magic was powerful, but she hadn't realized that it could completely disintegrate one of her kind. No one deserved that kind of power.

She cannot be allowed to live, not with the ability to do that. Hannah stared at the elf for another moment, knowing that thought was something her father would have said. Seeing how the elf's body was relaxing, her chest beginning to heave with the effort as the euphoria of using her power began to fade, Hannah understood why he would think such a thing. The elf shuddered, falling heavily to one knee, but she gestured quickly at someone Hannah could not see, someone who must have offered aid. Hannah closed her eyes, not wanting to see anymore. She lay limp on the floor, body aching as she tried to keep her teeth from chattering.

Gentle hands reached beneath her and turned her over, long fingers pressing against her neck to feel the pulse there. Hannah was glad that she was a born vampire yet again. Some fledglings no longer had a palpable heartbeat. Passing among the mortals was more difficult for them.

"She's alive," Rory said, and Hannah restrained the sudden urge to smile at the relief in his tone. Now that he was so close to her again, she could smell him, that musky blend of sweat and leather and trees, and her pulse sped up a little, body warming as heat flushed through her. He was so close. She could just reach out and take him. It would be so easy.

"He didn't bite her?" That was Gorn, and Hannah was glad to hear relief in the dwarf's voice too. It wasn't the chest swelling excitement that Rory's concern created in her for some silly reason, but it was nice to know that Gorn cared whether she lived or died.

"He didn't bite her. Why am I not surprised?" The last voice belonged to Jamison, and Hannah was pleased to hear a thud followed by a sharp cry of pain. Gorn must have hit the man.

"Hey!" Jamison exclaimed. "I just helped save her life, you know. I distracted it."

"Yes," Gorn commented, "your fog was a great distraction while I was trying to find the creature before it could kill wee Hannah."

"Hannah?" Rory asked, his face close to hers as he spoke in a low voice by her ear. She shivered, a delicious thrill skating across her skin, then she dismissed the last of her magic and opened her eyes. The relief on the elf's face was obvious, and he grinned at her. "Hannah," he said again, sitting back, an arm on hers helping her to sit up. "Are you alright?"

Hannah shook her head as if to clear it, trying to play it right. "I think so," she whispered. "My head…"

"Your poor head," Rory said, his other hand touching her cheek lightly before sliding to examine the back of her skull. "Did you hit it again?"

"I don't think so," she said. "It doesn't feel like that. I just feel muddled, like he tried to spell me maybe."

"He could have," Lira said, and suddenly the elf was standing next to them, her face returned to normal. "Vampires have the power to bewitch their prey. I understand it can be quite overwhelming. If you want, I can help."

"No," Hannah said quickly, trying to stand up. She didn't like being on the floor when Lira stood so near. It was too dangerous. "I'm fine," she told her. "There's no need."

"Jason?" Molly came into view then, her tall form throwing shadows inside the barn, the last of the afternoon light on her wet face.

Lira turned to the woman, face somber. "He is at peace," she said. Hannah restrained the sudden urge to shout at the elf. *Of course, Jason Saffron isn't at peace!* Lira had just obliterated him with her magic. If there was any peace to be found beyond life, Lira had just ensured that Jason Saffron would have none of it. And now she could stand there and lie to the man's widow, acting as if she had actually helped the man find salvation. It made Hannah's stomach turn.

Or maybe it was from hitting her head earlier, she thought as she leaned forward and was suddenly sick, the contents of her stomach emptying on the floor. As she leaned over the mess, Hannah was suddenly very glad that it was nearly dark inside the barn, and that once mixed with the dirt, the blood turned to mud that could have been anything. She felt Rory's hand on her back, a gentle pressure offering comfort, and she took a moment to wipe more dirt over the mess she had made. Then she sat back, raised a hand to her chin and wiped her mouth, hoping she had just smeared enough mud all over her face to cover any traces of Jason's blood.

Had it been because he was too much a fledgling? Was his blood not enough for her anymore? Or had it been a reaction to Lira's magic? Or maybe Rory was right, and she should be more careful with her head wound—even though she assumed that had healed days ago. Hannah wasn't in the habit of vomiting often and rarely when she had blood. She hoped it wouldn't happen again. Rory held out something cool in her direction, and Hannah accepted the wet cloth absently, wiping her face carefully and trying to calm her body.

"Easy now," he said, and she looked at him, seeing the honest concern on his face as he held a canteen in her direction. She accepted it and knew that she had to take him soon. Hannah nearly retched again, another wave of nausea keeping her on her knees, but she managed to hold herself in check, closing her eyes and breathing slowly, fingers tracing the worn leather of Rory's canteen.

"At peace...?" Molly asked, then Lira was speaking to the woman again.

"We did what was necessary, Mistress Saffron. Your husband was possessed. He would only have gotten worse. It was better to set him free now, when there was still a chance for his soul to see paradise."

The woman was nodding, a desperate hope fighting with grief on her face. "I knew it," she moaned. "I knew he was lost."

"He is not lost," Lira said gently, her hands coming to rest on the woman's shoulders. "He has been given the chance to meet his creator without the stain of devilry on his soul. He has been set free."

Hannah focused on her breathing, but she couldn't help but wonder if Lira honestly believed what she was saying or if she was just trying to comfort the widow. She made a mental note to study up on Lira's god when they reached Upsen.

"I see," Molly Saffron answered, sniffing and wiping her eyes. Then, she looked at Hannah, her eyes filling anew with tears. "I'm so sorry, my lady. My Jason would never have hurt you were he in his right mind." She looked to Lira. "Thank you for saving his soul."

Hannah looked away, trying to ignore the sudden heaviness in her chest. It had been a long time since anyone except Rory had referred to her as a lady, and having the new widow do so made something in Hannah ache. She looked down instead, eyes resting on her boots before looking up at Molly, and pushed the feeling aside. There were practical things to think of.

"Hey, you wouldn't happen to have a spare pair of boots, would you?"

VIII

For the next week, Hannah was convinced that every sound she heard was Malbrek leaping from the shadows. When Rory approached her to talk in the evenings, she was distracted, eyes skirting past him to the surrounding tree line, trying to determine where Malbrek was hiding, when he would strike.

After three days of her obvious preoccupation, Rory moved himself directly into her line of vision as he spoke. She had been nodding in agreement to what he was saying, but he broke off quickly, asking, "What are you looking for, Hannah?"

Hannah bit her lip nervously, struggling for an excuse. The elf turned to glance behind him, beyond the crackling fire in the center of their camp. His glance skittered over the hunkered shape of Jamison as he sat tracing shapes into the ashes around the fire pit and the distant lump that was Gorn as he rested against a large tree across the clearing, pausing for a brief moment on the still form of Molly Saffron who sat staring into the fire. Of course, the widow had chosen to come with them to Upsen. Rory wouldn't have left her behind, alone on her farm in a forest that may soon be teeming with goblins.

The elf looked at Hannah, pointedly into the darkening shadows of the forest, then back to Hannah. "What do you think is out there?"

Hannah hugged herself, consciously forcing her mouth to stop biting her lip in the nervous habit she had developed south of the Vanya. She shrugged. When it became clear that Rory wasn't going to speak until she did, she seized on something she thought Rory would understand and mumbled, "There may be more creatures like Jason."

The elf cocked his head to one side. "You fear more vampires?"

Hannah was aware of how true his words were.

He put a hand meaningfully on his sword. "No worries, Hannah," he told her. "We are perfectly safe here."

Hannah thought of how easily she had located Jason Saffron, knowing just what powers Malbrek had at his disposal, and let her worried skepticism show on her face.

"Look," Rory said, moving closer so he didn't have to speak so loudly, "I know how to deal with such creatures. Nothing will touch you as long as I am here."

"You've hunted..." Hannah swallowed, then asked, "vampires?" It felt weird to say the word out loud, as if she were committing some great heresy.

Rory shrugged a little in dismissal. "I've hunted a lot of things. You name it; I've probably tangled with it."

"Like what kind of things?" Hannah couldn't help herself. She wanted to know more about him, ridiculous as it was. When she killed him, she would absorb all of his memories anyway. There was no need for him to tell her anything.

Yet, I want him to tell me. Want him to trust me. Hannah was no stranger to desire, but this kind of wanting was new to her, and being dependent on someone else to provide her with what she wanted was disconcerting.

Rory looked around as if searching the sky for answers. "Let's see," he said, his hand leaving his weapon to rest lightly against his chin. "There were some demons outside of Severin. Three of them. Small, hairy, solid fighters, they were, but I eventually got the best of them. I took a beating though." He laughed a little, self-deprecating. "Taught me not to underestimate any foes like that ever again." He gave Hannah a pointed look. "Just because something doesn't seem dangerous does not mean it isn't."

Hannah grinned. "Why do you say that?"

He gestured at her small form sitting on her blanket. "Take you, for instance. At first glance, you don't seem very threatening."

Her grin turned into a chuckle. "Are you saying I am threatening?"

"Well, you survived the goblins and an attack by a vampire. I'd say you definitely know how to handle yourself in tricky situations."

"I was lucky," Hannah said. "You saved me from the goblins," she hesitated, "and from the vampire."

"*We* were lucky," Rory replied. "We were able to get there in time." He gave her a look then. "Still, I suppose you had a few remaining tricks. You would have gotten away from him, even if we hadn't been there."

"You think so?" Hannah felt an odd burning in her cheeks at the backhanded compliment. How long since someone had told her she did something well? That she was capable? "Thanks," she said, feeling the depth of meaning in the word.

"For what?"

His eyes were so intent. Hannah felt the slow beat of his heart as it sped up a little, the pulse echoing in her skin. She bit her lip, choosing her words carefully. "For your confidence," she said finally. "It means a lot."

"For me as well," he said, nodding his head seriously. He let out a breath, adding in a low voice, "I don't often have confidence in others." He seemed to realize what he had said and scrambled a little for something else to say, settling for, "I mean, most people always end up needing help, and you just seem like you can take help, but you don't need it." He shrugged, smiling. "It's refreshing."

Hannah felt the additional compliment warming her insides and decided that this was a terrible conversation to have, so she blurted out the first thing that came to mind in order to change the subject, repeating, "So, you've hunted vampires?"

He seemed to remember himself, settling in as he told the story. "It was a long time ago, just north of Firene. You know the Elven city?"

Hannah recalled the ancient maps Klauden had insisted on showing her as they read book after book on Elven mythology. Firene was the Elven stronghold to the east of the Vanya. Some said that occasionally an elf would get lost, separated from his comrades, and the child of the mountains who chanced upon him was blessed with the boon of Elven blood. Such was the case in Rory's story, at least.

There was a platoon of border guards running their rounds along the farthest borders when one of their number came up missing. By the time Rory had arrived to sort out the situation, several dogs and horses had also gone missing, and the men were restless, whispering stories of vampires. Rory had tracked the missing elf, a man named Javerus, through the rocky wilderness for several days, eventually catching up to him and killing him under the stars.

"He was a wild thing by the time I found him," Rory explained. "There was nothing of the old Javerus in him at all."

"You knew him?"

Rory shrugged. "I knew him when we were kids. He was never a close friend of mine, but what I killed among the rocks that night was not him. Not anymore."

Fehalon, Hannah thought. Javerus had gone crazy with the change. *But why was he left alone in the first place? What pureblood would feed on an elf and leave him alive? That doesn't make any sense.* Still, so close to Elven borders, that area of the mountains belonged to Gerter van Lartner, and Hannah wasn't sure how strict the ruler of House van Lartner was when it came to stray elves. Her own father would not have tolerated such sloppiness.

"Did you ever find the one who had bitten him?" she asked. When Rory gave her a sharp look, she added, "You said vampires infect through their bite."

He shook his head, brown hair falling in front of his eyes. His face grew hard as he spoke. "I never found the creature that bit him," he admitted, and there was regret in his voice, but then it was replaced by steel as he said, "but no others went missing from the east patrol while I was in charge."

"You were in charge of the patrol?" she asked, trying to steer the conversation away from a clearly unpleasant memory.

"No!" he scoffed quickly. "I wasn't part of the border patrol."

"But you were in the army, weren't you?" Hannah pressed, curious about him despite herself.

"It was a long time ago." He brushed her question off and leaned toward her instead. "So, tell me about you. Hunted many vampires, have you?"

"Oh, no," Hannah said. She looked away from him, hoping he wouldn't ask something that she would have to lie about. She firmly ignored the voice that demanded to know why she cared.

"Did you grow up in a smithy?"

"No," she said quickly, then frantically tried to think of something else to say before he could ask her anything else. Failing, she admitted, "I sort of fell into metalwork as an adult."

Rory smirked, a hand reaching out to trace the smooth skin of her palm. "You? I would never have guessed." He reflected on the skin of her wrist, eyebrows crinkling as his fingers slid across the perfectly healed skin.

Hannah pulled her hand away before he could ask, trying to hide the shiver as his fingers slid along her skin. "I did not have to do much manual labor as a child," she said quickly.

"I thought as much." He stared at her knowingly. "You have the bearing of aristocracy, Lady Hannah."

Hannah stared at him in disbelief, hands gesturing down at her travel-stained and simple clothing. "Me? I am no lady!"

Rory smirked. "You may not wear the clothing anymore, but I see it in you, Hannah *Smith*." He lingered on her new last name. "A childhood spent at court is not so easily hidden." He looked away, face lost in memory. "I would know."

Hannah gave him a sad look. "Who are you, Rory? Who are you really?"

He returned the expression, and then the melancholy left his eyes. "I could ask you the same."

She drew in a breath, biting her lip. "Rory..."

"Don't," he told her. "I won't ask." He searched her face, pondering. "Will you agree to a bargain then?"

She considered. "What are your terms?"

"I take you as I find you, and you extend the same courtesy to me."

She nodded slowly, liking the idea.

"Very well," he said, extending a hand in mock formal greeting. "My name is Rory, I am an elf, and I can protect you from vampires."

Hannah laughed, taking his hand. "Well met, Rory! I am Hannah, sword-fixer and magic user. I would love your protection, but apparently, I can survive just fine on my own."

When Rory laughed in response and tightened his grip on her hand, Hannah wondered if that last was true anymore.

IX

Hannah was still thinking about Rory's comments a few days later, thinking perhaps the elf was right, and he could protect her from attacks. She had seen no signs of Malbrek as they made steady progress east through the thinning forest, and she had started to think she had imagined that scream in her head. Maybe it was her overactive mind trying to scare her. It didn't make sense that Malbrek would bite a farmer in the middle of nowhere, let him live, allow him to die, then not confront Hannah for over a week if she was the magician's target. She wished suddenly that she could talk to Klauden, to ask her old friend if Malbrek had even left the castle, and her hands drew together in front of her body, fingers twisting the silver ring she wore on her middle finger, feeling the warmth of her body heat seeping into the metal. *I could probably do it,* she thought. The bond between them was strong, even for her kind. And there was always the spell he had given her, should she need him. But to call on Klauden after being silent for so long would be too much like failure.

She stopped herself, realizing that she was basically wringing her hands in worry, allowing her fears to run away with her until she was begging Klauden for help. It was exactly what Malbrek would want if he were out there. She let her hands fall to her sides, remembering what it was like to be Hannah van Kreeosk, First Daughter to Magnus van Kreeosk, and felt the strength of her name steel her spine. She looked around, taking in the small clearing that marked another night on the road. First Daughters did not wring their hands in worry, nor did they turn to lesser betrotheds to solve their problems. She frowned then, scanning the ground. First Daughters were not in the habit of sleeping rough on the forest ground either. She had spent way too much time lying on hard dirt, only the thin layer of her blanket between her and the earth. It hadn't been cold, so that wasn't a worry—not that the cold would bother her really, but that the others would expect it to—but the ground was hard, and even in Talperin, she had a soft bed of many blankets, stuffed with feathers and wool, and perfectly shaped to encase her small frame. It wasn't the luxury of the bed she had left behind in her father's castle, but it had been nice—and it had been hers. Sleeping out in the forest may seem a romantic idea from behind stone walls, but Hannah found the reality was much less satisfying.

At least the forest was thinning out with more of the slender trees that Rory had said marked the edges, but there was still enough foliage around them to warrant a clearing for a night's rest. The ground was growing softer too, fewer rocks digging in Hannah's side through her blanket each night, but Hannah still longed for an inn, a farm, something with a bed to sleep in, just for one night.

Arriving at a town or village large enough to support an inn would also make her feeding situation easier. There were still a few stragglers in the woods around them, but Hannah had to wander farther each time, and she knew that eventually her supply would run dry. *What then?* If Malbrek were still hunting her, biding his time while she worked herself into a frenzy, he would strike soon. For all that she was worried about the possibility, she had not gone off on a wild hunt for her father's magician. She had been careful, staying near the group at all times, only leaving to hunt twice since they had left the Saffron farm. She was thirsty, more so than usual, but still well under control.

She surveyed the ground with eyes newly accustomed to sleeping rough. She spied a promising place beyond a small tree, across the clearing from where Rory had let his bag fall with a careless thump. The elf never seemed to care where he laid his head, tree roots or rocks be damned. The elf just lay wherever he dropped his bag, sleeping soundly as soon as his blanket was on the ground. Hannah was more particular about her rest. She headed toward the edge of the clearing, booted feet scraping the ground to clear the few stray rocks in an attempt to make the ground more level. It was a decent spot. She was closer to the woods than to the others, so when she left to feed later that night, she didn't have to tramp through the campsite. She was also across what would become the fire pit from Rory, so she could watch him in the light of the flames without much notice.

She really liked watching the elf go about his nightly routine. He didn't seem to be much a creature of habit, but there were a few little rituals that he had, nothing quite so elaborate as Lira's prayer sessions each night and morning, or even so predictable as Gorn's humming, but she had noticed small things. He always straightened his blanket so that it was in line east to west, aligned with the setting sun. He did this even if it was after dark by the time they stopped to rest and even if that meant he had to move slightly farther away or a little closer to the fire to find enough flat ground. For someone who didn't seem to care where he slept, he always faced the same direction. Hannah was curious why—it seemed like something done without conscious thought. She planned to ask him about it when she got the chance.

The small group made their way around the clearing, each claiming a small area for personal space, dropping bags, and issuing sighs of relief. Molly let out a low groan and stretched, long arms over her head with her fingers reaching toward the sky. Hannah saw how the movement accentuated her bosom, saw the small marks of sweat across her sides where the straps of her pack rubbed, and glanced over to see Rory looking away from the woman, gaze intent on the rest of the clearing, probably deciding where to put the fire. Hannah smiled, pleased, even as she saw Jamison's appreciative look linger on Molly for another few seconds before turning back to his own belongings. Molly held her pose for another few seconds before letting her arms fall, emitting another sultry moan as she bent gracefully forward, this time bending nearly in half to stretch her back. Hannah was glad to see her black hair fall forward as well, loose curls hiding her face and what were probably fairly exposed breasts. She turned back to her own belongings, restraining the urge to roll her eyes.

Humans were so dramatic. Her own back and arms were sore from the walking too, but Hannah didn't need to share her relief with a wanton display of limbs and flesh. It reminded her of something Livenna, her father's other daughter, would do when they were younger, flaunting her height and curves while smiling with their father's purple eyes as she sashayed into the chamber that served as a classroom for the castle, eager to assert her place as first among the Kargin, second only to the three Firstborn children who always had their lessons first, who always had first claim to anything and everything in the castle. And Hannah had given all of that up to sleep on the ground in the middle of the woods in the middle of nowhere. She could see the look of smug satisfaction on Livenna's face even now.

I wonder if she has moved into my rooms yet, taken my place at my father's side. Another thought struck her then, more disturbing than it should have been—*Will Klauden marry her now instead of me?* Hannah didn't like the image that followed, her old friend standing cool and reserved with black-haired Livenna at his side, her hand possessively gripping Klauden's arm.

"Are you alright?"

The voice jolted Hannah out of the unpleasant thought, and she looked up to see Rory standing near her. His face suggested that he must have said something before his question, words Hannah had been too distracted to hear.

"I'm fine," she said quickly. "I was just … thinking."

"About what?" the elf asked easily, and Hannah looked down at her bag and the ground. She shrugged then, the image of Klauden still too raw to contemplate.

"Home."

"I take it you are not referring to Talperin?" Rory said carefully, the elf kneeling down next to her. Hannah knelt too and pulled her blanket from her bag. "Here, let me help." He took one end of the blanket and, in one swift motion, laid the fabric completely smooth on the ground, perfectly aligned east to west, without a single wrinkle or crease.

"Wow!" Hannah exclaimed. "Where did you learn that?" It always took her a few tries to get the blanket flat, and even then, she had to run hands across it to flatten the lumps.

"Lots of practice," he replied with a grin.

"You've slept outside a great deal?" Hannah tried to remember their bargain not to ask difficult questions, but she wanted to know everything about him anyway.

Rory shrugged, seeming not to mind her prying. "Some. You're thinking of home?" he asked gently. He peered at her intently, and Hannah was reminded of the way Klauden had looked at her when they were children. He always wanted to know what she was thinking too, though he could have easily guessed it. Hannah wasn't one to hide her thoughts or her feelings; that is, she hadn't been until leaving home and coming here. Now everything was secrets and deception. Hannah couldn't decide which she preferred—the open hostility of her father's castle, or the silent accusation in Jamison's eyes whenever she let her accent slip up.

Hannah had to be careful here, but she wanted to tell him something true anyway. "I lived in Talperin," she explained, "but it was not my home."

"I know what you mean. I've lived all over, but nowhere is ever the same as where I grew up."

She wanted to ask where that had been, but something held her back. She avoided the issue, asking instead, "Will you go home again, after all this is over?" She shifted her position, crossing her legs and piling her skirt in her lap as she settled in more comfortably.

Rory's hand tightened on his sword, his face clouding over with some remembered pain. He shook his head sharply. "No." He seemed suddenly very far away.

"Why not?" she probed.

"Because I can't," he said quickly, then shook his head again, returning to the present. He stood up abruptly, glancing at Jamison as he stacked wood for the fire. His gaze tracked over to Molly, pausing to watch the woman pull several cooking implements from her bag. "Molly will need meat for the stew tonight. I will go hunt."

Hannah tried to keep the disappointment from showing on her face. *It's always Molly this, Molly that...* "Good luck," she said lamely to his back.

Rory took a few steps, then turned back around to face her. "Hannah?"

"Yeah?"

"Will you go home again?"

Hannah considered. It wasn't a matter of will. After what she had discovered about her heritage, Hannah wasn't sure she could go back again. Everything had changed. In her cozy existence before that horrible morning of revelation, Hannah rested easily in the knowledge that her position, her bloodline, her future, even her mate, were all settled. No matter how hard the other girls had tried to belittle her for her abilities, or lack thereof, no one could argue with her breeding, and blood was everything to the people.

CHAPTER IX

Now, all that was gone. Hannah didn't even know if Klauden would stand by her now—he had been awfully quick to help her flee to the south, after all. Thoughts whirling, Hannah came to a realization. Though she did miss her homeland, the conveniences and familiarity of things known all her life, nothing could compare to the freedom she now enjoyed. After all, a few weeks ago, she had been alone in a village, and now she was traveling to an unknown southern city in the company of a ragtag band. Her father would never have approved of such behavior.

Hannah met Rory's gaze, allowing herself the pleasure of locking into those light brown eyes. "No," she stated. "I will not."

He flashed a bright smile, then turned and walked away. Hannah tried not to watch him go, focusing instead on how to get some supper without Molly chewing her ear off about her beloved Jason. *The man is dead*, Hannah thought, *and Molly should just get over it already. Talking about him incessantly won't bring him back, and what makes her think I care about any of it in the first place?*

Hannah began rummaging through her pack, wishing she had another set of clothes. Her current skirt and sweater were beginning to show signs of their days on the road and needed to be washed, but her only extra skirt was too thick to be practical for walking in this weather. Hannah thought of the river that lay beyond the tree line. Well, they didn't call it a river, not yet—to her companions it was still a stream—but to Hannah, the wide expanse of water was unnerving. She told herself that she wasn't afraid of it. *It's not like I'm going to drown, am I?*

Hannah looked up from her blanket to the woman setting up a pot with steaming water above the fire. *I bet she doesn't dislike the water*, Hannah thought. *I bet she jumps right in and swims like a fish, or a siren, and probably does laps in between scrubbing clothes and washing dishes.*

Hannah looked down at her own grimy clothing and wondered if she was beginning to stink. She hoped that wasn't why Rory had walked away from her, then hated herself for always thinking about the elf. *Ridiculous*, she told herself, scratching at a rather determined patch of what might be mud or blood on her sleeve. She didn't know how to get the stains out anyway.

Laundry had never been something Hannah concerned herself with. Even in Talperin, she had worked out a deal: Alice washed all of Hannah's clothes, and Hannah mended any of the laundress's cauldrons when they wore thin. Laundry had always been something someone else took care of.

There had been servants to do that at her father's castle. Hannah's rooms had been filled with freshly pressed dresses in the latest fashions. Her favorites had been red, of course, because her father had once told her how the red satins and silks complimented her red hair and pale complexion. Hannah always had an eye for fashion, the best dressed at any one of her father's galas. *The others always looked to me to see what to wear. Now look at me*, she thought dismally. *I'm a mess.* She looked up again at Molly, the woman smiling sadly as she measured small bits of shrubbery that must be spices into the pot. *I bet she is great with laundry*, Hannah thought with a mixture of bitterness and envy.

When Rory came back with several rabbits, Molly made short work of preparing them for the pot. The elf said something that made the woman's smile grow, but the happy expression was brief. Soon, she was back to her usual maudlin face, staring off beyond the fire with unnoticed tears tracking down her face. Hannah scowled, then forced herself to be realistic. She knew Rory wouldn't be so critical of Molly. *Look at him*, she thought, watching as he moved away to enjoy his meal. *He wouldn't ask her to forget her grief. He's too nice.*

But then, maybe his niceness was warranted. After all, the woman was far from home, too, out of her element, and likely as unsettled as Hannah had felt in her own early days. Maybe all of her dramatic sighing was her way of dealing with everything. Hannah tried to think kindly of Molly's plight, trying to understand the woman's position.

What in the hell is wrong with me? Last week I felt sorry for a fledgling who was none of my concern, and now I'm trying to empathize with a woman because that's what the damn do-gooder is doing? She shook her head, smoothing her wrinkled skirt, then turned to dig her dinner bowl from her bag. *What would Father think of me now? Filthy, traveling with elves for weeks instead of taking them, eating mortal food, and conversing with a farmer's widow... He would hardly recognize me.* Locating the bowl, Hannah ran her hands over the smooth surface and the worn runes carved into the rim. *Maybe that's a good thing.*

I have changed, she thought, sitting there looking at the crockery from her father's kitchen. Back home, it wasn't considered a nice bowl; in fact,

Hannah knew Klauden had taken it from the servants—her own people rarely ate anything in a bowl.

She stared at the bowl, running her fingers across the inlaid design. It was nice in its own way, she decided a bit uncertainly. She had no real head for appreciating artwork. She saw Jamison watching her then, and she quickly put the bowl down, out of sight. It was foolish to keep such a fine item with her—it marked her as wealthy when she clearly wasn't.

She learned that on her first arrival in a mortal village. Unaccustomed to her new surroundings, Hannah found a room in a crowded inn, only to have two men barge into her room in the middle of the night, intent on thievery and worse. Of course, Hannah made short work of them before she fled, but she had been very careful since then, making a point to fit in.

She stopped, the bowl forgotten. *Is that what I'm doing here? Do I really plan on spending the rest of my life, and a long life it will be, living among people and customs not my own?* Hannah had to admit that she hadn't fully come to terms with that concept yet; maybe she never would. *Do I honestly believe I will not go home ever again?* She shivered, the finality of her flight catching up to her. *Klauden knew*, she realized. She glanced down at the ring he had given her, the silver band on her middle finger still somehow bright against her dirty fingers. Hannah quickly altered the course of her thoughts. She held her hands out before her, ragged fingernails with dirt crusted underneath making strange shadows in the campfire light. She really needed to wash up.

She glanced at Rory, leaning against a tree and savoring his meal. He always managed to look so clean. As she watched him, he glanced over at her, raising an eyebrow in her direction. Hannah looked down. *Idiot!* She didn't want to admit what she'd really been thinking, the possibility that unnerved her even more than the easy idea of taking Rory as her customs demanded.

Let's have it, then, she told herself. *You're afraid that you'll break down and go back. You're afraid that, eventually, you will beg for any position in your father's castle, even among the Kargin, if only things would be normal again, predictable again.* She persisted, her innate brutal honesty forging ahead. *And if you really don't want to go back, you know that there's only one way to make sure you can't waver, one way to ensure that return is impossible.*

Her gaze wandered to Rory again, his long limbs and strong muscles. He would be kind and gentle, and it might even be fun—fun in ways she and Klauden had never ventured to explore. And he always smelled so good. She told herself it was foolishness, that he probably wouldn't have her anyway, but when he met her gaze again, a slow smile teasing across his lips, Hannah knew that it would be easy.

It hasn't come to that, she told herself, looking away from temptation. *Not yet.*

She decided that all these thoughts could wait for another day. Now, she just needed to do something, to act instead of think. She stood up, remembered her newfound intentions, and promised to be nicer to Molly. *I'll listen to her talk about Jason again,* she decided, *but only until I'm done eating. Then my time as a damn do-gooder is over for the night.*

X

Later that night, Hannah tried to imagine that the goblin struggling feebly in her grasp was not reeking with sweat and fear. The blood was warm and rich, but not as satisfying as she hoped. It never was these days.

She held the creature as it began to slump, then slowly moved to the ground with it in her arms, careful to hold the short sword in its belt against its hip to prevent any noise. Plates of metal wove into the goblin's makeshift armor, and though the clang the weapon might make would be minimal, Hannah wanted to avoid any notice at all. Her midnight meal's companions camped nearby; Hannah could see the flames of their dying campfire through the trees. She had watched as the one she held in her arms wandered off, no doubt to relieve itself, and she was there to relieve more than one of its fluids. She considered merely bleeding him at first but decided to go for the kill, not willing to risk the creature remembering anything about her. Even goblins would start to notice that something was preying on them.

As the blood flow slowed, Hannah released her hold, allowing the body to rest on the ground. Steeling herself against the stupor that would come, Hannah drew her dagger and set to work, quickly making the marks that would disguise this death as an animal attack. She dragged the corpse to a nearby bush and stashed it halfway beneath, remembering at the last second to draw the goblin's short sword and leave it lying a few feet from the limp hand, staining the blade with some blood so it looked like the goblin had at least made some small effort at defense.

It had been the same thing since leaving Talperin. She hunted for fresh blood, sometimes settling for a goblin, sometimes returning to her bedroll frustrated and burning, but something was changing. Normally, she only needed blood every three or four days, but lately, she had felt the need more and more often. It was being near the damn elves. Their blood burned at the edge of her mind constantly, a temptation that was getting harder and harder to resist.

As if that weren't bad enough, the dreams were back again too—the nightmare, her mind amended. Every night she lay down hopeful, wishing for undisturbed peace, and every night she woke, starving and ashamed, to hunt for something, anything, to sate her needs. On nights when she couldn't find anyone, she paced in the darkness, sweat running down her back, her body shaking as she tried to regain control for another long day.

Back in Talperin, she had rarely been haunted by the old faces, but they seemed to have returned with a vengeance, determined to wake her in a cold sweat at least once every night. She missed being able to sleep until morning. Even more, she missed the old days when she could just feed on humans. Even taking Jason Saffron hadn't exactly been the kill she remembered—he had been bitten already, and his blood was fast losing what her own body craved, not to mention that the whole thing had been rushed out of fear of discovery. *And look how well that turned out*, Hannah thought, repressing a shudder at the memory of Jason's fate. She was relieved when the numbness crept over her limbs and the fog encased her mind.

She kept walking, slowing down but still moving forward, heading back to the camp where the others still saw her sleeping form wrapped inside her blanket. *Sometimes*, she thought, *being a spellcaster has its uses. I always was good at illusions.*

The blood stupor was a relief, cutting off more coherent thought as she made her way through the forest. She could hear the dull roar of the river—stream—nearby and knew that she was close. The sound soaked into her, and the next time she thought of anything, she was aware that some time had passed. She shook her head to clear it, wishing she knew how long she had stood there motionless in the moonlight. She took a few tentative steps, stiff limbs obeying as she moved back toward the campground.

Just as she rounded a stand of trees, the worst of the blood stupor fading away, Hannah's foot caught on a root, and she stumbled, landing hard on her face in a puddle of black mud. The new boots were just slightly too big for her small feet. She restrained the impulse to curse, knowing it might rouse her companions, then rolled over and sat up. Despite the darkness, her nightvision allowed her to see the viscous substance coating not only her hands, but her sweater and skirt in sticky clumps. Her good mood evaporated.

Great, just great. How will I explain this? The sound of the water echoed in her sensitive ears, and she glanced in that direction, head cocked as she considered. *Without the others, I could get away with it.* She looked down at her clothes, sighed in acceptance, and got slowly to her feet.

Turning toward the sound, she made her way to the water, careful to look only at the ground and not at the heart-numbing expanse of the river itself. When she stood on the banks, she closed her eyes, concentrating a moment to restrain her natural nightvision, then opened them again. Without her night eyes, it was very dark. *Good*, Hannah thought, *now I can't see the other side. I can't see anything at all.*

It wasn't that she feared the water; in fact, Hannah knew there was no reason to. All that open space just made her uncomfortable. She assumed it had to do with the fact that she couldn't swim. None of her kind could. There was no reason to learn. Since arriving in the southland, Hannah had seen people swimming and marveled at the way they seemed to float on the water, their heads always bobbing on the surface as they breathed in the air they required. Hannah didn't need to breathe. She could, and did, but her body would survive without air, just as it could survive everything else. When faced with a river back home, Hannah simply waded in, trudged along the bottom, and walked out when a convenient exit presented itself.

Still, Hannah's method of dealing with water would hardly work while the rest of her companions watched. Rory would jump in, trying to save her from what he thought was drowning. While the act might increase his devotion to her, Hannah didn't think it was worthwhile. *After all*, she admitted, *don't I blame Molly for being in need of saving? Who am I to put myself in the same "dire peril" just so that I can be saved?* An image of a soaking wet Rory flashed across her mind, the lines of his shoulders outlined by tight wet clothing, and she scowled, annoyed at herself.

Taking a breath, she surveyed the dark water before her with night-blind eyes. She needed a bath, and dillydallying at the water's edge wasn't going to clean her body.

She stepped out from beneath a low-hanging branch and approached the bank, holding up her muddy hand as she walked—the ring on her middle finger glinted in the moonlight, another memory aching to be stirred to life. Hannah closed her fist and focused on the task at hand.

Her boot squelched in the mud that made up the riverbank, and she pulled her foot back as water began to seep through the leather to her foot. *Damn!* She put her hands out behind her and took several careful steps back to dry land. In the darkness, she did an odd little hopping dance to take off both boots. After another moment's consideration, she removed her belt with its daggers and laid it on top of the boots.

Having succeeded, she headed back for the water, reminding herself that this was no different from any stream back home. The water would be cold, the rocks would be sharp, and the current would do most of the work for her. She reached the bank again, squelched in her bare feet through the mud of the edge, then plunged into the water. It was surprisingly warm. *It would be*, she thought. *This far south it is warmer.* She took a moment to relish the novelty—her toes sinking in the soft mud, the warm water rushing around her knees. *I could get used to this*, she thought, taking a few more steps forward.

Soon, she was up to her shoulders, feeling the current as it tried to pull her downstream. She planted her feet solidly, then began scrubbing at her sweater. It became apparent quite soon that while this might work for her arms, she was going to have to take it off in order to clean it thoroughly. She turned back to the bank, convinced for a moment that someone was out there watching her. It was second nature to let her senses expand, tapping into her innate ability to feel the presence of other minds, but as she closed her eyes and reached with her magic, she felt a small hint of something—surprise perhaps? She tried to focus on the feeling, but it was gone as instantly as it had appeared, and she could sense nothing beyond herself in the water.

Giving up, she listened intently to her surroundings as she squinted her nearly useless eyes in an attempt to see if anything moved. There was a sliver of moonlight, but it only gave her a hint of the shoreline and the dark trees beyond. She felt suddenly vulnerable, then shook the thought away. There was no one there.

Besides, what could possibly happen to me? I doubt anything in this river, or even in this forest, could manage to kill me tonight.

She thought of Kelvin Malbrek, her father's wizard who was now hunting her, then pushed the thought away. He wouldn't come this way, she had decided. He would hunt for her farther north, convinced she would linger among the goblins, since they provided a steady diet of food. And if he did head south, he would never look for her near the river— stream—because he knew how she felt about open water.

Comforted, Hannah shrugged off her sweater, conscious of the tendrils of water that now caressed her bare arms and shoulders. After allowing herself a moment to enjoy the sensation, she focused on the task at hand.

She had been at this laundry business for almost an hour when she finally met her match. There were two spots on her skirt that simply would not come clean. She turned from her work to check the moon, which seemed to have dropped drastically as she stood there scrubbing. *I need to get back soon,* she thought. Giving up on the skirt, she finished washing her body, finally just dipping under the water and sitting on the bottom as she let the current pull her hair out in a stream behind her.

When she was as clean as she thought possible for such accommodations, she set out from the water. She squelched through the mud, wishing she had a spell that would levitate her over the dirty bank, then made her way by moonlight to where she had left her boots. Holding her wet sweater and skirt over one arm, she squeezed the water out of her long shirt and shook her head to rid her hair of excess water. Her hair always felt odd when it was wet, the weight of the water pulling her tight curls down below her shoulders, the cold tips brushing against her back as she shook from side to side. She attempted a finger-combing, then gave up, remembering the brush in her bag at the campsite. She shrugged awkwardly into the wet sweater, the sleeves pulled out of shape by the water, and stepped into the skirt, enjoying the feel of the smooth wet material next to her skin. Her belt helped hold up the suddenly heavy material. After wiping the mud from her feet on the grass, she slipped on her boots, not bothering to lace them up since she was just going to take them off again.

I can sit in front of the fire and dry off. No one will be awake anyway. Hannah made her way through the trees, approaching the soft light of the campfire in the center of the clearing.

She was about to enter the clearing when she noticed the goblin kneeling over the illusion she had left under her blanket. The creature held a sword, preparing to bring the weapon down into what it thought was her sleeping body. Hannah froze, trying desperately to come up with a solution before everyone else woke up.

Why did I think leaving tonight was a good idea again?

XI

Hannah scanned the surrounding trees for the goblin's companions. A lone creature would never be so bold as to stroll into a campsite like this. The others would have to be nearby. She reached out with her senses, choosing not to use her nightvision unless it was absolutely necessary. It wasn't hard to pinpoint each being's location. Two behind the trees opposite the river; two on the north side of the clearing; three to the east, congregating behind the tree Gorn leaned against, the dwarf snoring in little sputters; and three more to the south, hovering behind a copse of trees near Rory's blanket.

Rory's empty blanket.

Hannah came back to herself, what she was seeing in the light of the dying fire sinking in. Rory wasn't there. *Where did he go?* Jamison had been on watch, the one she had spelled into sleep. His slumped form still sat before the fire, head resting on his chest. She hoped the shouting would wake him once things got going. *So many goblins!* It was a miracle that she hadn't stumbled across one of the attackers when she made her way back into camp. She only had a few seconds to act.

She focused on the goblin leaning over her bed and silently slid her dagger out of her belt. The creature crouched on one knee, its rusty blade in hand, ready to stab the sleeping form huddled under the blanket. Hannah waited, dagger in hand, for the opportunity to present itself. The goblin thrust down with the sword, the blade slipping through the illusion, dispelling the magical image, and settling in the dirt beneath Hannah's blanket. The creature uttered a shriek of dismay, rearing up to look around for its lost prey, also displaying a decent square of vulnerable waist, and

Hannah let her dagger fly. The goblin's cry was interrupted by a gurgling wail as her blade struck home, but the sound had done its work.

Across the clearing, Gorn sat upright, an axe already in his hand even before he had opened his eyes all the way. "What in the hell?" he muttered, scanning the campground. His gaze settled on the goblin as it toppled over onto Hannah's blanket.

Lira also sat up, her blonde hair flying in disarray around her face as she scrambled to her feet. She too noted the goblin lying where Hannah had made her night's rest and began chanting.

Molly began to scream at the sight of the goblin, even though Jamison and the fire lay between her and it. Jamison sat up at her shrieks, looked confused for a moment, seemed to register that there was a fight going on, and began mumbling a spell. Seconds later, fog began to roll into the campsite from the surrounding trees.

As if brought on by the fog, the goblins pounced as one, all ten pouring out of the trees and into the clearing. Hannah darted into the fray as well, ducking to avoid one creature's swing as she crossed its path, and made a line for her blanket. The body of the fallen goblin was still, her dagger sticking out of its side. She made it to the body, collected the weapon, and put it up just in time to stop one of the eastern goblin's sword thrusts. She wasn't very good at close combat, her skill with daggers mostly with distance throwing, but she was managing to hold her own with each thrust. It was when the second creature's blade dug into her back that Hannah realized she was outnumbered yet again. Her options were limited. With so much action, she couldn't concentrate long enough to get a spell off, and it wasn't as if she could just bite them with everyone standing around. The goblin before her wavered at the appearance of its companion, clearly expecting her to fall now that she had been wounded. Never one to disappoint, Hannah fell to the ground with a cry, tucking her legs so that she would be able to spring up again quickly.

The goblins knelt down to finish her off, and Hannah took her chance. She swung hard with the dagger, catching one under his armor for a deep cut, then withdrew the blade, trying to catch the other goblin's weapon before it put another hole in her. She was just fast enough, the short sword slipping against her blade, veering off course from her heart to land near her armpit. She felt the impact in her breastbone, focused around the pain, and thrust up with the dagger. It took two tries to get around the creature's armored chest plate, but it was too busy trying to free its weapon from her shoulder to put up more of a defense. She felt her blade sink into its side, then the body collapsed on top of her.

Rolling over and letting the body fall to the side, she sat up, trying to take stock. The rest of the clearing was a misty mess of images. She could hear the sounds of metal clashing, but she couldn't tell who was fighting whom or how many of the goblins were left. A burst of light to her left caught her eye. *That's probably Lira,* Hannah thought as a goblin's cry cut through the general noise. Hannah understood every word.

"<Find the one who hunts us in the night!>" the creature screamed in its native tongue. "<Find the creature who would devour us all!>"

Hannah straightened, her skin going cold at the words. *They are hunting me,* she realized. *I've been a careless fool!*

She scanned the clearing, trying to pinpoint the one doing the shouting. The darkness and fog weren't helping her. She was about to close her eyes and allow her natural nightvision to come into play—damn the consequences—when she saw something just as useful.

Rory was fighting three of the creatures near the southern edge of the clearing, his sword whirling dangerously, but these goblins were better trained than the ones in Talperin. They were ducking and weaving around his thrusts, just as he was avoiding their own. It was only a matter of who could keep up the game longer. Hannah was sure that Rory would eventually win, but waiting around wasn't something she could afford to do. Molly was screaming again. *Maybe a goblin has her,* Hannah thought, trying to decide if that would be such a problem.

She avoided the issue, focusing instead on Rory, glad that she had memorized useful spells that morning. He was the only one she could see anyway. She closed her eyes, pulled the words from the bottom of her mind, and let the spell loose. At once, ten identical Rorys stood among the three goblins. One creature stayed focused, stabbing at the elf nearest him, then stood dumbfounded as the illusion first wavered, then vanished. Nine Rorys seemed to pause, then realize the new advantage, each moving exactly the same way. A surprised goblin took a sword thrust through the chest, then the remaining two creatures began swinging in random circles, trying to cut down anything elf-like that stood before them. It didn't take the real Rory long to cut them down instead.

The elf didn't hesitate in his attack as the creatures fell, moving across the clearing to where Hannah could hear more action. Through the fog, she heard more cries, more metal, then the thump as bodies hit the dirt. There were two more flashes of light from Lira's direction, a satisfied "humph!" from where Gorn had been sleeping, then a muffled sob that must be Molly.

"Is everyone alright?" Lira was asking. "Rory, where are you?" A surprised "what?" was followed by another question, "Hannah?" There was another silence as Hannah tried to answer, but then Lira was speaking again. "Jamison, do something about this fog, will you? Molly, are you hurt?"

Hannah stayed seated on the ground. It was suddenly so dark. Her spells normally took some energy, but this weakness seemed a bit excessive. She tried to say something and was half convinced she had spoken before she noticed that no sound had come out. *What is going on?*

She blinked, concentrated, then found herself lying on her back, the ground warm beneath her, staring up at the cloudless sky through an opening in the dissolving fog.

Oh, that's nice, she thought, seeing the stars, then three Rorys were leaning over her, concern on their blood-smeared faces. Hannah closed her eyes, then opened them again. The three figures were still there. "What?" she tried to ask, but her mouth only opened soundlessly.

Oh, she remembered suddenly. *The spell*. She waved her hand to dispel the images. Or tried to. Her arm suddenly weighed a hundred stone. She glanced over at it, and understanding finally dawned.

The goblin's short sword was still sticking out of her chest. *I'm bleeding*, she realized, noting that the warm feeling growing beneath her was her blood. *I'm bleeding badly*. Three Rorys were simultaneously seeing to her shoulder, strong hands tearing her sweater from her neck to her arm to reveal the wound. She wanted to tell him that it was alright, that she would be fine if he just left her there for a moment.

Then why is the blood still running?

Oh, she thought, *I need to get that out of me in order for it to heal up. That's the problem*. She moved her other arm to get the job over with, then realized that the Rory kneeling across her body was the real one as her weak movement collided with his backside. She closed her eyes, recited the words to dispel the illusion, and made the gesture that completed the spell with the fingers of her right hand. As she opened her eyes, the other two mirror images melted away into the vanishing fog just as Gorn appeared on her other side. The dwarf seemed fine enough, a random blood smear across his forehead the only evidence beyond his bloodied axes of the recent fight, but his eyes widened at the sight of Hannah's pierced chest.

As Rory reached for the hilt to pull the weapon out, Gorn put a hand on his shoulder. "Not that way," he instructed, moving the elf's hands away from the sword. "You hold her down. I'll pull it out, then you cover it right quick, or she'll bleed out."

Can I bleed out? Hannah wondered. *If my body can't heal because the skin is being held open, will I bleed to death just like a mortal?*

It was a shock to realize that she didn't know. The odds of a weapon sticking out of someone like her in an area that carried a lot of blood hadn't seemed very likely, so she had never thought about it, and because she hadn't thought about it, she had never asked anyone.

What would it be like to bleed to death, to die the same way that I've killed so many victims over the years? Would it be peaceful like it seems sometimes, or would it be strangling agony like when I haven't eaten in a long time and my body burns for blood? Would I die like a human? Can I? She knew her thoughts were wandering, and it was a bad time for it, but there was hardly anything she could do with an elf straddling her and a dwarf's boot pinning her wrist to the ground.

A wrenching pain brought her back to the moment, and she watched in sick horror as the dwarf yanked the weapon free. Her body bucked with the effort, and Rory put most of his weight on her chest, his hands moving to cover the gaping three inches of exposed bone from just above her left breast to her armpit. Hannah lay motionless, aware of how close his leaning body brought his neck to her mouth. She closed her eyes, trying to ignore the sight of that lean shoulder and smooth skin smeared with dust and blood, the pale blue traces of the veins below the surface throbbing in rhythm with his heartbeat. She realized she was rubbing her teeth with her tongue, a move that always led to poor choices, and forced herself to stop, thinking of the throbbing agony that was her left side instead. Focusing on the pain was a bad idea; the way to survive wounds was to avoid ever acknowledging the pain, but in this case, she thought it might be warranted.

It had been a long time since she allowed her mind to feel a wound up close and personal, disregarding the training of her youth, and never had she been wounded so badly as this. Unable to stop herself, she let out a scream. She reflexively breathed in, and with the renewing air came a waft of Rory—his sweat, his leather armor, his hair, his breath, his blood.

I have got to get away from here. Hannah began to struggle, rocking her little body under Rory's, trying to do anything to get away, just get away from the furnace that was her shoulder and the temptation that was just too close. Her body was singing for blood, her deepest primal instincts knowing that the only way to heal after this, to truly heal, was to drink blood, and not just any blood, certainly not any goblin's blood, but human blood, or better yet, Elven blood.

No! She struggled again, her free hand latching on to Rory's hair and yanking it up and away, anything to move his head, his face, his neck away from her mouth, which was slowly growing a mind of its own. She realized she was growling. *What kind of beast have I become?* The thought came absently, distantly, as her body tried to take over.

The hand in Rory's hair came loose with a ripping tear as his free hand forced her arm to her side. His other hand remained locked on her upper chest, his fingers holding the wound shut. He leaned forward, his arm bending across her chest to hold her down as he approached. "Hannah!" he shouted in her face. "You have to stop struggling! You're only making it worse!"

She wanted to scream at him that he was the one making it worse but couldn't. Her teeth were huge inside her closed mouth, and if she opened her mouth at all, he would see. *Calm down,* she ordered herself. *You can control yourself. You will not take him now, not when everyone is standing around. It goes against everything that you've ever learned. You know that!*

She was going to close her eyes, to turn herself inward and ignore everything, when she heard the tail end of Gorn's sentence. The dwarf was no longer standing on her wrist, had not been for some time, she realized, but now she could see him approaching with a dagger held out before him. A dagger glowing white hot. *Oh, no*, Hannah thought. *No.*

"—seal up the wound," Gorn was saying. "Otherwise, it will never close right."

Hannah looked back to Rory, the elf's face hovering only a few inches from her own. She began shaking her head violently back and forth. "No," she managed to mumble through barely opened lips, "he doesn't need to do that. I'll be fine." She knew she must appear to be rambling. Hannah had seen men seal off wounds like this before, knew that for delicate mortal constitution it was necessary, but it was not needed for her kind. In fact, searing her flesh would probably prevent it from healing normally. She would be scarred.

Hannah didn't want to think of herself as vain, but it was an easier reason to cling to than how much the fire-heated metal would hurt as they held it to her skin. She could deal with pain, she told herself, but she had already made the mistake of allowing herself to feel the damage in her shoulder. There was no turning back now. Whenever she had been wounded before, Hannah had never allowed her mind to recognize the pain for more than an instant—acknowledgement led to understanding, and understanding led to agony. Her body and brain were designed to avoid such a connection, but she had already managed to circumvent her own natural defensive systems. She would be naked before the pain. She would scream.

And when she screamed, she might lash out, she might lose control, and she might lunge and bite Rory, who was still too damn close for his own safety. Of course, she still wanted the elf, but such delicacies were for private moments to be relished, not stolen for a moment before the others killed her.

Gorn made his way to her side, kneeling and arranging the dagger.

"Please," Hannah managed, pleading for the first time in her life. Rory looked to Gorn, then back at her.

"I'm going to hold you down, Hannah. Try not to move until it's over," he said, and she could feel him settling himself on top of her, steeling corded muscles to restrain her thrashings. Hannah knew that if she had her full strength, she could easily push him aside. She tried to move the elf just a little, muscles straining with the effort, and was not surprised when he didn't budge. Losing blood took all the strength out of her. This was going to happen, and there was nothing she could do to prevent it. The idea galled her. *How did things come so far so fast?*

Gorn took her left hand in his, stretching her arm and pressing her shoulder against the ground to flatten the surface of her skin, and balanced himself. Hannah winced, feeling tears leaking from her eyes. "Now, this will only hurt for a minute, lass," the dwarf said. "Right."

Rory removed his hand from the wound, which, Hannah noted with horror, had not begun to mend at all. Apparently, she would need much more blood for her body to return to normal. The elf placed his newly freed hand and arm against her side, bracing as Gorn lowered the blade to her flesh. The pain was as Hannah had anticipated, a shrieking spike of agony that spread from her shoulder in growing waves. Her body began to buck wildly again, anything to get away from that heat, and Rory pressed himself closer. Luckily, his head was below her chin, his neck as unreachable as the stars, and Hannah was able to avoid the added temptation he presented. That left only the pain, the burning, boiling patch of metal against her skin. She did scream again, but both men were too engrossed by their doctoring to notice the insides of Hannah's mouth.

By the time Gorn pulled the cooling metal away from her shoulder—it came away with an audible pop—Hannah could smell burning flesh. She closed her eyes, her body going limp with the effort of the past few minutes, and a cold sweat covered her face. Trickles of sweat ran behind her ears. Hannah wondered if she was crying as well but could hardly muster enough energy to care. Her head flopped to the side, damp curls hanging across her forehead, across the smoothly healed skin she had lost when blowing up her forge so long ago. She felt her teeth recede as her body finally understood that there would be no blood forthcoming. She lay completely still for a moment, feeling the wrongness within her body, the body she had always relied on, knowing that what Rory and Gorn had just done to save her life would probably end up killing her—if she couldn't find fresh blood soon, that was.

I see serious problems ahead, she thought, then there were no more conscious thoughts for a while.

XII

Hannah came back to herself slowly; the first sensation she consciously noted was cool dampness on her forehead. Someone was washing her face. Time must have passed because Rory's weight was no longer on top of her, and the wetness beneath her was also gone.

She opened her eyes to see a somewhat cleaner Rory looking down at her. She blinked a few times until her sight was clear, then looked around. The fog was gone, the stars were gone, Gorn was gone, even the campfire was gone. The sky was brighter, the deep black she had been looking at faded to a deep blue that was almost purple across the water. *Water*, she thought. *The river—stream—I'm near the water.*

"What?" she asked, the word a hoarse whisper in her parched throat.

"Shh," Rory whispered, pulling a damp cloth from her forehead. Hannah heard the small splash of the cloth hitting water, but she wasn't lying on the bank—the ground beneath her back was harder, a rock of some sort. The elf was sitting between her and the water then, a bowl—her bowl, she realized—before him. He squeezed the cloth out into the stream, then dipped it back into the bowl, running the silky material across her cheeks. Hannah thought absently that it felt like part of Lira's shirt, as if Rory had pulled one of the sleeves off to use as a rag. The cooling wet felt so very nice on her hot skin. Hannah took a minute to drink in the sensation, then opened her eyes again, more details filling in her perception. Her head was propped on something soft, a rolled-up blanket perhaps, and she could look down at her body without much trouble. She was wearing only the thin material of her underdress, her shirt, skirt, and sweater having vanished along with her boots. *Who undressed me?* She looked carefully down at her shoulder and saw a swatch of clean white linen covering her newly seared skin. That was probably the rest of Lira's shirt. She looked back to Rory, sitting there doctoring her as if he had nowhere else in the world to be.

"What?" she repeated, wishing she could think of something more intelligent to say. Her body felt sluggish, warm and achy. Hannah knew it was the beginning of blood withdrawal. She had felt it occasionally as a child, not because of any enforced starvation, but because she had simply been too involved in her games or her exploration to remember to feed. She had felt it even more recently, too, in those first weeks after leaving home, before she had learned how to survive south of the Vanya. She knew the steps—it started with burning, fever; then progressive weakness, paleness; and finally, the degeneration into a raving creature desperate for blood, a madness that consumed everything. She knew that blood starvation was a slow process, a long road that would eventually lead to a mindless death in gasping agony. She had had her share of agony for now, however, and determined not to meet that particular fate. She and Rory were alone. She could take him now, be sated, and move on. It was the perfect moment.

But she couldn't bring herself to muster the energy. It was pleasant enough to lie there, basking in the glow of his attention, the gentle care of his hands. *To take him now, well, it just isn't practical.* She ignored the voice that spoke in her mind of the utter practicality of her plan, ignored the bone deep hunger she felt stirring, ignored everything except the feel of his hands on her face, the cool water running down to puddle in her collarbone.

"I thought you could use some cleaning up," Rory said, repeating his squeeze and dip procedure. "There was a lot of blood. Did you know you were stabbed in the back too?" He shook his head. "You're lucky to be alive."

"Are..." Hannah tried again, finding her voice. "Are we by the river?"

Rory laughed, glancing out at the water. "River? Not yet. But this will join the Marin eventually. We'll follow it down to Upsen."

"It's so big," Hannah said, knowing her thoughts were disjointed but unable to connect them at the moment.

"Not really. Are there no rivers where you come from, Hannah?"

"Not like this."

His hands rested on the bowl of water. "Hannah, where do you..." The question trailed off as he looked from her to the water. "Where did you get this bowl?" he asked instead.

"It was my father's," she answered, unwilling to lie. Besides, it was just a bowl. Owning an ornate bowl didn't mark one as a vampire.

"Is he the one you are running from?" The question was matter of fact, and it nearly caught her off guard.

She blinked, then raised an eyebrow, careful not to move her head and jar her shoulder. "I wasn't aware that I was running from anyone," she replied evenly, her fingers twirling Klauden's ring.

Rory looked at her intently, his own eyebrow raising. "Indeed," he said sarcastically.

At his tone, Hannah tried to sit up, moved her shoulder, and stayed where she was, closing her eyes as pain washed over her. She waited for it to subside, then opened her eyes and settled for a more comfortable spot on the pillow. "What makes you think I am running? Didn't you find me in Talperin where I owned a forge?" Her voice was sharper than she had intended, pain making her edgy.

Rory gently picked up her right hand. She stopped twisting the ring as he lifted her hand and flipped it palm side up. "Your hands are not those of a blacksmith, Hannah," he observed, his fingers carefully avoiding the silver circle on her middle finger. He moved to her wrist, positioning the inside so that it was level with her eyes. "And what of your arrow wound, Hannah? Why is your skin unmarked?"

Malfek, Hannah cursed silently. Still, she had a plan for this moment, at least. "I was only a blacksmith for a few months," she explained, then she displayed her wrist, "and I have a spell that helps skin heal without scars. It's in my spellbook." *It's not a huge lie,* she told herself. *This is about survival.*

Rory considered her reply, then cocked his head. "You do not strike me as the vain type, Hannah. Why would you care about having a scar?"

"It's a new spell," she invented, not anticipating his disbelief. "I wanted to try it out." She waved the wrist a little, then flinched as her shoulder twinged again. "It works!"

"You seem surprised. So, you can just create new spells?" he asked.

Hannah moved her shoulders in the start of a shrug, stopped instantly when the pain hit, and settled for slowly tilting her head back and forth. "Well, sort of. I'm not very good at it." In truth, she had stopped trying to make new magic when she was still in Essentials. After yet another incident of her magic exploding in her face—or more likely into Klauden's face—she had given up, accepting that while Klauden and even Vailen seemed to conjure new powers at will, she was limited to improving what she already knew or what Klauden wrote down in the book for her. She had focused on enhancing her spells from then on, making them even more powerful in force or range.

"Well, this one worked," he said, a finger tracing the smooth skin of her wrist. She tried to ignore the thrill that his touch raised, her body very aware of his heartbeat again, the low pull of his blood echoing in her fingertips.

"It did," she said. More to distract herself than because she wanted to brag, she said, "But I'm better at making the spells I know a bit better."

"What do you mean 'better'? Spells aren't a set thing?"

"No," she said, "not all of them. Some magic is fixed by the words, but a lot of it is malleable, shaped by the thoughts of the caster." She considered whether she should be telling him these things. Rory wasn't a magic user that she knew of, but maybe he had spoken of mortal magic with other casters. She didn't know how different her magic was from theirs, if at all. She had simply been glad to know that the people down here practiced magic enough that her own usage wouldn't be an oddity. "It's a little different for each caster, though," she added, just in case.

Rory seemed to accept this explanation, though Hannah thought it wouldn't last for long. *What the hell am I doing with this one? This is an excellent way to get caught. But I can't leave now*, she thought, a small movement jarring her tender chest. *Not until I am healed completely. Again,* the silky voice in her mind whispered. *How convenient for you. Honestly,* she told herself. *I need to mend, don't I?*

But the elf's blood... The voice in her mind began, but Hannah ignored it as she had more and more often lately. She changed the subject. "Where are the others?"

Rory gestured to the trees. "At the campsite. Molly was wounded by one of the goblins."

"That explains the screaming, then," Hannah commented, then remembered herself. "Is she alright?"

Rory smirked. "It's not as bad as yours, of course, but Lira used all her energy on mending that. She didn't know how badly you needed help, or she would have left Molly's side to heal naturally." Hannah was thankful for that; if Lira had tried to use her divine arts to heal her, Hannah would have suffered the same fate as the late Jason Saffron. Rory was looking at the bandage, as if checking for seepage. "That shoulder is a nasty wound. We'll have to watch it very carefully over the next few days. You too, Hannah. How are you feeling, by the way? You feel very warm."

"I'm fine," she answered automatically, aware that for someone who was fine, she would have a hard time standing on her own. "What about Gorn and Jamison?"

"Fine. They cleared up most of the bodies last night while Lira and I tended to you. They were almost done when I brought you down here."

"Why did you bring me here?"

The elf looked away across the water, shrugging. "I suppose because it's peaceful here. I thought you would like the water." He turned to her again and added, "Since you snuck away last night to go swimming."

Hannah felt herself reddening. "I didn't go swimming," she said quickly. It was not the best thing to say, and she cursed her stupidity.

"You didn't go swimming," he repeated, pursing his lips. "Then why were your clothes all wet?"

"I washed them," she answered. "They were starting to stink." She paused. "And so was I, I guess."

"You snuck away in the middle of night to do laundry." He seemed on the verge of laughter.

Hannah jerked, the movement jarring her shoulder and causing her to wince. This was going to be a rough few days. "Why is that funny?"

Rory shrugged. "I guess I thought..." He trailed off. "I don't know what I thought. You are a very strange girl, Hannah."

She grinned. "I know."

He seemed to think of something, then looked at her closely. "Do you want to swim?"

Hannah's eyes grew large. She could barely move, let alone float, even if she did know how. She looked at her bandage. "But my shoulder—"

"That's not what I mean. I know you can't really swim like this." He glanced down at her feet, which Hannah noted were quite muddy. "I thought you might like to wash up a bit. Since you thought it was important enough to sneak away and leave an illusion in your blanket, you shouldn't have to stay dirty all over again."

Hannah was suddenly very aware of how short her thin slip was and how Rory was now seeing more of her legs than anyone in her father's castle ever had. Even the slaves had the decency to look away when she was naked. Rory didn't seem to mind her flesh, taking it in as he took in the rest of her body lying on the rocks. Hannah was also aware of how the material seemed molded to her skin, highlighting her small curves. She restrained the urge to tug the material down on her thighs.

"Sneak away?" she asked, her voice rising a little. *Was he the one I sensed watching me?*

He shrugged, not the least embarrassed by his apparent voyeurism. "You said something right before you woke up. A name. It woke me. At first, I thought you were just going for a walk, but when you didn't come back right away, I thought I should go look for you." He looked out across the water, then back at her, curious. "What haunts your dreams, Hannah?"

"You were watching me from the trees?" she asked, changing the subject.

He gave her a pointed look. "I wanted to make sure you were alright. It's dangerous to wander around these parts alone," he gestured to her shoulder, "as you can see. You shouldn't wander at night, Hannah. If you can't sleep, just..." He let the thought trail off, a hint of embarrassment reddening his face when he saw the way she was looking at him.

"Come talk to you?" He seemed wary, uncertain of how to take her question. She asked, "Is that what you were going to say?" She didn't know what to make of someone who could be casual about watching her bathe and awkward about offering comfort.

He looked down, then back at her. "Yes." He seemed suddenly shy about it. "If you wanted," he added lamely. "I understand if you don't."

She cocked an eyebrow. "Why didn't you come talk to me last night?" When he just stared at her, she said, "When you couldn't go back to sleep. When you followed me to the river." She realized that if he had seen how long she could sit underwater, he would have killed her already.

"Stream," he corrected.

"Whatever. Why didn't you say something?"

"You looked like you wanted to be alone."

"I did." It came out a bit harsher than she intended. He recoiled a bit from her tone but softened when she said, "But maybe next time, I'll try talking to you first." She didn't know why she said that, but it seemed the right thing to do. She was rewarded with a wry grin.

"The swim will probably help more," he said. "It always helps me."

"Maybe, but I don't swim."

"Well, not with that wound, but if you wanted to wash off some..." A smile began to sneak across his face. "I could hold you up," he offered.

"No, thanks."

Her tone must have been harsh again because he sat up straight. "I'm sorry, Hannah. I wasn't suggesting anything!" *Gods, is he blushing?* Considering her own thoughts of last night, she was thankful that the fever hid her own red cheeks.

"No," she stopped him. "It's not that. I just don't..." Now it was her turn to blush.

"What, then?" he asked, his legs stretching out as he prepared to help her up.

Hannah gave up. "I can't swim."

He gave her a searching look. "You're serious?"

She looked out at the watery expanse, nodding slowly. "I only stay near the bank. I didn't want you to know."

He considered. "I guess the swim is out, then?" When he saw the extent of her embarrassment, he got onto his knees. "It's not a crime to not be able to swim, Hannah." When she said nothing, he smiled. "Alright, I'll teach you sometime, then." He looked at the bandage wrapped around her shoulder and under her armpit, thickly padded over the wound on her upper chest, and his smile faded. "Not now, of course."

"Not now," she agreed. She had a sudden urge to tell him that there wouldn't be a "sometime." That she would be leaving very soon. The urge passed as soon as she shifted slightly, and the agony that was her shoulder washed over her again. Maybe not so soon, then.

"I can still help you wash off, though. Lira and I did the best we could, but you could at least wash your hands and feet, maybe your face, before we leave again."

Hannah wasn't certain that she could even sit up, never mind do all the washing he detailed. *Well, start at the beginning*, she thought. She gritted her teeth against the pain, then allowed him to help her to a sitting position. Rory waited a moment while she regained her strength, then he helped her swing her legs over the water's edge, holding her steady as she lowered her feet to the water's surface. She used her free hand to splash water where she could, then gave up and let Rory splash her with water, managing to get them both fairly wet in the process. When her hair was soaking wet, Rory's pants were dripping with water, and her own slip was clinging to her in rather awkward places, she let him help her to her feet. Rory had dumped some water over her head with the bowl, and wet ringlets curled in front of her eyes. She wobbled a bit, feeling the fever stealing her equilibrium, but she fought against the dizziness and stood on her own after a moment. She wanted to brush the hair out of her face, but moving was a trial, and she decided the hair could wait. Standing was more important at the moment.

Rory ducked and retrieved the pillow, which was actually a bundle of what looked like Molly's clothing. As Hannah stood there wobbling and dripping, Rory wrapped the dark blue material around her back, draping one side over her right arm and securing the rest toga-style around her wounded shoulder before tying the belt at her waist. The wrap dress was much too big for her. Molly's curves required much more material than Hannah's slight frame, but Hannah decided she didn't care what she looked like at the moment. She was just doing her best not to fall down. When Rory looked up at her face again, he seemed to notice the hair in front of her eyes, and he reached out to tuck stray ringlets behind her ears. He gave her a long penetrating look, his fingers still resting against her cheek. He was so close to her, and she became aware of the blood speeding up a little in his veins, the low thrum of life within him sparking something primal in her nature.

Hannah wanted to stand there longer, but her vision was starting to spin a little at the edges from the intensity of her need. She looked down at the ground to reorient herself. Rory's fingers left her face and retreated to his sword hilt, his distance taking the temptation of blood with him.

"Where are my clothes?" Hannah asked when she had calmed herself, looking down at the rather large dress she now wore.

Rory gestured beyond the trees. "They are drying before the fire, though I doubt you should wear them again until tomorrow. Especially the sweater, since we tore it." He looked at her sheepishly. "Sorry about that, but you were bleeding quite a bit."

Hannah smiled weakly. "No trouble. It's not like I can wear anything over that arm now anyway." She thought for a minute. "So, Molly washed my clothes, then?"

Rory looked surprised. "Molly? No. She's been sleeping since last night."

"So, who...?"

The elf smiled, checked to see if she was in immediate peril of toppling, then bent down to collect the bowl and few cloths. "I did."

Hannah stared at him, taking in his own unstained, though newly damp, pants and shirt. "You did."

"Of course. I always wash my own clothes." He quirked an eyebrow, securing the bowl against his waist with the wide leather of his weapon's belt. He tucked the damp cloths inside the belt as well, then settled his blade so all were facing the usual direction. "I can do laundry, you know."

"I know," she said quickly. "I didn't mean..." *Hell, where is my brain this morning? Why do I always sound like a blithering idiot when talking to Rory?* Hannah focused. "I just didn't think you would wash my clothes. Thanks."

"It was the least I could do after your help in the battle."

"Help?" She looked at her shoulder, a weak shiver working its way through her blood. She couldn't keep standing like this for much longer. "I didn't realize that getting speared and falling down was a great help to you."

Rory chuckled. "No. Although that was an amazing performance of fortitude, I meant before you went down. The multiple images. You are very useful in a tight spot, Hannah."

She smiled, suddenly shy. When had someone last told her she was useful? When had anyone ever commented on her abilities except to say where she was lacking? She risked a look at him. "Thanks again, Rory."

"You are quite welcome." He was watching her with an appraising eye, as if waiting for her to fall over. "Can you walk?" It seemed almost like a challenge.

Hannah took a risky step to prove it. Though the rock was steady under her bare feet, her knees buckled, and she started a watery slide to the ground. Rory caught her good arm, then held her motionless until he had established himself under her right arm, one of his arms around her waist. "Step with me," he said, illustrating slowly. Hannah did.

Rory laughed under his breath as they made their way off the rock onto the bank nearby.

"What?" she asked, a bit sharply. "What's so funny?"

"Just you, Hannah."

"I'm funny to you?" She didn't appreciate his joke, whatever it was.

"No. I'm just glad to discover that you aren't as indestructible as you seem. I would have thought a girl," he seemed to catch himself, then went on, "I mean, anyone, with the beating you took last night would sleep for days, and here you are, trying to walk around on your own." He shook his head, his arm tightening around her back as he helped her around a tree stump. "It's nice to know that you do have a limit."

Hannah took in a deep breath, concentrating on walking, and said, "Everyone has limits. It's just how far beyond them one can go that makes the difference."

"Oh, does it?" He looked at her, then back at the path ahead. "Watch that root."

Hannah avoided the tree in question, then glanced at him. "Yes, it does." She took a few more steps, leaning more against his weight than she was comfortable with. She had never truly been unable to walk on her own before. The weakness was unnerving. *I need to feed soon,* she thought again. *Soon.*

"And how far away is your own limit?" he asked, his other arm coming around to hold her waist, his embrace making a solid circle for her to rest in.

Now it was Hannah's turn to laugh. "I passed it when Gorn yanked the sword out of me. Everything since is just sheer determination."

"Well then, Hannah," he said, bracing himself and moving around to face her. "Take a rest now." One arm looped under her legs, then he was carrying her easily, her wounded shoulder singing with the movement enough to make her break out in a cold sweat. He settled the other arm around her back and on her elbow. "Hold your side steady with your good hand," he instructed. "You won't bounce as much that way." She grabbed her wrist, risking a slight movement so she was comfortable and wincing against the pain.

As Rory began to walk slowly back toward the campsite, she wondered how much time she had until the blood sickness really began. Then she closed her eyes and stopped thinking about anything at all, simply disappearing into the solid comfort of Rory's chest.

XIII

"What we really need are horses," Jamison said. "That's the only way to keep moving south. We can't keep carrying them like this."

They were camped barely ten thousand wheels from where they had fought the goblins the night before. What would have taken an able-bodied party a morning to cross had taken them all day; Gorn and Rory had shared the burden of Hannah, passing her gently between their arms as the group progressed, and Jamison had been Molly's crutch the entire trip. Only Lira had been able to move at her regular speed, and she had been forced to slow down to keep pace with the wounded.

"Where are we going to find horses, Jamison?" Gorn asked, brushing a loose chunk of hair off his sweaty forehead. "We haven't passed any towns since Talperin, and wild horses don't live in forests."

"We can't keep moving like this. We need a place to rest. An inn would be ideal, even a farmhouse would work, but we can't stay out on the road," Lira said.

Hannah lay near the fire, her blanket wrapped around her as she fought cyclic bouts of chills and fever. The blood loss that would have killed a mortal was doing the same to her, though a fresh infusion would likely reverse the illness she felt coursing through her. In her weakened state, she couldn't get away from them to make a kill, and although their constant supervision was well intended, it was going to be the end of her. Of all the things Hannah had envisioned going wrong on the road, lying helpless near a fire, starving slowly from lack of blood with five helpful companions nearby was not something she had ever anticipated. She tried to think of what Klauden would say, but his somber face in her memory remained silent. Even her father's image, one which often spoke to her in desperate moments, was quiet.

Of course, her mind already knew the only solution to this situation—she would have to kill one of them and take her chances with the rest—but she just couldn't bring herself to do it. She knew she was being irrational, but she couldn't find the justification.

Hannah had to laugh at the irony—she who had always been able to justify even the cruelest acts was now incapable of saving her own life; her people would laugh at her. Worse, they would scorn her. She supposed they already did. She had become weak. She couldn't explain how the group hunched on the other side of the fire had helped her, had gone out of their way to make sure that she survived. Such selfless actions would not have happened north of the Vanya. Maybe that was her trouble—she had no precedent for the behavior.

She shifted in her blanket, the baking heat from the fire combining with the heat in her veins and causing sweat to run in rivulets, stinging the still open wound in her lower back. The sweat grew chill in the night air, and the cool dampness sent her into yet another spell of shivering. She gritted her teeth and tried to hear what they were saying.

"There is one place we could go," Jamison suggested. *<I've always wanted to see the hidden city,>* Hannah heard him say.

"Where?" Gorn asked. *<I hope he's not going to say Kalford,>* the dwarf offered in a very uncharacteristic observation. Hannah tried to focus even more on the conversation, then understanding dawned—*I'm hearing their thoughts.* The ability had come so easily to the others back home, but Hannah had needed a spell to read even the most surface thoughts of those around her. Her abilities allowed her to sense rough intentions but never this detailed look into the minds of others.

"Kalford," Jamison said, and Lira began shaking her head violently. Hannah couldn't get much of a reading from the elf beyond a thorough negative. Lira seemed cloaked somehow. How odd that Lira's mind would be hidden. *What is the elf hiding?* Or maybe it wasn't Lira. Maybe Hannah's own abilities were fading away again.

"No," Lira declared. Or maybe the elf just always said what she thought?

"Why not? We need to stop. You said so yourself," Jamison defended. "Tell her, Gorn."

"I will not bring two defenseless women into that place," Lira answered, "and that is final."

"They will not be defenseless, Lira," Gorn said, hands on his axe handles. <*What does she take us for: fools?*> Hannah heard the question clearly, but she was trying to separate the spoken words from the sudden onslaught of ideas. *This is how everyone always knew what was on my mind back home. Can they do this all the time? No wonder they thought I was an idiot.*

"You know what I mean," Lira snapped. "Kalford is a den of thieves, murderers, and cutthroats. Even I would have to be careful there, and I am not wounded." She was shaking her head. Hannah realized that Lira was willing to do anything except go into Kalford. The elf seemed almost afraid of the city. "There has to be another way."

"What then?" Jamison asked. "Would you have Hannah die because we cannot get her to a proper bed in which to rest? Would you have Molly collapse in the middle of this never-ending forest? They cannot get better on the road, Lira. You know that." The man was hoping that appealing to the elf's generous nature might help. Hannah got the impression that Jamison said what he thought people wanted to hear more often than not.

"We can make it to Upsen," Lira suggested instead, though Hannah knew she was reaching for any alternative. "The people at Valerius's temple will be able to help them both mend." There was something about buying time, Hannah sensed then, a need to slow their progress down so that—

The thought broke off abruptly, a wall slamming into place, and Hannah felt Lira's eyes searing into her own for a brief moment before she turned back to the group. "Molly's wound could be healed entirely."

"Maybe the rest of us don't share your faith," Gorn commented, remembering that Valerius hadn't saved his brother when the elves had rescued him from the goblins, but then the dwarf focused, trying to keep the conversation on track, "and besides, Upsen is still a week's travel from here, and that's regular walking—not dragging two wounded behind. The girls won't last that long."

"No one even knows exactly where Kalford is," Lira tried. "Trying to find the hidden city might take a week or longer."

"We know it's north of Upsen along the Marin," Jamison noted. "How hard can it be to find?"

Gorn shrugged, then admitted, "I've been up and down this bank many times, and I've never seen any city. The path to Kalford is supposed to be cloaked by magic."

They looked to Jamison. "Could you find it?"

The man shook his head. "No. You know I'm only good at one thing." *Stealing*, Hannah heard clearly.

"Making fog," the others said in unison.

Jamison shrugged. "But at least I'm good at making fog." *And stealing*, he added silently, thinking of the spellbook that had held the fog spell he cherished so dearly. He had stolen it from a silly woman in Tel Ran, Hannah understood, *<Yet another idiotic female who no doubt left her loving mate behind while she chased ridiculous ideals.>* Hannah's curiosity was piqued, but the thought was lost as the conversation continued.

"Conjuring fog won't find the path to Kalford," Lira claimed. She looked to where Hannah lay shivering again near the fire. *She's worried about me*, Hannah realized, oddly relieved for some reason. She had never had any real sense of how Lira felt about her. It was nice to know the elf cared if Hannah lived or died. "She might be able to find the way, but I don't know if she can do anything in this state."

"Why is she so sick?" Jamison asked. "The wound is healing clean."

"She lost a lot of blood," Rory said. It was the first thing he had said since the discussion of the infamous city had begun. He seemed to be considering something, but Hannah couldn't get a feel for what it was.

"So she did, but she's got some kind of fever. Maybe the sword was poisoned," suggested Jamison.

"Ridiculous. Why would a goblin poison a sword?" Gorn asked, snorting.

"Maybe it wanted to make sure she died." Jamison thought a moment, then said, "What was it the creature shouted? 'Find the one that hunts us in the night'? Something like that?" He looked over at Hannah, his old suspicions returning. *<Could she be one of them?>* "Maybe she's the one they were after."

"Because Hannah hunts goblins at night," Rory said. "Right."

"What a surprise. You defending her yet again," Jamison observed wryly. He was thinking of Matthew again, Hannah heard, and a woman. Matthew, she knew now, had been his brother.

"I'm not defending her," Rory defended. "I'm simply pointing out that the very idea of Hannah creeping around at night killing goblins is ridiculous. She's a spellcaster, Jamison, not a fighter. She couldn't even defend herself from two of them, never mind waltzing into one of their camps to hunt them in the night, as you put it." Rory gave the man a disgusted look. "You've had it out for Hannah since she got here. Why?"

Jamison held his ground. *<She's a woman from the North,>* Jamison thought clearly. *<Need I say more?>* "Since she got here, she's brought nothing but trouble. First the goblin attack when we're passing by, then the vampire bite at the farm, then the goblin attack last night? Nothing like that happened before she started traveling with us."

"Well, nothing like that happened to me before you started traveling with us, Jamison. Maybe you're the problem," Rory snapped. He didn't like what the man was suggesting. Rory had his own doubts about Hannah, but now she also knew that it bothered him to hear those thoughts coming out of Jamison's mouth.

"Now that we've sorted that out," Gorn interjected, "maybe we can get back to the issue at hand. Kalford?" He looked at the two scowling males, then to Lira, who had her eyes closed and was shaking her head in that same silent negation. She opened her eyes and breathed out slowly.

"If we could find the city, maybe it would be better for them," she conceded. "But it's a pointless debate, much like the one you two were having," she glared at Jamison and Rory, "since we don't know where it is."

Rory seemed to consider for a moment and looked across the fire at Hannah's shivering form. *<Can I go back?>* Hannah heard, then *<Yes, for her, yes.>* She wanted to read into this, wanted it to be about her and the way she felt him looking at her sometimes, but she was afraid of assuming anything. *He's just concerned for my welfare, like Lira. He doesn't want me dying while they are with me. Maybe he just doesn't want to be bothered with digging the hole to bury me in.* Rory spoke. "I know where it is."

Everyone looked at him. "You do?" Lira asked, a bit shocked.

Rory nodded, a bit uncomfortable with all of their attention. *<You knew this would happen,>* Hannah heard.

"Were you there before?" Jamison asked, his question tinged with suspicion. *I knew it!* "Why was the almighty paladin in such a place?"

"I am no paladin," Rory stated in a low voice, "and you would do well to watch yourself, Jamison. I can do a lot more than just make fog." Hannah heard a low mumble that sounded something like <*Rory, watch your temper,*> but it was gone too fast to place. Whose thought had it been? Hannah closed her eyes and tried to concentrate, forcing herself to isolate the swarm of thoughts that overwhelmed her. There was a moment when she thought her mind might split under the strain of so many voices, then everything was quiet again. She was alone, her awareness reduced. She listened in to the conversation again.

"Is that a threat?" Jamison was asking, his voice raising in a mocking pitch. "Tell us, Rory, what one such as yourself would be doing in a place like Kalford. Does someone have a little secret he's not telling?"

"Shut up, Jamison," Gorn ordered, his own tone growing annoyed. "You're not helping yourself." The dwarf looked at Rory. "Do you remember the way?" The elf nodded. "Can we get there tomorrow?"

"If we carry them again, we should get there by tomorrow afternoon." Rory looked to Lira. "Will you go?"

Lira sniffed loudly. "Will I go?" she repeated. "What would you have me do, Rory? Leave you behind to care for those girls alone? Please." She looked over to where Molly lay, the woman curled up in a blanket under a nearby tree. The widow's wound was not so bad as Hannah's, but the woman didn't have nearly the constitution of the younger girl. Both would need a place to rest for a few days. Any place with a bed and a fire would do, preferably with a roof over their heads. She met Rory's gaze, making the question in her eyes clear. "I will go, but there is one thing I would know."

"What?" Rory asked, preparing to stand up.

"Why were you in Kalford?"

Rory stood up with a sigh, arranging his sword and running a hand through his hair. He rubbed both hands over his face, then shrugged. "It was a long time ago. I needed a place to stay for a bit. Kalford was nearby, and I found someone who led me to it." The elf walked away, his hands working on the hilt of his sword as he made his way to his blanket. He stopped to check on Hannah, a worried frown creasing his forehead, then moved away to rummage in his pack. Hannah deliberately avoided watching him, turning instead to the flames and the conversation that was still going on.

"And that's as much as he's likely to tell us," Gorn observed, still sitting near Lira.

"I don't like this," Jamison complained. "What was he doing in a place like Kalford?" The man turned to Lira. "What if those goblins really were hunting Hannah, huh? What if she's the reason they're chasing us? And who is Rory, anyway? Where does he come from?"

Lira stopped his questions with a raised hand. "Jamison, I don't know. But I do know Rory, and I know he has his reasons." She looked at Hannah and Molly, then exhaled heavily. Hannah closed her eyes, feigning sleep. She could think about all these things later when her body wasn't burning for blood. She heard Lira sigh again, and the elf said in a resigned tone, "And I do know that we have to get them off the road, and Kalford is the only opportunity available." Lira asked sharply, "And weren't you the one who suggested it?" Hannah opened her eyes again, relieved that Lira wasn't looking directly at her anymore. The elf was glaring at the human, who stared back nonplussed.

Jamison shrugged, big shoulders causing his cloak to flutter. "As a theory, yes. I didn't think we'd actually go there."

"Well, we are," Gorn said, getting to his feet. "Best get a good night's sleep for it." The dwarf began to walk away, then turned back to face Jamison. "Hey, you," he began, "did it ever occur to you that the one who would be hunting goblins might be the same creature that did for old Jason Saffron?" At Jamison's silence, the dwarf tapped his head with a finger. "How's that for brain power, eh?" With a chuckle, he set off to find his own bed among the rocks and branches that littered the ground.

Lira took a deep breath, then stood and walked to her own blanket. Kneeling, she began to unbraid her hair, clearly taking comfort in the nightly ritual before she began her prayers to Valerius. Hannah turned over again, hating the sweat that pooled under her head, the fire warming her back again. She could feel Jamison's eyes on her as he sat near the fire, the man splitting his gaze between her and the elf. When Rory came back to the fire with the carved bowl and the water bag to settle himself next to her shivering form, Jamison got up and moved over to check on Molly.

XIV

They stood on the banks of the Marin River, staring out across the wide expanse of water that their little stream had emptied into. Hannah's awareness had expanded again, and she was making an effort not to talk for fear she might answer an unspoken thought.

Her plan had been aided in part by the miserable weather, which couldn't seem to decide if it was actually going to rain or not, the still air filled with humidity that clung to everything. The travelers were not in the best of moods.

Lira was out of breath and sweaty, her blonde braid coming unbound in little wisps around her face. Gorn's arms were aching from his turns at carrying Hannah, though the dwarf would never admit to it—the combination of sturdy support and gentle ease had caused his muscles to alternate between locked and loose in a way that no amount of axe slinging had ever done. Rory was feeling much the same way, though his arms were more accustomed to heaving weight around, but the constant need for caution, for steady steps and careful motion, was making his muscles jumpy with the need for some all-out action.

Standing on the bank with Hannah cradled against his chest, he was looking forward to the chance to move freely again. It wasn't that he minded carrying Hannah—her small frame was not much of a burden— but the restriction on his movement was making him crazy. The elf couldn't help speculating what he would do if they were attacked while he was carrying Hannah and couldn't get to his weapons—would he just drop her?

Molly had been staggering along all day under Jamison's aid. The man seemed to have attached himself to the widow as Rory had attached himself to Hannah, taking care to help her walk, talking softly to her of this or that as they moved. Hannah knew that Jamison was glad that Molly hadn't had one of her sobbing episodes since the goblin attack. The widow seemed quiet, pensive.

Jamison knew a thing or two about grief, especially when it came to vampires. Hadn't his own brother been taken by the creatures? And then his own bride had been taken as well, run off into the damn mountains to chase after his brother when she should have stayed at home with him. Wasn't it bad enough to have lost a brother to the monsters in the Vanya, never mind adding a wife to the numbers of the lost? Jamison had reason to distrust Hannah's Northern accent, for it had been a woman of the North who had seduced his brother away from hearth and home. He knew the pain of losing a loved one to such monstrosity, and this he confided to Molly as they walked, partly to distract her from the trial of walking with a healing slice along her hip, and partly because it had been so long since he'd had anyone to commiserate with, especially one who had recently had the same experience. Though, Jason Saffron hadn't willingly gone to his doom, and that, he repeated, should be a comfort to Molly. She had not been abandoned, not like his woman had abandoned him so long ago.

Hannah had tried to ignore Jamison's thoughts as they walked, but his overwhelming anger at what had happened to him was difficult to block out. She dismissed the idea of telling them that Jason Saffron actually had abandoned his wife, left her because he feared hurting her, left her because he was a coward, left her because he could not cope with what happened to him, but to explain such things would have been cruel, and Hannah didn't have the strength to be cruel anymore.

The actual day had passed in a blur of thoughts, images, and fears for Hannah, the fire in her blood growing steadily worse. Surely the blood withdrawal had never come on so strongly before, not to mention so quickly. She had hoped for more time to get away, more time for a chance to feed. Lying weakly in Rory's arms, she knew that any time was slowly dwindling, not only for a chance to slip away, but a chance to feed at all. When she felt Rory cease walking, she forced her eyes to open, taking in the scene.

The stream they had been following had emptied into the marin River. *And rightly called a river,* Hannah thought, looking over the expanse with a shiver. *So much water.* Though, she didn't see why they had stopped. There was no city here—only trees, the same trees she had grown accustomed to as they traveled, growing along the banks. Rory walked to the edge of the river. "We're here."

"Is Kalford on the other side of that?" Lira asked, skepticism clear in her tone. She squinted at the distant trees lining the far bank, then back to the elf. When Rory nodded, she shook her head in defeated resignation. "How do we get across?"

Rory adjusted Hannah in his arms, then tossed Lira a grin that Hannah had only glimpsed before. Hannah liked the expression. He looked like he was almost excited to be here. "Do you know where Kalford gets its name?"

"No. Should I care where a group of thugs and murderers got the name for their fabled city?" Lira retorted.

"Kal Langeson was one of the best thieves in Upsen." Rory stepped closer to the waterline, watching the ground carefully. "This was, oh, a hundred years or so ago, when Kal was in his heyday, but like any thief, he eventually got sloppy. He was chased for a week along the riverbank as every able-bodied man in the city came after him." Rory took a few more steps, seemed to find what he was looking for, then motioned for Gorn to come over. "You see, what Kal had stolen was a magical item of great worth—a crystal ball with the power to shield whatever its wielder wanted hidden—and the visiting priestess whom he had taken it from was quite eager to get it back. They said she was bringing it north to some secret tribe in the mountains, but it never made it that far." As Gorn approached, Rory looked down at Hannah, thinking how her pale face and hollow eyes looked much worse in the dull afternoon light than they had by firelight. "Hannah, hold your arm steady. I'm going to hand you to Gorn."

She moaned a bit as the two men shuffled her between them, trying to cling to the words of Rory's story. She had always loved stories, and this one was familiar for some reason. *Wait... a shielding crystal that was supposed to go to the north. Ha,* she realized, a slight smile creasing her cracked lips, *so that's where Ajira's Bauble went. It was too bad Father had her killed for arriving without her promised prize—the woman* had *been robbed.*

"Anyway," Rory said, reaching into the water to retrieve a flat stone. He said a word, then passed his hand over the smooth face of the rock. Hannah watched from within Gorn's arms as letters began to form on the surface. "Kal was right about here when he realized that he'd never make it to safety. So, he stopped, yanked out his prize, and recited a spell he'd found in another book he managed to acquire."

"You mean steal," Lira said pointedly, but Rory ignored her.

"It turned out that the spell was the right one—Kal always had the best luck—and he ended up shielding this whole place, including the way in, from anyone who didn't know the password." The words on the rock had fully formed, and Rory read the magical incantation slowly, carefully enunciating each word.

When he finished, there was a tearing sound like rending fabric, followed by a hollow pop, then the view across the river Marin shifted. One second there was nothing but trees and water and the sound of the current and a few lone birds, and then it was as if a curtain had been shuffled aside, and the companions could see a wooden bridge that started a few feet from where Rory stood at the water's edge leading to a bustling metropolis of haphazard wooden shelters on the far side. They could hear shouts, whistles, and singing from across the bridge, and Lira's keen eyes identified the shuffling forms of what were probably drunk men along the far bank. A cool breeze ruffled the sweaty ringlets on Hannah's forehead, and she risked a deep breath.

Men, she thought, *and blood. So much blood.*

"Of course, there wasn't anything here then," Rory said. "Kal would swear that he thought he'd lost his mind in those first few minutes, when everyone chasing him vanished into the fog and he was all alone."

"So, how'd all this come to be here?" Molly asked. Hannah felt Jamison's surprise. The woman had barely spoken all day, and he hadn't thought she was listening to Rory's history lesson, just as he assumed she wasn't listening to him talk all day either. "More magic?" she asked.

Rory shook his head. "No." He gestured at the buildings and bridge. "Everything was built by Kal's friends. He promised them a city where they wouldn't have to worry about being chased, captured, or hung." Rory shook his head, then bent to replace the rock where he had found it, noting the white stone marker that showed the touchstone's place. "I never thought I would come back here again."

He turned to the others. "Come on. Let's go find a bed and a roof."

Gorn followed him onto the bridge, then Jamison ushered Molly through the ankle-deep water onto the wooden slats, a wiry arm around her back. The woman was looking a bit better, but she would recover much more with a good night's rest in a real bed. It was Hannah who looked like death. Lira stayed on the bank for a moment, then took a deep breath, and stepped toward the bridge. There was another of those tearing sounds as her feet hit the first board. "This is a bad idea," she muttered as she walked, turning around at the bridge's halfway point to note that the far end disappeared into a thick fog.

Shielded indeed.

XV

They entered the town without much fanfare, and Hannah marveled at how the passersby just seemed to accept their appearance as normal. She supposed the denizens were accustomed to strangers appearing out of the air. Then again, their little group with three women, two of whom were wounded, was something a bit out of the ordinary, Hannah decided, considering the expressions of three humans who gawked at Lira's smooth skin and licked their lips at seeing Hannah's obviously wounded form in Gorn's arms and Molly's exaggerated limp. Hannah thought women might be scarce in Kalford, and she repressed a shudder at the memory of that first night away from her father's castle and the men who had opened her door seeking easy prey. Maybe the only members of the fairer sex who dared to enter the shielded city were those thoroughly capable of protecting themselves since these men seemed to look on any woman as a prize to be hunted, captured, and taken. In all of her studies with Klauden, Hannah had never heard of Kalford.

Still, each of the men also glanced at Rory, and whatever they saw in his face made them recall some other errand, and their little party of six was quickly lost amid the regular street traffic. Hannah wished she could see the elf's face, but all she could see was a narrow band from within Gorn's arms, and feeling the slow burn of his arm muscles was making her tired, so tired that it seemed easier to close her eyes than keep them open. She tried this, but as she began picking up random thoughts from those they passed in the street, Hannah thought it best to remain vigilant. After yet another vision of someone pouncing on Gorn with a quick dagger to the back as another distracted the elf in front, Hannah began to hope that Gorn would set her down for just a moment so one of those men could try to grab her. A few seconds was all she would need. But Gorn kept a solid hold on her, grunting in defiance as they made their way through the crowded streets.

Rory seemed to know where he was going, leading them steadily forward, ignoring the looks of passersby as he made turn after turn. He had been fairly tight-lipped about his previous visits to this place, and even though she was awash in thoughts, she couldn't make out anything specific through the jumble of images and thoughts in her mind.

If this keeps up, she told herself, *you will go mad, and the bloodfever will be the least of your worries.* She tried to block it out, closed her eyes and steadied her breathing as she had seen Klauden do when readying himself for a challenging spell, and for a few seconds, the wave of other people pulled back, but as soon as she let herself relax, it crashed back in again.

This time, though, the noise was bearable, a cacophony of voices that reminded her of where she was and the potential therein. *A city,* she thought, *a real city, filled to the brim with people, living, breathing people, and bad people at that, so I don't have to feel guilty about taking any of them.*

Wait, she thought, *bad people? What are you thinking? Rory is here—is he a bad person? Besides, when did you ever feel guilty for feeding?* She shook such issues aside, focusing instead on the sights and sounds of Kalford to distract herself.

The buildings were made of wood with thatched roofs, each lopsided porch brushing up against the porch of the building next door. Each structure seemed to be either an inn, a tavern, or a specialty shop, though Hannah noted that there were more goods on display on carts and makeshift stands than actual stores. Kalford seemed an excellent place to find odd items or to get rid of them quickly. Hannah saw that everyone they passed was armed, which wasn't odd in and of itself—the world was a dangerous place—but the sheer number of deadly weapons was disconcerting. Each man carried at least two blades easily accessible on belts. Some accentuated the blades with crossbows, maces, and quivers of arrows; Hannah saw one dwarf carrying something that looked like a pike with an elongated tip in one hand and a scourge in the other, the metal tips jingling against the metal knobs on his armor.

Gorn made a point to step over to the side to allow the dwarf easy passage. Hannah caught a glimpse of red rage in the stranger's thoughts, then he was gone, lost in the fray of bodies, his murderous intentions fading into the crowd. Hannah felt a moment's pity for whomever his rage had targeted but then reconsidered; at least in Kalford, the person would be armed.

Back in Talperin, only Burke, the mayor, had carried a sword at all. Hannah decided that the people here were more concerned with protection from one another than any outside threat. Looking at the mixture of races on the streets—humans, elves, a few halflings lounging here and there—Hannah tried not to stare. Cricking her neck to follow each character as they passed was too much effort, so she settled for quick scans as they came into and out of her sight. She had seen the little people before, so it wasn't so peculiar. One of their women had passed through Talperin just after Hannah had arrived, and Hannah had gotten over her initial impulse to treat her as the child she resembled. Hannah knew what it felt like to be mistaken for a child, so she had made a point not to insult the woman, though she had secretly smirked at the thought of taking the woman's tiny frame. *So cute, but probably not very filling;* Hannah had never been very interested in taking children anyway.

There were also half-elves on the streets, a sight Hannah had not seen before, and it took her a moment to realize that what she was seeing was not more elves, but a curious blending of elves and humans. Of the three they passed, one was stocky, like a human, but with the long ears of an elf; another was tall and willowy, like a taller version of Rory, but the man's features were the squarer, more choppy features of a human; the last was a woman, the first Hannah had seen since their arrival, and she was tall, like Lira, though her ears were short, and only her eyes held the somewhat angular look of the elves. It seemed that crossbreeds came in all shapes and sizes. Hannah thought of her grandfather and stifled a snort.

The sound would make her throat begin aching again, though the burning of her veins was already making her crazy. She needed to drink, needed something, anything. She willed Gorn to put her down but had to settle for him carrying her into a larger building that sported a second story. Apparently, they had reached the inn Rory sought.

Hannah tried to hear what Rory said to the man behind the bar in the common area they now stood in, but the babble of voices and thoughts from the men sitting at the tables was overwhelming. There were at least twenty people inside, a motley group including two elves and a dwarf playing some type of card game in one corner—Hannah knew one of them was cheating and starting to get cocky—another group of very drunk men and one halfling singing an off-tune song in front of the fireplace, and a female elf, looking rather the worse for wear, was batting her eyes at five rather determined suitors who surrounded her place at a table near the stairs. She was clearly armed with a small dagger, and Hannah puzzled over how often she killed her clients and how often the murder was warranted.

When she found herself wondering if that was what had happened to Mara, she realized that the thought wasn't hers. She focused, narrowing her senses to find that the thought had come from Lira, the elf looking at the woman in the room with horrified disgust. Hannah doubted Lira had never seen a whore before. Hannah had seen them; even back home, though never within her father's castle, there were women who exchanged favors for the pleasure of sharing their beds, though there were a lot more of them south of the mountains. Hannah assumed this place would be good business for such a woman.

Rory finished his talk with the barkeep, returning to them with three brass keys. He handed one to Lira and one to Jamison, holding the other as he motioned for Gorn to trade Hannah to him. "I got us three rooms," he said, adjusting Hannah's weight in his arms. The movement pushed Hannah's face close to his chest, and she breathed deeply of his leather armor, his sweat and blood thrumming in her skin. She closed her eyes and stopped breathing, hoping Rory wouldn't notice if she just took a small moment of relief. "Each of the women will stay with us. I would have put us all in one room, but that would give the wrong impression," the elf said to the others.

Lira looked from the key to Gorn. "And this gives the right impression?" Rory laughed at the thought of Lira sharing her bed with a dwarf, in fact, at the thought of Lira sharing her bed with anyone, Hannah picked up. "Better to pair up with a dwarf than be taken as free." At Lira's puzzled expression, he continued, "If we all share one room, they will assume you are..." he tried to phrase it delicately, then gave up, "open for business. They will wait for their turn outside the door."

Lira shook her head. "They would not!" She seemed to notice the appreciative glances she was receiving from some of the singing group and looked up the stairs to where the rooms were. "I see," she said, then grabbed Gorn's hand. "Come with me."

The dwarf grinned, then muttered, "If only I didn't know she will have me sleeping on the floor in front of the door..."

Jamison put a possessive arm around Molly's waist to meet the one already around her back, swinging her onto the first step. "Up you go," he said in a teasing voice. Molly smiled vaguely, her own thoughts a muddled haze that Hannah avoided exploring. The woman was tired, that much was clear, but she was also sad, sad in a bone-deep way that all of Jamison's talk had not relieved. Hannah hoped that her thoughts about the woman showed that she was caring about her and was suddenly sure that Rory would not think so.

Rory followed everyone else up the stairs, balancing Hannah as he unlocked the last door on the right, then walked into the narrow room, kicked the door shut behind them, and laid her gently on the rather narrow bed. Hannah knew that he remembered these beds being slightly bigger, but he had learned that time had an odd way of warping the memory over the years; either that or Tom had swapped out the old ones for cheaper new beds. Hannah allowed herself to breathe again as Rory moved away from her, twisting her face to the pillow and inhaling a mostly refreshing waft of clean linen.

Across the room, Rory unshouldered his bag, then untied Hannah's bag from his waist and put the two on the room's only chair. He took a minute to stretch, and Hannah felt the release of tense muscles, enjoying the unencumbered feeling of not having to carry anything. His hands moved to unbuckle his belt, then thought better of it as he glanced at the window with its two wooden shutters between them and the world, then at the room's door, also wood that could turn flimsy with a few good kicks.

Better to be safe, then, Hannah agreed silently. He did take off his boots, though, before he settled on the edge of the bed, which was harder than he recalled, and began pulling off Hannah's shoes. Once both boots were on the floor, he hesitated.

<She would be more comfortable,> he thought, looking away from her to the crackling fireplace. When he looked back at the bed, Hannah was looking at him. It was so strange to feel him like this, to see herself as he

saw her, to know his surface thoughts, to sense his deeper self. *How do the others back home stand to live like this?*

"I'm hot," she said, raising heavy arms toward him. "So hot."

Hannah sensed the impulse those words raised in him as he reached for her, ignoring the desire to touch more of her when he helped her to a sitting position. She could feel him behind her, one hand on her back to hold her upright, the other hand untying the knot that held Molly's dress on. She stayed still, letting him do all the work, reminded of earlier days when servants would dress and undress her, when all she ever had to do was stand still and let them do everything. That life seemed very far away from this room, but also very recent, a queer doubling in her mind that must be the bloodfever working in her. She was suddenly cold, the air causing her bare arms and legs to break out in gooseflesh as he tossed Molly's dress onto the chair. Hannah was thankful for the warmth of his hand through the thin fabric of her slip, leaning back against it as he fumbled with the blankets at her feet. There was more shuffling, then he was easing her down again and pulling the blanket over her. Hannah took another moment to relish the feeling of lying in a real bed with cushions beneath her and a warm clean blanket over her. *How long has it been since I last slept in a real bed? More than a month,* she figured.

She let her eyes close, her mind wandering into the dream that came more and more often, the nightmare. *But it isn't really a nightmare, is it?* It had all happened. She had been in her rooms, wearing her favorite red dress, when the humans were delivered. There were two of them that time, a rare treat, a young man and woman who stared at each other and at her with fear in their eyes. Hannah nearly turned them away, but then Malbrek, who delivered her evening meal, closed the door and stood to one side, clearly intending to watch her this time. Warnings sounded in Hannah's mind as she recalled the last time she had seen her mother, before the sickness killed her; hadn't Malbrek and her father led her into the room with her mother's favorite slave trailing reluctantly behind? Hadn't they looked at her mother with the same questioning condemnation? Hannah knew that she had to perform better than her mother had, or she might suffer the same fate.

The man was first, she decided, though it made her uncomfortable to take a victim who was so obviously unwilling. She waved her fingers in the arcane pattern, stunning him in place as she approached. Everything had been going according to plan, a routine that she had followed hundreds of times before, but then the woman had spoiled everything. She had screamed. Not a wordless scream either, but a word, "Please!"

Normally, Hannah wouldn't have been overly moved by her pleading, but there was something in her voice, something in the eyes that Hannah reluctantly met that caused her to waver, a pause that had nearly cost her life, when she thought back on it. That didn't make her feel any better about what happened next, of course, but survival was always the most important thing, wasn't it? She had seen the look on Malbrek's face, and she knew that she had to prove herself, prove that she had the viciousness that had come into question lately.

Afterward, she told herself that it had to be done, and at the very least, she felt badly about it, but the truth, as her dreams revealed, was that she hadn't really felt bad at all. In fact, she relished the look on the woman's face as her hand latched on to the victim's throat, a nail sinking into the soft flesh of her neck but not allowing her to bleed out. She held the woman, letting her struggle against Hannah's grip, and she enjoyed the pain and fear that overwhelmed the man when she let the glamour drop, her face inching closer to his neck as she made sure he could watch the struggling of his mate. She had been thrilled when the man began to weep in frustrated agony, and she took his life in a vicious snarl, for the first time allowing the blood to spray on her clothes, to matte her hair and smear her face. She had been joyous when she took the woman next, not taking the time to make her death painless as she sometimes did with the less than willing, and when she stood over the bodies, licking her lips and smoothing her sticky hair, she even appreciated Malbrek's leer, the approving nod he gave as he stepped carefully over the victims on the floor, the way he lifted her chin and licked the blood from her cheek with a lazy tongue. It had been the only time she allowed Malbrek to get so close to her, and she still didn't know why she let it happen.

Later, as she sat in the tub soaking the blood out of her hair, she told herself that it had been a fluke, an act, the need to prove herself a necessary evil for survival in her father's castle, but deep down, she knew the truth. She dreamed the truth in her nightmares. She wanted Malbrek at that moment, craved his approval, reveled in his admiration. The thought made her stomach crawl now, but she couldn't deny what she was. "No!" she yelled at the smirking face in her memory. "No."

"It's alright, Hannah. It's alright." A soothing voice was talking to her. The smirking face faded.

When she opened her eyes, the room was hazy, her eyes dimming as the fever returned more strongly, and Rory was sitting on the edge of the bed again, slowly mopping her forehead with a damp rag. Hannah saw a tray on the floor with two steaming bowls of what smelled like soup and a sweating pitcher that must contain the water he was using to mop her brow. *When?* She wanted to ask, but then she knew, heard the knock in Rory's memory, saw the young man who delivered the food nod as he accepted Rory's gold, then she was burning again.

"Drink," she moaned. "I need to drink."

Rory heard her, tried again to force her to drink some water that ended up running down her chin, and wished Tom's healer would arrive soon.

XVI

T om's healer ended up being an elf, Hannah saw when she opened her eyes to see another angular face looking at her. She smelled him, sensed the low thrum of his heartbeat speed up a little as Rory let him into their little room, but she avoided looking at him until she was fairly certain she could control herself.

The healer was thinner than Rory, she noticed as he leaned over her, with green eyes instead of Rory's brown, and his hair had a subtle wave to it that kinked around his forehead. Hannah thought she should find him attractive, but she kept thinking of Rory's face instead, the lines subtly different and more pleasing to her eyes. *But he's an elf*, her mind insisted, *and all elves are beautiful; all elves are desirable; all elves have the power you need...*

She closed her eyes, halting the litany of her childhood, forcing herself to relax as she restrained the ever-growing urge to lunge and feast. When she thought she could refrain from any sudden leaps toward the unprotected neck, she opened her eyes again, noting that he was much too close to her, his hands too familiar on her body through the thin blanket.

"She was wounded?" the elf asked, looking over his shoulder at Rory, who stood frowning by the fireplace. The movement drew his neck into the light, and Hannah looked away from the relief it promised. She watched as Rory approached instead, tracking his movement as he pushed the blanket aside so that the healer could see Hannah's upper chest. Gentle fingers unwrapped the wound, then began to poke and prod her uncomfortably. The healer seemed to be mashing the skin around along the line of burned flesh. Hannah squirmed but managed to avoid crying out.

"No seepage," the elf observed, "no redness, nothing out of the ordinary." He let her arm go, leaving a festering ache behind, and began touching her face. His hands were cold on her skin as he pushed her eyelids open, examining her eyes. "No yellowing of the eyes." Then he bent to smell her breath, spidery hands leaping down to press on her chest. "No foulness within." Hannah bit her tongue, holding herself in check by taking deep breaths until the elf sat back and cocked his head, clearly pondering.

"What's wrong with her?" Rory asked.

"Tell me everything that happened," the elf countered.

Rory shook his head. "It was just a wound. A bad one, but nothing special beyond that. We sealed it off two days ago, but she's just been getting worse." Rory began a subdued pacing from side to side in front of the fireplace. "I thought maybe it was poison," he suggested. "Couldn't that give her a fever?"

"It could, but a poisoned blade would leave signs around the wound itself. Her wound is healing cleanly." He stopped, then looked sharply at Rory. "You say this happened two days ago?" The healer bent again to examine Hannah's shoulder, this time running a finger along the extent of fresh pink tissue along the angry red welt of the burn. Hannah closed her eyes tight and tried to ignore the scent of masculine sweat and clean linen that washed over her. He would taste so much better than the goblins had; hell, anything would be a relief at this point. She held herself motionless, the effort causing sweat to bead up on her forehead, the dampness giving her a chill. Hannah held onto the thought that although she may not be the pureblood she had always thought she was, she could at least be grateful that she had never been a fledgling—nor was she subject to the bloodsweat that marked a turned vampire. If that had been the case, there would be no mystery as to the cause of her illness. This way, she still appeared human, though she was hoping she didn't end up dying like one.

"What?" Rory asked as the healer sat back up.

"She has healed a great deal for only two days, especially if the wound was as bad as you say."

"I could see the bone," Rory stated, shaking his head as he recalled. "There was so much blood."

"She bled a lot? Hmmm... Blood loss would explain the weakness. That will pass, but not the fever." He put a hand to his chin, rubbing it across his lip.

Rory said, "She has a smaller wound on her back as well, but that wasn't serious."

The healer reached out and lifted Hannah with sturdy hands, rolling her to the side with a practiced move that spoke of long years in the profession. Her shoulder objected but not too strenuously. She did stiffen when the strange elf rucked up her slip without a word, baring her flesh as his hand slid across the small stab in her lower back. His fingers pressed on it, and when his motion elicited a small moan of discomfort, but nothing more than that, he lowered her back down, replacing her slip with the air of a professional. Hannah considered the elf in a new light. He must have been a healer for a long time now to be so comfortable with the bodies of his patients. She wasn't a woman to him at all—just some flesh with holes in it that needed doctoring. It was somehow refreshing to be seen that way, though the feeling was fleeting. Her shoulder was aching again.

"There has to be another explanation," the healer said, hand to his chin in thought. He seemed to recall something, his hand darting out to touch a lock of her red hair, and he looked sharply at Rory. "Who is she?"

Rory seemed surprised by the elf's question. His brow furrowed, and his voice was a bit firmer than Hannah thought was necessary. "Her name is Hannah," Rory said, "and she travels with me."

"Where is she from?" The hand didn't leave her hair, and the healer was studying Hannah's face closely, his eyes skating down to take in her forehead, cheeks, and chin. He seemed to be memorizing her face, and Hannah wanted him to stop looking at her like that.

"Why does it matter?" Rory was cautious now, and Hannah knew that he didn't like the way the healer was looking at Hannah, and he certainly didn't like the way the elf was touching her hair.

"I'm trying to help you here, *sir*," the healer had taken an officious tone, one Hannah knew that he must use often with patients. "Maybe if I knew more about her, I could figure out why she is so sick." He stopped staring at her, and Hannah had the sense that he had made some important decision, but she couldn't tell what it was. The elf's mind was a blur to her bloodfevered mind.

Hannah looked from Rory to the healer, her breath coming in sharp gasps as the blood withdrawal gave her another shudder. This was intolerable. She had to do something, to get away and feed, or she was going to die in this bed tonight. If only her body could understand that and do something besides shake and shudder.

"Will she get better?" Rory asked, and he seemed unable to stop the question before it came out, face hesitant as he stared hard at the healer.

The healer looked at him, an eyebrow quirking. "She's dying. I thought one as astute as you would know that by now."

"Please," Rory said, and Hannah felt his struggle to maintain a civil tone. "Can you help her without knowing exactly what is wrong?" Hannah heard the strain in his voice and wanted it to mean something, but she didn't know exactly what she wanted it to mean. Everything was confusing when it came to Rory.

"Are you begging, Rorinvalranus?" the healer asked, and Hannah didn't miss the look on Rory's face as the elf said his full name—shock, self-recrimination, stolid expectation. "It is not becoming in one such as you."

"How do you know my name?" Rory asked, a hand moving to the hilt of his sword. "Do I know you?" He was tightly wound, his body tensed for confrontation.

The healer shook his head. "No, but I know who you are."

"And who am I?" Rory's hand had not moved from his belt.

"Everyone knows who you are around here. Did you think no one would notice the way Tom fell over himself to get you and your friends a room? You're a legend in Kalford, Rory," the elf sneered the nickname. "The man who singlehandedly took down the ruler of Firene. You must be so proud." He looked to Hannah lying weakly on the bed. "Is this your new woman, now? Picking them kind of young, aren't you?" He seemed to consider. "Does she know about you, Rory? Does she know who you really are? Or were, I suppose?"

Rory was staring hard at the healer, his face tight in warning. "You don't know what you're talking about." Hannah waited for him to explain that she was not his "newest woman," whatever that meant.

The healer scoffed. "Do you even remember Galina? She died, of course, but you knew that, didn't you? Died of the shame after what you did." Lying forgotten on the bed for the moment, Hannah realized that for all she might find appealing about Rory, there was still a great deal she didn't know about him.

"Shut up," Rory grated. "You don't know anything about it."

"I know it took Jasper nearly five years to put things back together after you left. I know that you left Firene a disaster. I know that not only did they lose their beloved prince, but their warmaster all at once." Seeming to realize that Rory did not appreciate his speech, he added in a more subdued tone, "And I also know not to cross you, and for this town, that's more than enough." The elf looked back to his patient. "She should know, though. She should know what she's getting into." He looked to Rory, and Hannah felt the flood of righteous indignation fueling his words. "That's more than Galina ever got."

Wait one moment, Hannah thought, astonishment trying to work its way through the haze of her fever-clouded mind. *Could it be possible?* She remembered the old story—how Firene had nearly been destroyed by a civil war thirty years before her birth, how it had all started over a fight between the lord and his master of war, and over a woman named...

Hannah lost the motion of her thought in a wracking spasm, unable to conjure the name of the mythic lady who had unknowingly sparked a civil war that lasted five years. She knew Klauden would remember, but her old friend wasn't here to remind her. The whole idea was ridiculous, of course; her Rory couldn't be the Rorinvalranus of the history. Then again, stranger things had happened.

Rory seemed on the verge of saying something to the healer but bit his lip instead, trying to gather himself. He was reminding himself that he needed the healer, Hannah knew suddenly, and that without the damn elf's help, Hannah might die this night.

It was so odd to think of herself in his thoughts, and she pulled away. She heard Rory take a few deep breaths, watching as he made an obvious effort to remove his hand from his weapon. He crossed both arms across his chest, carefully holding his hands in place. Hannah thought he might be deliberately tying himself up so he didn't do anything stupid. "Can you help her or not?" The words were icy.

"I can try," the healer said, snickering as he placed one hand on Hannah's chest and the other on her forehead. *What the—?*

Hannah didn't get the chance to finish the thought before he began chanting something low under his breath, and it took her a moment to recognize what he was doing. He was calling on his divine powers, his holy magic, to heal her.

I'm going to die, she thought clearly. *I've been so stupid.* There was a sharp pain on her forehead where his hand rested against her skin as she felt the power begin to stream out of him and into her.

Desperate, she called on every last reserve of strength she had left, and then she was shoving his hands away, scrambling up and away from him in a flurry of blankets and holding herself up against the wall. There was a low pop as the power vanished into the bed instead of into her body, and she looked from the pinprick of white light that faded from view on the blanket to the elf who was staring at her, face aghast.

"What's going on?" Rory yelled. "Hannah, what happened?"

Hannah felt herself slipping down the wall, the strength that had buoyed her fading, but one look at the healer's face strengthened her spine. There was something more than outrage there, something closer to mad desire that made alarm bells ring deep in her mind. She could not let that elf touch her again. She looked from the healer to Rory and back again, utter confusion paralyzing her limbs.

"Do you know what she is?" the healer hissed, slowly adjusting in preparation for a lunge at her.

Rory's sword was drawn, and he held the blade between the healer and Hannah, the metal shining in the firelight. His voice was calm, collected, and filled with steel. "What are you talking about?"

Hannah looked frantically around the room, searching for an escape route. The door was beyond the two elves, so that was out, but the window was only a few feet to her right. It was still shuttered, but she thought she could throw herself through it and get out. They would follow her, but it was the only chance she had. Now, if only she could get her muscles to understand the urgent need for action.

"Demon," the healer hissed.

Hannah's body was still frozen, trapped between bursts of adrenaline. Stalling seemed her only option now. "What are you talking about?" she croaked though a sore throat, fingers gripping the wooden wall behind her to support her weight.

"Demon?" Rory echoed. "Have you gone mad?" he scoffed, sword moving a little bit to discourage the healer from moving toward her. "Hannah is no demon."

The healer addressed Hannah, "I know who you are, and I know who hunts you."

"I don't know what you're talking about," Hannah repeated, trying to find the strength within to make a desperate lunge for the window. The healer had to be talking about Malbrek.

"Leave her alone," Rory said, his free hand reaching for the elf to pull him away from Hannah.

"You are mine!" the healer screamed, lunging at Hannah across the small bed. He pushed the sword aside, blood spraying the bed as his hand took the blade's impact.

Hannah managed to duck to the side, felt herself beginning to fall, and made a desperate wrenching motion that extended her movement beyond the end of the bed and into the shutters. The wooden slats splintered beneath her weight, and then she was falling through open space. The impact on the street below jarred her, and for a moment, she stayed there, hunkered on one knee, head hanging down, the burning in her veins pulsing through her. She heard shouts from the window above but didn't look up.

She closed her eyes, allowing the beast to come forward, giving up conscious control of her body to the demon that coursed through her tainted blood, and then she was scampering off down the street into a darkened alleyway that smelled of fresh human blood.

XVII

Hannah regained conscious thought after what she assumed was her third victim. The man still lay a few feet from where she leaned against the stone wall of what smelled like a smithy. The scent of hot iron was comforting, and the memories attached to it—of days swinging her hammer in Talperin, the warm glow of steel causing sweat to stream down her face—forced her slowly back to herself.

She glanced at the man nearby, trying to recall how she had killed him—had it been the neck wound or had she strangled him first? A cautionary exploration of his neck revealed both teeth marks and a reddish purpling that suggested she had done both. She sat back hard, wiping her hand against the side of her slip, realizing as she did so just how battered the material was. The blood soaked immediately through the cloth, smearing her thigh instead. She curled her feet up, bare feet cool against the dirt of the alley, shrinking against the wall as she recalled the two previous victims. She remembered them vaguely, the images dreamlike as their faces contorted from violent intentions to stark fear, then into the pliable blankness of death. She could feel the blood surging in her, the silky smoothness cooling her fever, stealing through her limbs and deadening the ache in her shoulder.

Her arms unconsciously went around her body. She wasn't cold, but she was exposed and recently sated, her skin still sensitive. Her arm brushed against the spot where her shoulder wound had been, the bandage long gone, and she glanced down at it. Blood crusted the edge of her slip, but the skin was puckered now, the bleeding stopped. She didn't know if the wound would heal correctly from here, but the blood had restored the balance to her body. She could move on her own again, her strength returning. She didn't know how long she had been sitting there or how much time had passed since she jumped to the street from the inn's room.

Her memory was hazy, the pictures and words blurring together. One thing she did remember, though she would rather not—the healer denouncing her to Rory. He had known, and likely the others all knew by now of the demon that had been traveling with them.

As she sat there, huddled against the alley wall in the dark, she tried to believe that this was better. It was better to leave them behind. The whole thing with Rory was getting too intense. Now she wouldn't have to be so conflicted. She just wouldn't see him again.

For some reason, that thought hurt worse than the wound in her chest had. She drew her knees together, realizing that while finally leaving the group was a great idea, she had left all of her belongings behind. She had only her slip, the thin material barely covering her to the knees. She had no weapons, no money, no spellbook—that was a jolt—and no clothing, not even her boots. In a place like Kalford, it wouldn't take long for trouble to find her.

She looked at the body lying a few feet away; trouble had already found her.

She shook the last of the blood daze away, then crawled over to where the man lay—Hannah avoided looking at his face, somehow ashamed of her kill even though the man had threatened her... hadn't he? She tried to remember, couldn't, and settled for drawing the man's sword and turning the bite mark on his neck into a fully slit throat. Glancing around, she spotted the refuse bin from the smithy and dragged the man's body into the dark shadows behind it. She dismissed his clothing, knowing that although she did need something more than a shift if she was really going off on her own again, wearing ill-fitting, bloodied clothes would probably draw even more unwanted attention. She held onto the sword, hoping it wouldn't mark her as the man's murderer but might come in handy the next time she was attacked.

The next time... she thought. *I can't hold my own in this place with just a sword*, she thought, thinking of her daggers and, more importantly, her spellbook. *I need to get my things back.*

She held the sword out in front of her, practicing a few quick moves drawn from the man's memories. She decided she could use the weapon if the occasion called, but it would take a lot of practice to make her proficient. That was the problem with the blood memories—it was one thing to know something in the abstract; it was another to have the muscle memory necessary to perform under pressure.

She needed to think, to take stock of the situation. Her bag was in the room at the inn. If Rory or the others were out looking for her, she might be able to sneak back in and get her things. *And money,* she thought, although she knew that her few silver pieces were not enough to buy rooms in the towns along the way. Along the way to where? She didn't know.

A plan, she thought, *I need a plan*. Klauden would have a plan. *What would he do?*

She twisted the ring on her finger, a desperate desire for her old friend nearly overwhelming her.

Oh, Klauden...

Wait. Think, she ordered herself. *Feeling sorry for yourself is not helping anyone.* She thought of the small pouch in her bag back at the inn, pictured the worn leather bag with its promise of relief.

No, she decided fiercely. *I don't need him. I don't need anyone.*

She took a deep breath to calm herself, trying to ignore the mounting panic that was so uncharacteristic.

Get a hold of yourself, she demanded. *You're no worse off now than when you first left home.* This seemed to work, but then her thoughts started running away again.

Except then I had a bag of belongings and money... She forced herself to stop. *It's the same thing. It's just me now, and it was stupid to spend so much time with them, with him, because now I've gotten used to their protection. I've let myself become weak.*

She stood up, scanning the alley for life and finding none, then crept around the corner and began walking down the street. She hid against the wall as much as possible, sticking to the shadows, moving silently so as not to attract any more attention than necessary. She had lost her bearings in the blood stupor and only managed to reorient herself when she reached the riverbank.

Deciding it was worth it to wash the condemning blood from her face and hands, she stowed the sword in the dry grass and knelt along the edge. She splashed herself with cold water until her skin glowed like marble in the moonlight again. Her anger shielded her from the fear the water should have conjured, and she washed more vigorously than necessary. She shook herself to dry off, then examined her shoulder, flexing the muscle and relishing the novelty of motion without pain. The line of burned skin was silvery-white in the moonlight, the outline of the blade Gorn had used to cauterize the wound clearly visible against her pale skin. *At least it had healed,* she thought, but she knew it would scar. It didn't matter though; a scar would make her look more human. She couldn't see the wound on her back, but a quick examination by touch revealed only smooth skin where the sword had cut her. The blood had done its work.

She scanned the water for the bridge they had crossed when entering Kalford and saw the dim wooden outline to her right. She tried to remember how they had gotten to the inn from the bridge, then decided she would have to walk around the entire area in order to find it again. She thought she would recognize the two-story building if she saw it. Either way, she could always look for the broken shutters.

She stayed along the riverbank, following the clear path to the bridge, allowing the lapping water to wash away the footprints her bare feet left in the mud. The man's sword was awkward in her hand, the weight much heavier than the daggers she was accustomed to, but the mere presence of the weapon was reassuring. Hannah pretended the comfort did not stem from memories of Rory's weapon and the careless ease with which he used it. She had made it three streets in from the river's edge when a voice spoke in the darkness of the alley in which she was creeping.

"I thought you would find your way back here."

Hannah turned, squinting in the darkness, debating if she should use her nightvision or if the red of her eyes would cause more trouble. She recognized the healer's voice. He stepped out of the shadows, his tall form reminding her of Rory's smooth grace as he moved.

An elf, she thought. *I could take him and be even stronger.* The thought was habit, though, not something she took seriously. She would no more take this elf after her earlier feasting frenzy than she would have taken Rory as he tried to help her. It wasn't necessary.

Hannah sighed. *Can this night get any worse?*

"What do you want?" she asked, gripping the sword tightly. The question was a waste of time. She knew what the elf wanted. He wanted to destroy her.

But as she watched him, another possible purpose became clear. If he had wanted to kill her with his divine power, he could have done so already. He didn't need to be so close to her.

In fact, she realized, he could have killed her in the room before she managed to escape. He just needed to call on his power and release it in her general direction. Hannah's wariness increased.

She tried not to think of the spellbook in the room; even if she had possession of it now, the spells within wouldn't help her. She hadn't studied in two days, the fever too much of a distraction. She tried to remember the few spells she could throw and managed to recall three— the ice shard, a hypnosis, and an invisibility. Not much to work with. The ice shard was her best bet since elves weren't likely to fall for hypnosis, and invisibility only worked if he hadn't already seen her. Even so, it was better to keep him talking; her spells were sometimes unreliable.

The healer was still approaching her, and Hannah began taking steps away from the elf, pacing him to keep the distance between them. "What do you want?" she repeated.

"I think you know, demon," the healer said, pausing in his advance. He looked her over, a lewd grin contorting his lips. "You did well to attach yourself to Rorinvalranus," he observed, "but I think that he got the better end of the deal by far. You know, Malbrek never mentioned how attractive you were."

"Oh, he didn't?" she asked, thoughts racing. Malbrek was here. This elf had spoken with him. *How many others does the wizard have looking for me?*

The elf shook his head, blonde waves bouncing. "Nor did he mention how young you appear, but it didn't take me long to figure you out." His face creased in curiosity. "How did you manage to get so sick?" he asked. "Your kind are supposed to be indestructible."

"Someone has misinformed you," Hannah said.

"Or was it a trick?" he asked, eyes gleaming with the thought. "A way to lure another elf to your side?"

"Oh, please," Hannah sneered. "I don't use such tricks." *Anymore,* she thought silently.

"Of course not," he said, "why use tricks when you have Rorinvalranus at your side?" He shook his head. "You do aim high, Lady van Kreeosk." His use of her old title was disconcerting.

"Speak plainly," Hannah demanded, old habits surfacing. "Are you here to bring me to Malbrek?"

The healer started to nod. "Of course, but..." His voice trailed off, his nod turning into a suggestive leer. "Maybe I have changed my mind."

Hannah felt her skin start to crawl, wishing she had more clothing to cover with, to shield her body from his lascivious gaze. She steeled herself, remembering how to behave around men like this. *Haven't I been doing this since childhood?*

She sneered, looking down her nose at him. "Kelvin Malbrek does not look well on those who *change their mind*," she commented. "In fact, he would be very disappointed if any harm were to come to me." As soon as she spoke, Hannah knew the words were useless. He wouldn't heed her warning because there was no threat of her father or Klauden behind her. She was alone. Still the familiarity of the routine was comforting, and she felt her confidence returning. He was just one elf, and he hadn't made any move to use holy magic against her; he obviously wanted something from her, and that gave her the edge.

"Would he now?" the elf asked, taking a step toward her. Hannah held her ground, knowing that if she moved, he might just jump the rest of the way, and she didn't know if her strength had completely returned yet.

"Yes."

"Then it is fortunate that I have no intention of harming you."

"What are your intentions, then?"

"I wish to serve you," he said. Hannah wasn't sure she heard him correctly.

"I'm sorry?" she asked, aware of the wall a foot behind her, knowing that if she was going to flee, she had to get out of this corner.

"You heard me," he said, holding out both hands toward her. "You are powerful, lady, one of the strongest of your kind," the elf said, biting his lip in anticipation. Hannah considered telling him she was actually one of the weakest of her kind but thought it best to keep silent. *What has Malbrek been telling his spies?* "You will share such a gift."

It took Hannah a moment to understand what he was saying. *Gift? For Cairn's sake, does he want me to make him one of us?* She had known he was a fool, but this made him an utter buffoon. No one who had any idea of the trials of fledglings would willingly ask for such a curse.

She scoffed. "And why would I do that?"

"I will be a better guardian than Rory," the elf claimed. "With the blood, I would be unstoppable." *No, you would be miserable*, Hannah thought, *if you lived through it*. "I would protect you always."

"I don't need your protection," Hannah said. She had never had anyone ask her to convert them before. It was flattering in an odd way. She knew she would refuse—she was not interested in a follower—but the idea was intriguing.

"But you do," the elf insisted. "Think of it—a vampire who wielded holy magic," he posed. "I could destroy any who threatened you. I could serve you."

Hannah considered. The very idea of a vampire using divine power was ridiculous, and she was rather surprised that the elf didn't realize it. Whichever god granted him his power would almost certainly withdraw any abilities the moment he became one of Cairn's children. *And who knows if he would even survive the transformation?* She had never heard of an Elven vampire before. Maybe it couldn't be done at all. If she did bite him, he would probably sicken and die or at best become a mindless wraith. *Who has been filling his head with such thoughts? Malbrek*, she answered immediately. *Who else?*

"You are a fool," Hannah said finally.

The healer's face shifted, and Hannah remembered that he could just use his power to destroy her. She should try to be nicer to him. "I am no fool."

"That's right," Hannah said. "No fool would willingly choose to become a demon."

The elf approached, menacing as he drew both hands together before him in the universal preparation for spellcasting. "You will do this, or I will destroy you right now."

Hannah laughed, unable to stop herself, cloaking her nervousness with haughtiness. "You won't do it." She decided to stick with arrogance. She dropped the sword she had been holding, the point sticking into the dirt of the alleyway, and took a few bold steps toward him. "You can't destroy me. Not if you really want what you claim."

He watched her, licking his lips again. "You will do it, then?"

"That's not what I said," Hannah reminded him.

"I will not be denied," he stated. "I will have such power."

"You know nothing of my power," Hannah observed, scanning the alleyway for any hiding places. Not that hiding would help her get away at this point, but any edge she could get would help.

"But I will learn," he said. "You will teach me." As he finished speaking, he leaped at her. Hannah had been prepared, but the force of his full weight smashing into her still knocked them both down, Hannah's upper back and head smacking into the stone wall behind her.

There was a moment of dislocation, then she was aware of him on top of her, his hands trying to hold down her arms. He was strong, Hannah noted, but she was stronger. *Aren't I?* Now that she was no longer playing the role of defenseless human, she could utilize her full strength—provided her midnight snacks had replenished more than her blood alone.

She moved an arm cautiously, checking to see if she could just pry him off, and was a bit dismayed to note that while her strength seemed to have returned somewhat, it was not yet at its full potential. She was evenly matched. That would make things more difficult.

She struggled, managing to get her arms in the space between their bodies. He was kneeling on top of her, his legs worming between her own as he tried to force her to lie down. The stone wall behind her scratched her back as she began to slide to the ground, an elbow landing uselessly against the wall instead of connecting with his head. *Damn, he really is strong.* This was going to get ugly.

She knew what he was doing, of course. He wanted to force her to bite him, force her to defend herself in the only way she knew how. But Hannah had learned a few tricks since leaving home. She let herself be pushed flat to the ground, uncomfortably aware of how thin her dress was and how he was prying her legs apart with his knees. *What the hell are elves coming to these days?* For a race that was supposed to be pure and holy, they weren't anywhere near what the reports claimed.

All those stories we read as children, she thought, *and not one elf misbehaving. I meet two elves in real life, and one knows thieves and has a violent past, and the other tries to rape me to convince me to bite him. Some heroes.*

Hannah waited until she could grab both of his upper arms with her hands before making her move. When she had a good hold on him, she jerked up her left leg, her foot landing solidly on the wall, then pushed off with as much force as she could muster. The movement forced both of them rolling to the right, and Hannah dragged him with her by the upper arms, managing to get on top of him as they came to a stop. His hands were caught somewhere around her waist as he tried to roll them again, but Hannah focused on locking her legs under his knees to stop his attempts to buck and kick her.

"Bite me," the elf demanded, throwing back his head to reveal a smooth throat. Hannah caught herself, the impulse to take him suddenly boiling up in her, the need for not only fresh blood to increase her strength, but an elf's blood, the pure blood that would make her a god.

Ridiculous! Remember how true those myths about elves were? The stories about Elven blood are probably just as true as that tripe was.

She reared back, feeling her teeth huge in her mouth, and tugged at his hands on her waist, trying to get free so she could stand up. As she did so, the healer lunged up at her, mouth open, teeth bared, and bit her unmarked shoulder. Even though he didn't have the teeth for it, the force of the attack was enough to break the skin, then he was clinging to her, mouth working desperately as he tried to suck her blood. The move shocked Hannah into stillness—no one had ever dared to bite her before.

She was Hannah van Kreeosk, First Daughter to Magnus van Kreeosk, and her blood was her most precious commodity. She had never shared it with anyone, and this filth, this leech was trying to steal it from her! She leaned forward, regaining her balance as he clung to her chest, her arms scratching uselessly at his back, trying to pry him off of her. She could feel the blood leaving her, the power of his suction pulling her precious blood into himself. She tried again to force him off, but she could feel her strength leaving her.

Oh, no, she thought. *I will not be weak again.*

She thought frantically of any spell she might use to defend herself, but nothing she could recall would be of any use. Her only weapon was her mouth. She could bite him, make it hurt so badly that he would let go of her, then be certain to drain him to the point of death so there would be no chance of conversion.

Her hands still gripped his shoulders, trying to pry his head back, but he was determined, his arms wrapped around her small frame unyielding as iron.

"Get off!" she shouted, frustrated that his neck didn't snap under the strain of her pulling hands under his chin. He did move slightly though, his neck turning just enough to make it an easy target for her own mouth, her eager teeth.

Fine, she thought, *but only because I have to. He has to die now.*

She bent slowly, knowing there was no other alternative but still hating herself for giving in to the urge, her teeth breaking the skin easily, the blood flowing into her mouth. She had a moment of pure ecstasy as the elf's blood filled her, such a change from the goblins of the previous weeks and even the humans of a few hours before. She marveled at his strength, his power, then remembered that the leech was still attached to her, recalled how he had tried to steal from her, and doubled her efforts, her normally meticulous feeding habits forgotten as she mauled him in earnest. The elf's desperate grip on her shoulder loosened and disappeared, his head lolling in her arms.

Try to steal my blood! How dare you!

She could feel the strength coursing back into her body, strength she had not known since living back home where willing humans had been plentiful. It was just so good to finally feast again! And the elf had asked for it, hadn't he? There was no need to feel guilty, no need to regret what she was, no need to wish to be something other than what she was, even if it would make Rory think she was worthy...

Her thoughts were spinning, her body taking over, forcing the healer back and to the ground.

The whirling kaleidoscope of images from the elf's memory—a dancing girl, a man standing on a riverbank, another man (*Malbrek!*) sitting across the table in an inn promising glory and riches to the one who could deliver his prey, then she pulled away, unwilling to see anymore. As she retreated, she noted that he was barely alive now, but she still clung to him, determined to get every last drop.

"What in the nine hells are you doing?"

XVIII

Hannah jerked upright, dropping the body to the street as she turned away from the voice she knew so well. She wavered, then got clumsily to her feet, staggering to the opposite wall of the alley, hands wiping at her face. When she reached the wall, she turned to face him, her back against the wall holding her up as she reeled from the blood stupor.

It was Rory looking at her, Rory looking from the elf on the floor to the damning evidence smeared across her lips and chin, Rory with his weapon drawn and his eyes questioning and surprised. Hannah stood completely still for several seconds, at a complete loss for thought. Then the look on his face broke her paralysis. She retreated, an arm against the wall supporting her weight as she took several staggering steps down the alley and away from him.

"I'd hate to think I'm interrupting what I think I saw," he said, the words tripping over themselves as they came out. Rory stepped toward her, glancing suspiciously at the body on the ground. "What are you doing? Hannah, did he attack you? Are you alright?"

He glanced from her face to her slip, his face clearing of any expression, and Hannah's gaze followed his. The bite mark on her shoulder was raw and bleeding, a trail of red running down onto her clothes. The shift was a little worse for wear, if that was possible, a long tear now running up to her hip on one side, apparently torn in the struggle. She moved her hand away from the wall to cover the wound, ignoring the dull ache, hoping the elf's blood would get to work healing her body, while her other hand went to cover the rip in her clothes. "You're bleeding," Rory observed, his face blank. "Again," he said.

Hannah continued her retreat, hoping the shadows could hide her face. "I'm fine," she said in a strangled voice, trying to think of an excuse.

"Are you sure?" He had reached the body by this point and, noticing the curious wounds in the neck, knelt down for a closer inspection. Finding no weapon either on the elf or lingering on the ground, he turned his suspicious gaze to Hannah. "What were you doing?"

Hannah looked at the barely breathing elf on the ground, knowing that she had to finish him off or he would get his wish. She couldn't do that with Rory standing here, so she tried to compose herself as the implications of this encounter dawned on her. "None of your business," she said coldly, unable to meet his gaze. She couldn't bear it quite yet. It was too fresh, too new to grasp.

He knew. He had to know.

"Oh, I think it is my business," he said in clipped tones. Hannah noticed that he did not sheathe his drawn weapon, as if she were a threat to him. She felt horribly exposed, and it made her angry. "Tell me what happened here."

"What do you think happened here?" she asked, trying to avoid the question.

Rory knelt, placing his free hand on the healer's chest. "He's still breathing," he stated, "so that's something at least."

"Not for long," she whispered.

"I'm a bit lost here, Hannah," Rory said, his sword dropping to his side. But he didn't put it away. "This guy starts calling you a demon, and you jump out the window and run away. It's ridiculous, of course, I know that, but you're not helping your image by having sex with him while you bite each other." He laughed bitterly. "I know the women of the north are known for some voracious appetites when it comes to men, but I never pegged you for one of them."

"It's not like that," Hannah tried to explain. "We weren't... I mean... It's not what it looks like."

"Well, I'll tell you, Hannah, it looks pretty bad. And I thought you were such a nice girl."

"It's not like that," she repeated, looking at her feet.

"Then what is it like?" he asked. "You looked like he scared you half to death. Now I find you necking... or whatever... in an alleyway." He stopped to catch his breath. "You jump through the shutters to get away from him and land without breaking any bones, and only two seconds before that, you were lying in bed dying! Am I losing my mind here or what?"

His face was red when she looked up and made the mistake of meeting his eyes. What she saw there frightened her. There was outrage, yes, and disbelief, but the most disturbing thing was the look of disappointment, as if she had somehow failed him. *Damned if he'll make me feel bad for who I am*, she decided, holding his gaze without flinching. He groaned in annoyance, seeing the determined set of her jaw.

"He attacked me," she offered, trying to get as close to the truth as possible.

"I believe that much," he agreed. "And?"

"And I defended myself," she completed.

"Defended yourself," he repeated, "by biting him. Why wouldn't you use a spell on him?"

Hannah said the first thing that popped into her mind. "He bit me first." It was childish, and suddenly, she felt like a little girl again, trying to explain to Malbrek why her clothes were torn, except that Klauden had always been standing beside her when she got in trouble, and this time she was alone.

"Why would he bite you, Hannah?"

She shrugged. "I don't know."

"He called you a demon, and when he tried to heal you, you flinched away," he recalled. "Lira tried to heal you when we first met, and you nearly fainted." His voice was picking up now as he remembered. "And with Jason Saffron, you kept trying to get away from me. I thought you were disoriented from his attack, but it was really Lira again, wasn't it? You were trying to get away from her. Why? Are you cursed?" He stood, leveling her with his gaze, his blade raising. "What are you, Hannah?"

"I am your friend," she said quietly.

"Fine," he agreed. "Then do what friends do—tell me the truth."

"He attacked me," she said again. "He wanted me to..." She trailed off, not knowing how much to say, or how to phrase it, or if there was any way to get him to stop looking at her like that.

"I know what he wanted," Rory said quickly. "That's not what I'm talking about."

"Then what *are* you talking about?" she demanded.

He moved toward her, the weapon still in his hand as he closed the distance between them. Hannah turned, sagging against the wall, defeated. He lifted her chin with the tip of the blade, the metal cold against her skin. "We agreed not to lie to one another, Hannah. What in the hell is going on?" At her silence, he sheathed the sword, replacing the metal with warm fingertips. "At least look at me."

She did.

"I want to believe you, Hannah, but you give me nothing to believe." He looked back to the healer lying on the ground. "And I'd like to say that I'm upset at what you've done to him, but I can't because he probably asked for it. Do you know him?" He shook his head. "It doesn't matter." He returned his gaze to her. "Why won't you give me an explanation?"

"There's nothing to explain," she said.

"Nothing to explain," he repeated, his voice growing lower, dangerous. "When bodies keep piling up around you, Hannah, there is something to explain."

"It's none of your concern," she tried.

"It concerns me when I'm constantly having to defend you to the others."

Now she looked at him. *Defend me to the others? What is he talking about?* "You shouldn't defend me, Rory." She took a deep breath and gave up. *Oh, the hell with it*, she thought, the weeks of frustration and silence catching up to her. *He already knows anyway.* "I am what he says."

"What? You don't honestly expect me to believe that you're a demon," he said, shaking his head. "You can't be."

"Why not?"

"Because…" he floundered, "because demons are creatures who escape from one of the nine hells," he settled for saying. "Demons possess people and wreak havoc on the living." He smirked a little. "Demons are not young women with a penchant for getting in trouble."

This was something Hannah had not expected. Of all reactions she had anticipated, this flat-out denial was not one of them. "Rory, I'm telling the truth."

"Sure," he gave a self-deprecating chuckle, drawing away from her. "I get it," he said, glancing at the healer on the ground, "though I don't understand it." He sighed, shaking his head. "Look, whatever kinky business you've got going with the healer is fine. Why didn't you just say so in the first place instead of this elaborate charade?"

"Charade?" she repeated, dumbfounded.

"You didn't have to go through all of this ... pretense ... of being interested in me so you could get here. If he was what you were after, you could have just said so."

"What are you talking about?" she asked, struggling to follow his logic. *Does he think he interrupted some sort of sex game between me and the healer?*

He looked at the body lying on the floor. "Though you did bite him a bit harder than necessary." He looked to her shoulder, where blood was still slowly dripping out from between her fingers. "Not that he didn't do the same to you. You've got some teeth on you, huh?"

"Rory," she said, "I told you it wasn't like that."

"Listen," he said, "you don't have to lie anymore." He waved both hands before his body, backing up. "I'll just leave you two alone, alright?"

"No!" she had shouted the word before she could think it through. *I do want him to leave, don't I?* That way she could finish this business with the healer and get the hell out of there. Malbrek could be anywhere.

Still, she just couldn't let Rory leave thinking her some sort of whore. *It's better than letting him know what you really are*, the voice whispered, but she ignored it. Her mouth was open, the words tumbling out.

"I wasn't having sex with him," she insisted. "I was feeding on him," she said instead. At the look on his face, she looked away at the ground. "He knew what I was and wanted me to turn him, and I refused, so he attacked me, and he bit me, so I bit him, and I thought he would die so it wouldn't matter, and then I could get away from here, but then I needed my bag, and I just didn't want you to know the truth." She stopped, amazed at the floodgate her mouth had become. She opened it again, unsure what might come out next.

"But I guess I do want you to know because... because I like you, and because you've always been kind to me, and because you didn't care who or what I was, even though I knew I was wrong, even though I knew I should get away from all of you before it became too obvious, even though I knew it was stupid to travel so long with mortals, but then there you were, always talking to me, being nice to me, helping take care of me, even though your care almost killed me last night..." *Gods, I am rambling.* At the thought, the words ran out, a pitcher empty of water.

There was a long moment of silence, then Rory spoke. "What kind of demon are you, Hannah?" He still didn't believe her.

"I am a vampire," she whispered.

He chuckled. "Right. Look, if this is your idea of a joke..." He looked around the alley as if expecting someone to jump out at him, to mock him for falling for her foolish game.

"Do I look like I'm joking?" She held her bloodstained hands out to him. "I really am a vampire."

"Hannah, everyone knows that vampires are dead, the souls of the damned possessing the bodies of the living. They can only be destroyed by holy magic or fire. You nearly died from a fever," he pointed out.

"I lost a lot of blood," she explained in a low voice. "I needed more, or my body would have died."

"But... but you look normal," he said. "Vampires have red eyes and big teeth." He peered at her eyes, then reached a hand around to open her mouth. She helped him, allowing her teeth to grow in her mouth and displaying them in a disconcerting grin. He narrowed his eyes, less skeptical. "Lira would have known," he said at last. "She would have said something."

"She should know, but she was distracted. I don't think she has had a chance to realize it yet, but she will. I have to leave before that happens."

"Why did you stay?"

"I was wounded," she said quickly. "I needed your protection."

"But you healed. Why stay after that?"

She shook her head. "I don't know." She looked up, taking in his slowly believing eyes, the desire for a different truth warring on his face. "I'm so sorry."

"You're sorry?" he asked. "There's no reason to be sorry for what you are. Clearly, this is some sort of curse. You were bitten, yes? So, if we find the one who bit you—"

"Rory," Hannah cut off his recitation of the oldest myths about her kind. "I was not bitten."

"What do you mean? What happened, then?"

"I was born this way," she stated.

"There are no born vampires," he declared.

"There are not many of us," she explained, "but enough for the old Houses to still hold sway over the villages north of the Vanya."

He looked at her seriously, a hand rubbing his chin. "Let me see if I've got this right—you claim to be a vampire from a whole group of born vampires who live in the north?" When she nodded, he shook his head. "You don't seem like a vampire to me, Hannah."

"What does a vampire seem like, Rory? Like poor Jason Saffron who was unlucky enough to get bitten?" She remembered how eager Rory and Lira had been to destroy the man. "Or Javerus, the elf from the border patrol you spoke of?"

He looked incredulously at her. "Did you bite Jason Saffron?"

"No," she said instantly. "Well, actually..."

"Actually what?" He seemed to be growing indignant as his belief sank in.

"Someone else bit him. I agreed to end his life." She waited for Rory to absorb this.

"So, when we walked in..." he began, "you were biting him."

"The life of a fledgling is difficult. He didn't want it."

"Why did you bite him, though? Did you need a victim or something?"

Hannah shook her head. "No, I had already had my share of goblins."

"You were hunting the goblins?" At her nod, he shook his head. "So, they *were* looking for you that night. Jamison was right. I don't believe it." He seemed to recall his direction, then asked, "So why did you bite Jason Saffron if you didn't need him?"

Hannah remembered her own confusion at her sympathy for the man. "I think... I think I felt sorry for him."

"You say that as if it were a new concept, Hannah."

"For me, it was. It is. I mean, being down here with everybody is changing me." She stopped, marveling that her ability to keep her mouth shut had gone. "I just don't know anymore."

He cocked his head, considering a moment. Then he closed his eyes, turned away from her, and began pacing up and down the alley, careful to avoid stepping on the unconscious healer. When he had made three rotations, Hannah spoke. "What are you going to do?"

"I don't know," he admitted. "It's too bizarre to decide right now."

"Are you going to kill me?"

He scoffed. "Now that was something I hadn't considered." He paused in his pacing, drew his sword, and flipped it in an intricate swirl that Hannah recognized from his morning ritual. "Should I kill you?" After a few turns with the weapon, he slid his dagger out as well, twisting the two in an expertly choreographed move that Hannah knew was his way of calming himself. Her confession had caught him off guard, and if he needed a moment alone, so be it. She kept an eye on him, ready to flee if he made any sudden moves.

When it became obvious he wasn't going to come flying down the alley to chop off her head, but rather, seemed focused on his pacing exercise, she knelt beside the fallen healer. Putting a hand on his chest, she felt the shallow breaths that marked excessive blood loss, then traced a line up to his neck. She wanted to hit him, to make him pay for trying to steal from her, but she thought his fate was enough. At least, it should have been enough, but for some reason, she knew it wasn't. She felt dirty, soiled by her contact with him, and pulled away. Suddenly, she didn't want to finish him off, didn't want another drop of his blood.

She looked around for the sword she had dropped, spotted it sticking in the ground a few feet away and crossed to it. She plucked the weapon out of the dirt, amazed at the strength in her now, knowing that it came from the elf she was about to kill.

Better to kill him than to let him suffer, she thought. *It's one of our rules,* she recited, one of the rules she and Klauden had sworn as children. She couldn't explain why they had decided not to pass on their blood to others, to forge an army as other Houses had tried, but it had been a pact in earliest childhood, and like all secrets sworn in childhood, it never occurred to her to break it.

She was kneeling over the body again, her hair hanging in her face, when Rory stopped his inner debate, walking purposefully toward her. She sat back on her heels, sword tip resting on the ground, waiting for his decision.

"So?" she asked when he didn't say anything.

"I have a few questions." He sheathed his blades and knelt before her, the body between them. He put both hands on his knees, preparing himself.

"Fine." Of everything she had envisioned, this calm explanation of her condition had never been an option.

"Do you absolutely need to kill people?"

"If I bite them, yes," she said without hesitation.

"You need their blood?" he asked, trying to sort everything out.

"There's that," she admitted, "but I never leave a victim alive. I don't want anyone of my blood running around."

"Is that all it takes? One bite?"

"Usually. Sometimes victims can recover, but it's not common. More often the victim will become what we call fledglings, new vampires who fall inevitably into one of two categories—the fehalon, mindless savages with no thought beyond blood, like Javerus, I imagine, or young creatures who grow to power over the years. They never get the status of a born vampire, but some have come quite far." *Like Kelvin Malbrek,* she thought. That was a story for the old legends—the fledgling who became advisor to the most powerful House in the Vanya, and now he was more obsessed with the bloodline than any born vampire.

"How often do you need to … eat?"

"Every three or four days is good, but I can go for a week if the blood is good."

Rory cut her off, placing a finger across her lips. "I see."

Do you? she wondered but couldn't bring herself to bring it up now to destroy the mood.

He pulled his hand away slowly, eyes creasing in consternation. He seemed about to say something else, then looked over at the body instead. "So, what about him?" he asked, gesturing to the healer. "Will he become a vampire now too?"

"No."

He seemed confused, "Why not?"

"Because I'm going to kill him first."

Rory started a bit at her tone. "You can't do that."

"I will not let him become a fledgling, Rory. I have never made another of my kind, and I don't plan on starting now. Especially after what he did to me."

"What did he do to you?"

Hannah gestured to the wound on her shoulder, the fresh scab barely visible through the rest of the gore. "He bit me."

Rory stared at her, nonplussed. "So? Apparently, you bite people all the time."

"Not all the time, and I only kill when I have to. I don't take pleasure in it like some do." *Don't you?* She ignored the question, putting a finger against the healer's cheek and turning his face toward her. "You will not become one of us," she told him. "I will not allow it."

"Hannah, wait..." Rory's hands reached out to stop her.

"Ah, Hannah, always so damned greedy with that tainted blood of yours," a voice said. "You never did understand the joy a fledgling could bring."

XIX

B oth Hannah and Rory looked up to the shadows. Hannah, who recognized the voice, immediately closed her eyes and focused on her nightvision. When she opened her eyes again, everything was clear, the shadows vanishing into subtle planes of grays and whites. She saw Kelvin Malbrek lounging against the wall a few feet away, an elegant finger poised before his face, as if he were examining it. Hannah knew the gesture meant he was ready to cast a spell. Which one he had ready, she did not know. She ran through her own available spells and winced. Malbrek was the best wizard her people had; she was no match for his skills.

Upon seeing him, her body tried to make the instinctive kneeling response and a deferential nod. She caught herself before she moved, reminding her body that such niceties were no longer needed. She was no longer north of the Vanya. She was free.

Or I could be if I survive this.

"Rory," she said slowly. "Run."

"Yes, Rory, do run. Please?" Malbrek suggested. "It's so much more fun to chase my prey down."

"Leave him alone," Hannah argued. "It's me you want."

"Dear Hannah, you have no idea what I want." The wizard stepped out of the shadows, and Hannah felt more than saw Rory get to his feet, weapons drawn. "Oh, look at this," Malbrek jeered. "You have picked a fine defender, my lady."

"He is not my defender," she said, still resting on her heels, her body crouched low to the ground, the sword lying to her right. It didn't matter though. Kelvin Malbrek was her superior in every sense—wizardry, weaponry—even his position as her father's advisor outranked Hannah's somewhat forfeited position as First Daughter of the House. If he wanted her to leave with him, Hannah knew that she would. Fighting might delay the inevitable, but she had always known that when he caught up to her, that would be the end.

Still, Rory didn't need to die tonight. She could save him. "He's nobody. Let him go, and I'll go with you."

"Go with me? What makes you think I'm not here to kill you and get it over with, Hannah?"

"Are you?"

He shook his head, blonde hair waving around his face. "You always were too much like your mother for your own good. I told Magnus not to marry that woman. I knew even then that she wasn't pure."

Hannah scoffed, tired of the old line. "You just wanted her for yourself," she said, the words out before she could stop them. She seemed to be running at the mouth this night. At the shocked look on Malbrek's face, Hannah realized what her body had already accepted. She would never have said such a thing at home. *But I'm not home, am I?* She wasn't in her father's castle, and she wasn't anywhere near the territory that delineated her position in society; she was free, in Kalford, a southern city without any rules at all. She didn't have to submit. She didn't have to go back, and she certainly didn't have to accept his death sentence.

She stood, the realization nearly overwhelming her. "You know what, Malbrek?" she asked, the intoxicating freedom making her careless. "I'm not going back with you. I'm not going to do anything you tell me to, not anymore. I don't have to obey you, you worthless fehalon!" She shouted the last word, knowing that calling him a fehalon—the name for those fledglings who went mad with the bloodthirst—was the worst insult she could probably use. She tipped her neck from side to side, feeling the small cricks as the stiffness left her, then concentrated, feeling the strength from the elf's blood coursing through her.

Malbrek stared at her for a moment, his face reddening, then flicked his open hand. Hannah was moving before she even thought about it, dodging whatever spell he was throwing at her, but when she stopped a few feet farther down the alley, she saw that he hadn't directed the attack at her, but at Rory. The elf was wrapped with black bands of power, each thread binding him where he stood. Hannah saw the sweat break out on his face as he struggled to get free. She had seen the spell before—a Malbrek Special, she and Klauden had called it—and luckily, knew how to defend against it. Those restraints only worked horizontally, not vertically.

"Fall," she commanded, reversing her direction to swing past Rory, pausing long enough to shove hard on his shoulder and force him to the ground. He didn't resist, and when he was lying on the ground, the black bands dissipated into mist. He didn't wait but rolled to his right, his hands collecting his fallen weapons as his feet tucked neatly underneath his body, then he stood in a smooth movement that had Hannah marveling at his grace.

Malbrek was chanting again, but this time, Hannah was ready. She thought desperately of her own measly supply of spells, settled on the only one likely to be of any use, and released the magic in a slew of words that put Malbrek's careful recitation to shame.

There was something to be said for winging it. The shard of ice hit the magician square in the chest, the edges melting outward as the spell sought to encase the victim. The distraction would only give them a moment, so she was moving behind Rory again, hands on his back to usher him away.

"We need to run, run now!" she was shouting, and it took her a second to realize that he wasn't moving. In fact, he seemed rooted to the spot, weapons out in a defensive stance. Hannah pulled on his shoulder, turning him ever so slightly to see that his eyes were closed. As she watched, horrified at the seconds ticking away, he opened his eyes, cricked his neck, shrugged off her hands, and stalked toward Malbrek.

Malfek, she cursed. *He's going to fight him.* And on the heels of that thought—*He's going to get himself killed.*

Hannah glanced around, wishing desperately for her daggers, then her eyes settled on the forgotten sword. She leaped to it, getting to her feet just as Malbrek dispelled the last of her ice shard, the patch of ice on his chest disintegrating into useless mist. She tried not to think of how much heavier the blade was than her normal throwing weapons as she lifted it to her shoulder. She held it by the tip of the blade and let it go, flinging it end over end at Malbrek. He ducked aside, but the blade still managed to nick his cheek, a small trickle of blood running down his face. He seemed about to charge her, then noticed the enraged elf barrelling toward him and changed his tactic. He loosed another spell, this time a bolt of electricity that Hannah had never been able to duplicate, but Rory ducked easily to the side, the spell crashing into the stone wall behind him. Malbrek seemed to realize the capability of his newest foe and drew his rapier. Hannah began scanning for another weapon, knowing that while Malbrek was an expert spellcaster, he was also a master swordsman, and Rory, amazing as he was, might not be able to hold his own against a vampire who had no doubt enhanced his natural skills with magic.

Hannah watched the first few blows nervously, then looked back to the alleyway. There had to be something she could do besides stand here like an idiot.

Yes, she thought suddenly. *There is something you could do. You could run.*

She stalled for a moment, seriously considering the option. The men would be fighting for some time, she knew, a few minutes at least, long enough for her to disappear.

But, Rory, she thought. *I can't abandon him to Malbrek. It's my problem, and he's defending me even though he knows what I am. I cannot leave. Well then,* she thought, *you need to find a way to defeat Malbrek. It's impossible... The only thing strong enough to defeat someone like him is holy magic and I don't have...*

She stopped, looked down at the fallen healer, and jumped on him. She began patting down his pockets, knowing that any healer who could wield divine magic would have his god's sigil somewhere on him. *A necklace, a dagger, a ring, something!* She found what she was looking for in his pocket, a small red medallion that burned her hand when she grasped it. She steeled herself against the pain, plucked it out of the pocket, and rested it on his slowly rising chest. The elf was still alive. *Oh, hell*, she thought, *he can wait*, then focused on the fight between the two men, waiting for her opening.

Rory was swinging both blades carefully, alternating between low jabs at Malbrek's undefended side and high passes that would take off the wizard's head. Malbrek's own sword was zipping before his body, defending each blow as Rory tried to sneak past his guard. Both men were tiring, sweat running down their faces as they ducked and dodged—the blood-sweat on Malbrek's brow blending with the small cut on his face.

Hannah measured their steps, counting the beats of the whirling dance, and then she saw it—when Rory circled back her way again, he would draw Malbrek's sword out to the left. Hannah could dart in to the right with the stone. She grabbed the holy relic, aware of the smell of sizzling skin as the item began burning into her palm, and pounced just as Rory stepped past.

She reached out to touch Malbrek's exposed side with the palm of her hand, the medallion between them. Her hand connected with the side of his face, the disc sinking into his cheek with a sickening putty-like stretching, and her father's wizard screamed. Rory managed to sneak a blade past the vampire's distracted defense, and Malbrek screamed again as the blade slipped into his side. Hannah forced the relic farther into Malbrek's face, then shoved the man away, relieved as the symbol lost contact with her hand and ceased the unbearable burning.

She staggered back, then watched as the necklace on Malbrek's chest glowed brightly and exploded, the magic contained within arcing toward the one who was still holding the weapon that had stabbed him—Rory. The black spear coalesced around the elf, tightening into iron bands around his chest, these designed not only to hold in place, but to squeeze him to death.

Hannah stepped back, suddenly aware that her nightvision wasn't working as well as it should. Everything seemed foggy, a low curl of mist covering the entire area.

Jamison?

She staggered toward where Rory had been. She heard a wet sound that must be Malbrek spitting out the medallion that had eaten through his cheek into his mouth, then a scrape of metal that was Rory's blade hitting the street.

"You will not escape me, Hannah," she heard the man grate through a ruined mouth, then she heard a shuffling, and then silence. Had he fled? Had Kelvin Malbrek just fled from her—Hannah of the Tainted Blood? She fell to her knees, feeling through the fog for Rory's body.

She felt coldness beneath her searching hands, the sensation cooling the burn mark on her palm, then realized that the contingency spell had not left with its master. Rory's face was turning red as the bands continued to constrict around his chest; the spell trapped in Malbrek's necklace had been rigged to kill anyone who managed to wound the wizard. Hannah placed her hands on the bands, knowing that most of Malbrek's magic was beyond her skill, but desperate all the same. She still had the elf's blood in her—maybe that would give her the edge she needed.

Closing her eyes, she concentrated on conjuring the counterspell that would dissipate Malbrek's magic. She tried to recall anything Klauden had taught her about sending power away, and suddenly, she could hear the words she needed, a low chanting in an accented voice she had loved once upon a time. She recited the words along with the voice in her mind, Klauden's pronunciation guiding her over the difficult portions, and she felt Malbrek's spell wavering, then disbanding. She opened her eyes to see the last of the bands dissolve into mist, then sat back as Rory began coughing.

He sat up quickly, gasping and gagging as air finally passed into his chest. "Ha..." he tried, then a few gasps later, "nah..."

"Easy," she advised. "Take slow breaths."

He did as she suggested, staring at her with shocked eyes.

"The next time I tell you to run," she commented, "you should listen to me." She heard someone approaching behind her and was about to leap into action again, when she heard Jamison's voice.

"I heard shouting, so I thought you might need a hand. What's going on?" The fog was thinning. "Who did you anger this time, Hannah?"

Hannah was about to turn around to face the man when Rory grabbed her arm and pushed her gently to the side. "Eyes," he gasped, then pulled himself to his feet. She remembered her nightvision, silently thanking the elf for his presence of mind. That was all she needed tonight—for Jamison to see her glowing red eyes. She closed her eyes, focused, and dispelled the ability. When she opened her eyes again, it was very dark. It took a moment to identify the dim shapes and shadows she was seeing, then she was standing as well, an arm around Rory's waist to hold the still gasping elf steady.

"Hannah didn't anger ... anyone," Rory explained in hitching breaths. "It was ... a wizard who attacked me," he choked out.

"Always making friends with the locals, huh?" Jamison commented but said no more when he saw the look on Rory's face.

Rory grimaced. "He killed ... the healer, too."

"Healer?" Jamison glanced around the alley, hands resting on his hips. "What healer?"

Hannah turned to where the elf had lain on the ground. "The one who healed my fever—" she started, then stopped as she saw the empty ground. There was no one else in the alley. Had Malbrek taken the elf with him? *Why? A snack or another spy?*

He will turn, she started to think, then stopped herself. *No, he will die. They usually died, didn't they?*

"He's gone," she concluded. "He must have fled when the wizard showed up."

Kelvin Malbrek just ran away from us, she thought stupidly, the novelty of the idea difficult to grasp. *The great bastard of my childhood fled.* She wanted to scream with the sheer joy of it, remembered Rory and Jamison standing there, and held in the sound.

"Wizard, eh?" Jamison was still talking. "Too bad I wasn't here to fight him with you."

Weren't you, oh great maker of fog? Hannah scoffed, the sound close to an escaped laugh. She composed herself, feeling Rory's confused glance on her. "Too bad," she agreed.

She really looked at Jamison then, noticing that he had a new necklace, a small pink pendant on a chain around his neck. It seemed very delicate and a bit out of place on him. Hannah wondered if Molly had given it to him. "What are you even doing out here?"

"You're looking much better, Hannah," Jamison noted, ignoring her question completely. "Except for the blood that always seems to cover you, that is. Whatever that healer gave you must have worked."

"I got cut in the crossfire," she explained, grateful that Rory's arm was covering the bite mark on her shoulder. That would spark too many questions, but Jamison seemed distracted anyway.

"Whatever," Jamison said, started to walk away, then stopped and turned back to them. "Are you going back to the inn?"

Hannah looked to Rory. "Yes," she said. "You?"

"Would you tell Molly I'll be back in an hour?" he asked.

"Sure," Hannah agreed, curious as to why Jamison found this a perfect time to relay messages but also glad that she wouldn't have Jamison walking back with them. As the man walked away, she wanted to ask what he was doing out so late but decided that was a mystery best left for another night.

Lucky, she thought as she helped Rory back to the inn. *We were just so lucky.*

XX

With an arm around his back to help support some of his weight, Hannah let Rory direct her back to the inn, the somewhat haphazard streets solidifying to a map in her mind. She wouldn't get turned around in Kalford again. When they approached the two-story structure, she opened the door with her free arm and helped him through. Ignoring the stares of the patrons enjoying their late-night meals, she eased him up the stairs, careful not to squeeze his wounded ribs too hard. Silently accepting the key he withdrew from a pocket, she opened the door and helped him onto the bed.

Turning about, she faced the splintered shutters hanging on the hinges, shrugged, and took the four steps across the room to the window, grabbing the shutters by the hanging edges, careful to avoid scraping her burned palm against the ragged wood. She held the broken pieces of wood together, then mumbled a minor spell she had always been able to do. She watched as the wood mended itself, not completely filling in the hole her small body had made a few hours before, but making enough of a patch to keep the shutters from fluttering open all night, an invitation to anyone walking beneath.

She turned to her right, facing the foot of the bed and Rory, who seemed to have wiggled something out from underneath his butt. As Hannah stepped closer, she could see that he was pulling clothes out from under him; apparently, they had been lying on the bed when she sat him down. When he held them out to her, she accepted, noting the expensive material of a brown skirt and thick brown sweater woven with a lighter brown pattern on each sleeve. They were fine clothes. She held them before her, also noting how they would probably fit her body. "What's this?" she asked.

Rory chuckled, the sound obviously painful. "I got you some clothes when we arrived. I thought you might like a new outfit after we tore your sweater."

Hannah held the clothes at arm's length, very aware of her bloody slip and bare feet and unwilling to get the new outfit dirty. She was moved, stupidly, ridiculously moved by the gesture. "Thanks," she whispered. "They're beautiful."

"Sure," Rory said. "They're lovely." He winced, his hands pausing as he tried to remove his weapon belt.

Hannah gently placed the clothes on the chair, then sat on the bed next to him. "Let me do that," she said, pushing his hands away.

"I'm fine," Rory said, but he let her unbuckle the belt. He breathed a bit easier with it off, but Hannah thought that the leather armor he wore was probably not helping. "You should take that off, too," she said, hands reaching under to pull the buckles into view. She realized how much she was invading his personal space, looked up to his quirked eyebrow, cocked her own head in response, then continued her work as he signaled his consent.

She moved slowly, working the armor over his head gently so as not to jar his ribs. He seemed to breathe easier without the leather restricting him, but his shirt was still covering his ribs. Hannah reached to pull it off without thinking, only aware of what she was doing when their eyes met as the shirt cleared his head, his hair falling onto a bare shoulder criss-crossed with silvery scars.

Suddenly shy, she looked away from his eyes to the old wound, face creasing in curiosity. The burn mark on her shoulder was the first she had ever had, and the novelty hadn't worn off. She reached up to trace the skin and caught sight of the new burn on her palm. Would the twisted serpent and staff fade, or would she have a new scar? She hoped it would heal—having a divine sigil burned into her hand would cause questions. She turned back to his body. "What happened?" she asked, a tentative finger reaching out to trace the series of bumps.

"Morningstar," Rory said. "I learned fast to avoid those at all costs." At his low chuckle, he winced, and Hannah looked down from his shoulder to his chest. It too was crisscrossed with random scars. She ignored these for the moment, focusing instead on the red area beneath his right nipple, where Malbrek's spell bands had caused the most damage. She traced the area lightly, closing her eyes to focus on the sensation. She counted in her head, one, two, three ribs, then a sinking sensation, then another band of bone. She opened her eyes, frowning a bit. "It's your fourth rib," she explained. "It's damaged."

"How do you know? Are you a healer too, Hannah?"

She shook her head. "No, but I know a lot about the body."

"Do you?" She didn't miss the teasing note in his voice. She glanced away from him, eyes settling on the shutters, and a new idea struck her.

"Rory?" she asked and looked back at him, eyes tracing the line of the wounded rib.

"Hmm?" He leaned backward a bit on the bed, allowing her to get a better look at his chest.

"I have an idea," she said shyly, "about how to help your rib."

Rory took another one of those tortured breaths, then said, "I'm all ears. This isn't some kind of vampire trick, is it?"

She gave him a look, relieved to see that he wasn't serious. "No," she told him anyway. "It's a magic trick." She traced the line again, contemplating. *Bone isn't that different from wood, is it?*

"What's your plan?" he asked.

She traced a line across his chest. "I think I can mend the bone," she told him. "It probably won't help with the swelling, but the break itself..." She trailed off, shrugging. "It may help a little."

"Give it a try," Rory said, lying down flat on his back. Hannah moved closer to kneel beside him, hands tracing the line again and again. The spell was simple enough, nothing like the magic spells she had been casting tonight. It was just a matter of picturing the smooth band of bone without any blemishes, just as she had fixed the shutters.

She closed her eyes, hands pausing above the place she wanted, then concentrated. She felt the power try to slam out of her, and she took a quick breath, holding it in check. Maybe some of what they said about Elven blood was true after all. She breathed out slowly, channeling the magic in a slow line, just enough to mend, not enough to affect anything but bone. She was almost finished when she took another slow breath, this time getting a whiff of Rory's scent instead of the stale air of the room. Her hands jumped, and she quickly pulled them away from his skin, from the neck that was so close to her.

She looked at Rory then, at his eyes bright with remembered pain as he watched her carefully. Hannah was reminded of the way he looked when hunting, that carefully controlled face a mask hiding his ability to move at any second. The moment stretched out, then Rory took a low breath of his own, and his expression changed from wariness to awe. He moved his arms, one hand moving to touch his chest, and took another cautious breath. His skin was still red and would likely turn purple by morning, but he seemed better.

"How does it feel?" she asked.

He smiled at her. "Better!" He sat up, winced, then moved closer to her, a hand on her shoulder. "Not perfect, mind, but worlds better. Thank you, Hannah."

She sat up, pulling away from him, suddenly aware of how close she was to him, how she was wearing nothing but a torn slip, and how he wasn't wearing a shirt. "You'll heal," she said, then stood. "I'm going to get some water. Do you want anything?"

When Rory shook his head, she moved to the door. "I could get Lira," she offered, turning back to him.

"No need. As you said, I'll be fine," he said, lounging a bit against the headboard. Hannah slid the bar off the door and started to open it. "Wait," he said.

Hannah turned again. "What?"

He was moving, leaning over the footboard to tug his bag from the chair onto the bed and began digging through it. He tugged free a length of black material that Hannah recognized as his cloak and stood up, one hand to his side as the other shook out the flowing garment. "Put this on," he suggested, his hand leaving his wound to drape the cloak around her back, fingers lingering on her neck as he tied the front shut. "Better to avoid any trouble."

"I never get into trouble," Hannah said, again acutely aware of how close he was to her, aware that, for once in her life, the desire she was feeling was not blood related. She had to get away from him before she did something irreversible.

"Of course you don't," he agreed, a hand brushing a curl out of her face, then wiping at her chin.

"If you want to take a bath," he suggested, "just tell Tom, and he'll have them pour you one." At her surprised look, he said, "The tubs are in the kitchen, quite private and quite comfortable."

XXI

The bath was everything Rory had suggested and then some. Hannah had not had a bath since leaving home, and although the wooden tub was a far cry from the elaborate steel bath she was used to, the water was hot, the soap smelled divine, and there was a pitcher that she used to dump water over her head.

She scrubbed the blood from her shoulder, wondering if a day would go by when she wouldn't get covered in blood, then stood up, water sluicing off her naked body. She was shielded from sight by a linen screen, as were two other tubs that were in the kitchen, but Hannah was still self-conscious. There was no door, after all, and anyone could just walk back here.

She grabbed the towel Tom had provided and dried off, careful to dab the bite on her shoulder and not rub, lest the newly healed skin slough off and start bleeding again. Her hand had stopped throbbing, though the red tracing of the burn was still visible. She made a mental note to keep that hand in a fist at all times until she could get a glove.

It was only after she had dried off that she realized she had only brought Rory's cloak and the bloodied and torn slip with her. It was a bit unsettling that she, who had always been so concerned with clothing, would have completely forgotten to bring fresh clothes to a bath.

She didn't want to put the slip back on now, not after she had gotten so clean, so that left either the towel or Rory's cloak. She draped the cloak over her shoulders, using the towel to soak up as much moisture from her curly hair as possible, then tied the neck closed. She stood, uncertain for a moment, then settled for wrapping both sides of the cloak around her hands and crossing her arms, twirling a bit in either direction to see how much the material moved.

After making some minor adjustments, she decided the cloak was as secure as it was going to get. She stepped carefully out from behind the screen, bare feet leaving wet prints on the wooden floor, and walked to the kitchen door. Tom stood behind the bar, wiping down a few mugs, and the fat man greeted her cordially as she passed. She hurried to the stairs, fiercely aware of the few patrons left in the bar who were staring at her fleeing form. As she passed the halfway point on the stairs a voice catcalled after her, "Easy, lass! Rory's not going anywhere!"

She blushed at the comment, then remembered her state beneath the cloak and blushed some more. She made it to the door and managed a subdued knock, the material cushioning the blow as she tried to keep the cloak closed. "Rory," she said, her mouth up against the doorframe. "It's me," she added, hoping he hadn't fallen asleep.

She was so close to the door that when it opened, she fell inside, practically tumbling into Rory's arms, the cloak flying open as she put out her hands to brace her fall. "Woah," Rory said, hands carefully neutral on her waist as she righted herself. He had not put his shirt back on. "Easy there, Hannah."

"I tripped," she said, covering her embarrassment by stepping away and readjusting the cloak so it covered her body. When she turned around again, Rory had shut the door and was sliding the wooden bar into place.

"You don't need to throw yourself at me, Hannah," he teased, a hand against the spreading bruise on his side. "Though I appreciate the gesture."

Hannah felt herself reddening again, suddenly aware of just how small the room was, not to mention the bed itself. *Am I really going to sleep here tonight? Where? On the floor? Or will we share the bed...?* She let the thought trail off, aware that for all her eighty years of life, there were still some mysteries she had never explored. She had never really wanted to, either, knowing that such things were in her future with Klauden when they decided to have a child, normally when they reached their mid-hundreds, a good age for childbearing, the elders always said. *Am I really going to permanently forfeit that future tonight?* But here she was, Klauden miles away and a memory of a forgotten life, standing half-naked in a room with a shirtless elf.

Damn, she thought, *how far things have come.*

But there are rules, she tried to remind herself. She stopped the thought, choosing to stare at Rory instead. *There are no rules here*, she decided. *Not tonight. Maybe not ever again.*

"Hannah," Rory said, taking a half step toward her, then fell back to where he was.

Hannah said the first thing that came to mind. "I don't have a slip."

Rory blinked, glanced down at the bunched fabric between her crossed hands, then looked up at her face. His gaze shifted to the chair where the new skirt and sweater lay, then back to her. Hannah noticed a pair of boots tucked neatly under the chair—they matched the skirt and sweater. She tried to quash the upwelling of thankfulness in her belly. "I didn't think to get you one," Rory admitted. "Sorry."

"It's okay," she said, then looked down at herself. She thought of the extra shirt in her bag, considered sleeping in the sweater, realized that either way she would have to change in front of him, and just pulled the smooth material of the cloak tighter. "Can I just keep this on?"

He seemed about to say something, then thought it over and settled instead for a nod.

"Thanks." She moved, darting past him, her feet moving in little steps to keep the cloak from billowing out, then climbed deftly onto the bed, pulling the blanket over herself and wedging close to the wall.

Rory laughed a little under his breath, turning to stare at her pale face in the firelight. He took the two steps to the bed and sat down on the edge, one leg tucked underneath him. Hannah realized he had taken off his boots as well. "Do you need anything?" he asked, gesturing to the tray sitting on the floor with a bowl of what had probably been hot soup and the pitcher of water next to it.

"No," she said, board stiff under the blanket and cloak.

"Hannah," he said, breaking into a smile, "you are ... adorable beyond words."

She felt the blush creeping back up her face. "I'm not adorable," she said, sitting up and adjusting the covers accordingly, resting against the head of the bed. "I'm a demon if you would recall."

That threw him a bit, and Hannah was relieved to see that she wasn't the only flappable person in the room. He looked down at his hand on the blanket. "About that..." he began.

"What?" she prompted.

He looked up at her abruptly. "Why is that wizard hunting you?"

Hannah swallowed, biting her lip. "Because I ran away."

"Why did you run away?" He moved across the bed, settling himself against the wall at the foot of the bed, occupying space her feet had just vacated.

"I found out the truth," she said, aware of how silly she sounded. "I mean, I found out about my grandfather." Rory watched her, clearly waiting for her to go on. "He wasn't a..." She trailed off. *How do I explain centuries of blood lineage and family history to one not of the blood?* "Blood is very important to my people."

"I imagine it is," Rory said neutrally, nodding slowly in agreement.

"No, not *blood* blood." She realized she wasn't making much sense. "I mean blood, like history blood, family blood, lineage blood."

"I see."

"And my family is one of the longest lines," she said, "of the purest lineage."

"Go on."

"And my grandmother had an affair," Hannah stated, appalled at how simple the truth really was when it came down to it. "With a human."

"Not something looked kindly upon," Rory guessed.

"Not at all, but lucky for her, no one found out about it."

"Then how do you know?"

Hannah didn't answer right away, deciding that if she was going to be honest, she should just get it over with. "We found her diary." She exhaled, then said the worst part, "I'm not truly a pureblood. I'm a halfbreed, or my mother was. Worse than one of the Kargin, even." She shook her head, wishing she hadn't used the word "we."

"Kargin?" Rory asked instead. "What's that?"

"Anyone not first born to the families is considered one of the Kargin," she explained. "It's a way of determining rank in our society." She looked at him. "Being one of the Kargin would be bad enough, but with human blood, I would be something even worse. A few steps up from a slave, per-haps, depending on who was willing to speak for me."

Rory shook his head, clearly not understanding the importance of what she was telling him. "Your people seem ... interesting."

Hannah didn't know why, but his attitude toward her people offended her. *Who is he to pass judgment on thousands of years of tradition?*

"What's that supposed to mean?"

He shrugged. "Nothing. I just think that your people seem a bit ... strange."

"A bit strange?" she repeated. "Well, I'm sure your people have just as many *strange* customs."

"It just seems odd that they can justify killing people for food but can't understand someone following through on natural impulses."

"It's more than that! There are rules for a reason, Rory. Women share their bodies with their mates until they have a child, then anything is acceptable as long as everything is done discreetly. It's to ensure that the bloodlines stay pure." Hannah questioned why she was defending a way of life that made less sense to her every day.

"Like your bloodline?" He sighed, shaking his head in exasperation. "Hannah, what is so important about who your ancestors were? You're here, aren't you? Why do you focus so much on where you came from?"

Hannah shook her head, a bit annoyed at his lack of knowledge. "Blood determines everything, Rory. Don't you know that? I am the person I am because of my lineage. I lack basic abilities that my people have because that bloodline was ruined. I'm a perfect example of why pre-serving the bloodlines is so important to the people."

Rory was shaking his head again. "So maybe you can't do all the spells that everyone else could do. So what? Hannah, you have an amazing gift for magic, but beyond that, you're still you, regardless of blood, and it doesn't matter who your grandparents were. I don't see why you place so much value on people long dead." He paused in his critique. "Though I guess you would value anything to do with blood, since you seem to be steeped in it."

"I won't apologize for what I am, Rory." She was getting angry now, and she pushed the blankets aside, standing up to walk across the room and away from him, cloak edges tucked up under her arms. She knelt on the floor in front of her pack and started angrily pulling things out of her bag. Organizing her belongings might distract her enough to calm down.

She heard Rory sit up, his voice beginning to rise with heat of its own. "I'm not asking you to apologize, Hannah. I guess I just don't understand some of your customs." She tossed a glare at him, and he responded with a scowl as he reached for his own bag. He dumped the contents in a pile on the bed, then started to fold a lump of material into a vaguely shirt-like shape.

He shook his head in dismissal, clearly trying to find the right words. Finally, he gestured to his bruised side. "Take that wizard," he said, recalling the name, "Malbrek, for instance. He killed, what, two men tonight while looking for you? And he's going to judge someone for having an affair?" He shook his head again, shrugging as he reached for another bundle that could have been pants. "I don't get it."

Hannah's hand hovered in mid-air, her father's bowl hanging above her pile. "Malbrek? But he didn't kill…" Her voice trailed off as Rory's own hands rested mid-fold, his head snapping up to look at her.

"What?"

Hannah contemplated lying, thought it would probably make things easier, but knew it would eventually cause a problem. Besides, if they had any chance at a future, he had to understand what she was, a fact she thought he still hadn't quite grasped.

Anyway, Klauden and I never lied to each other, she remembered. It hadn't been the same sort of thing—there had never been a need for concealment—but it was her only model for a relationship, and she thought it best to follow it. She looked down at the floor, resting the bowl on top of her folded blanket. "I mean *he* didn't kill them," she repeated, wanting to tell him the truth, but also wishing he would stop looking at her like that.

"Please don't tell me what I think you're going to tell me," he whispered, eyes closing. He opened them again, his gaze a bit desperate. "Sometimes up to a week, you said, didn't you? Was that the truth? Please tell me the truth, Hannah."

She met his eyes, hating to hurt him, but knowing he had to accept the reality sooner or later. "What do you want, Rory? Do you want me to tell you the truth, or do you want me to tell you Malbrek killed them?"

He got to his feet, belongings forgotten in their pile on the bed, and began pacing. "Why?"

She glanced at the barely mended shutters, then to him. "I was dying. I needed blood."

"But the healer," he said, as if that explained everything. "Wasn't he enough for you?"

"He probably would've been, but I didn't meet him until after all the rest."

"Why didn't you tell me?"

"You didn't ask."

"I'm not kidding, Hannah," he said, pausing in his pace at the window, both hands gripping the sides of the opening.

"Neither am I," she replied, annoyance bubbling up inside.

"How could you not mention the fact that you had killed two men before you nearly killed that elf? How could you just leave something like that out of your explanation?" His voice was low, angry.

"I didn't purposely leave it out," she snapped. "You never gave me a chance to explain."

"Yes, I did. I believe I sat you down and asked a number of questions." He took a deep breath. "One victim, you said, one every three or four days, sometimes up to a week. Why lie about it?"

"I didn't lie," she said. "I usually do fine with one every few days."

"So, what was this? Dessert?"

She didn't think about it, but her father's bowl was suddenly in her hand, then flinging across the room at his head.

"How can you say that to me!" she shouted as he dodged out of the way, the bowl clanging against the wall behind him and then clattering to the floor. He leaped toward her, dodging around the bed and kneeling on the floor in front of her, arms grabbing her shoulders.

"Because it's true!" he yelled back. "You don't even feel bad about it, Hannah! You killed those men, and you don't even care!"

"Why should I care?" she spat back at him. "And don't act as if you've never killed anyone!" She stopped struggling with his grasp and allowed her true strength to come forward. She was glad to see she was completely recovered.

Effortlessly, she pushed him up and away from her, his body hurling toward the opposite wall. She got to her feet, fists clenched at her sides as she stood in the center of the small room. "I will die without blood, Rory. Could you say the same for all of your victims? How many truly threatened your life?"

He stood reeling against the wall for a minute, as if trying to comprehend that Hannah had just tossed him across the room. A hand went to his chest as he took several steadying breaths. "You don't know anything about my life," he said finally.

"You haven't offered anything," she noted.

"You never asked," he mimicked, straightening himself and standing away from the wall.

"Ah, so then it's all okay then, right?" She crossed her hands over her chest, careful to keep them away from other items that were meant to be thrown at deserving targets. "Except I know what's really happening here. It's not that I didn't tell you the details, or that you didn't ask the right questions. It's that you just can't deal with the truth!" she shouted, face reddening as her anger grew.

"Do you enjoy killing people?" he asked in a low, sarcastic voice that she hated.

She wanted to throw something else at him, to at least curse at him and his condescending tone. "I don't delight in killing people for sport," she explained in a tight voice. "I only needed that many because I was dying. I didn't even want the elf's blood."

"You couldn't tell that from where I was standing," he said, and Hannah heard the temper that would have killed the ruler of Firene. "No, Hannah," he said, turning to look at her, "from where I stood, you seemed to be enjoying yourself a great deal."

"Well, you couldn't have been standing there very long," she snapped in return, "or you would have seen me trying to *avoid* biting that bastard." Her hand went to her shoulder, the skin newly healed under the cloak.

Rory shook his head. "I don't know what to think, Hannah. If you could avoid mentioning a double murder, then what else are you not telling me?"

"A double murder?" she repeated, realizing that if this was going to be it, then he should at least get the facts. "If you want to know the truth of it, I think I killed three people tonight," she said, enjoying the shock on his face. "Maybe even more than that."

"How—?" he began, but Hannah cut him off.

"How dare you?" she hissed, restraining the urge to yell.

"How dare I?" he repeated. "I'm not the one committing triple murders, Hannah."

"How dare you judge me?" she asked.

"I didn't know that you could kill three people in cold blood and not think the occurrence important enough to mention!"

"Really?" she asked, sarcastic now. "And how many people have you killed in your lifetime, Rory? How many men besides the prince of Firene have died at the end of your swords?" At his surprised look, she said, "Oh, you didn't think I heard that bit, did you?" She backed up to the bed, sitting down heavily on the edge as she stared at him. She knocked over his small pile of belongings, and a knife slid off the bed onto the floor. Hannah left it there, the fight drained out of her. "It looks like I'm not the only one with a few secrets."

"That's not fair," he said.

"And you blaming me for my life is?"

Rory took a deep breath, and Hannah felt his heart slowing as he calmed down. He ran a hand through his hair, rubbed his jawline, then put both hands up in the air in defeat. "Look," he said in a conciliatory tone, "this is just a lot to take in." He sat down next to her, close but not touching. After a moment of silence, he reached out to gently take her hand. "I'm sorry. I shouldn't have said that."

Hannah pressed her palm against his. "I'm sorry too. I shouldn't have shouted." She looked up from their linked hands to his bruised chest. "And I'm sorry for that," she said. "You shouldn't have gotten involved in my fight."

"So, who is this Malbrek?"

"My father's wizard," she explained. "My old teacher."

"Why do you think your father wants you back?"

"I don't know." She let go of his hand and leaned her head back on the bed, looking up at the wooden crossbeams of the ceiling. "I don't know if Malbrek meant to bring me home or to destroy me."

Rory winced a bit as he adjusted himself on the edge of the bed. "Remind me not to meet any more of your family."

"He'll be back," Hannah said. "I'm sure of it." She rolled her head around, moving her gaze from the ceiling to the small fireplace. "In fact, I shouldn't even still be here. He'll find me. I should be running for a new hiding place." She moved to sit up, remembered the cloak at the last minute, and tucked her arms around herself, the blanket modestly covering her lap.

"Relax," Rory said. "He probably thinks you did just that—took off for the hills to hide from him. He won't think you bold enough to stay here right under his nose."

Hannah acknowledged the reasoning. "You're right, you know. He would think I had taken off alone after his contingency spell killed you." She glanced at him. "I guess I'm safe for one more night with you."

"But am I safe with you?" he asked, an eyebrow quirking.

Hannah scoffed. "I think I'm done biting people for the evening, thank you."

"Are you?" he asked.

"Why? You want me to bite you too?" She meant it as a joke, but the words fell flat.

"No," he said. "In all honesty, Hannah, I don't know what to do with this."

"With what?"

"With you."

"What would you do with me?" she asked, surprised to hear the teasing note in her voice.

"Hannah, I..." He reached out to touch her. She leaned into him.

"I'm not good for you," she whispered from within his embrace.

"No better than I for you," he whispered, his chin resting on top of her head.

"But it's impossible." She tried to move away from him, but he held her closer.

"Didn't your own grandmother have a thing for a human? Apparently, illicit relationships are in your blood." He allowed her to retreat to arm's length.

"But—"

He tugged her close again, silencing her objection with a kiss. His lips were soft and warm. "Stop," he told her.

"Stop what?"

"Trying to leave me."

"I'm not trying to leave," she insisted, face close to his. "I'm trying to be honest."

"I was shocked, Hannah. I thought you had lied to me."

"I didn't lie about it," she said. "Just left it out."

"Well, don't leave things out in the future, alright?" He kissed her forehead, his arms resting around her waist.

"Rory?" Hannah hated to destroy the peace they seemed to have, but she had to know.

"Hmm?"

"What happened in Firene?" He pulled away from her, something like shame crossing his face.

He bent down to pick up the knife from the floor, spinning it between dexterous fingers. He watched the blade. "It was a long time ago."

"I know. I read about the civil war when I was younger."

He cocked his head, looking up at her. The knife continued to spin, hypnotic in the firelight. "How old are you, Hannah?"

"I'm eighty-two," she said, looking away from his hand. "How old are you?"

"Two hundred and twenty-seven."

"Wow, you're an old man."

He grinned. "That's a hell of a thing to say."

She moved closer to the edge of the bed, feet tucking under the blanket as she assumed a comfortable position. "So, you were just over a hundred when it all happened? Isn't that young for an elf?"

He sighed. "When I think of it now, I was very young, but at the time, I was considered an adult." Rory stepped to the scattered pile of his belongings on the floor, dropped the knife on top, and knelt to push the pile together again. "I was in charge of the prince's war council, his confidante, and his cousin. Marten and I grew up together." He scooped everything into his arms, then dumped it unceremoniously on the chair.

"What happened?"

Rory turned away from her to face the fireplace, a hand resting on the mantle. "Galina."

"Who was she?"

"My wife."

Hannah started at that. "You're married?"

He looked at her without smiling. "Not anymore. It was an arranged match, Hannah. I didn't much care for being married at all, but if it had to happen, Galina was nice to look at."

Hannah didn't quite know what to do with that bit of information. "So...?"

"So, one day I came home and found her in bed with Marten." He looked grimly at the floor. "I may not have loved Galina, but I was proud then—still am, I suppose—and she was my wife. I got angry. Words were exchanged. I drew my sword. There was a fight. At the end, I was the only one standing." He gave the speech flatly, the words falling like chips of iron from his lips. "I left and am forbidden to return."

She waited a minute, trying to attach this new bit of information to the Rory she had in her mind. To her surprise, it was an easy adjustment. Rory was the type of person who would kill a man for sleeping with his wife. Still, there was something that had never made sense to her, even when she read a version of the story as a child. "So, you killed the prince?" When he nodded, face constricted in grief, she asked, "Why didn't they kill you?"

He snorted, then gave her a wry grin. "My people are not so eager to execute their nobility as yours are. I am still blood kin to the ruling family, and as such, I am beyond the reach of normal laws," he said bitterly. "Besides, I killed the only man who stood between me and the throne. I'm sure some thought that's why I did it." He spoke matter-of-factly, but Hannah's mind was whirling with this next piece of information. Rory was the next ruler of Firene? Hannah tried to picture him as a prince but couldn't make that image mesh with her newest concept of him.

"Who rules now?"

"Jasper," Rory said the name with some scorn. "He's my brother."

"I didn't know you had a brother."

"I have two. We don't speak."

"I'm sorry," she whispered, aware that she truly was sorry for making him tell her. Still, it did clear up a few questions. It also brought up the question of Rory's temper, but Hannah didn't want to think of that at the moment. She was so tired of thinking all the time. She stood, moving toward him. When it became clear that he wasn't going to face her, she stood behind him and wrapped her arms around his waist.

"What do you want, Hannah?" he whispered.

Hannah pushed away from him, sitting back down on the bed. "I don't know," she whispered. "It's different."

"What's different?" He sat down near her, a hand resting on her foot. She shook her head, nervousness taking over again. She stared intently at the fireplace, avoiding any glances in his direction. *Why is this so awkward?* She heard him shift again, probably leaning back against the wall. "Who's Klauden?" he asked casually. When she whirled to look at him, he cocked his eyebrow curiously, an arm draped lazily under his head.

"How...?" she began.

"You mumbled in your sleep," he said, "when you were sick. You kept asking for someone named Klauden."

"Oh," Hannah said, embarrassed beyond words. When she realized that he wasn't going to stop staring at her like that, she mumbled, "He was my friend."

"Your friend?" Rory asked. "Interesting. Did he give you that ring you always twist when you get nervous?"

Hannah looked down at her hand, visible through a rather immodest gap in the cloak, to see that she was twisting Klauden's ring again, and forced herself to stop, bunching the cloak back together again. "Yes," she whispered.

Rory took a deep breath. "Is he your mate?" When Hannah's eyes widened, he said, "I thought so. It's alright, Hannah. I won't force you to break any vows tonight." He moved, sliding to the edge of the bed, his feet dipping to the floor. "I can find another room." Hannah found her voice.

"He's not my mate."

Rory paused in his shuffle. "No?"

Hannah shook her head. "We were promised as children, but I left before anything more was done," she explained. "He was my friend. He helped a lot with my magic. In fact, he taught me the spell I used to dispel the contingency."

"So, you're not bound to him." Rory was watching her carefully.

"No," Hannah said.

"Are you bound to anyone else?"

"Just you," she said, the words falling out of her mouth and landing heavily on the bed between them. "I mean…" Her voice trailed off. She was turning into a gibbering idiot.

He turned to her, the firelight glinting off his bare chest, the scars glowing silver in the flames, his face earnest. "Would you tie yourself to me, Hannah?" The question was a whisper, the desire on his face plain even to her virgin sensibilities.

"I could…" She started, then he was moving toward her, his mouth covering hers in a soft kiss. When he pulled away to look at her, Hannah put a hand to his chest.

At his wince, she looked down at the bruise she was pushing against and pulled away. "But your rib—"

"I'll manage," he assured her, then kissed her again.

Okay, she thought, *you wanted to live like a mortal. Here goes.*

There was no more talking for a long time.

XXII

A few hours later, Hannah lay half on Rory's chest, listening to the elf's somewhat labored breathing. The rhythm was comforting, and she was trying to memorize the feeling, trying to immortalize the moment in her memory. Of course, she knew it had to end. This whole mess had to end. Hannah didn't know the exact moment she had decided to leave him, but she knew this was the time. After waiting another moment, she rolled onto an elbow to peer down at him. She concentrated a moment, hoping she had the words right.

"Rory," she whispered in a soft voice.

"Huh?" His voice was sleepy, not really aware of her at all.

"Rory, listen to me," she whispered again. "I'm sorry," she said. "So sorry to do this. Maybe someday you'll forgive me." She closed her eyes to block out the sight of his contented face, then began reciting the syllables of the spell to make him sleep. It was a good spell, but only effective when the victim was willing or off guard, both of which Rory was. When he had settled into a deeper, steadier rhythm of breathing, Hannah climbed over him, cautious of the black bruise on his chest, and out of the bed.

She picked up her new clothes from the back of the chair, stepping carefully into her skirt and trying not to hear the soft snuffles he made as he shifted in the bed, subconsciously aware of her missing body and trying to compensate. She wiped her nose, unwilling to let the tears fall as she gathered up her bag. It was still half unpacked, her spellbook poking out of the top.

Am I really going to do this? Can I really just leave him without any explanation?

Hannah began picking up random items and shoving them into the bag. She had managed to get half of her items inside when she realized that the laws of the universe regarding how much stuff will fit in a designated area were against her. She dumped the entire bag out and began packing things in a more orderly fashion. Her few clothes she buried at the bottom with her mother's mirror and hairbrush. The silver set was the only true memento she had taken from home other than Klauden's ring. Her blanket went on top of that, then her spellbook. Finally, she stuffed the last remaining space with the leather pouch of ashes from her homeland—the spell components she had never needed to use, though Klauden had insisted she take them just in case she needed him.

She couldn't stay with Rory. She had come so close to biting him when he kissed her, so very close to losing control when he touched her, and she knew that her restraint would not last long. It was a miracle that he had made it through the last few hours unscathed.

If she stayed, she would do nothing but drag him down to a place he shouldn't have to see. Or at least, judging from the somewhat checkered past he had revealed, he shouldn't have to sink so low to again.

He would be fine on his own.

And so would she.

She finished her packing, pulling the straps tight. As she did so, Rory twisted on the bed, moaning a little. Hannah froze but was reassured when he turned on his side, settling more firmly into the mattress. She stood, tying her boots and shouldering her pack, then surveyed the room.

She snuck a last look at Rory and turned to leave. Her hand was on the bar to open the door when she heard Rory's voice from the bed. He whispered her name. She froze, guilty, and waited for him to say something more. When the silence dragged out, she risked a look over her shoulder.

Rory was still deep asleep, a hand tossed above his head against the headboard, his face content.

Hannah sighed. *I can't just leave without any explanation.* Setting her bag on the floor, she slumped against the door. *I owe him more than that, at the very least.*

Deciding to at least leave him a note, she opened her bag and retrieved her spellbook. Kneeling, she rooted around near the bottom of the bag, reaching past her mother's mirror and a group of candles wrapped in waxed paper to retrieve her inkwell and stylus. The pouch Klauden had given her popped out, then refused to fit back inside. She tied the leather bag to her belt instead, deciding she would get the thing into her backpack later. When she managed to worm her writing tools out around the rest of her few belongings, she rested the book on the floor, then popped the cork of the inkwell and set that to her left.

She opened the book to a blank page, aware of the low thrum of magic running up her arms from where her fingers touched the pages. Klauden had done a magnificent job with the book, capturing a great deal of energy within its pages, and Hannah was almost sorry to have to tear out a sheet.

She did, though, closing the book and laying the blank sheet on top. She thought a moment, dipping the stylus into the inkwell, then began to write.

XXIII

Hannah was walking slowly down the street that led back to the bridge over the river, knowing that she made an easy target for anyone to attack but not really focusing on her own safety. She knew that it was foolish to behave in such a way, but she couldn't help herself. She deserved at least a few moments of mourning, and some part of her was almost hoping someone would try to attack her. It would give her a chance to focus her nervous energy.

Still, she counted herself lucky that the man she did eventually encounter in the street was Jamison. She didn't notice him approaching, but when he said her name, she looked up, suddenly sad to even bid a fool like him goodbye.

"Hey, Jamison," she answered his greeting.

"Where's Rory?" the man asked, glancing around the street for the absent elf.

"He's not here."

"Why not?"

"Because I left him sleeping."

The man peered at her, confusion clouding his face. "Why did you leave him?" Understanding crossed his expression in a flash. "Are you leaving us, Hannah? Has the time come for you to be on your way again?"

Hannah was unwilling to explain, though she knew he expected her to.

He looked her over, taking in the pack, clothing, boots, weapons, and the determined set of her chin. "No wounds to hold you back this time, eh?" When she glared sharply at him, he shook his head. "I meant nothing by it. You just always seem to be hurt, so I thought that might be why you stayed with us. It's why I stay." He saw her creased brow, and explained,

"Not because I'm hurt, but because they offer protection so that doesn't happen. Rory is amazing with those swords of his."

"He is," Hannah agreed, wishing she could forget about Rory altogether. "Was there something you want from me, Jamison? If not, I'm on my way. Tell Molly I'm..." She let the thought trail off. *Tell Molly what? That I am sorry for biting her husband? Ridiculous.* "Tell her I appreciated her soup," she settled for saying. She took a few more steps down the street before Jamison cut her off.

"Where are you going?"

"Does it matter?"

He shrugged. "Maybe. I got horses for everyone. You should at least take yours. It's paid for."

"A horse would be wonderful, Jamison. Where is the stable?"

He led her down a different street, parallel to the river but creeping ever closer to the bank. Hannah didn't make any small talk on the way. She was ragged and worn out, the loss of Rory—however intentional it had been—weighing heavily on her mind. She worked on putting one foot in front of the other, eyes on the dirt road. She eventually noticed that Jamison was no longer in front of her and didn't know how long she had been walking alone. "Jamison?" she asked, glancing around in puzzlement.

"I hoped to see you again, my Maker."

The voice brought Hannah instantly out of her thoughts and into the present. She was in an alley that ended in a stone wall before her with two wooden walls on either side. There was no smell of horses anywhere. She was so distracted by her emotions that she'd walked right into a trap. She was immediately on her guard, tossing down her bag and drawing a dagger as the healer strolled into the moonlight before her.

Her blood had been good to him—his eyes were bright with fever or hunger, his skin flushed with vitality, his muscles corded with borrowed strength. She realized with horror that she could feel the elf as well, an awareness of him that ran just below the surface of her skin. She felt dirty, disheveled, and wished that she could cut him off, could shut off this too personal connection with a person so despicable. She knew she couldn't though. The blood bond could only be severed by death, a blow Hannah was more than willing to deliver, her fledgling or not. She began planning her attack around the fog that would no doubt appear soon.

"I'm sorry to hear that," Hannah said, flinging the dagger at him, "because I swore to kill you if we met again." The dagger landed with a solid hit, sinking into his stomach to the hilt. He snarled, narrow fingers reaching for the handle to pull the blade out. She was not surprised to see that she had scored a hit—she was fairly decent with her daggers—but the wave of agony that spun out from her stomach was nauseating.

She felt the dagger in her own gut, felt the blade as it pulled free, felt the blood dripping down her belly. She glanced down, half expecting to see blood covering her, and was mildly relieved to see she was unharmed. The pain faded from severe to aching, but Hannah knew one more thing about the blood bond now—she would feel the elf's pain. They were tied together. *That's fine,* she decided. *I can deal with pain.*

"Now, is that any way to treat our child?"

Hannah whirled to the source of the new voice, fingers already retrieving her second dagger from the small of her back, ready this time for what she would see. Kelvin Malbrek was lounging against the wall, a small knife working out the dirt from beneath his fingernails. His face was no longer the flawless perfection she recalled, his cheek marred by a circular symbol, the burn from the healer's holy sigil imprinted on his skin. Hannah knew it would not fade, just as the matching scar on her own palm had not faded. It pleased her to have left her mark on him. Malbrek shook his head. "I suppose I can't fault your lack of maternal instinct, though, since you left the job half done."

"Why?" Hannah whispered, her mind frantically working on a way out of this mess. She knew what Malbrek was saying. Obviously, he had finished what she had started, had shared his blood with the healer to ensure the elf's survival. Hannah was amazed that it had worked. She wondered if Malbrek could also feel the elf's pain. Looking at his face, she didn't think so. Hannah considered—her blood was in the healer's body, he was mostly her creation, and so the bond was mostly between them. Malbrek had merely supplied the extras; if he shared any bond at all with the healer, it wasn't physical.

What was I thinking to wander around Kalford without knowing where Malbrek is? What kind of an idiot am I to leave my protection sleeping in the inn? She tried to regain her waning confidence. *You survived him last time; you can do it again.*

Yeah, right, her mind retorted. *Last time you had a very strong, very angry elf to back you up.*

She forced herself to remain calm, noting how Malbrek had not moved from his position along the alley wall, measuring the distance to the newly turned healer, and trying to judge the odds of running past him and leaping over the wall. She ran a quick glance up to the top of the stone divider—it was at least twice as tall as she was. There would be no leaping that boundary, but if she could buy some time, maybe she could climb it. It was her only chance.

"Why what, Hannah?" Malbrek was saying. "Why finish what you started? Why am I hunting you? Why can't you escape?" He chuckled, the soft sound full of contempt and confidence.

"No," Hannah said, twirling the dagger between her fingers, watching the healer's slow and unpracticed attempt to sneak up behind her. "Why are you such a *krangesh*?"

She didn't wait to watch Malbrek's face as she used the Dwarven curse, but spun, forcing the dagger into the healer, scoring another solid hit on his chest before turning to flee.

The pain exploded in her own chest, and for a minute, she wasn't sure about her tolerance, but she swallowed the scream and focused on running. Ten steps to the wall, then a jump to grab a handhold, then a few seconds to scurry up the rest of the way and tumble over the other side. Hannah made it to the wall and was preparing to jump for a handhold when her hand shrieked in more than phantom pain. She saw the rapier sticking out of her hand, the blade wobbling in a singing tone as she began to bleed. She heard the elf shriek in agony—apparently theirs was a two-way connection—but ignored him, turning instantly to pull Malbrek's weapon out of the wall and free her hand. It came loose with a sucking sound, the elegant blade clattering to the street, and Hannah fisted her wounded hand and leaped for a handhold with her other hand. She caught the edge of a stone block and was reaching around to secure more purchase with her elbow when she heard something more disturbing than any Elven scream or Malbrek Special. Her skin prickled, a silent alarm running through her body. Someone was casting divine magic.

At her.

She panicked, the need to move suddenly overwhelming, then she was scrambling up the wall, bits of stone and dirt grinding into the hole in her palm. She reached the top of the wall, ready to throw herself over the edge to the unknown other side, when the blast hit her. Instead of the burning agony she expected, her muscles froze, her unsecured position giving way to gravity as she first tottered, then plummeted to the ground on the same side of the wall. The shock knocked the wind from her, but the real problem was the sluggish, honeyed movement of her limbs.

What kind of holy magic is this? Hannah lay there a moment, staring up into the black night sky, wondering why she wasn't dead. She had seen what such magic could do—hadn't Jason Saffron disappeared before her eyes, burned beyond ashes? Yet she was still here, a bit dazed, but alive.

She managed to turn her head to find the speaker of the spell and was astonished to see Jamison standing a few feet away, a scroll of worn parchment in his hands. His face was calm, determined, as he looked from her prone form to Malbrek and back again.

Jamison had intentionally turned her over to Malbrek. He had betrayed her.

Bastard! She wanted to throttle the man, cursing herself for not taking him more seriously, for being too caught up in her own obsession with Rory to notice the man's descent into what was obviously Malbrek's mind control. She knew Malbrek could influence humans with ease, but she also knew that Jamison had to be somewhat willing for it to work.

I have been so blind.

Whatever spell he had used, it appeared to be wearing off. Hannah could make her arms obey a bit more, but she didn't have nearly enough control to stand up yet. She wiggled, trying to reach something, anything that might be of use. Her fingers clambered over her belt, the worn leather smooth against her touch, then the bump of another string—something tied to her belt. She remembered how she had rifled through her bag for her stylus and inkwell, the leather pouch that refused to fit back inside, and her hasty decision to tie it to her belt instead.

The fingers of her unwounded hand closed on the pouch, then began working the knot free from her belt. If she was going to do this, she needed the damn thing open. Now, if only she could remember the words...

Malbrek was speaking again, but she ignored him, turning inward, returning to that last frantic morning in the catacombs beneath the castle when Klauden had shoved the pouch into her reluctant hands. Her newly acquired slave's clothes had felt loose and droopy, the boots heavy on her feet, the pack an unaccustomed weight on her back. He had been clever about it of course, almost boasting.

"If you ever need me," he had said, *"use this. Take it out, pour the ashes, and call for me. I will hear you, and I will come."* She insisted that she would be too far away. *"You will never be too far away from me, chaivin."* She hugged him, a wave of appreciation welling up inside for her dear friend, her love, her future mate.

Hannah hoped he had been right.

She had worked the pouch from her belt and was untying the top when someone stepped over her. It was Malbrek, his feet planted on either side of her hips, his face looking down at her with that damn disappointment she remembered so well from her youth, though the addition of the marred cheek thrilled her a bit. Hannah stopped her struggle with the bag, letting her hand fall limp to her side and out of sight under the swath of her skirt on the ground. Her fingers continued to move, slowly, quietly under his gaze.

"Hannah," he said, and Hannah took a deep breath. That was one of the things she hated about this man—how he always used her name, the way he seemed to either be reminding her of it because she was too stupid to recall or claiming it for himself with an underlying ownership that made her skin crawl. Either way, she hated the sound of her name in his voice. "You seem to be having some trouble."

"I'm ... fine," she gritted, fingers twisting and tugging under the skirt. *Distract him*, she thought. *Get him talking. You know how this one loves to hear his own voice.* "How did ... you do it?" she asked.

"Do what?" He gestured to the alley, taking in the healer and Jamison, who stood to either side of her. "All of this?" He smiled, baring vampire teeth. "It was so easy, Hannah, you wouldn't believe me if I told you."

"Try me," she suggested, a sudden muscle spasm causing her head to snap to one side and back again. The spell was wearing off. *Maybe if I keep him talking...*

He looked down at her, calculating as always, then motioned to his right. To Jamison, Hannah noted, tracking his gaze with her eyes. The man bowed his head and pulled another scroll from inside his cloak. Hannah's skin prickled, sudden fear threatening to freeze her more completely than the spell. She struggled with the pouch, fingers working more frantically to loosen the last loops. Of course, Klauden's spell wouldn't do any good if she couldn't move around enough to empty the pouch. She had to wait for the right moment.

"Hannah, my lady, it is time for you to return to your home. Your father is most displeased with your behavior, as you must have guessed, and fortunately, he has at his disposal a magician who has found the solution."

"The solution?"

"Yes, dear, to your tainted blood." He smirked at her. "You will learn what it means to be a true pureblood. You will be purified."

"Can I be purified? I know you have a great deal of magic at your disposal, but no spell I've heard of can restore that much purity." At Hannah's question, Malbrek had taken a deep breath, smelling her, then his face darkened, the scarred symbol flaring white against his red face. "You did not—" he began, but she cut him off.

"I did," she confirmed, "so there's no reason to bring me home. Not now, not ever." She smiled at him, relishing the angry maelstrom brewing on his face. A voice in her mind asked politely if she had truly gone mad to push him like this, but Hannah's fingers closed around the pouch, Klauden's words crowding in her memory. *He needs to hit me*, she thought, *then I can break free.* "You can still smell him on me, can't you?"

"Filthy whore!" he screamed, reaching down to pull her upright. One hand closed around her throat, the other tangling in her hair as he lifted her clear off the ground and held her in the air before him. Hannah's feet kicked uselessly, a reflex that she couldn't control. She fought to keep her hand on the pouch, knowing that was her only way out now. There was one more vicious jerk, then her feet were on the ground again, the hand loosening its iron grip from her throat, hot air burning her lungs. She staggered back, but the hand in her hair tugged her back, her feet tripping over themselves under her skirt.

"It doesn't matter," Malbrek said. "It won't matter what you've done to this body once we're through with you." He looked to Jamison, the tall human standing pale-faced against the wall, one hand frozen on the still rolled up scroll. "Kindly start reading, Jamison. I've got her."

Hannah watched Jamison unroll the scroll, then, as if remembering a detail, he reached under his cloak again to retrieve the small pink crystal pendant on the chain around his neck, lifting it slowly over his head.

He held it out in her direction, then cleared his throat and began reading the scroll in his other hand. Hannah didn't need to listen to the words to know that this was bad news. She found her feet, stood firm in Malbrek's grip, then upended the pouch in her hand.

The ashes of her grandmother's journal spilled free in a thin funnel of dust, and Hannah whispered the words to call Klauden. She felt the strength in them, the power in her focused by the sound of Klauden's soft voice, the magic draining out of her into a tall, thin shadow that began to materialize. Malbrek lost his grip on her hair, the curls tearing free in his fist as a figure formed between them, pushing him back.

Hannah could still hear Jamison's voice, could feel the threat growing from that direction, knew the pendant was spinning and glowing in the human's grip, but she ignored all that, focusing her will on completing the spell.

Klauden was standing before her. He was as tall as she remembered, a bit thinner than usual, but that was probably because he spent so much time studying that he often forgot to feed. She hadn't been there to remind him. His hair was shiny, the blonde wisps hovering around his ears, and his dark eyes stared at her in confusion, joy, then dawning horror.

Malbrek screamed something indecipherable, reaching for the newcomer whose face he could not yet see as her old friend stepped toward her. The black material of his robe rippled with the movement as he opened his arms to enfold her, and Hannah had a second to think, *He's here. He's really right here!* She practically fell into his embrace as Jamison's voice rang out on the final verse of the spell, and the world exploded.

She was being torn inside out, a wrenching, shrieking pulling that was unbearable. She thought she might be screaming, heard something that was probably the healer screaming, and something that might be laughter—Malbrek—then everything was the dark of Klauden's cloak overwhelmed by a soft, soothing pink.

The Man

J amison Hunter watched as Hannah collapsed, her body falling in an empty heap on the street, the shadowed figure that had swallowed her disappearing. He stared, amazed, at the bluish-gray cloud that streaked toward him, or rather at the crystal in his hand. The glowing pendant absorbed the blue light, there was a sound like a coin falling onto its side on a wooden table, and then everything was quiet. The pendant swung a few times, then stopped. He lifted his hand, trying to peer inside the pink stone.

Is Hannah in there?

He looked at the body lying limp on the ground, then back at the stone. *What have I done?*

Malbrek approached and snatched the pendant from his hand.

"Well done," the man said approvingly, and Jamison felt a warm glow inside, as if Molly had just complimented his intelligence.

"Thank you," he whispered, head down as he watched the vampire hunter turn to the elf at his side. Kelvin Malbrek was indeed a man to be reckoned with, he thought. It had been a good idea to go to him. Of course, at the moment, he couldn't remember exactly what had made him seek the man out, but after that first meeting in the woods outside Talperin, Jamison had known what must be done.

He didn't particularly like Rory, but he wasn't about to let that girl lure him to his death. She was dangerous and needed to be contained. He knew that he couldn't do it, not with the elf bewitched the way he was, but Malbrek had been the perfect solution. He could contain Hannah, he promised Jamison, capture her and keep her where she would no longer be able to harm anyone. Jamison knew it was for the best.

He had told Molly about it, of course; he had been telling Molly everything, it seemed. She understood. She knew what a danger vampires could be, knew that destroying them was the only solution. After all, hadn't there been times when he had been tempted to fall for Hannah's beguiling innocence? To believe her smiling face as she tossed her red curls and pretended to be human?

I will not be a Matthew, he had decided. *Nor will I lose another woman to those monsters.* Matthew had been seduced, lured away from home and family, taking Jamison's wife with him, in a manner completely beyond his own volition. Jamison would not allow another to suffer such a fate.

He stared at the vampire hunter. He watched as the elf knelt to pick up Hannah's body, the limbs dangling uselessly as he adjusted her in his arms. Malbrek leaned down and collected her pack.

Jamison stood quietly to the side, wondering if the pair would say anything else to him.

They didn't.

When they rounded the corner and disappeared from view, Jamison knew he didn't have much time. He had to get back to Molly, and they had to leave Kalford immediately.

He checked the sky. There were a few hours left until dawn. With luck, he and Molly would be on their way to Upsen long before the others even noticed they were gone.

XXIV

The only thing Hannah was aware of was pink. Not just the color pink overwhelming her eyes, though it was a bit overpowering in its softness, but a sense of distant, satisfying pinkness that called her to lie down, to rest, to sleep as she hadn't in months, to disappear into that pink blanket and know peace.

But someone was shaking her. The someone wasn't pink. It was black, a darkness piercing the perfect pink cocoon and dragging her back to reality, to herself, to her body—a body that should by all rights ache in one punctured hand. She heard a noise that might have been a groan, realized that the sound had come from her throat, and sat up, her head nearly colliding with Klauden's nose.

Her friend knelt before her, head shaking in exasperation. "I nearly lost you there, Hannah. What in the nine hells have you been doing?"

Hannah was so struck by the similarity to Rory's comment when he found her with the healer that she just sat there for a minute, staring like a drooling idiot. Hearing her native tongue again snapped her into motion.

"Hannah?" he asked. "Are you—" His question deflated into a grunted "oomph" as she threw herself at him, burying her little body into his embrace, so grateful that her friend was with her that she didn't want to think of anything else.

"Easy, it's alright. You're alright, chaivin, you're alright." Hannah felt the tears running down her cheeks as he used the nickname, his hands running up and down her back in a soothing gesture. *Chaivin*, fiery or fire-soul in the oldest Elven texts, a reference to her red hair and, she often thought, her temperament, Klauden had used the word since their earliest days in Essentials. Even then, it had been a private thing, the first secret of what would be many between them through the years. Hannah knew she should get a hold of herself, but for the moment, she was content to stay in his arms. *Why did I ever leave home?*

The thought brought more important memories to mind, and suddenly, she was calm, the emotional whirlwind subsided, the tears cold on her cheeks as she recalled her predicament.

She sat back on her heels, taking in her surroundings. Everything really was pink, a pink room with pink walls and a pink floor. She traced a finger along the ground, trying to determine precisely what kind of room this was, but her fingers slid across an indefinable surface, something between the smoothness of her daggers and the silkiness of Rory's hair. The thought of Rory brought her hand away from the floor, and she stood up, testing the give of the ground with a few steps. It seemed solid enough. She walked ten steps to one of the walls, not surprised to find the same blend of smooth silkiness under her hands. She turned back to Klauden, who still knelt in the center of the odd room, hands folded on his lap in that age old posture of contemplation. She had loved that pose once upon a time. Now it was comforting, but the old feeling of warmth it used to conjure was absent, replaced by a fierce desire to see Rory again, just once more.

"Where are we?" she asked, trying to focus.

"Inside the Star of Elgiva," Klauden replied. "You've made some powerful enemies since you left."

"Oh, no," she said. "Are you sure?"

"Unfortunately, I am."

"How are you here?" She took a few steps toward him, sinking to a knee. She studied his face, which seemed to be shifting ever so subtly every few seconds. "*Are* you here? What's going on?"

"Think, chaivin," he snapped, and Hannah's coldness was warmed by a memory of that voice always dragging her back to attention and forcing her to focus. If it hadn't been for Klauden's mostly patient lessons, she would never have lasted as long as she did among the people of her father's castle. "What do you remember?" he prompted.

"They used a spell to hold me, divine magic that I hadn't seen before." When he motioned for her to continue, she said, "I summoned you, but Jamison was already reading the binding spell. It was too late to escape."

She realized something horrible and gave him a desperate look. "Did I trap you in here with me?"

He shook his head, the features she remembered blurring a bit. "I am not bound to this place, not like you are. The spell allowed me to travel with you, but my soul is free to return to my real body at any time."

"Where is your body?" she asked, knowing that Klauden had always had a gift for dreamwalking, the ability to send his spirit wandering far from his body—it was why he always forgot to eat enough. She hadn't known he had grown quite so adept at it, though; the castle must be thousands of leagues from Kalford. *Has he ever traveled so far before?*

"In my rooms," he replied, "though I have to get back there soon. When I heard you call, it was just before evens. I have to be downstairs by nines, or I will be missed."

"My father will miss you," she completed the thought for him. She almost asked after her father, then decided against it. Magnus van Kreeosk hadn't changed in a hundred years—*Why would he start now?*

"Among others. Things have changed since you left."

Hannah doubted that. "Did they give you a hard time about my leaving?"

"They didn't know I had anything to do with it. Do you think I'd be here if they did?" He shook his head in quiet derision. "They don't even know how far I can range. I hope Malbrek didn't see me, or I won't enjoy the same freedom for long." He looked at her with something like surprise. "Your father would consider me a threat. Can you imagine? *Me*, a threat."

Back when she had known him, Hannah wouldn't have thought Klauden a threat at all, but since she had traveled and seen new things, she wasn't so sure. Anyone could be a threat, even handsome boys with inquisitive eyes and flyaway hair. The irony struck Hannah—*Why did I need to travel so far to learn what Malbrek was always trying to teach me?* She shook her head, remembering the lay of the land in her father's castle, knowing the rules of engagement, the fine nuances of power shifts and new alliances.

"He won't tolerate anyone growing powerful enough to overthrow him. You know that. You should be careful." His eyes blurred, then focused as they found hers.

"Speaking of careful," he said, eyes narrowing even more. "What were you thinking to go against Malbrek?"

"He cornered me," she explained. "I had no choice." She was about to continue her explanation but couldn't help her distraction. "Why does your face keep doing that?"

"Doing what?"

"Shifting and blurring. Why does it move?"

He gestured to the room. "It's the magic." He pinched an arm swathed in the black material of his robes, and Hannah watched the material stretch and blur, then reform to his forearm. "None of it is real. I'm not really here, so what you see is a mental projection of my self-image. I thought I'd gotten better at keeping it fixed, but apparently, I was wrong." He smiled. "Leave it to you to point that out."

"A mental projection of a self-image?" Hannah repeated, the concept vague in her mind. "So, you look the way you *think* you look? Am I doing that too?"

He shook his head. "Not at all. In fact, you look exactly like your mother."

"My mother?" Hannah looked down at herself, somewhat comforted to note that she was wearing the sweater and skirt that Rory had given her, the gifts of his consideration that had meant so much to her.

Is this how I see myself now? What has become of the elaborate dresses Klauden would expect? She noted that her backpack was gone, along with her boots and all four of her daggers. She looked at her hands, amazed to see the smooth skin of an unblemished palm that had never been burned and the unmarred back of a hand that had never been speared with a rapier. As she thought about it, the seal began to reappear on her palm, the burn a livid red against her pale skin. *Well, there's something my mother never had*, she thought.

Klauden was nodding. "You must recall her face very well to project it so clearly, since it's not your face that I'm seeing."

"Can I make something reality here?" she asked, still unclear about the parameters of this new prison. When Klauden nodded, she thought about her dagger and looked down when she felt the reassuring weight in her belt, the pommel resting against her hip. She pulled the blade out and began to pace, another habit she had picked up south of the Vanya.

Ignoring the question of why her face would appear like her mother's if it was her mind doing the projecting, a mind perfectly aware of what her own face looked like, she focused on more important issues.

First things first—take stock.

"So, I'm trapped inside the Star of Elgiva?" She remembered the pink pendant in Jamison's outstretched hand, recalled the pink shimmer as it began to spin with the spell. She knew what the artifact was, of course; she and Klauden had done their share of studying.

The Star was a repository for a soul, a holding pen for the spirit of a person unlucky enough to get trapped by the spell. In the old stories, heroes used the Star to transport villains back home, where just rulers offered judgment of the condemned in the spirit world. Usually, the Star functioned as a waiting room for any number of spiritual dimensions, typically hellish worlds of fire and pain. Hannah tried to reconcile what she knew about the artifact with her own situation. She looked to Klauden. "How do I get out?"

He looked away, seeming to focus on something elsewhere. When he came back, she repeated her question. He ignored her. "I have to get back." He got to his feet, hands pressing together in front of him as he closed his eyes.

"Wait!" she yelled, grabbing his hands and breaking his spell, aware as always of the surprising strength in his frail grip. For all of his leanness, Klauden was still a vampire, blessed with the strength that only human blood could give. Hannah remembered herself. "I have to get back to my body! Where is it? Does Malbrek have it? What are they going to do to me?"

Klauden opened his eyes, his face sympathetic. He took a breath, wiping a hand over his chin and mouth. "Come here," he said, motioning to one of the walls. Hannah obeyed, stopping in front of the pink barrier. "Look."

Hannah looked at him, then at the wall. "At what?"

His head leaned to one side, the eyebrows raising in the classic will-you-at-least-try-to-pay-attention stance she remembered so well. "It's a magical construction, Hannah. The wall in front of you isn't real. It's just a way for your mind to visualize what's happening to you. Just focus, and you can see what's going on outside of the magic."

Hannah did as she was bid, closing her eyes to the pinkness and reassuring her mind that this room wasn't real. The only real thing was that she was trapped in some sort of extraplanar space connected to the Star of Elgiva. That was understandable—the world was filled with such holes and doors. She just needed to find the window to the outside, and she should be able to see.

When she opened her eyes, she was standing before a glass window in the pink wall. The scene outside was jumpy and dark. It took her a few moments to recognize the rhythm of a rider on horseback traveling swiftly through the trees. It had to be Malbrek. She caught a glimpse of the scenery to the right and left—dark twisted shapes that were more trees—then pulled back. He was alone, heading north and moving fast. The artifact must be around his neck.

She stepped back from the window, watching it mist over with pink as she stopped focusing on it. The frame stayed, though, and she was intrigued to see that it was the same worn, slightly off-center window frame of the inn room in Kalford. She knew it would stay there now, her own mark in this ancient magic.

She faced Klauden again, who was standing there with an approving grin on his face. "You remembered," he observed. "Well done."

She smiled. "I had an excellent teacher."

Klauden shook his head. "Now she says it!" He looked away, face distracted by something else. "I've been here too long already. I must go." Hannah heard the familiar sound of the rushed scholar and smiled again. Klauden hadn't changed a bit.

"Can you come back?"

"I think so. I won't know for sure until I try, but I know the spell bound me to you, and since you're here…" He let the thought trail off.

"Be careful," she warned, old habits returning as she looked him over again. "And remember to eat—you're too thin." At the mention of his body, the startling thought returned to her. "Klauden," she began, turning back to the window and watching the same scene reform out of the pinkness. Malbrek was still riding north through the forest with the Star of Elgiva around his neck, placing her line of vision about level with his chest. Alone. There was no other horse tied to the saddle, no other figures clambering along nearby. Totally alone.

"Klauden, where is my body?"

THE DWARF

Gorn Haversont knew something was wrong the moment Rory came down the stairs to the inn's common room. He was alone; that in itself was odd—he didn't think the elf would let Hannah out of his sight, not in Kalford—but worse was the expression on his face, a mask of worry tightening his features. Even his shirt was in disarray, the ends hanging over what was clearly a hastily donned weapon's belt. His bag was slung haphazardly over one shoulder; his hair had not been combed.

Gorn stopped with a piece of bread halfway to his mouth, staring as the elf sat down hard on the opposite bench. Lira put down the water she had been drinking, face calm as she waited for an explanation.

"She's gone," he said without preamble, looking at both of them as if they had personally dragged the girl away.

"What do you mean 'gone'?" Gorn asked, brushing breadcrumbs from his beard. "Where is she?"

"I don't know." Rory gritted the words. "Have you seen her?"

Gorn and Lira shook their heads. "Not this morning," Lira said, looking around. "Have you seen Jamison or Molly?"

Rory shook his head. "No. They're probably still upstairs." He glanced around, catching the barkeep's eye. "I'll be back," he said, rising jerkily from the bench.

"Where are you going?" Lira asked.

"To find her."

Gorn watched him walk over and have a quiet word with the barkeep. He took the last few bites of his bread, washing it down with some ale, then looked up at a shout from the bar.

Rory was leaning against the counter, shoulders tense, deep in conversation with a young boy that Gorn recognized from the kitchens. He asked, "Where?" then practically dragged the child out of the room.

"We're going," Lira said, rising from the bench and gesturing for Gorn to finish up his meal. The dwarf took his last swig of ale, following her with cup in hand. He finished his drink and set the cup down on an empty table as they crossed the room to the bar.

He wiped a sleeve across his mouth. "What is it?"

"I don't know," Lira replied. Rory and the boy had disappeared out of the door.

"I'll find out. You follow him," Gorn told her, gesturing to the exit. Lira seemed relieved to have a plan and slipped out the door after the elf.

Gorn made his way to the bar, noting the interested gaze of several patrons at the commotion. Gorn put a hand meaningfully on his axe handle, and the intrigued looks faded away. The barkeep moaned as he approached, setting down a mug that he had been towel drying.

"What did you tell him?" Gorn asked.

"I told him that your friends left," he announced. "Earlier today. They seemed in a hurry." That wasn't much of a shock. It wasn't as though they had all promised to stay together. It was a bit odd, though. *Why would Jamison forsake our protection to leave alone with Molly? Maybe something made them leave,* he pondered. But that wasn't what sent Rory running out the door.

"And?" he prompted.

Tom looked down, face contorting in sympathy. "And they found a body. Burned. They pulled it out of the river."

Gorn felt the heat rise in his belly, thinking of the small slip of a girl alone in this town, and hoped it wasn't her. He thanked the man and headed out the door.

He was down the street when he heard the noise of people gathering. In a place like Kalford, it was not a pleasant sound. When he turned the corner, the scene was what he had expected, though he didn't want to admit it. Lira was holding Rory away from a scorched pile that vaguely resembled a human body. A small crowd of onlookers had gathered to see what was going on. Gorn pushed past Lira and Rory, steeling himself for what must be done.

He knelt beside the body, breathing through his mouth to avoid the smell, and set to work, carefully pulling away strips of burnt clothing and flesh. Another man, one who had been working by the river's edge by the look and smell of him, was hovering nearby. "I found it downstream," he said. "It got caught up in my fishing net. I thought maybe we could help at first, but then we could see it was useless."

There is no helping the poor soul now, Gorn thought, but he had to be sure. Holding his breath, he reached down to a shriveled arm, following the blackened appendage to a withered clump of bony fingers. The fourth finger bore a silver ring. He pulled it off carefully, not wanting the finger bone to crack, though he doubted it mattered at this point. He rubbed the ring against the ground, noting the blackened soot that coated his fingers and wishing he could wipe off that greasy smell as he did the blackness. He held the ring up slowly toward Rory, and Lira released him long enough for it to land in his palm, heavy with implication.

"No," he whispered, falling to his knees before the body. "Please."

"I'm so sorry, lad," Gorn whispered, wishing there was something more to say. He turned back to the body, noting the bag wedged partially underneath, and began to carefully pull the pack out. He was amazed that no one had stolen it; apparently, they had gotten here in time. The leather had burned through in most places, the bag barely held together in a sodden pile, but there were still some items within that appeared unmarred. *Magic.* He withdrew a small bound book, blew the damp ash from the cover, and placed it before Rory's knees. On top of that, he placed a muddy silver bowl and a still dripping silver mirror.

There was no more room for debate. This was Hannah's body.

Rory picked up the book, bowl, and mirror carefully, delicately placing them on top of his own belongings in his pack, then he got slowly to his feet. The elf took a few dignified steps away from the body, then a few more, and soon he was moving briskly down the street. Gorn nodded to the man to stay near the body—there would be arrangements to make, even in Kalford—and he and Lira hurried to catch up with the elf, eventually cornering him in the stables.

He was saddling a horse.

"Where are you going?" Lira asked.

"Away from here."

"I see that. But where?"

Rory looked at Lira, his eyes red with unshed tears, his face a pale mask of death.

"You're going to do something foolish," she observed. "Is that what Hannah would have wanted?"

"Don't you say her name," he whispered. "Don't say it."

"Getting yourself killed won't change anything," Gorn said, thinking of the vengeance in his heart after the death of his brother. If the elves hadn't found him, he would probably be dead now, body lying next to a mountain of goblin corpses. It still wouldn't bring his brother back.

Rory glared at him in defiance. "I'll see her again," the elf declared, his voice steady.

"Don't be ridiculous," Lira snapped. "Hannah's soul wouldn't be anywhere near yours, and you know it." Gorn stared at her. *Why would she say such a thing to the clearly distraught elf?*

"What do you mean?" Rory's face was dangerous, barely concealed anger showing around the edges of his mask.

"Come now, Rory. Hannah was a vampire. Her soul would return to the underworld. She was damned. You know that."

Gorn stared at her. "What nonsense is this?"

Rory's hand shot out and grabbed the collar of Lira's shirt, jerking her forward a little bit. "She is not damned," he growled. Gorn put his hand on his axe handle and stepped forward.

"Fine, she wasn't damned," Lira said, face annoyed, but it was clear she didn't believe what she said. She didn't seem worried by Rory's rage or his hand on her shirt. If anything, she was disappointed. She looked at his hand pointedly, then added, "But you cannot get to her, wherever she is now."

"Watch me," he said, releasing her savagely and getting swiftly on the horse.

"Jamison and Molly have left," Lira tried. "Don't you want to find them?"

"Why?" He was settling himself on the horse, adjusting his feet in the stirrups and tightening the ropes in his hand.

"Maybe they know what happened," Gorn offered.

He looked at them, eyes derisive. "I know what happened."

"Oh? Do enlighten us, then," Lira snapped.

"The bastard caught up with her. He was going to take her home, and something must have gone wrong, and instead she..." His voice caught, and he hiccupped a bit, stifling his sobs.

"Rory, we need you here." Lira spoke softly.

"I can't stay here," he said, giving the horse a small tap to get it moving.

"Please listen to me," Lira said. "We've traveled together for nearly a hundred years." Gorn blanched a bit at that. He hadn't realized just how old the elves were. She reached out a hand to touch the horse's bridle. "Don't go."

Rory shook his head, her words beginning to work on him, but then his face hardened. "And in a hundred years," he said in a low voice, "I never met anyone like her."

"Rory—" Lira tried again, but he wasn't listening to her anymore.

Rory turned the horse away. "And now I will kill him," he swore. "I'll kill him."

Gorn wondered who he was talking about. Rory maneuvered the horse skillfully around them, then kicked the beast into motion, his bag jerking up behind him and smashing down into his back as he took off at a gallop. Lira shouted after him, but he didn't turn around.

"I suppose we'll see to the body, then," she said to Gorn. "And find Jamison and Molly while we're at it."

They headed back down the street to where the man was waiting with his burden. It was just the two of them now.

XXV

The tall vampire standing in front of Hannah sighed, a deep sound that echoed in her heart. His features softened, the dark eyes turning down with sympathy. He ran a hand through his hair, pushing the stray strands behind both ears. "I had hoped you would not ask me that, chaivin. Not yet." A hand reached up to touch his face, the fingers long and elegant as they rubbed his chin.

Hannah looked down at her own stubby fingers, the small smooth pads on her palms marred by the divine sigil scarred into the center. She held herself perfectly still, refusing to allow her thoughts to run as they would—*Alone, Malbrek is alone, he doesn't have my body with him, what are they going to do, what is going to happen to me, what did he mean by purification*—as she waited for Klauden to continue.

"I think he burned it. I'm sorry."

Hannah felt her knees give way as she sank to the floor in a puddle. *Malbrek burned my body?* The thought was too strange to conceive. She looked at her hand, so solid in the pink room, the scar on her palm vivid in the half light, then looked at her other hand, noting that the ring on the middle finger was gone. *What happened to my ring, the ring Klauden gave me? Ring*, she thought, *you idiot! Focus!*

As she thought about it, the circlet appeared, but there was no comfort in the worn silver band. *What about the rest of my body? And what happened to the healer? Is he dead?*

"Am I dead, then?" she asked finally. "A ghost?" She looked up from her puddle.

"No."

Well, that was a relief. "So, what happens now? Where will I go? Where *can* I go?"

Questions of the afterlife had never been something Hannah spent much time with. She knew the theories, of course, had even listened to Lira long enough to have some concept of the Elven paradise—a place of green fields high above a white city, an endless forest filled with rivers—definitely not Hannah's idea of perfection, but she had never considered her own concept of heaven. It hadn't been necessary—it wasn't as if she was going to die any time soon. Her body was practically indestructible.

Or so she had thought. Now, she didn't know what to think. Given the circumstances, a belief in some sort of afterlife was probably a good idea, but she didn't know which one, or if she even got to pick at all.

Klauden took another deep breath, and Hannah braced herself for the additional bad news he had yet to share. "They mean to give you a new body, a pureblood that will not have your previous … flaws."

So that's what Malbrek meant by purification. "Is that even possible?" she asked.

"Yes. In fact, it's quite simple. You might say it's what the Star of Elgiva was made for. The ceremony requires a soul and a body and someone able to read the incantation and control the transfer. It takes a lot of power, though, otherwise everyone would do it all the time, I suppose, and sometimes the body will fight it." He looked at her. "Forgive me, chaivin. Here I am, going on about magic… I never was very good at this."

She sniffed, her mind frozen. "At what?"

"At you." He shrugged, his face in the open expression she recalled from their youth. It wasn't often that they spoke frankly to one another about this, but she knew the look when she saw it. "I thought maybe that was why you left." When she would speak to contradict him, he said, "I guess I always knew there was something else out there for you, something that would give you what you wanted."

"What are you talking about?" Her head was spinning.

"Rory." The spinning stopped. *Rory! Did he find my body? Does he think I'm dead? Will he be alright? Will I ever see him again?*

"How do you even know about him?" she whispered. *Could my old friend be in on it?* Looking at him, she thought he wasn't, but one could never be too sure among her people. *Everyone can betray, even promised mates*, she realized, and thinking of her father, *especially mates.*

"It doesn't matter now," Klauden said. He got that faraway look again, then returned, all business. "I have to go. I'll be back if I can."

She watched as he placed his hands together before him, chanted a quick verse, then faded from sight. She was alone, bodiless, trapped in an ancient artifact, and on her way to be transferred into a new body. What else could possibly go wrong?

THE WARRIOR

Rory Tallerin had been riding for three days, trading out his exhausted horse at a farm up the river from Kalford, a stop along the Marin River for those who kept the trade routes from Upsen to the northern lands. He was heading back toward Firene and knew he would have to veer to the east soon or risk capture, and then probably death. He considered for a time if his death would be such a great loss—to Firene, to the royal family there, to his few remaining friends, or to himself.

He had been dreaming, of course. Even while riding, his body knew what to do, his unconscious mind taking over what had to be done to keep the horse pointed north and keep his body on the beast's back. His conscious mind had been elsewhere, searching, scanning, looking ... and finding nothing.

Maybe it wasn't so odd, he considered, since Hannah was a born vampire. It had always been his Knack to find people in dreams, to focus on a person and draw his mind close to that soul, wherever it lingered.

He had spoken to Galina, just the once, days before she had finally given in to her despair. That had been a conversation worthy of memory, but Rory still wished he could forget. Even after all these years, he realized, he was still angry with her. For all the grief she had caused him, and he her, he reflected sourly, Galina had been easy to find.

Hannah was proving to be much more difficult. He had been reaching for her, calling to her, wishing he could find her by recalling her face, her eyes, the scent of her skin, the way she always grinned in the midst of battle, a certain familiar bloodlust lurking behind her gaze. Sometimes the pictures helped him to focus; sometimes they shattered his concentration. It was useless. He would never find her. He would never get to say goodbye the right way.

The new horse jumped a fallen trunk across the path along the river, jarring him back to reality. There had been a bad storm up here, perhaps a month ago judging by the overgrown look of most of the fallen trunks.

Rory wondered if it was the same storm they had weathered that night in the cave, the night he had comforted Hannah in her nightmare, the night he had first considered her as anything except another traveling companion in a long line of companions over the years. The horse landed smoothly, but the move made his vest bump against his chest, the soft thump of the folded paper in the vest's inner pocket a reminder that he hadn't needed.

He still didn't know what to make of the map. Obviously, Hannah had left it for him, a clue of some sort to her whereabouts. It had been resting carefully on top of his bag when he had woken alone in the room.

His head had been fuzzy, his mind coated in a strange haze that left a bad taste in his mouth; he wasn't positive, but he thought something magical had happened to him. It had to be some sort of magic, a sleep spell or a charm, that had kept him from noticing Hannah's departure. What worried him was who had cast it. Maybe Hannah had spelled him and left, but then why leave the map?

He slowed the horse to a trot, pulling the worn page from his pocket and unfolding it. He knew where it led. Anyone could decipher the little crosshatches that resembled mountains, the swirls of treetops that represented the endless forest, the wavy lines of the Marin River and several tributaries.

What the average person would not recognize, however, was the small square near the top of the page, the black mark labeled Kreeosk. His eyes traced the page, the clearly delineated line running from Kalford, a city never visible on any map Rory had ever seen, up along the riverside and across the foothills, through the Vanya Mountains, around several clearly posted "routes to avoid" and "potential hazards" to a castle that could only belong to Hannah's father.

He thought he recognized the spiky handwriting but couldn't recall if it belonged to Hannah or not. He thought he had seen it in her spellbook. He folded the map again, the thought that plagued him resurfacing.

If Hannah is dead, why would she leave me a map to her father's castle?

It made sense to think that the reason was because she wasn't dead but had been captured instead, and was even now being dragged back to her homeland. The possibility was compounded by the fact that he couldn't find her soul, not anywhere in any of the realms beyond that he searched in his mind.

Still, dreamwalking was only Rory's Knack; he hadn't any true skill in the area. He clung to the knowledge that before, whenever he had looked for someone, he had found the soul quite easily. And, he thought, he and Hannah had a tie, more of a bond than any he had shared with Galina, so she should be even easier to find.

And yet three days of nothing.

He was fairly certain, despite the ring he now wore on a chain around his neck, that Hannah was not dead at all. Even if they had killed her body, there were other ways of living, other planes of existence, and if Hannah was in one of those places, he would find her. He had to.

It had been a long time since he had felt such a drive to do anything. These past few decades of aimless drifting had passed in a blur; the only thing that had caused him to notice the world at all had been Hannah's cautious smiles, her blunt questions, her quirks and curiosity.

So, is that it, then? Am I risking life and limb heading back to Firene because I am that desperate for a purpose again?

He wasn't sure, not yet. All that he was sure of was that Hannah might still be out there, and he had to find her. He had to know what had happened, at least. And if he couldn't find her, then he knew who could.

Caganasti was an old friend, a recluse who lived among the people of Firene, running an odd shop of magical items, spells, artifacts, weapons, and anything else he could find or trade for. The elf had been roosting in his store for at least four hundred years, his clientele the eager young elves seeking adventure and wishing to arm themselves as best they could. Caganasti was the one to see for any and all magical questions, not to mention his reasonable rates for identifying any found items.

The elf was also a renowned dreamwalker.

If anyone could find Hannah, it was his old friend. Rory just hoped it was worth the price. It wasn't that Caganasti would charge him a lot, though he might relieve Rory of a few gold coins. The money wasn't an issue; it never was. Rory had left Firene well taken care of. The trouble was getting to Caganasti without getting caught. Even if they didn't keep their promise and kill him for returning, they would certainly hold him for some time, and that was a delay he couldn't afford, not if Hannah was on her way even now to the mountains.

If Caganasti could find her, *Which he would*, Rory assured himself, *he would*, then Rory would follow the map to the north. Something in him wanted to follow it anyway, skipping the stop in Firene and charging head-long into battle. Of course, it wouldn't help Hannah, if she could still be helped, for him to get himself killed before he even got there. Caganasti knew other things as well, and one of those areas of knowledge was life beyond the Vanya, west of the dwarven mines and in the unknown territories. Such knowledge might make the difference between salvation and disaster.

Okay then, he decided. *It's time to go home.*

XXVI

There was no concept of time in the pink room, but Hannah occupied herself. She had conjured the spellbook, and she realized that either she already knew everything in it in order to reproduce it so well, or the magic of the artifact recognized other magic and conjured it for her. Either way, the words were here, written in Klauden's familiar spidery handwriting, and it was even missing the page she had torn out to leave Rory her note.

Her stupid note.

She spent some time mentally kicking herself for that, then some more time angrily pacing the small room. She hadn't had a choice about leaving him, really—she knew they had no future, not if he was going to touch her like that again—but she had been foolish to leave herself so unguarded.

Eventually, though, her anger faded, and she turned back to the book for comfort. It was a testament to just how bored she was that she sat and spent some time diligently at work memorizing her spells. She didn't know if she would even be able to cast them but decided the effort was worthwhile anyway. She had to do something, or she would go mad.

She tried to recall everything she knew about magic and the body; she knew that casting a spell used energy of a sort, but had it been physical or spiritual? She didn't know but hoped it was spiritual. Apparently, there was still enough of her spirit to go around, enough to keep her alive—if she was alive. But Klauden had said she wasn't dead, and if anyone knew about these things, it was Klauden. She had to believe him.

She even spent some time trying to solidify her own reflection in her mother's mirror, but her features kept swirling, the eyes slowly widening and slanting, her lips morphing from a thin line to a lush pout.

Klauden still had not returned, and Hannah couldn't bring herself to look out the window anymore. The night had passed into day, but she didn't know if it was the next day or a week later. The forest was still the same, but it had been much the same since Talperin, and that was four weeks by walking from Kalford. A horse could move faster, but Hannah wasn't sure how much faster.

She was taking a break, lying on her back on the floor—she had thought about conjuring a bed, but figured it would clutter the small space, especially since she hadn't figured out how to un-conjure things yet—when something different finally happened.

Someone yelled her name.

The sound was distant, a hoarse cry muted by the walls, but it had Hannah on her feet instantly. She moved to the wall opposite the window and closed her eyes. She told herself that it had worked before, that she had been able to see her way through the magic before, and that doing it again would be easy.

This time, instead of picturing a window, she imagined a door, a wooden door with slats and metal hinges and a bar to keep unwanted people from entering. When she opened her eyes, the door from the inn in Kalford was there. She reached out to remove the bar, setting the wooden beam gently on the floor, but hesitated as she reached for the handle. *Where does it go?*

She heard the voice again, muffled through the wood this time and not filtered through pinkness. *Why didn't I conjure a door with a window?* She thought there probably wasn't time to adjust the image.

Oh, the hell with it. Anywhere is better than stuck in here.

She took a deep breath, opened the door, closed her eyes, and stepped through. There was some resistance as she crossed the threshold, but then the force released, like a parental hand realizing the child only meant to run to his father instead of into the firepit, and she was free. A cool breeze caressed her cheek, a wonderful change from the soft stillness of the Star.

She opened her eyes. She was standing on a green hill overlooking a wide river, what Rory would no doubt call a mere stream. Far beneath her and across the river-stream was a city, a sprawling construction of white towers and black gates that seemed large enough for a school of midges at this distance.

Where am I? She looked around, taking in the soft blue sky, the looming mountains to her left that looked vaguely familiar, but in a mirror image way, the sounds of birds chirping and water splashing, then the cry again.

"Hannah!"

It was Rory's voice. She recognized it even before she saw him slide into view. First his head as he cleared the other side of the hill behind her, then his chest, his sword, and his boots as he crested the ridge and approached her. *Am I dreaming?*

"I'm here," she said, surprised by how calm her voice was when her heart pounded at the sight of him. "You can stop yelling now."

He seemed glad to see her too, arms outstretched to enfold her in a hug. She accepted, his embrace so much thicker than before, so much more real than any solace Klauden had offered. When he leaned down to kiss her, she forgot Klauden completely, her senses overwhelmed by the new man in her life—the only man in her life now. Or elf, as it were.

"I was so worried," he said, his lips soft in her hair.

"I'm fine," she said. A quiet sense of urgency was building in her chest. She was with Rory now. What could go wrong?

"Good," he said, then took her hand and led her toward the water.

"What's going on?" she asked, trying to recall how she had gotten to this place, to explain the knot churning in her stomach. There was something important to do, but she couldn't remember what it was. Following Rory's lead, it didn't seem all that important anymore. She was here. Rory was here. Everything would be fine.

Rory looked back at her as they neared the bank, reaching down to remove first one boot, then the next. "Isn't it obvious?" he asked, a sly grin on his face.

"Should it be?" she retorted, a matching expression crossing her own face.

"I'm teaching you how to swim," he explained, releasing her hand to pull off his shirt, eyes sparkling like the sun on the water. There was an underlying ebullience to the elf that Hannah couldn't resist, a childlike fascination that demanded a response in kind.

Laughing at the oddity of it all, Hannah pulled her own sweater over her head, then stepped out of her skirt. She was delighted to discover her slip, the material untorn and clean against her body as she walked to the water's edge. Rory took her hand, stepping into the water and leading her deeper. When the water reached her shoulders, a depth that lapped mid-chest on Rory, he stopped, planting both feet in the sandy bottom, and pulled Hannah closer.

"Now," he began, hands on her hips suspending her off the ground, "you have to trust me."

She smiled uneasily, the sight of all that open water making her a bit queasy, the idea of getting swept into the current and dragged away a very real possibility in her mind. That was why she always stayed on the bottom of such waterways when crossing them became unavoidable; floating left one so vulnerable.

"I trust you," she breathed, hands resting on his shoulders. There was something more there, she thought, her mind struggling with this dream, the knot of fear in her gut amplified by more than just a phobia of the water. "You know I trust you," she repeated, then watched in growing confusion as his face twisted, seemed to turn inward as if he were trying to remember something.

"Hannah?" he asked, head cocked to one side as he held her. "What's happening?"

"I don't know," she answered, trying to pull the answer from her memory. "There's something..."

He pushed her away to arm's length, peering at her intently. "I can't remember," he said. "*What* can't I remember?"

She started to reply that she didn't know any more than he, but her eyes caught the glint of something shiny around his neck. It was a silver chain, a necklace with a single object on it—a ring engraved with runes that only she could read. Her hand reached out for it tentatively. "Why are you wearing my ring?"

He looked down, then understanding flooded his face. "Your ring, Hannah! The ring was on your body!" He looked down at the water between them, then up at the sky, and Hannah noticed what he had already seen—the sunshine was fading, the wind picking up, the formerly inviting scene fast disappearing. He started to force his way back to shore, propelling her before him. They had retreated to water as high as Hannah's thighs when the rain began.

"What's happening, Rory?" she yelled over the growing storm. "Why are you here? What is this place?"

"It's a dream, Hannah!" he shouted, his steps slowing as the wind increased, the rain plastering his hair to his head, his long ears sticking awkwardly out of the mess. "I couldn't find you, so I went to someone who could. Where are you? Tell me how to find you!"

"What do you mean 'find me'? Malbrek burned my body! I think I should be dead, but I'm still alive. I'm trapped inside the Star instead!" She was shouting to be heard over the roar of the rain. Lightning struck nearby, the thunder deafening her for a moment, and she couldn't hear what Rory said next.

"Caganasti... dreamwalker... truly dead... map... find your soul... sent me... look..."

To Hannah's horror, Rory was fading from her sight, his shoulders becoming less substantial under her hands, his face taking on a ghostly hue as his words grew softer. "Wait!" he yelled, then vanished altogether, the space where he had been tingling with spent magic. She stood for a moment, letting the rain soak her, the drops stinging her face, then she screamed his name.

As if her shout had conjured it, a lightning bolt struck a nearby tree, the limb severing with a crash and knocking into her, pushing her into the water. She splashed to her knees and lost her balance as a rock sliced her palm. She toppled sideways, and then the water was pulling her along. She struggled to get control, to stand up, but the current was too strong. *Isn't this what I was afraid of?* She yelled for Rory once more, then her head went under, and everything was dark for a time, a swirling maelstrom of water.

XXVII

Hannah woke to someone shaking her shoulder. She sat up fast, the insistent hand slipping down to the crook of her elbow.

"Why are you all wet?" Klauden asked, his hand retreating to his side to wipe on his robe. Hannah was glad to see the gesture; it made what happened inside this pink room more realistic if he bothered to dry manifested hands from manifested wetness.

"Rory," Hannah said breathlessly, looking around for the wooden door again.

"How did you know?" Klauden asked, following her gaze to the blank slate of pinkness that had replaced the door she had walked through to Rory. She ignored his question, her thoughts spinning. *Was it a dream? Was Rory really there?* She reached down to her dripping sweater, twisting the bottom out of habit, letting the water drip onto the floor.

"I saw him, Klauden."

When he frowned at her, she insisted, "I did! I heard him yelling my name, pictured the door, and *bam*!" She smacked her fist into her palm. "I was there! It was amazing..."

She let the thought trail off, then looked sharply at Klauden. "What was it? Was it real? Can I get into people's dreams from here?" Recalling the endless moments before Rory's visit, she added with some asperity, "And where the hell have you been? How much time has passed?" She forgot about her wet clothes.

Klauden was shaking his head at her, the classic slow-down-you're-making-me-crazy gesture she remembered from their earliest days of study. He took a deep breath before speaking. "It's been two weeks since I was last able to visit you."

Hannah felt a sinking in her stomach. *Two whole weeks?* "Has Malbrek returned to the castle?" A nervous hand brushed her sweater, and she was perplexed to find that it was dry. *Do things really work so fast here?*

"But that's not the problem."

The sinking feeling intensified. "What's the problem, then? Why couldn't you come back sooner?"

"Much has happened."

"Like what? Are they going to do the ceremony soon? How much time do I have?"

"There has been a slight complication," he said mysteriously. Hannah wanted to shake him. *Why can't he just answer my questions?*

That was his way, of course. Klauden never told her what she wanted to know; he made her work it out on her own. Hannah thought it was his way of making her slow down since her rapid twists and turns were one of the things he never accepted, especially in her lessons. She took a deep settling breath, Klauden's expectant face the signal to calm down and be patient.

"Fine," she said when she had steadied herself. "Tell me."

"Rory came to find you," he said simply. Hannah stared at him.

"What?" *How could he find me?* She was trapped in here. She remembered him saying something about a dreamwalker in the dream they'd shared, but was that even possible? "How could that be? I just talked to him in a dream..."

Klauden crossed his arms, assuming his lecturer's face. "Think about it, Hannah. Your spirit is trapped in the Star of Elgiva, an artifact designed to hold souls in an extraplanar space. All such spaces are connected in some way or another, and finding the doors only takes some concentration. Your elf must have been searching for you, even in his dreams, and he found you. It's not so surprising, given your connection."

Hannah glanced sharply at him. "So, it was a dream then?"

"In a manner of speaking. Is he a user of magic?" When Hannah shook her head, he said, "Then he must have sought out someone who could help him get into the spirit world, probably a dreamwalker of some sort."

"Caganasti," Hannah muttered.

His face sharpened. "Caganasti? Where did you hear that?"

"Rory said it, right before he disappeared. Why? What does it mean?"

"Caganasti is an Elven dreamwalker who lives in Firene. He's mentioned in the old tales. If you want to find someone in the worlds beyond and you live south of the Vanya, Caganasti is the one to see." Hannah got the impression that he wanted to add that if you lived north of the Vanya, then Klauden van Sherinak was the one to visit. He looked hard at Hannah. "That explains it. You must have made quite an impression for him to travel all that way to find you."

Did Rory go back to Firene? Hannah couldn't be sure. He had said he was banished. *Why would he chance discovery to visit a dreamwalker?* She wanted to think she knew the answer to that question but couldn't bring herself to admit it. She had been the one to leave him, after all.

"But how could he do it? I just saw him." Hannah tried to puzzle out the chronology, uncomfortable with Klauden's searching look.

"He had a horse," Klauden remarked, "and he's a much better rider than Malbrek. He made excellent time."

"To Firene. That I believe. But you said he came to find me. Where is he now?" She stopped, something clicking in her mind. "And how do you know all of this?"

Klauden answered her second question. "Because he's wearing your ring."

"What do you mean 'my ring'?" She looked down at her hand, noting the white band on her middle finger, the mark left from a ring no longer there. "You mean your ring?"

"He took it from your body when he thought you were dead."

"So, what are you saying? That you can follow him through the ring?" Hannah narrowed her eyes suspiciously at him, an unnerving possibility becoming clear. "What exactly have you been doing?"

Klauden looked down at the ground, his feet shuffling under his robe.

She glared at him, hands on her hips. "Klauden!" she demanded.

He looked up finally, his eyes hooded with something like regret. "I had to make sure you'd be alright," he said quietly. "I had to know."

"I was fine!" she yelled, the implication slowly sinking in.

"You're not fine!" he yelled back, his face showing more emotion than she had ever seen in the restrained scholar. "First, you let Malbrek track you; next, you took up with a group of mortals. You nearly let yourself die of the bloodthirst, and then, then—" he sputtered, face reddening.

"No, Hannah. You have not been fine. I'm astonished you lasted as long as you did."

"You've been watching me the whole time, haven't you? That's why I could remember the spell to undo the contingency on Rory. I heard you in my head, but it wasn't a memory, was it? It was you!" She shook her head, too betrayed to speak, then managed to whisper, "You've been spying on me." She looked at him, face reddening in embarrassment and anger. "How could you do it?"

"I had to know," he repeated, his voice quiet and stubborn again, all traces of emotion gone. He was the same old reserved Klauden again. "At the very least, my spell has allowed me to track your Rory, and that has been fortunate."

"What do you mean? What happened?"

"He made it here."

"You mean he's there? In the castle? How did he find the way? Pass the guards? Cross the mountains?"

"That's not relevant now. What does matter is where he is now."

"And where is he?"

"That's the complication." He looked away, gathering his thoughts before speaking. "The ceremony for your purification was supposed to be tonight, but now it's been postponed."

"Postponed?" Hannah echoed. "Why?"

"Because that elf showed up, followed every rule of the Vangard code, and demanded the chance to fight for his boon." Klauden was shaking his head ruefully. "You sure know how to pick them, Hannah."

Hannah was trying to follow events. Rory had found her father's castle, managed to avoid all of the traps and pitfalls along the way, and had not been waylaid by any of the other Houses. A bloody miracle in itself. On top of that, she couldn't figure how he could have known about the Vangard code, the detailed treaty that kept the Houses steady in their alliance and unable to subvert one another. Of course, the guidelines were clearly outlined in the old books, but there were always those who managed to circumvent such laws; her father had been excellent at such maneuvers.

It was strange that her father would have honored Rory's request for a boon at all—Hannah would have expected Magnus van Kreeosk to laugh at any newcomer before ordering his painful death. Or maybe he would have put him in the games, the to-the-death tournaments populated with fledglings, goblins, ambitious Kargin seeking to raise their status, along with anything unfortunate enough to wander into the castle's far-flung security nets. Rory would put up a good fight in such games, but the result would be the same. No one ever really won.

"What was his boon?" Hannah asked, unwilling to ask what had become of an elf who knocked on her father's door.

Klauden gave her an even look. "You."

Hannah closed her eyes. She had tried to tell him in the dream that it wouldn't do any good. Her body was gone—*What can my soul do for him?* "And what did my father say?"

"He allowed him the privilege of fighting for you."

Hannah opened her eyes, giving Klauden a pleading look. "No."

"Yes. Rory will fight in the tournaments tonight."

"Who will he face?" She tried to remember who had been the reigning champion when she left. Someone named Marten? Mayhew? She couldn't recall. The games had never been her favorite pastime, required as they were for someone of her position, yet another flaw her father and teacher had berated her for at every opportunity.

"The reigning fledgling—Matthew." So that was the name.

"Is he good?" It was a foolish question. Anyone who survived long enough to be considered the reigning anything had to be amazing.

Klauden shrugged. "I am not qualified to judge such things. He has been champion for some time now, though. For your sake, I hope your elf knows how to use his blade."

"He'll die," she said, more for her own benefit than Klauden's. The idea was crippling, the knowledge that she had damned him, had caused his death as clearly as if she had bitten and condemned him herself.

How did he find me?

She knew Rory had some vast resources at his disposal, but she didn't think maps to the Vanya were plentiful, even for one in the know. Men like her father had spent millennia preventing such knowledge from spreading beyond their own kind.

"Maybe." Klauden took a breath as he knelt beside her. "I have an idea, chaivin."

She looked at him, eyes burning with unshed tears. "What?"

"I think you can come with me."

"Go with you where?"

"Hear me out. You left this place to find him, right? It didn't last long, but you managed to find your way through the worlds to his side. That's the kind of concentration you'll need for what I propose."

"I'm listening."

XXVIII

Hannah wondered if this was what real demons felt like—the ones who escaped from the hell dimensions and hitched rides in unsuspecting human hosts. She was inside Klauden's mind, her awareness limited to his scope of vision and his physical form.

It was strangely comforting to have some sense of a body again, even if the body in question was male and not entirely under her control. Klauden was walking down the corridors of her father's castle, his long strides careful and sure, the way she probably used to walk these halls. They looked different now, and she didn't know if it was Klauden's vision—his eyesight perhaps—or her own widely increased perception of the world that altered the stone walls.

This place seemed so big to her then, so impregnable, the thick stones of the walls melding into the bedrock of the mountain and under it to create a fortress thick and mighty. She had never thought to see life outside these walls, beyond the castle courtyards and cliffs and valleys below.

Sure, she had explored as a child, had even gone so far as Valrane, the human village half a day to the east, to watch the people there, but she had always thought to end up back here, safe in her suite of rooms, which would have eventually become their suite of rooms, she realized, thinking of Klauden and their promises.

It had never been their promise at the start; the marriage of two firstborns was always left to the parents. Of the three families who lived in her father's castle, the Kreeosks, Sherinaks, and Joosens, it had always been clear that she was for the Sherinaks. The Joosens also had a son, Vailen, but their family was the lowest ranking of the elite, and so Hannah had gone to Klauden as soon as she was born, some twenty years after he was. Typically, Houses would marry among themselves to secure loyalties, but occasionally a feud was settled or an alliance forged by uniting two firstborns from different Houses. Hannah had always been glad that she wouldn't be sent away to a strange castle to live, had always been grateful that her mate was right here.

And then I went running away south of the mountains, she thought wryly. *Who would have thought that scared girl would ever find the courage?*

Klauden was on his way to the games held in the arena adjacent to the castle proper. Though Magnus van Kreeosk had been ruling the place for nearly a half millennium, the castle was ancient, the stones built by ancestors thousands of years before.

Specifically, Hannah recalled from her endless lessons from both Malbrek and Klauden, the castle had been crafted by Warren van Harner, the great architect who set up the Vangard code and ended the senseless violence that had kept their species so limited in number. Warren van Harner even set up the Houses, only three at that time, and their society had flourished; there were seventeen Houses north of the Vanya now, seventeen strongholds with three families in each, and there had been talk of starting another House soon.

Hannah had been taught to feel honored that her family lived in van Harner's castle, even though the last van Harner had died ages before, to take pride in the craftsmanship that linked the living areas to the arena. But Hannah had never liked the tournaments, so the open-aired arena with its black stone benches and dark earth floor—the dirt stained from so much blood spilled over the years—had always made her uncomfortable.

The proximity of Cairn's Temple probably had something to do with her unease; it was convenient though, making it easier to bring those disgraced in the tournaments to be sacrificed, or even worse, to finish off those who didn't have the decency to die right away.

<<*Stop that.*>>

The voice was insistent, accented, and spoken in a familiar language. She thought Klauden would be giving her one of his patented looks by now if she wasn't already in his body.

<<*Stop what?*>> she thought at him in their native tongue.

<<*Stop being so maudlin. The tournaments have always been and always will be. Get used to it.*>>

A typical Klauden response, but somehow it made her more aware of how much she had changed since leaving home. <<*This is the only place where things are and always will be,*>> she thought. <<*This is the only place where nothing ever changes.*>>

<<*Except something has changed, hasn't it?*>> Transferring souls and accepting Elven requests for boons were definitely not standard fare at her father's castle. Hannah hoped that other things would change as well, like the fact that no one ever escaped.

<<*You did.*>>

It was unnerving to have him answer her thoughts like that. It was even more unnerving to know that for all that he must hear from her, she could hear nothing from him. He had practiced and perfected the art of shielding his mind since everyone else could easily read surface thoughts—everyone but Hannah of course. She had never been very good at that skill. She felt very exposed, aware that Klauden was seeing far more of her than ever before, a closeness even more revealing than her night with Rory had kindled.

She stopped herself, cutting off that line of thought completely. Still, it wasn't quick enough because suddenly she felt a wash of heat from Klauden, something like anger. She had time to be amazed that the studious and reserved Klauden could harbor such emotions behind his stoic face, then Klauden was talking to someone.

"Greetings, Lord van Kreeosk." It was her father. Magnus was as tall and imperious as ever, the purple of his gown accenting the flecks in his eyes, his dark hair falling in perfect waves over his shoulders.

Her father made the appropriate gesture for greeting a beloved underling, a finger to his forehead that moved to tap on Klauden's right shoulder as he spoke his own greeting. "Klauden van Sherinak, always a pleasure to have you in my sight." The two continued down the hall, through the archway that led to a brief catwalk, then into the arena. Klauden waited for Magnus to sit on the cushioned chair on the dais, then took his own seat to the man's right.

After Klauden sat, another young man took not the chair next to him, but the one two seats down. Hannah recognized Vailen van Joosen, the strapping, strutting imbecile no smarter today than when they were all in Essentials together. She had never had much use for him, the boy who had been skilled in weaponry but unable to add simple sums in his head.

<<*Vailen's looking well.*>> She tried to remember her manners.

Klauden was not so cordial. <<*As always, but there is still nothing beneath that shining veneer.*>>

Next to him, and hovering far too close for propriety's sake, was Livenna. Hannah had known she would see her father's other daughter again, but she hadn't expected to find her here among the elite. Livenna was one of the Kargin, the second-class citizens who lingered in the middle of the social ladder, ever looking upward but unable to climb due to their tainted blood. They weren't treated as slaves, not like the humans in the castle, but they certainly weren't equals, and Hannah had never expected to find one of them lingering on the dais where the three families sat. Livenna should be sitting up above with the others.

<<*What is she doing here?*>>

She felt Klauden's grimace. <<*She's been hanging around Vailen, hoping to mate her way into the elite. Your father hasn't said anything against her, so she stayed. She's even started calling herself Venna.*>>

<<*Really?*>> Hannah knew how the girl longed to be one of them, knew even more poignantly how her own father probably wished Hannah had been more like Livenna as a child, more calculating, more ruthless, more brutal, but shortening her name to the two syllables of the elite was a childish attempt to gain status.

<<*That's why she'll never be one of us,*>> Hannah thought. <<*She just doesn't understand at all. Next thing, she'll be adding the "van" to her name, as if the honorific could magically purify her blood and propel her onto the dais.*>> As she thought the words to Klauden, Hannah realized she didn't understand it anymore herself. There was a time when everything was so clear, but not anymore. Now everything was foreign to her, even the small subtleties of home.

<<*She chased me for a time.*>>

Now Hannah was really surprised. <<*Did she?*>> An image flashed into her mind, one of Klauden's memories, she assumed, as she saw Klauden's room. He was sitting at his desk, a pile of parchment and scrolls spread across the working surface, and Livenna, wearing a red dress to accent her pale skin, sat on top of the desk, her leg exposed as the tight material hugged her hips and the slit that made walking possible expanded.

Hannah thought the dress looked an awful lot like one she had worn on special occasions, and for a moment, she was convinced that Livenna had stolen her clothes. Anger spiked through her at the thought, and then faded—*What would I need those clothes for anyway?* Her old wardrobe was probably still hanging in the closets of her old rooms.

Livenna was smiling a charming smile, but Hannah could feel Klauden's own emotions at the girl's face, and it was clear the smile wasn't working. He was annoyed at her presence, but even more so by her casual abuse of his papers. Her bottom had slid a bit when she hopped onto the desk, the motion creasing the top paper and tearing the ones underneath.

"Livenna," she heard him say. "Get off my desk."

"Why?" she giggled, still unaware that her seduction attempt wasn't working. "Would you rather move to more comfortable quarters?"

Watching the scene unfold, Hannah stifled a giggle herself. <<*She actually said that? Like you would even think of being with her!*>> Hannah knew that while having sex with future mates was seriously discouraged, having sex with one of the Kargin, and his mate's half-sister at that, was cause for a final trip into Cairn's Temple, with a brief stop in the arena if he was lucky and could get killed there first. <<*You would never!*>>

<<*Wouldn't I?*>>

The question was angry, the tone distant, the implications damning. Here she was, assuming that Klauden would have waited for her when she had no intention of returning. And she hadn't waited either, had she?

<<*I'm sorry. I didn't think—*>>

<<*No, you didn't think. You never do.*>>

<<*I...*>> She let the thought trail off, not knowing what to say. A moment passed. <<*What happened, then?*>>

<<*She spilled my inkpot all over my desk. I kicked her out and told her never to come back.*>>

Hannah hoped he couldn't tell how relieved she was. It was selfish, but she couldn't help it. Klauden was hers—or had been. Of course, she had been his once too, and here he was, helping her to get back to her new lover. Not to mention risking his life in the process. If Malbrek or her father suspected anything was amiss, Klauden wouldn't stand a chance, his amazing gift of dreamwalking or not.

Hannah followed Klauden's gaze as he greeted his parents, Jorus and Keller van Sherinak, when they took their seats between Klauden and Vailen. The lord and lady were looking well, Hannah observed, seeming to have suffered no ill effects from the flight of their son's betrothed.

Hannah had always like Keller, Klauden's mother; though the woman never came close to replacing her own mother, she had always been kind to Hannah, never openly begrudging her anything. Hannah didn't know what to make of Jorus, but she knew Klauden admired his father, and they shared the same love of papers and stories.

Hannah could hear the other guests seating themselves in the rows up above the central dais, and as she turned to look that way, felt Klauden's resistance.

"I have heard about the elf's request, Mother," he was saying, "and was interested to—" He broke off as Hannah attempted to push forward, shouting a loud, <<*QUIT THAT!*>>

Something must have shown on his face, for his mother asked, "Are you feeling well, dear? This must be difficult for you. You seem a bit pale."

Klauden regained control. Hannah remembered what he had told her about coming forward—mainly that she shouldn't try to do so at any cost because others might be able to tell. At the very least, he had pointed out in his rooms, his eyes would change colors as possessed people's eyes always did, revealing the true nature of the spirit in charge. People would notice if Klauden's eyes suddenly turned green. They might not know what it meant, but word would travel, and Malbrek would certainly know what such a change signified. "Mother, I am quite well."

Keller reached a hand out to caress her son's cheek. "Have you been eating, Klauden? I know you've been pent up in your room researching that spell for Magnus, but you really shouldn't neglect yourself like this."

"I'm fine," Klauden repeated, ignoring Hannah's questions: <<*What spell? What is she talking about?*>>

Klauden was spared a reply as the bell chimed, signaling the start of the matches. Klauden turned to face the arena, his gaze lighting on the dirt floor, the archways that led from the dungeons below, before skipping to his left and Magnus. Hannah saw that Malbrek had joined her father, taking the seat to the lord's left. He was still wearing the Star of Elgiva, the crystal pendant resting against the leather of his vest. He spoke quietly to Magnus, and the two shared a chuckle. Hannah noted the smooth expanse of his cheek and wondered what magic he had used to conceal the scar.

<<*What's that about?*>> She didn't move his head but sent the bent of her thoughts in that direction.

<<*No doubt they are speaking of you.*>>

<<*This is bad,*>> she thought, then followed Klauden's gaze to the floor once more. They were bringing out the first round of prisoners, a ragtag assembly of goblins, orcs, a few battered humans, and one hulking, but barely breathing, troll. Hannah wanted to look away as the youngest fledglings came through the opposite archway, but Klauden's gaze stayed fixed.

Hannah realized that for all his distaste for the tournaments, Klauden couldn't help but watch them in awe. On the heels of that revelation, she also knew that part of the reason for his fascination was his own inability to fight at all—Klauden could use a short sword in extremity, but he was no warrior. He was almost jealous of the fighters, wishing he had their skills, the skills that had obviously attracted someone like Hannah, since she had left him for an elf with such capabilities, since that must be what she wanted—

<<*Kindly get out of my thoughts. It's rude.*>>

<<*Sorry. I didn't mean to pry.*>>

<<*Yes, you did. Now, stop it.*>>

<<*Fine.*>> Hannah tried to focus instead on the fights below, watching as the fledglings cut their way through the horde of unfortunate creatures. The troll didn't prove much of a problem as three of the fledglings cut the wounded beast down. She followed Klauden's gaze to one of the humans as he managed to steal one of the fledgling's blades and began to defend himself with it quite nicely.

<<*He shows promise,*>> she thought. <<*Father will want him if he lives.*> The man's sandy hair was flying in his face, but he seemed to ignore the distraction, darting here and there with the weapon, finding openings in first one, then two, then three of the fledglings' defenses. As the third victim slid off his blade, he turned to face the remaining two new vampires,

the three of them beginning a dangerous dance, stepping carefully over the bodies of fallen foes.

Hannah saw the trouble immediately. The two fledglings had the advantage, but they weren't using it properly. She felt Klauden's curiosity and thought more clearly. <<*They aren't working together, see? They both want to be the only one left standing, so they are still fighting alone. They could join forces and kill the human, but they won't. Tactical error.*>>

As soon as she said it, the human seemed to realize the same thing, backing his way to the far wall to keep them from flanking him from behind, then cutting out at one fledgling when the man checked his right to make sure his comrade wasn't going to attack him. The first fell with a groan, then the odds were evened, and even with his enhanced blood, the newbie wasn't much of a swordsman. He soon fell to the human's blade. There was a polite smattering of applause as the human bowed, then fell to one knee in supplication.

Magnus stood and spoke in a clear voice. "Take him back to his cell," he ordered. As the guards, two of the Kargin, approached, Magnus continued, "You fought well, and you will be rewarded for your display. See that his wounds are tended, and clean him up. He will be blessed tomorrow."

The second-sons bowed and herded the man through the archway. Other Kargin guards came out and hauled away the bodies. There were three more such bouts before the one she had been waiting for.

The blood flowed, and the survivors were promised another night of life, if not more valuable prizes like the blood-gift. Hannah tried to ignore it, her old dislike for the tournaments surfacing like bile.

She focused on Klauden instead, reveling in the feel of a body again, the sense of solidity and control. It wasn't long before she was analyzing the differences between her own body and this one, the way Klauden held himself in the seat, the way his arms were slightly longer than hers had been, the way his eyesight was just a bit fuzzier at the edges. No wonder he always preferred reading to living; he couldn't see nearly as well as she could.

She was cataloguing the subtleties of chest and arms when she found herself curious about other parts of his body, the mysteries they had never explored together, mysteries that she now knew a lot more about than he did. The feeling was odd, to realize that something existed about which she knew more than Klauden—the role reversal was refreshing. Her mind wandered, considering what Klauden would do in such a situation, what he would say, if he would whisper or cry out or remain entirely silent, his face that inscrutable mask he always wore when things got emotional—

<<*Hannah, please!*>>

She came back to herself immediately, intensely embarrassed. She had forgotten her predicament entirely, reverted to old habits among the stones of the arena, allowing her mind to wander as it would while the violent images occurring below wandered across her eyes, unseen and unrecalled. She refocused her attention, aware of some strange shifting in Klauden's body as he readjusted himself on the seat.

<<*Here comes your lover now.*>>

She watched Rory enter from the northern archway, the one that led to the deepest of the dungeons, the foulest holding pens. She didn't know if he'd been placed there as an insult or out of practicality, to keep the blazing temptation of Elven blood out of reach of everyone else. It didn't matter.

<<*He's looking well.*>>

It was ironic, of course. Rory wasn't looking well at all.

He was pale, his face drawn and haggard, lines of dirt and grime lining his neck and arms. He wasn't wearing his armor, but only had on his shirt— thoroughly grayed with road dust and dungeon slime—and pants. He still had his weapon, a mark of honor in the tournaments, a courtesy normally extended only to fledglings. She was glad to see he still wore the chain around his neck, her ring resting against his chest.

As she watched, he tucked the necklace beneath his shirt and drew the blade from its sheath. He pushed it into the soft ground, letting go of the hilt long enough to remove his belt and set the wide band of leather with the dangling scabbard against the wall next to the archway. He tucked his hair behind his ears, and Hannah didn't miss the low hum of anticipation from the onlookers—*An elf*, she could almost hear them thinking. *An elf right in front of us. Who will get him?*

Rory closed his eyes for a minute, straightened his shoulders, then pulled the blade from the dirt and strode across the open floor of the arena. He stopped in the center and bowed deeply, blade held across his body. "I come to seek a boon according to the Vangard code," he announced formally, and Hannah was glad to hear that the tiredness of his face had not reached his voice.

Her father stood. "Very well. According to the code, you must defeat a champion of my choosing." He looked to the eastern archway, the one that led back to the castle where Hannah assumed the amazing Matthew must have his rooms. "I call Matthew Hunter."

Hannah thought the name was familiar, then understood as Jamison walked through the archway.

But it wasn't Jamison, not really. The man had the same features, the same dark hair around the same brown eyes, but his stance was different, the steady pace of a warrior, not a coward who used fog and stolen spells instead of direct confrontation.

<<He's Jamison's twin,>> Klauden explained. <<He was turned three years ago but has progressed rapidly through the ranks. He has been undefeated. There are those who say that if he'd been a magic wielder instead of a fighter, he would have rivaled Malbrek.>>

Hannah knew such speculations were pointless; anyone who could rival Malbrek would have suffered an unfortunate accident long before he became a threat. <<So, Matthew has been winning for years now?>>

She studied the man, noting his gait, the familiar way he handled the longsword at his waist, and taking in the elaborate shirt and vest he wore, the elegant boots that came to just below his knees. The clothing looked restrictive, like all of the clothing worn by her people, and a thought occurred to her.

<<Does he always fight dressed like that?>>

<<Yes. Matthew's very conscious of the latest fashions. Why?>>

<<No reason,>> Hannah projected, but she knew Matthew had just given Rory an advantage. She remembered the fight with the goblins, recalled how Rory's clothes moved with him, allowed his limbs to react as they would, how even the armor he customarily wore had more give than Matthew's embroidered jerkin. The vest might give him some protection, but he would suffer greatly in mobility. Of course, the blood would help him there. She hoped Rory's advantage would be enough.

The two figures stood facing one another in the center of the ring. Rory held his blade down before him, carefully balanced in what she had always thought of as his prep stance. If Matthew's appearance had startled him at all, he didn't show it.

The current champion was idly moving his blade from side to side as he stood, taking lazy strikes at the air between them.

<<*Another mistake,*>> Hannah noted. <<*He's showing how he fights before they begin. Rory will know what to expect from him now.*>> The strikes were quite skilled, though, and Hannah hoped Rory would be able to get out the way.

Matthew reached out with his free hand, snapping his fingers, and a Kargin scuttled into the arena, carrying a short sword. Matthew gestured at Rory, and the Kargin handed him the extra blade.

"To give you a fighting chance," Matthew sneered, watching as Rory lifted the new blade, testing its weight and balance. He adjusted his stance for the second blade, still leading with his sword, but holding the new blade backhand as though it were a dagger. <<*It must be light,*>> Hannah explained to Klauden. <<*And he's not sure if he can trust it not to break in a direct hit.*>>

Magnus raised his finger, and a bell sounded from somewhere below them. Matthew moved instantly, stepping forward with a quick swipe intended to decapitate his foe. Rory ducked easily out of the way, then sidestepped and tried to stab Matthew's side. The blow was deflected, but not before Rory's new blade darted in to score a hit on the vampire's cheek. Hannah remembered that move; it had been the one that defeated Malbrek. She scanned Matthew's neck, relieved to find no necklace on him—no contingency spells there, then. *Good.*

The two exchanged a few passing blows, nothing serious, just a slow feeling out of the other's defenses. She could tell that Rory was pacing himself, not moving unless he had to, conserving his strength for an opportunity.

The two seemed evenly matched until Rory's blade slid along the outside of Matthew's upper arm, slicing through the elaborate jerkin as if it wasn't there. The material sagged heavily. The move left Rory's right lower half undefended for a second as he retracted his blade, and Matthew's wounded arm darted inside his jerkin to retrieve a second blade of his own; the dagger flicked with deadly precision into Rory's unprotected thigh. The elf staggered as his leg gave out but managed to right himself as he spun past the vampire instead of pulling back. Matthew anticipated a retreat and stepped forward, moving through Rory's threat range and earning a slash across the back for his mistake.

Rory hopped a second, trying to regain his balance as Matthew turned around to face him again. The elf decided to use his sword as a crutch, sticking the blade in the ground and pivoting around the cane on his good leg, his remaining short sword extended in a defensive stance.

As expected, Matthew lunged at what he assumed was a somewhat weakened foe, his sword scoring a hit against Rory's side as the elf used his blade to take another slice at the vampire's sleeve.

<<*What is he doing?*>>

Before Hannah could reply, Rory's plan became clear, Matthew's sleeve tore free from his shoulder, first curling down, then spilling forward, the heavy material wrapping around his sword hand, effectively tying up his weapon. Matthew moved to tug the piece of purple material free, but not before Rory had whipped the sword he had been using as a cane into Matthew's side, the blade sinking deep into the man's middle. Before Matthew could recover himself or his sword, Rory completed the move with his new sword, using his hips to spin around and lop off the vampire's head.

The body fell heavily to the ground, and Rory nearly followed him, catching himself at the last minute as his sword tip found purchase in the dirt. He wavered, pulled the dagger from his thigh, tossed it aside, and stood up straight. He lifted the sword from the ground, crossing both blades before his chest in salute, and bowed his head.

There was a stunned silence. Hannah wanted to scream in relief.

Then she caught motion out of the corner of Klauden's eye; her father was standing up. He held his hands out, looking as if he meant to give the signal for the guards to rush Rory and put him down, but instead he put his hands together, beginning a slow clapping that rushed through the spectators like wildfire. There were a few hoots of approval as Rory lifted his head and slowly approached the dais.

"My lord," he said, his voice a bit strained between heaving breaths, "I beg the boon promised by the code." He held a hand against his side, but Hannah could see the spreading stain of blood through his shirt. Matthew's hit had been solid.

Hannah was surprised that she couldn't feel Klauden's bloodlust. If she were sitting there near all that blood, that Elven blood, she would be fighting to control herself. Klauden hardly seemed to notice the blood at all.

Magnus narrowed his eyes, considering something. *Oh no*, Hannah thought with a pang of terror. *No.* She knew that look.

"And what would you ask of us, Master Elf?" The question was polite, the appearance of propriety with an undercurrent of malice that Hannah recognized. <<*He won't do it,*>> she understood. <<*He will never give me up.*>>

"That you uphold your end of the bargain." Rory's voice seemed a bit annoyed, as if he had not expected this formality and resented it.

"And what was that bargain?"

Now he was clearly annoyed. "I have bested your champion. You must give me what I ask for."

"What precisely do you want?"

"You know what I want," he retorted angrily, then took a breath, letting it out slowly. "I came for Hannah van Kreeosk. You will return her to me."

"Hannah is not here," Magnus replied smoothly. "Therefore, we cannot grant your immediate request." After a short beat of silence, Magnus added, "However, should you find Hannah again, she is yours. I relinquish all rights to my child and surrender all that is hers to you."

"Why you son of a—" Rory began, then caught himself. "You're lying. I know she is here. Give her to me." He tightened his grip on his swords again, eyes slowly taking in the landscape. Hannah knew he was calculating the odds of escape. <<*Klauden,*>> she thought slowly, <<*you have to stop him.*>>

<<*Stop what?*>>

<<*He's going to do something stupid! Stop him! Do something!*>>

She felt Klauden tense in his seat, the spell forming in his mind.

"I am afraid we cannot do that," Magnus replied. "I think you should be more concerned with your own fate than that of my daughter."

"I should have known. *Felcher.*" Hannah grimaced internally at his use of the Elven word for an oath breaker. He held both swords at his sides, all traces of formality gone from his demeanor. Apparently, the time for civility had passed. "Fine. If you won't give her to me, then I'll just have to take her."

He darted forward, clearly intending to leap over the arena wall and onto the dais, but before he had gotten three steps, Malbrek was speaking. Hannah watched the black bands appear around Rory's middle, the restraining circle that she had always called a Malbrek Special. Rory remembered that spell from their last encounter, however, and instantly stopped resisting, letting his body weight drag him to the ground and out of the trap.

The elf took another few steps as Malbrek sputtered, and Klauden spoke his own litany. Hannah felt the spell ripple out of him, a stream of controlled magic that was nothing like the wild maelstrom she was used to feeling when she cast. Rory froze in place for no apparent reason, his face a permanent scowl of determination. Hannah allowed herself a moment to appreciate the power of such a spell.

Magnus was looking at her, at them. "Well done, Klauden." He seemed surprised. "That was most effective." He glanced to his left and the pale-faced Malbrek. "Most effective," he repeated.

"My lord," Klauden acknowledged.

Magnus gestured to Rory, standing frozen below. "He will be held in the dungeons for now. I think he would make a fine fledgling. Perhaps you would enjoy the privilege of making him?" The last was directed at Klauden, who bowed his head in acceptance of the honor being bestowed upon him.

"I would, my lord."

Hannah screamed at him, << *You will not!* >>

"I thought you would, given the circumstances. Very well. After the ceremony, you shall be rewarded with some Elven blood. Perhaps that will make up for the trouble my daughter has caused."

"Thank you, my lord." Hannah hated Klauden at that moment, hated him with a ferocity that she had never anticipated, hated his subservience, his meekness, his willingness to accept whatever judgments her father made. As Magnus turned to leave, Klauden spoke once more, "My lord, I would ask a favor."

Magnus turned back, pleased. "Yes?" Malbrek was glaring at them from behind her father's back.

"May I see the elf to his cell?" Klauden asked. "I would speak to him."

Magnus laughed. "Very well. Just try not to kill him until *after* the ceremony."

Hannah watched her father walk away, signaling the end of the games, then tried to watch Rory out of the corner of Klauden's eyes as her friend turned to accept the congratulations of his parents.

XXIX

The dungeons were dark, but Hannah had always known that. *Didn't I go through these halls when making my escape months ago?* Still, the weight of the stone walls above them was palpable, the dank wetness overwhelming, and she was glad she wouldn't have to stay here long. She knew the thought was selfish since Rory would have to stay there, but she couldn't help herself. The place disturbed her.

She watched Rory as he walked before them, his movements tired and sore, the uneven gait caused by his wounded thigh making him lurch from side to side. She ached to reach out to help him, to offer her shoulder as a crutch to get him to the cell where he could sit. Klauden glanced at the three Kargin flanking them, sighed, and moved forward a few steps, shrugging underneath Rory's arm and helping him move a bit faster.

Hannah wished she could see the faces of the surrounding Kargin, but then ignored the impulse. They wouldn't comment; they were trained to stand by and be silent. Klauden would be fine. Rory rejected Klauden's aid at first, then relented when his leg gave out on the next step. Hannah thought he must be much more wounded than he let on to let a stranger help him, especially one of his captors.

It was good to feel Rory again, the strength in his muscles, the musky smell of his sweat, the scent of his blood, the pounding of his heart, the grimace that was halfway between pain and a rueful grin on his face a welcome reminder of what she loved in him. Because she did love him, she saw now; it had been foolish to leave him in the first place. She should have just bitten him and gotten it over with.

"Why are you helping me?" Rory asked as they limped down the hall, genuine curiosity in his voice.

"Because I haven't got all day to follow you to your cell," Klauden replied shortly as they rounded a corner and went jouncing down another flight of stone stairs.

At the bottom, Hannah watched as Klauden used his nightvision, the blackness dissolving into planes of gray and white as the light from above faded behind them. "Wait here," Klauden ordered the Kargin, and they paused at the foot of the stairs, arms at the ready.

Klauden helped Rory take the final steps to a cell with a thick barred door standing open, crossed the threshold and into the room, and settled the elf onto the stone bench against the wall. Rory's eyes moved around, but she knew he couldn't see anything in the darkness.

"You're lying to me," Rory said to the darkness. "I can tell, you know."

Hannah felt Klauden's scowl, knew he wanted nothing more than to leave this elf alone in the darkness for a very long time. But then she felt him subdue that desire, focusing instead on what Hannah needed to be done. "You are right, elf. I am lying."

"So, why help me, then? You're the one who cast the spell on me, right? Didn't your lord promise my blood to you? What do you care if I limp a little?"

Klauden waited a moment, thinking idly that it was no surprise Hannah liked this elf; he asked as many questions as she did. <<*They must make one another crazy with them.*>> "It's not about what I want," he said finally, and Hannah felt the heavy weight of the truth.

"Then, who?" Rory's gaze sank to the hand pressed against his leg as he winced, then jerked back up again, scanning the darkness. "Are you talking about Hannah? Is she here? Where is she?"

"She's safe for the time being, but she won't be for long." Hannah marveled that Klauden could keep his head with the scent of blood so thick in the air down here.

As she thought it, Klauden made a choice, put both hands on Rory's shoulders, concentrated, and spoke a brief slew of words. She felt the magic stream out of him into the elf, a perfectly controlled arc of power, and she felt the pull of jealousy, all thoughts of bloodlust forgotten. It never felt like that when she cast a spell. Klauden was so controlled in everything he did.

She recognized the healing spell from their lessons in the library beneath the castle. The ability to heal was not widespread among her people, whose natural metabolism allowed them to heal from most wounds, but Klauden had found it useful for keeping the human slaves healthy. Hannah had never bothered to learn any of it, even though it did require words like the rest of her magic. She couldn't imagine a time when it would come in useful. *Why would I have ever needed to heal a mortal?* She would have just ended the person's suffering and enjoyed a meal at the same time.

She had to marvel at how very much she had changed since she left this castle.

Rory allowed Klauden to finish his spell, the elf's hand against his leg pulling away as deft fingers felt for a wound that was no longer openly weeping. "Thanks." Rory looked up at the only thing he could probably see in the darkness, Klauden's glowing eyes, and cocked his head. "Why won't Hannah be safe for long? Where are they keeping her? What are they going to do to her?" Hannah didn't want to admit it, but she enjoyed the worry in those words, more proof of his feelings about her.

<<*What more proof do you require?*>> Klauden snapped. <<*He came all this way to fight for you. It's fairly obvious how he feels about you. Honestly.*>>

"It doesn't matter," Klauden said. "For now, all you need to know is that you should be ready. You need to rest up, get some sleep, and be ready for tomorrow."

"What's tomorrow?"

Klauden hesitated, and Hannah sensed that there was something he wasn't telling either of them, some plan buried deeply behind his walls. She started to pry, but an iron grip forced her back. "Well, you'll either be traveling through the mountains again, a feat which requires more energy than you have at the moment, or you'll be turned into my fledgling. Whichever way things turn out, you'll need your strength."

Rory accepted both possibilities with aplomb. "I'll be ready, then."

"Good." Klauden walked to the door and began to push it shut behind him.

"Who are you?" Rory's question hung in the darkness between them.

Klauden wished he could have at least disliked the elf, then spoke quietly, "I am called Klauden."

There was another pause, then, "I figured it was you. She spoke of you often, you know."

"Did she now?"

"Yeah. She cares for you a great deal." Hannah wished Klauden would look back at Rory so she could see his face, but he kept his gaze on the door instead.

"I am glad to hear it." Klauden slid the bar that locked the cell into place and headed back toward the stairwell and the waiting Kargin. Hannah didn't want to admit it, but the cold ball in her stomach was fading, replaced by a small blaze that might be hope.

XXX

When they finally reached Klauden's rooms, he shut the door carefully, whispering a soft spell to shield the place from prying eyes. Hannah was going to ask when he had started doing that, but the answer was obvious—since Malbrek had started to see him as a possible threat. She was comforted by the sight of his rooms, even the cluttered mass of papers that covered his workspace. Klauden walked to his desk and plopped down in the chair, hands automatically pushing the papers into a single pile.

Hannah caught a series of spells in a language she thought might be Ancient Elven, and a diagram involving a circle and a number of carefully drawn squares and angles. She wanted to ask what it was but sensed Klauden's fatigue and quelled her curiosity.

<<*I should leave you alone,*>> she thought. <<*It's been a long night.*>>

She felt more than heard Klauden's agreement. When he told her to concentrate, she did, and the next time she opened her eyes, she was staring at pink walls. She had a body again, her own remembered body, and she wrapped her arms around herself, relishing the feeling. A moment later, Klauden was standing before her, shoulders slumped and a thoughtful expression on his face.

"What?" she asked, aware at first of how loud her voice was, then how she was alone again, separate from Klauden and able to think her own thoughts without worry. It was a relief, but something in her also mourned the loss of their connection.

"There isn't much time."

"There never is. What will become of me?"

"To be honest, I don't know. Some say that you will retain your essence, others claim that the process causes irreversible changes in personality."

"Do you know who..." She tried again, her voice stronger this time. "Do you know whose body they plan on using?"

Hannah tried to think of available purebloods that her father would consider expendable. If the question was her blood, then making her a fledgling was out of the question, but Hannah couldn't think of where they had found a host. Unless they had made a body, conjured it whole through magical arts she had never conceived. *Didn't Keller mention something about researching a spell for Magnus?*

"Maybe you should sit down."

Well, that doesn't sound good. "More bad news? Look, why don't you just tell me everything all at once? That way I can stop thinking things are the worst they are going to get." At his look, she squatted, hands tracing patterns on the pink floor.

"Do you remember Anna?"

That made Hannah pause. Of course, she remembered Anna. How could she forget her father's daughter, the girl who hadn't quite been one of them, but hadn't been sent to live among the Kargin either? Then again, Neira van Joosen had been a pureblood herself, and that had made Anna one as well, second child or not; Hannah knew there had been quite a scandal when Ranik van Joosen had discovered that his mate had become her father's mistress, but no one had been willing to shun Magnus's second daughter. It had been settled when Hannah was still in swaddling clothes, but Anna had been raised in a semi-elite place, ever hovering on the lines between the first children and the Kargin. Hannah had always hated her father for that, for causing her own mother such pain at the betrayal she must have anticipated, then seeing the girl raised next to her own daughter... Then again, Hannah was realizing that she hated her father for a lot of things.

"I remember Anna." Hannah hadn't spoken about her half-sister in many years. Since the end of Essentials, when the nearly inseparable trio had gone their own ways, Hannah and Klauden to hours spent working with magic, and Anna off to study with the blades that matched her own skills. They hadn't been as close as they once were when the accident happened, but Hannah had still been scarred by the loss of her only female friend, a girl who was nearly her sister. Of course, Livenna was also her half-sister, but there had never been any warmth between them, not like the relationship she had with Anna. Livenna was clearly Kargin, half-blooded and lowly. *Besides*, Hannah thought, *Livenna is intolerable. Anna was my friend, my confidante.*

It hadn't been long after Anna's accident that Hannah's own mother had died. Barely ten years between the loss of both women in her life.

It was a disease of the blood, Hannah recalled. Infected strain of humans. Nothing to be done. She remembered the last time she had seen her mother, the short woman's bowed head as she walked into her chambers, Magnus and Malbrek standing at the door. They had ushered in a frightened human slave before shutting and barring the doors. They told her it was to keep the others safe. Her mother had to be isolated. The old explanation seemed thin now. The likelihood that a virus that affected an entire family of humans, a family that Malbrek had wiped out in the days following that morning, could have killed her mother was simply preposterous.

What was more likely: that my mother was infected, or that she was starved to death in a room with the human slave she had always been too kind to?

Hannah realized how foolish she had been, how blindly she had wanted to believe her father, and how she had wasted so much time worrying if the same virus would someday rise from her blood and claim her as well. It had all been lies. *And if they could lie about my mother, what kept them from lying about...?*

"She's not dead, is she?" When he nodded, she added, "You knew." She couldn't explain the betrayal she felt; it was too large to categorize. How could Klauden have lied to her, have listened to her cry for hours about the loss of their proverbial third wheel when he had known all along that she still lived? "Tell me," she whispered.

"There's not much to tell. There was an accident. She was severely wounded. Everyone expected her to die, but she didn't. Not exactly."

"What do you mean 'not exactly'?"

"Her body lived, but her mind... Well, it went somewhere else." He looked away. "They say she went mad."

"But why lie about it?"

He gave her a stern look. "Magnus van Kreeosk does not have daughters that go mad," he stated. "Or he didn't, until you ran away. People knew then that she hadn't died, but they only whispered it among themselves. But since you left, those whispers have become soft insistent voices worrying away at his control. You see why he had to do it."

The sad thing was that Hannah could see perfectly. She knew what her father had to do to stay in control of his House. She knew what he was willing to do to keep things in line. Hadn't she heard her mother screaming through the locked doors? Still, there was Klauden's betrayal to consider. "How could *you* not tell me?"

He shook his head, kneeling before her. "Do you remember how you were, Hannah?" He reached out to touch her sleeve, the rough material of the sweater pinched in his fingers. "You were not like this." He sat back. "You certainly wouldn't have dressed like this, that's for sure."

"So what? I had a fashion sense. Maybe I was a bit spoiled. But did that give you the right to keep such secrets from me?"

"Would you have wanted to know?"

"Of course!"

He smiled. "Please, chaivin. The second you found out only one of these secrets you decided to run away. There was no way you would have stayed if you had known everything."

"You should have trusted me."

"It wasn't a matter of trust, and you know it." He took her hand in his grip. "You've grown strong in your months away from home. You've changed so much that I hardly recognize you."

"I'm still me," she insisted, placing both hands in his. "I'm still that girl."

He shook his head ruefully. "Yes and no."

"What should I do?"

"Don't you know?"

She shook her head.

"You don't even have a plan?" He leaned back, hands still holding hers. "I am amazed. Truly. The girl who always had a plan for everything, including how to get out of every single obligation we ever had, has not even a ghost of an idea of how to get out of this one."

"Don't mock me," she said, a bit hurt by his attitude.

"I'm not." He lifted her hands to his face, kissing each as cordially as possible. "We would have made a fine couple, you and I, but that's not in your future anymore."

He pulled her to her feet. "Then what is?" she asked, confused by the sudden take-charge attitude he was displaying.

"The ceremony will go forward as planned. That I cannot change. But there is hope."

"What is it?"

"You will be placed in Anna's body. She's not very strong, and she won't fight you at all. It shouldn't be too difficult to hold onto yourself during the transfer." Hannah wanted to ask about her one-time sister, wanted to know what really had happened to her, but he was still speaking. "When the ceremony is over, you must pretend to submit. You will still be yourself, but you must convince them that you have been purified, that you are willing to reform your ways and become a perfect pureblood." She wanted to ask how he expected her to do that, but again, he was moving on. "They will watch you closely for a time, but eventually they will let down their guard. That's when you can escape again. You remember how to do it, don't you?"

Hannah looked at him. "*That's* your plan?"

Klauden crossed his arms before his chest. "You have a better idea?"

"What happens to Rory?"

Klauden shrugged. "If I can't get him to leave you, I'll make him into a fledgling. When you leave, you can take him with you."

"What? You can't do that!"

"You would rather I kill him, then?"

"You can't do that either!"

"So, you have a better idea?" He cocked his head at her silence. "Do you?"

Hannah stood perfectly still. No matter how she looked at it, Klauden's solution was the only feasible answer. *Maybe I can talk to Rory, get him to see reason and leave before Klauden has to turn him. But how? My father will never let me talk to him. And how can I just allow myself to take over my half-sister's body? Where have they been keeping Anna all these years? What kind of life has she known? Klauden said she wouldn't put up a fight; what does that mean?* It was all too much, all at once.

She wanted to scream but settled for running a ragged hand through her hair and over her face, scrubbing the skin that seemed so real in this magical place.

"What is it that you really want, chaivin?"

She looked at Klauden, eyes brimming with tears. "I don't know anymore." She wiped her face. "No, that's not true. I know exactly what I want." She looked at him, hands on her hips, bare feet squared with her shoulders. "I want to live a normal life away from this place. I want a body that I don't have to steal from a sister I thought was dead. I want Rory to escape without being bitten, to live his life the way he was meant to."

"With you, you mean."

"Maybe," she agreed. "If he wanted. If I could somehow manage to not turn him..." She shook her head. "But it doesn't matter anyway. None of that will happen now. I'll get pushed into Anna's body, and maybe I'll even become what they wanted me to. I'll stay and become your mate, and the precious bloodlines will be preserved, and I won't think of poor Rory fighting his way through the tournaments every night. He'll live, of course, I know he will, and you'll take his strength and become even more powerful among our kind. My father will respect you, and one day, you'll replace Malbrek, maybe you'll even replace my father, and then Rory will be your Malbrek, a bloodthirsty fledgling with no memory of me or what I might have meant to him centuries before." She could see it quite clearly, a future that shouldn't be so bad, a life that involved surviving with a body, a possibility that should make her happy. There was a time, not so long ago, when such a road would not have been a problem at all. But now...

She looked at Klauden, realizing how much that future would suit his purposes. "And maybe one day you'll lock me in a room with a blood disease, and no one will hear my screams."

He looked hurt, the expression crossing his face and fleeing, leaving only a blank surface behind. But she could see the feelings lingering in his eyes. "I wouldn't do that."

"Of course, you wouldn't. Not now. But see how much I've changed in a few months? Think of what you could become in a few years, decades. Think of what it would be like, living all your days knowing that I had loved another first, and that other would always be there, lingering, maybe even hovering on my mind the way he would stay in yours. You do know the links between master and fledgling, don't you? You would never be free of him." She sniffed, wiping her eyes. "No, Klauden. It wouldn't be long before you were just like my father."

He stared at her for a long moment, then took three steps toward her. He wasn't a warrior, but he could still move quickly when he chose, and his grip on her wrists was firm. "No." He shook her, moving her arms to emphasize the word. "I would *not*." He pulled her close, the movement sharp and sudden, her feet tangling over themselves as she collided with his chest. "I love you, Hannah." She stared at him, at his use of her name, at the sudden longing on his face, at the words that neither had dared to speak before. There was no talk of love in her father's castle. Still, he had lied to her. He was still her father's lackey.

"And my father loved my mother," she reminded him.

He jerked back as if she had slapped him, hands releasing her wrists. He seemed about to say something, then bit his tongue, considering. "Hannah," he finally said in a low voice, "no." He stepped away from her, hands folding across his chest, his face a mask of control. "Your father wanted your mother. He never loved her. He has never loved anything in his life." He gave her a searching look. "I would have thought you knew that by now."

"Klauden," she began, but he cut her off.

"No. Don't say anything else, chaivin. I know where you stand." He backed up a few paces. He pressed his hands together as if he would begin the spell that would allow him to leave, then lanced her with his glare. "I know you may find it hard to believe, but I really do love you, fool that you are, and I have since we were children. I always thought to spend my life with you, and I was thankful for the opportunity." His lip quivered. "And, much as it pains me to know how little you think of me, I still hope that your elf deserves you."

She said his name again, suddenly sorry for everything she had said. It had been cruel, and he hadn't deserved her scorn or her suspicions. He had gone out of his way to help her, even risked his life for her sake on more than one occasion. Before she could explain, he put his hands back together, whispered the spell, and faded from sight.

XXXI

Hannah looked up at the sound of her name. She was sitting in the middle of the floor, forgotten tears running down her face as she tried to figure the exact moment when she had gone wrong. It didn't matter anyway. She was here, and no thinking could undo her present predicament.

The voice was familiar, but she couldn't place it.

"Hello?" she asked, standing up. She walked to the window, concentrated, and looked out. The pink mist swirled and faded.

She was staring at a familiar face. Yet, it wasn't familiar at all. The face was the same as her memory recalled, the small nose, the sharp chin, the brown eyes all surrounded by the same dark brown locks, but the expression was all wrong. It was the look of an idiot, a blank-faced drooling fool without a mind, a body that lived but wasn't controlled by anything or anyone.

It was Anna.

And she had obviously gone mad.

Klauden said there would be no resistance. She tried to see around the face, to discern the layout of the room beyond her half-sister's face, knowing that Malbrek was probably holding the gem before the body. Time was very short.

Am I going to do this, then? Am I going to steal a body? She didn't know what would happen if she refused. Maybe she really would die.

She could hear the spell now, the chanting words echoing off the walls of the prison, filling her head. She had a moment to think, *I'm not ready yet*, and then she was being turned inside out.

She remembered the wrenching pain from before, the agony that threatened to twist her apart, and she thought she probably screamed, but there was no sound. She could hear Klauden's voice as he controlled the spell, got a vague sense of self that she gathered about her mind like a shield, and prepared to be dumped into an empty vessel. Any life was better than this emptiness.

At least with a body I can kill Malbrek, she thought clearly, preparing to leap at the man holding the gem before her new body as soon as she could. Her anger gave her purpose, focused her soul into a tight knot that would not break under pressure. *I'll kill him*, she thought. *Maybe I'll get away and free Rory, or maybe Klauden will do it*. Either way, the magician had to die.

She could see the body before her, a kneeling form held in place by Malbrek's strong hand on its shoulder. Concentrating on holding herself together, she assumed that the pain of re-entry would probably be something like being pulled out. She realized that she had become something like a ghost, her body outlined in dim light before Anna, a trail of glowing light still attached to the spinning gem dangling from Malbrek's other hand.

She was close enough to reach out and touch her half-sister. She focused all of her energy and was about to move to the vessel when something shifted. Suddenly, instead of heading toward the kneeling figure on the floor, her essence was slipping deftly to the side, as neatly diverted as water poured onto a spoon instead of into the bowl, and she felt a connection with solid flesh with a crash. There was a struggle, a tangle of battling wills as she sensed that this host was not quite so pliable as Anna had been, and she fought to keep hold.

There was a series of negations, an overwhelming disbelief that someone could defile her body in this way, then Hannah was gaining the upper hand. She could feel a body again, the weight of it crushing against her spirit, the cold air dimpling what was her new skin, a wracking spasm that shook her chest in a series of coughs. The person whose body she had stolen was weakening, the voice growing quieter every second as Hannah's own awareness of the form was growing. She took stock, determined to hold onto this body, no matter what. Her knees hurt as if they'd been scraped and bruised raw. Her arms were tired, a muscle soreness that probably resulted from carrying something heavy, and she could feel the congestion in her chest, a sickness that made it hard to breathe.

Whose body is this?

She opened her new eyes, listening for the inhabitant's voice and hearing nothing, then looked around. She was kneeling on the ground, her bare knees aching from the contact with the cold stone floor.

Cold, she thought with delight. *I feel cold. Amazing!* She could see a worn sleeveless dress covering a much ampler bosom than the one she had before, and scrawny arms that clutched at her sides. She fell back onto her butt, coughing harder. She saw that her feet were bare, the toes covered in dirt. There was a hand on her back, and someone whispered in the language of the slaves, "Easy, Solyn. Take a breath. It will pass."

Hannah motioned that she was fine but coughed again for show. *Solyn? The slaves? What the hell happened?* She coughed once more, allowing the movement to turn her head to the right, hopefully the center of the room. She knew they would be in Cairn's Temple, but this was a new perspective for her, the upper levels where the slaves were permitted to watch the festivities.

The circle below was mayhem. Everyone was shouting. Hannah tried to get a sense of what had happened. Clearly, Klauden had sent her into this body instead of Anna's. *But why is my body up here with the slaves?*

Her eyes sought him out in the chaos below, heard his calm explanation as Malbrek sputtered accusations. "The ceremony was a success," he was saying, pointing at Anna's still form. "Hannah is in there. Somewhere."

"Liar! Something went wrong! I felt it go wrong!" That was Malbrek shouting, the pink pendant still in his grasp and flinging back and forth as he gestured at Klauden. Magnus silenced them both with a gesture.

He turned to Klauden. "What happened?"

"I told you there was a chance that the soul might not withstand the transformation intact." Klauden was calm, the patient scholar explaining the results of an experiment gone awry with foreseen complications.

When Magnus nodded, he said, "She went in there. We saw it happen." He walked over to Anna, touched her cheek gently, and spoke softly. Hannah couldn't hear what he said. It seemed this new body couldn't hear very well. Hannah hoped it was because of the sickness lodged in its chest. She forced a cough, aware of the attention of the people around her. *Other slaves*, she thought slowly. *I'm standing with them.*

A horrible thought struck her then, and she lost interest in the rest of Klauden's explanation. She looked down at her plain dress, taking in her dirty hands and the familiar way the hand on her back rubbed comfort against her coughs.

He didn't. He couldn't.

She stood up on wobbly legs, smiling weakly at the man whose hand was still on her shoulder. "Are you alright, Solyn?" he asked again.

Hannah found her new voice. "I am well," she said, hoping that she had the words right. The voice of this body was lower in pitch than hers had been.

The slave before her said, "It is time for us to go, you know."

She looked around, noting the small doorway that marked the slave's entrance and exit from the Temple. "Go where?" she asked.

He shushed her, taking her hand in his calloused grip, and began leading her away. It took her a moment to find her feet, noting that this body was balanced quite differently from her own, having less strength in the arms and more weight on the chest. She reached up with her free hand to touch her hair, noting the coarseness of long snarls that had not been washed in eons. She also became aware of a low musky smell that must also be coming from this body.

I'm a slave, she thought stupidly. *Klauden made me a human. What the hell was he thinking?*

The man led her down several flights of stairs. Hannah followed along meekly, trying to map out their path in her mind. At first, she was sure he was going to take her to the slave's quarters behind the kitchen, but he passed the cooking fires without a glance, heading down another stairwell into the storerooms below. Hannah's mouth watered. She was thirsty too—but not for blood.

"Where are we going?" she asked her companion, noting the rank smell that was wafting off of him as well. *Did the slaves always smell bad?* She couldn't remember, but she didn't think so.

The man shushed her again, leading them past rows and rows of stored food and casks of ancient wine. They scurried down another hallway, then stopped abruptly before a wooden door. The wall sconces were lit, and Hannah could see the condensation that meant they were far below ground. The man released her hand to open the door and led her inside, barring the door behind them. Hannah could see a single candle burning on a table in the center of the small room. A bag rested next to it, and the man walked over to it and dumped its contents unceremoniously on the tabletop. Hannah approached cautiously, her arms wrapping around herself against the chill. *Are mortals always this cold?*

Sudden smells assaulted her nostrils, and her stomach clenched. The man picked up a chunk of what looked like bread in the dim light and waved it in her direction.

"Eat," he commanded. "He said you would need to eat."

Hannah wanted to ask who had said but was distracted by the surge in her gut as she took a bite of the bread. It was delicious! She wolfed down the piece, then helped herself to the cheese the man pushed toward her. She was sucking the last drops of what tasted like wine from the water-skin when a sound caught her attention. The man stood up, back against the barred door, and Hannah watched as a section of the wall beside the table slid away.

Secret panel, she thought dully, wiping her mouth. *Am I in shock?* It wasn't too hard to believe, given recent events. When a shape passed through the new opening, Hannah knew she should be on her feet, finding a weapon and defending herself, and in her mind, she was doing all of that, but in reality, her new body sat there instead, stifling a wet burp with a dirty hand.

"Hi," she said as Klauden's face swam into view in the candlelight. The man near the door fell to one knee in the customary pose of slaves before their masters. Klauden took in her dirty dress and filthy hands, then approached the kneeling slave. He tapped the man on the shoulder, the signal to rise, then smiled as the man obeyed.

"You did well, Kar," he congratulated in the slave's tongue, then lunged forward to bite his neck. Hannah watched in horror as the body first stiffened in resistance, then sagged in defeat as Klauden ended the slave's life. *It is a fascinating display to watch a vampire feed,* she thought idly, then considered whether the thought had been entirely her own. *Where exactly did this body's host go?*

"Why did you do that?" she asked, surprised at the calm tone of her voice, when Klauden laid the body on the floor.

Klauden looked at her, cocking his head to one side, then wiped his mouth, sniffing at his hands in distaste. "I couldn't risk him telling anyone about this, could I?"

Hannah, aware of the resistance her hair made as the rough strands tangled around her neck, only said, "I see."

Klauden walked toward the table, stopping just before he reached her. "How are you?"

"Fine," she replied. "Just fine. Considering I've been made into a human. Why did you do it?" When Klauden didn't answer, she asked, "*How* did you do it?"

"Isn't this what you wanted?"

She coughed. "You couldn't find a healthier slave?"

Klauden gave her a look. "It's nothing a little food and warm clothing won't cure."

"What about the others? Won't they know what you've done?"

"They think your soul split apart during the transfer. That you're trapped somewhere inside Anna."

"Is that a good thing?"

He shrugged. "Well, at least they'll take better care of her from now on."

She looked at him, her mind straining under the events of the last few moments. "Why didn't you tell me?"

Klauden gave her a long look. "Would you have wanted to know?" he asked quietly.

Hannah honestly didn't know how to reply. Her instinct was to say yes, of course, she wanted to know the plan, but if she had known, would she have gone along with it? She hadn't been entirely willing to occupy a mostly empty body; would she have consented to steal a body, a human body at that, from an unwilling person? She focused on something she was certain of instead.

"What happens now?"

XXXII

Hannah followed Klauden through the tunnels that led toward the dungeons. She was wearing a new dress, the long-sleeved black material covering a clean slip, the boots on her feet the right size and made for crossing the mountains. Her hair had been managed, the snarls combed out by a gentle Klauden who maneuvered the entire mess into a long braid that hung just below her shoulder blades. She was trying to get used to the body, the way it moved. The calloused hands possessed a decent grip, she discovered, as she held the pommel of Rory's sword. She was wearing his weapon's belt, the blade a heavy, unbalanced weight around her hips but entirely covered by one of Klauden's black hooded cloaks.

Klauden had been well prepared for this, Hannah realized when she saw the tub of steaming waters in his bedroom. He led her through the tunnels and through several secret compartments before reaching his rooms and allowing her to clean up, then set about arming and preparing her for a long trip. The backpack she wore was filled with food, an extra set of clothes, his hairbrush, and a warm blanket. He had given her a dagger as well, knowing her skill with the weapon, but had decided on only one blade when she tried to throw with her new body. Apparently, Solyn wasn't one for dagger tossing. That would take some practice. The longsword had been more comfortable, the hands knowing how to hold the pommel, the blade not too heavy in her grip.

They waited some time before leaving Klauden's rooms again, ducking out through the secret panels that they had used as children and making their way through the tunnels to Rory's cell. They hadn't spoken much, Hannah too overwhelmed by her new body and its implications, and Klauden obviously preoccupied with making her escape.

She watched him as he led the way down the corridor, his steps silent in comparison to her clunky boots. This body had never learned to move silently, that was for sure. Hannah tried to move softly but couldn't. Eventually, she settled for moving quickly, hoping that any sound she made would pass before anyone would pay attention and sound the alarm.

She asked Klauden where everyone thought he was, and he explained how the ceremony had exhausted him and he needed his rest. Hannah observed that his failure had done double duty, both freeing her while removing him as a threat to Malbrek's position. Magnus wouldn't want a wizard who couldn't manage a simple soul transfer ceremony. Still, she feared for Klauden's safety, knowing that her father did not view failure very well. Klauden would have to be very careful not to disappoint her father again.

They were approaching the dungeons, the smell of decay and mold assaulting Hannah's new nostrils. This body certainly had a sensitive nose. She tried to ignore the scent and followed after Klauden. He slowed as they turned a corner and descended some stairs. She recognized the place. This was where he had left Rory in his dungeon.

Klauden turned around with a finger to his lips, then put up three fingers and motioned to the bottom of the stairs. Three guards, Hannah understood. Shrugging off the pack and laying the cloak on top, she slid the longsword from the scabbard, relieved that Rory always took such good care to oil the blade so that there was no sound. She settled her body weight, then followed Klauden to the landing. She was glad to hear no sound from her awkward feet.

Klauden took the first one by surprise, snapping his neck in a swift movement she would not have expected from her scholarly companion. She took the advantage of surprise as well, spearing one through the back, then pulling the sword free as he fell forward with a groan. The remaining Kargin stood paralyzed for a second, then reached for his own blade. The hesitation cost him as Hannah stepped on the fallen guard and used his body as a springboard to fling herself into the last guard. She hit him hard, catching his arms in her own and preventing him from freeing his blade. For a moment, she was sure she had him, but then he seemed to remember himself and his training as he easily pushed her aside. He was so strong! He wrapped one arm around her shoulders, spinning her around and holding her in front of his body as a shield. He began to back up, eyes on Klauden as he headed for the stairs.

She thought a moment, had an idea, and prayed it would work. She whispered the words softly, the spell building more slowly than she was used to, but the magic still spilled out of her, the ice encasing first his arm, then slipping up to enclose his shoulders and head. She wrenched free from his frozen grasp, watching as the spell spread, the ice covering every inch of the Kargin's body. Slowly, she picked up Rory's fallen sword, about to run him through, when Klauden walked in front of her and snapped the guard's neck through the ice with a resounding *pop*. Hannah stood uncertainly, adrenaline making her feel weak and giddy.

She could still cast spells. It had worked.

She had nearly been killed by one of the Kargin. This body was so weak.

"Come," Klauden demanded, grabbing her arm and propelling her forward into the darkness. She stood where he left her, listening as he opened the door to a cell somewhere in the distance, a muffled grunt and a "What—?" bringing her back to reality as she heard more shuffling and movement.

She spoke without thought, the spell working instantly—*Did I get better at this?*—a ball of light hovering just behind her right ear. The cell door was open and inside were two bodies wrestling on the dirty floor.

"Stop that," she demanded, approaching the opening and allowing some of her light to enter the room.

Both men covered their eyes as they sat up, pulling apart. Klauden began brushing the front of his robes as though Rory had somehow gotten him dirty.

"What the...?"

Rory, she thought, relief spilling through her at the elf's voice. He sounded so much healthier than yesterday. *Was it only yesterday?*

"Not so much light," Klauden ordered, getting to his feet and squinting at her. Hannah concentrated, redirecting the light to where it would help her and Rory's sight and not interfere with Klauden's nightvision.

"What the hell is going on?" Rory asked, blinking a bit as he stood up. "Who is this?" he asked, motioning to Hannah. "And why is she wearing my sword?" He looked at Klauden, who stood, brushing off his robes with annoyance. "Oh, it's you. What happened?"

"You would think I was the only one with ability to think around here with the way you two ask questions," he snapped, glaring at Hannah. "I think you deserve one another."

Rory seemed about to say something else, then stopped, head cocking as he looked at Hannah. His eyes narrowed, and he walked slowly toward her. She held her ground, wondering what his reaction would be to her new body, to her humanity, to her presence in the first place. "Who are you?" he asked slowly, his gaze taking in the weapon, the new curves of her hips and breasts, then settling on her eyes. "I know you," he said finally, a hand reaching out to touch her cheek. "Do I?"

Hannah tried not to breathe, realized it was a necessity with this body, and bent over with a coughing spasm.

"She's not well," Rory said, a gentle hand patting her back. "Why is she here?" The last was directed at Klauden she saw as she straightened up, wiping her mouth.

"Don't be a fool," Klauden snapped, then shook his head in the classic oh-forget-it-you'll-never-understand-anything look and strode past her toward the stairs. She was about to ask him where he was going when Rory looked at her again.

He moved to touch her face, then asked, "May I?" When she nodded, he placed both hands on her cheeks, staring intently into her eyes. "I know you," he repeated. Hannah noticed movement out of the corner of her eyes, then heard Klauden drop her backpack next to her feet. He placed the cloak around her shoulders, allowing Rory to tie the front closed. The elf looked at the vampire over her shoulder. "How is this possible?"

"Magic," she heard Klauden say, felt the rush of his breath against her ear.

"Is it really you?" Rory asked, eyes focusing on her again.

She was not quite able to speak.

"I thought I'd never see you again."

She wanted to say that he wouldn't *see* her again, not in her old body, but it didn't seem appropriate. She found her voice. "Then why did you come here?" It seemed once she opened her mouth, she couldn't stop the words. "You almost got yourself killed. What kind of hero are you trying to be, you idiot? I told you not come here, didn't I?" She was opening her mouth for another barrage, but Rory cut her off with a kiss. Hannah felt Klauden's hands release her shoulders as Rory's arms went around her back. It was a brief meeting of their mouths, but it was enough to shut her up.

"Are you alright?" he asked, taking a step back and looking her over again.

"As well as I can be," she replied, "for a human."

"It's still you though, right?" He looked at Klauden. "What about the girl who..." His voice trailed off as he tried to find the right words.

Klauden shook his head. "She is gone." At both Hannah and Rory's horrified look, he added, "Sleeping, if you prefer."

"What if she wakes up?" Hannah whispered, searching her mind for that other voice.

Klauden said, "Then we will put her back to sleep. It is not something that needs to be resolved today."

Rory gave the vampire a long look, calculating, but then turned his attention to the bodies on the floor, obviously assessing the current situation instead. "How do we get her out of here?"

Hannah turned around to see Klauden's chin gesturing deeper into the mountains. "She knows the way. Stay off the trails and mind the goblins. You remember. You did it before."

"Yes," Hannah said, nodding. She looked at Rory, taking in his ragged clothing and dirty face. It would be cold in the passes by now. She looked at Klauden. "He needs warmer clothes."

"He also needs his weapon back. Give him his belt."

"Oh!" Hannah exclaimed, remembering the weight on her hips. She began untying the belt and handing him the weapon as Klauden walked farther into the gloom. Hannah could only see a pair of glowing red eyes making their way back toward them as he returned. *Is that how I used to look?*

He was holding something, another backpack, Hannah realized, along with a sack of some sort. As he neared them, he set the backpack on the ground and began pulling clothing out of the sack. He tossed them to Rory in slow succession, watching expressionless as the elf first donned the heavy long-sleeved shirt over his stained white one, arranged his weapon's belt across his hips, then added a thick hooded cloak and a pair of leather gloves to the ensemble. Klauden took in the elf's new gear with a practiced eye, settling at last on the scuffed boots.

"I couldn't find a pair that would fit you. Those will have to do."

"They've done well so far," Rory said, testing out the movement of his clothes before strapping on the backpack that Klauden handed him. "They'll get us out of here."

Hannah arranged her own pack, noting her lack of a suitable weapon and hoping she stumbled upon something this body could use fairly soon. She looked at Klauden, who stood there with his hands clasped before him. "You're very prepared," she said, thinking of just how much thought he must have put into this little escape plot. "You knew."

"I hoped," he admitted.

Rory offered him a hand. "Thank you," he said as Klauden accepted the gesture, hands bobbing up and down in the age-old parting of male equals. "I hope I can repay you someday."

Rory took a few steps down the hallway, pausing when he reached the edge of her circle of light. Hannah knew he was giving them as much privacy as he could. She looked at Klauden, emotions swirling in her congested chest. She wasn't angry at him anymore, didn't hate him, couldn't fault him for anything, and she was feeling quite guilty. He had done so much to ensure her safety, her happiness, and she had never really thanked him, never really believed that he hadn't betrayed her in at least one way, if not many.

What it came down to was simple—Klauden was still a vampire, a pureblooded van Sherinak, and he always would be subject to the ploys of power and betrayal that thrived in her father's castle. She couldn't blame him for surviving.

"Klauden," she breathed, knowing that she would never be able to say what she wanted.

"Hannah," he replied, arms carefully crossed.

"Thank you just doesn't seem like enough."

"It is."

"Fine. Thank you. For everything."

"Go, chaivin." He gestured to Rory, his face shifting a bit as if he concealed some great emotion. "Time is short."

"I know." She tried to think of what to say. Their last parting hadn't been quite so difficult. "Be careful," she settled for saying, taking a step toward him. She wanted to hug him but didn't know if he would allow her to get so close to him.

Looking at his face as he slowly worked his lower lip, she shook her head, took two steps, and wrapped her arms around his frail frame. "<I loved you too,>" she whispered into the front of his robe, lapsing into the tongue of their youth. When his arms returned the embrace, pulling her against his chest, she looked up, memorizing the lines and angles of his face. "<You know that, right?>"

When she tilted her head back again, closing her eyes, he didn't ignore the offer, accepting her soft kiss with a delicate formality that thrilled her new human body. His lips were cool. She moved from his lips to his cheek, whispering, "<I always thought it would be you.>" She felt him nod in understanding, then he pushed her gently away.

"<Go, chaivin. Live.>"

She stepped back, nodding her head in the formal parting gesture of her people, then restrained the urge to sob when he tapped her shoulder, the signal that released her from his presence. "<I will,>" she whispered and walked quickly past him to where Rory stood in the hallway. The elf was looking carefully away from her, studying the layout of the wall and ceiling as she approached.

He took her hand without a word and started to lead her down the hall.

"Wait!"

Hannah looked back to see Klauden approaching, something held in both hands. He thrust the short sword at her as soon as he got in range, the scabbard decorated by three vertical symbols, the mark of Klauden's people, his family. It was his sword, the one he'd earned by right of being the First Son but had never really learned to use beyond the basics.

"I can't take your sword," Hannah said, trying to hand the blade back to him.

Rory was looking back and forth between them.

"Yes, you can," Klauden insisted, pushing the blade firmly into her hands. "You must." He looked to Rory. "It will be dangerous. She will need a weapon. Tell her."

Rory seemed to size up the weapon, Hannah's new arms, and Klauden's determined face. "He's right, Hannah. You should take it."

"You deserve it," Klauden added.

Hannah acquiesced, knowing both men spoke the truth. She slid the scabbard onto her belt, reassured by the weight there.

The next time they started down the corridor, Klauden did not call out again. Hannah did not look back.

XXXIII

It took them the better part of five days to clear the outlying defenses of her father's castle, and Hannah learned just how frustrating a human body could be. The girl must have had some endurance, Hannah had noted, but the chest cold combined with the general frailty of a mortal coil made their progress a lot slower than it should have been. It seemed like Hannah was hurting herself at every turn, here a sliced elbow against a rock as they climbed around a corner, there a nearly twisted ankle from a pile of loose rock. Hannah was amazed that Rory hadn't abandoned her useless self in the passes.

They had made it through, however, unseen and mostly unscathed, and now they stood in the foothills, the sheltering treetops of the endless forest below them, a stinging breeze blowing their hair away from tired faces.

"We should find some shelter nearby," Rory said, head cocked as he considered the weather. "I think it might snow tonight."

Hannah scanned the foothills for a likely shelter. They could probably find a cave somewhere to hole up in.

Rory headed off down the slope of the hill, and Hannah followed him. A thorough search revealed a small opening behind a group of pine trees, and after he determined that nothing else was using the space at present, Rory crawled inside, dragging their packs and then Hannah in after him. The inside was cozy, but still big enough to stand up in, with a wide enough base to build a fire against one wall and a bed against the other. Hannah began sweeping up the dead leaves that covered the floor, marking out a firepit with a few large stones and pushing up the dirt to form an embankment. She considered using a spell to light it, then settled for finding flint and steel. There wasn't any in her bag, so she tugged Rory's closer, untying the clasp and pulling out the few items on top.

She had put aside a waterskin, a blanket, and a packet of candles when she came upon the book. Pausing, she flipped open the cover, amazed to see Klauden's spidery handwriting on the first page, "Chaivin, so that you will not forget." Then in smaller writing on the bottom: "Always remember to study." Her eyes welled with tears, and she wiped them quickly, marveling at the clear liquid on her fingers. She hadn't cried so easily before.

Rory noticed her discovery and sat down, leaning against the wall as he looked at her.

"How?" she asked, motioning to the book.

He looked down, his face darkening. "We found your body," he explained. "I took what I could before heading north."

"What else was there?" she asked, glancing back at the bag, still a bit uncomfortable with this talk of her corpse.

He sat up, tugging the bag toward him. He rummaged, then withdrew her bowl, the silver runes clear in the fading light; her mirror, the polished surface gleaming; and then two daggers. "I couldn't find anything else," he explained, pushing the items toward her. He seemed to remember something and tugged his necklace over his head. "I believe this belongs to you."

Hannah took the ring slowly, considering. She knew what this ring meant for Klauden, but she just couldn't bring herself to throw it away. She tried to put it on her middle finger. It wouldn't go beyond her knuckle. She slipped it back onto the chain and handed it back to Rory. "Why don't you wear it?"

"Are you sure? It is your ring."

"I know. I want you to wear it." She felt the heat rising in her face a little and looked away. She still didn't know if he meant to stay with her; she was in a different body after all—maybe he didn't like blondes. She shook the thought away and looked back at the pile of things she had assumed were lost. "What happened?" she asked.

"I woke up and you were gone." He gave her a dark look. "Please don't do that again." He slipped the necklace over his head, tucking it beneath his shirt. "We can at least talk about it first."

"And?" she prompted.

"I went downstairs to find the others. I had your map and—"

She interrupted him. "My what?"

"The map."

"What map?"

He gave her a concerned look. "The map you left me. Are you alright, Hannah?"

"I didn't leave you a map," she insisted. "I left you a note."

"A note?" he shook his head. "I didn't get a note. I got a very detailed map to the castle, including trails to avoid and where the other Houses held their ambushes."

"What?"

"What do you mean 'what'?"

"Where did it come from?"

"I thought you left it for me. You didn't?"

"No. I wouldn't leave you a map. Why would I?" She knew the answer to that question. Who else would have the power to make a map take the place of her foolish words on a page of magical parchment in a book that he had crafted? Klauden had been helping her even then. *Who am I to deserve such loyalty?*

"I didn't know," he said, leaning back again and pulling her back into the conversation. "We found your body, what was left of it. I was very angry."

"I bet," she said, the words slipping out before she could stop them. "What then?"

"I headed north. I was looking for Malbrek," he said.

"What about the others? Did you find Jamison?"

Rory frowned at her. "Jamison? No." He sighed. "Though it was odd to fight his brother. There's a story there, I imagine. I guess that explains why he was so suspicious of you."

Hannah had wanted to hear that Jamison was dead, but then something inside her resisted, hoping instead that he had lived. It was a strange feeling, Hannah noted. Maybe it was mercy.

"He and Molly were gone before I even woke up. Lira and Gorn went to find them, and I went to seek you." Hannah wondered if he knew Jamison had betrayed her and assumed that the elf did not know. They had a lot to talk about.

"What made you think I wasn't dead?" she asked.

"It's my Knack," he said, as if that explained everything.

"Your what?" she said, nonplussed.

He grinned. "Most elves have a talent, a Knack. Some can walk the spirit worlds when they dream. I'm not so good at it, but I can manage when I want to."

"What does that even mean?" That was something none of the old tales had mentioned.

"I looked for you," he said simply. "I hunted everywhere I could think of, and then I got to thinking that maybe you weren't dead. I'd seen what magic Malbrek could wield, and I asked myself if he could have used that somehow to trap you." He shrugged, face reddening a bit. "I was desperate." He shook his head. "Lira thought I was crazy, of course, but she let me go. I think she thought it would clear my head or something."

"Caganasti," Hannah whispered, remembering the dream.

"Yes, my old friend Caganasti, renowned dreamwalker. He showed me the way, and I finally found you. That was all I needed to know to follow the map and get you back."

Hannah sat for a minute, hands numbing in the growing cold. "But why?"

He gave her a searching look, then glanced at her hands as they rubbed one another. "You're cold. Let me start that fire."

"I'm fine," she said but moved to let him use the flint and steel. When the fire was crackling nicely and the small cave was quite warm, Hannah settled herself on the blanket next to Rory. She could hear his breathing, but that was all. No pulse of a heartbeat, no echo of blood calling to her. He was just warm and alive and right next to her, and she really wanted to touch him. This body may be weak, but it certainly had its perks.

"It's so strange to be here," she said, staring at the uneven bumps of the cave's ceiling.

"I know," he said, "but we'll be on our way when the snow stops." Hannah rolled onto her belly, staring out the cave's opening to see the small whirls of ice spin to the ground.

"That's not what I mean." She rolled onto an elbow to look at him. "I mean, who am I now? What should I call myself? Hannah? Solyn? Something different altogether?"

Rory rolled onto his own side, a hand perched against the side of his head, his ears clearly visible above the waves of his hair. "I think you should call yourself Hannah, since you're still you, no matter how you look." He said shyly, "How about Hannah Tallerin?"

"Tallerin?" She tried to recall her Elven. She thought a tallerian was a noble of some sort. Maybe that was the root. "Why that name?"

"Because it's my name," he said quietly, "if you'll have me, that is."

"If I'll have you!" Hannah shouted, throwing herself into his arms. The new body was still awkward, the limbs not the same balanced weight she remembered, and the lunge was a bit wobbly, but he caught her up easily, rolling on top of her in the small cave.

"Would you, then?" He looked down at her searchingly.

"Of course, I will." Looking up at him, Hannah realized there was nothing she wanted more.

HANNAH'S STORY CONTINUES IN SOLYN'S BODY...

...Volume Two in the Klauden's Ring series!

Please take a moment and visit Amazon and Goodreads.com. Leaving a review on *Klauden's Ring* is the best help you can give!

Also, feel free to reach out to JM at authorjmpaquette.com!

About the Author

Author of the Klauden's Ring Saga and the Conjuring Fascination series, JM Paquette writes fantasy and paranormal romance novels. When she isn't writing, she can be found teaching English to college students as Dr. Paquette or watching her favorite Russian shifter romance movie, *I Am Dragon*. Her areas of expertise include the history of the English language and the intricacies of grammatical rules, but her favorite class to teach is on *Lord of the Rings*. (If you've ever wondered why English is a crazy language, watch her video series on YouTube under Editor JMPaquette!) She enjoys editing manuscripts for academic and creative writers alike, and she adores tabletop roleplaying (THAC0, anyone?) where her halfling ranger/Twi'lek adept/vampire wizard/[insert race and class here] is often underestimated. You can also find her guest co-hosting the podcast Drinking with Authors—even though she doesn't drink, she loves getting to know fellow authors! Check out JM Paquette at authorjmpaquette.com and 4horsemenpublications.com and as Author JM Paquette on Facebook and Instagram.

Connect with JM:
www.authorJMPaquette.com
www.facebook.com/authorjmpaquette/
Email: authorjmpaquette@gmail.com

OTHER BOOKS BY JM PAQUETTE

Solyn's Body (Klauden's Ring #2)
Hannah's Heart (Klauden's Ring #3)
The InBetween (Klauden's Ring #4)

Call Me Forth (Conjuring Fascination Prequel)
Invite Me In (Conjuring Fascination #1)
Keep Me Close (Conjuring Fascination #2)

Heart of Stone (Rock Star Fairy Tales #1)
One Mummy to Go, Please! (Shawarma Warrior King #1) with
Beau Lake

The General Guide to Worldbuilding

BOOK CLUB QUESTIONS

1. One of the main themes of the book is the tension between Hannah's upbringing in her father's castle and the life lessons she learns on the road with her new companions. In what ways does Hannah grow during the course of the story?

2. Hannah's people place a lot of value on heredity and blood lineage, a tradition that Rory is quick to dismiss as foolish. What do you think? Are blood and family genetics more important than lived experience?

3. As a vampire, Hannah easily discards the lives of others, often choosing to kill rather than risk the chance of infecting another and creating a fledgling. Is this the way you would live your life if you found yourself in the same circumstances?

4. When Rory's violent past is revealed, Hannah finds herself even more drawn to him as a romantic partner. Why do you think she reacts that way to his history?

5. Lira knows about Hannah's true nature from the start but chooses to say nothing to Rory despite seeing his growing attachment to the vampire. Would you have warned your friend about the danger of his potential love interest?

6. Jason Saffron becomes a fledgling who, afraid of what his new nature means for his wife, begs Hannah to end his life. Would you embrace the life of a fledgling?

7. Jamison distrusts Hannah from the start, a suspicion rooted in his wife's desertion years ago, and he is easily convinced to turn her over to Malbrek. Is there any way to justify his actions?

8. Klauden declares his love and then helps Hannah start a new life with her new love. What do you think truly motivates his behavior?

9. Klauden and Hannah were betrothed at birth, and though they have been apart for some time, they still share a close connection. Do you think they would have had a happy marriage? Why?

10. This volume ends with Hannah in a mortal body. What do you think will happen to her and Rory now that she is no longer a vampire?

11. You knew it was coming: Team Rory or Team Klauden? Who should Hannah end up with? (Spoiler: Read *Solyn's Body* and *Hannah's Heart* to find out what happens next!)

SNEAK PEEK AT SOLYN'S BODY

KLAUDEN'S RING SAGA BOOK 2

Hannah Tallerin was standing over her forge, eyes squinting against the waves of heat baking off the blade she worked, when the stranger opened the door to the smithy. Though her senses were by no means what they had been, she still had the uncanny reflexes of someone who spent lots of time barely dodging lethal blows, and so she turned as the door began to swing inside, her long limbs ready to react if the visitor proved dangerous. The turn was a bad idea, as the hammer in her right hand continued its arc of movement and connected with the second finger of her left hand, mashing the tip and sending a shriek of agony up her hand and into her arm. She cursed, dropped the hammer to the anvil with a clatter, and cradled the wounded hand against her chest as she completed her turn.

A man had entered the smithy. He hovered in the shadowed front of the room, and Hannah's mortal eyes could only make out a sense of height marred by stooped shoulders, the lump of a traveling bag, and a slow measured step as he moved to one wall, examining the weapons hung there. When she saw that the newcomer wasn't intent on harming her, at least not outright, she relaxed a bit, but she couldn't ignore the little thrill that had been building in her chest as it was suddenly and distressingly dashed.

I've got to get out of here, she thought, remembering a time when she had been so thankful for slow time like this, for days and weeks of mindless simplicity, she working away with metal, Rory shaping the local farmers into serviceable soldiers, the two of them carefully sharing the small bed each night.

Safety. Comfort. The regularity of a common life. *And plenty of smashed fingers along the way,* she thought bitterly, taking a cloth from her apron pocket and carefully wrapping the injured digit, blotting at the blood seeping from beneath the broken nail, remembering a time when blood meant something so much more. Now it only meant pain.

The stranger hadn't approached the wooden counter that divided the customer area from the black bellied forge, squat anvil, and large water barrel that took up her work area, and so Hannah ignored him for a time, allowing him to take in the plethora of short swords, axes, picks, and shields that lined the walls near the ceiling. The lower portion of the front area was filled with pots and pans, and Hannah had a new display area for her knives right next to the counter. She surreptitiously watched as the potential customer scanned her wares, noting how he seemed to focus on the weapons, some dusty from lack of interest.

Maybe he would actually buy something. It had been a while since anyone in this village had needed the weapons Hannah excelled at producing, though she had a nice business in knives, pots, and metal clasps. The idea of someone able to talk shop with her was exciting. Still, she had learned that it never paid to seem too eager to sell, so she left him to his examination. Her finger throbbed, and she checked to see that the blood had stopped flowing. It hadn't. She sighed angrily and pressed down with more force.

This was what she had wanted. This had been what she was thinking of when she told Klauden almost a year ago that she wanted a simple life with Rory, a life without the complications that had plagued them both. Of course, that had been when she thought she was dead, or dying at best, and anything was a preferable alternative to what she had been expecting. She clearly hadn't thought this whole thing through.

Simplicity was nice, but it was boring. Unimportant in a way that made her wonder if all humans felt like this all the time, the days running together into a blur until the body grew old and withered and died. She would die now, too, just like them. Old and ugly like a mortal woman.

She shook the maudlin image away—thoughts like these came too often these past weeks—to check on her customer, another man doomed by time. He was standing idle before the counter, eyes scanning the walls still, but she could see he wasn't really looking at the weapons anymore.

"Help you?" she asked in the low voice that she sometimes still thought of as a stranger's.

The man looked at her, then seemed to realize something as he gave her a closer look. Hannah waited patiently for him to speak. The double-take was nothing new. She was accustomed to people giving her odd looks, though lately, the reasons for them were a bit less clear than they had been. Before, they had looked at her because she made some blunder, some awkward revelation of her origins that marked her as a foreigner, as a freak, as something different. Now, they still gave her that look, but only because she was breaking their accepted notions of whom a blacksmith should be and what he should look like. Rory had warned her, of course, and she had known it would be hard at first. She had been a smith in Talperin for a few months before meeting Rory and encountered some resistance there, too. Still, it hadn't taken the people long to recognize skill, and that Hannah had. Of course, she didn't tell them where her knowledge had come from, and they hadn't asked, and then it hadn't mattered, but she and Rory had been in Severin almost eight months now, and some of the people here still gave her odd looks. She knew they were farther away from other towns, knew that the southern people were known for their particular expectations of what men and women should do, and she could understand that, having the background of her father's House in memory, but that didn't make it any less annoying when men stared at her for a few minutes before asking if she could get her man to come help them with something.

Some wouldn't even go that far. Some just walked out. Some gave her their esteemed opinions about female smithies. One had even gone so far as to grab her during one of these impassioned speeches, and he had learned the hard way that trying to strong-arm the new smithy was a bad idea, even when her man wasn't there to protect her. Rory had asked her if she wanted to leave after that, to go somewhere to the north, where people were less rigid.

She had declined, still lost in the fog of relief that was her life with him: the two of them sharing a home, eating breakfast together, doing all the little things that had seemed so impossible when she had first confessed to him in Kalford so long ago. *This is the life,* she kept telling herself. *This is what I wanted.*

And it was.

Sort of.

Except that when she told Klauden what she wanted, she hadn't imagined old men staring at her like this while she stood sweaty and disheveled, arms and back aching from a long day's work. She didn't mind the work. It was the waiting, the constant waiting, like she knew this fairy tale would end, and her real life would start up again. It just didn't feel right to be so secure, so settled, with no one chasing her, and no goblins, and no beast keeping her up nights.

Then again, Rory did his share of keeping her up at night, so that was a fair trade off. Better than that, even. She was fairly certain she had gotten the better deal on that exchange.

"You?" the old man whispered in front of her. Hannah focused on him again. He seemed ready to talk now, though she wondered what he was asking. She gave him a once over—traveling cloak, staff, pack—he definitely wasn't a local.

"Me," she replied, wondering if it was a language barrier. "What can I do for you?" She gave him a closer look when he paused. He had no visible weapons. *Maybe he really is looking to buy?*

She took in the state of his cloak, a bit tattered along the neckline but well mended and obviously cared for. His feet were covered in old boots, worn as well, but in decent shape. The man did his share of walking, but he had chosen well in his footwear. Hannah's own shoes would never have lasted so long. He seemed a simple traveler, a man she had seen a thousand times over, an old man wandering from here to there, stopping in shops when fancy and finance took him. His eyes were low set in a deeply lined face, a face used to the elements. Hannah wondered if he had ever been north of the Vanya, then stopped herself. He would not have returned if he had been. Few mortals did.

"You don't remember me," he said, and this time Hannah tried to pick up his accent. She had been a keen student of language patterns once, back in her father's House, but it seemed the gift had left her over the months. Either that, or her new ears had never developed the ability to listen the way she once had. Whatever the cause, she couldn't place the man's history. *Remember him?* She ran through the list of towns that she and Rory had traveled through before settling here in Severin. *He doesn't seem familiar, but then again, why would I remember him? And who would recognize me now anyway?*

And then it hit her. He didn't recognize her. It was the body he knew: the slave girl who had been in the wrong place at the wrong time, the girl Solyn whose body Hannah had taken over during the ceremony that had been meant to purify her tainted soul. *Thanks again, Klauden,* she thought wryly, absurdly conflicted whenever she thought of her old friend. He had meant to help her. Surely that had been his intention. He just hadn't realized what putting her into a feeble mortal body would do to her. Nor had she. Then it had just been a novelty, an exciting new toy to try out, a vehicle by which she could escape the castle with Rory and live out her childish ideas.

"Should I remember you?" she asked cautiously.

"What have they done to you, Hannah Hunter?" he asked, approaching the counter and placing large big-knuckled hands over hers. She pulled away, disgusted by the gesture, confused by the name, but then something in her surged, and she was allowing the old man to caress her hands. *What in the nine hells*—she began, Rory's phrase coming easily to mind, but then stopped as she realized more was happening. Someone was speaking, saying something rushed like "Where have you been?" in a low voice that was familiar.

Something was moving her mouth.

Someone else was speaking through her.

"Oh, hell, Malfek, fehalon," she cursed in a rush of words, jerking back both control of her voice and her hands. She withdrew toward the forge, staring at the man.

What did he do to me?

He reached for her. "Oh, my dear," he whispered, his face filling with pity, his eyes a well of sadness. "What did they do to you?"

"Nothing," she spat at him. "No one did anything." She realized she was breathing hard, like there was something trapped inside her chest trying to break free. She ruthlessly shoved it back down. She calmed herself, regaining the emotional cool that had gotten her through so many difficult situations. "I don't know you, old man," she said stiffly. "I don't know why you're here, or who you think I am, but you're wrong."

He paused, the emotions on his face loosening a bit as he considered her. She felt something snake out of him then, a low stirring across the room that prickled along her skin, and she recognized the feel of magic.

The old fool was using magic on her. She brought up her own defenses, ready to see what this spell would do, but when nothing beyond a small tickle of her face happened, she just stood there. She wanted to throttle him, to send a spear of ice into his chest that would make him regret coming in here, to use her magic to push him back against the walls and maybe even through the door to where he wouldn't bother her anymore, but there was something else in her now, too, a desperate need to keep him safe, to see him set free. She struggled with herself for a moment, then conceded the battle.

"Fine," she declared, "you can go free. Get out of my shop, and don't let me see you again."

"You are not yourself." It was not a question.

"I am not the person you are looking for," she said, as if that was obvious already.

"Not anymore," he observed, then his hands were raised in front of his chest, and Hannah knew that he was casting a spell again, and she wondered why she had been so stupid as to stand there and let this man into her shop and leave herself completely defenseless, when there was a sudden break in the room's air and a soft whooshing noise as the old man vanished.

Hannah stood from the semi-crouch she had assumed, ears popping, to stare at the space where the man had been.

Damn, she thought. *Vanishing magic. Serious spellcasting.* Even at her best, Hannah could manage a few offensive spells, but everything was memorization and stress for her. The power needed to simply disappear from the room was astounding. Or maybe he hadn't disappeared; maybe he had just gone invisible, as she could on occasion.

That was a hell of a lot of fuss just to go invisible, she thought, but she checked the room anyway, careful to cover every available space to make sure he wasn't still hiding in the building with her. When she was fairly certain she was alone, she barred the door and went to secure the forge for the night.

She had had enough of this for one day.

Discover more at
4HorsemenPublications.com

10% off using HORSEMEN10